Hard Magic

BY JOHN CARUSO

Also by John Caruso

Lightbearer

The Art of Finding

For John

And the Lord said unto him, Therefore whosoever slayeth Cain, vengeance shall be taken on him sevenfold. And the Lord set a mark upon Cain, lest any finding him should kill him.

And Cain went out from the presence of the Lord, and dwelt in the land of Nod, on the east of Eden.

And Cain knew his wife and she conceived and bore Enoch: and he builded a city, and called the name of the city, after the name of his son, Enoch.

Genesis 4: 15-17

The mountains of things we throw away are much greater than the things we use. In this, if in no other way, we can see the wild and reckless exuberance of our production, and waste seems to be the index.

John Steinbeck

"Ellen, only last night, asked, 'Daddy, when will we be rich?' But I did not say to her what I know: 'We will be rich soon, and you who handle poverty badly will handle riches equally badly.' And that is true. In poverty she is envious. In riches she may be a snob. Money does not change the sickness, only the symptoms."

John Steinbeck, The Winter of Our Discontent

Prologue

THE LEAD CLIMBER crossed the traverse between the last two trees. He looped the lanyard around the branch above his head and anchored himself to the big, black walnut tree before releasing himself from the line. The tree stood on high ground in the midst of a mountain bog. Swamp maples and cedars—all fifty or sixty years old at most—grew among tussocks of sedge grass above the water. Yellow birches had grown out of the rotten stumps of old growth trees and their roots gripped their nourishment like the tentacles of silver octopi around their prey. The canopy was broken in the bog, making it easier to site and move the line, but offered little choice of route. They had only to traverse six trees, but each was spaced a bit farther than the last, and the final traverse measured 120 feet. Nobody wanted to find out what would happen if a branch broke and one of them was to fall into the calm, green-black water.

The man let himself down until he was suspended in front of a hollow in the walnut tree. He flicked on his helmet beam, adjusted it down and looked into the hole.

"There it is," he whispered, as though the exceeding stillness of the forest in the heat of noon, or the object in the hollow of the tree demanded reverence. He lifted a platinum rectangle—what looked like a fireproof box—out of its hiding place. He hitched its heft to a metal clip on his waist, and anchored his weight to the traverse line (letting down the loop from the upper branch) and glided through the dappling of broken canopy back to the anchor tree. Two men stood silently there, as if waiting for his return to take a breath. One with a dark beard unclipped the platinum case and loaded it into the third man's back pack. The lead climber then tossed the throw bag to the limb of the next tree and shot the line six times, feeling the sweat on his neck and forehead build with each miss, before the grapnel caught the bag. He took off his hard hat, revealing a great shock of tawny hair, and wiped his forehead with the back of his arm.

The three retraced their route through the bog back to the solid forest floor. When they reached the penultimate tree, the last inside the clutches of the bog, the lead climber said, "Do you want to see what happens?"

The others were anxious to be free of the place and shook their heads.

"I'm not throwing your lunches down there." He broke a dead branch off the trunk and dropped it down. The moment it made contact, there was stirring down in the muck below and a drain-like sucking sound. Then the branch went down entire in a murky depression with a gulp. A smell wafted up to them out of the bubbles and muck. Something dark and rotten. Something dead.

"What is that?"

"It's like something in there sucked it down."

"Let's tighten this line and get across while this branch is still holding us."

PART I

1.

The Wreck Appears

THE SMASHED ROOF and the web shatter of glass froze Jude Corgan as he reached into the dish rack for a bowl and saw the wreck out of the kitchen window. Funny how a new wreck had a way of turning him to stone. Even after enduring the humiliating incantation in the front yard last night, Jude couldn't have imagined this. Jet had teetered on Everest—their sublime heap of No.1 aluminum—waved his hands like a magician, then staggered like the drunk he was, and recited in Bewitched Bible-ese: *"Scatter ye scraps of my toiling years; take up the incubus that lieth here; whither it came from take it whence; remove its wicked waste beyond my fence."* Presto! And just like that they wake up to another wreck.

The problem was always how to tell Aster. Tomorrow was the anniversary. This was going to put her in a tailspin big time. Jude looked grimly at the inedible lake of milk and drowning cornflakes in his bowl. "Mom, why don't you sit down?"

Aster didn't react. She leaned, shoulders hunched and the small of her back against the slender edge of the kitchen sink, clutching a mug of instant coffee in both hands like some rare gourmet brew. With her eyes half-closed and her back to the gray light seeping through the kitchen window, she looked asleep. It was late June, yet her face was winter pale, as if she'd been living all the while with her back turned toward the sun.

Jude knew she'd heard him perfectly well, but his mother's hearing worked on some weird delay mechanism in the morning, as if all his words were lined up single file and he had to keep talking to push his first ones deep enough into her ears. "Why would anybody drink coffee made out of freeze dried mouse turds?"

When Aster still didn't react, Jude lost patience and just came out with it: "There's another wreck in the yard."

Aster turned suddenly, sloshing coffee up over the rim of her cup. "Good Lord in heaven."

It was plain as all the other wrecks lining their frontage, a silver Volvo with the roof smashed in so bad it had to be a proper rollover. "Jet!" Aster screamed and stomped down the narrow hallway toward her bedroom at the end of the mobile home, splashing instant coffee everywhere. By the way she said 'Jet', in two syllables, you could tell he was dead meat. On the other hand, his father could probably snore through Judgment Day to avoid one of Aster's verbal thrashings. By the time she roused him, the worst of her fury would be spent.

Jude had grown up with junk—twisted car fenders, window frames, bicycles, card tables, tarps (black with mold, still shrouding something that had once been "valuable"), palettes, apple crates, mufflers, mangled scrap metal, rope, car engines, oil cans, busted chairs, plywood, washing machines, rust brown 55 gallon drums, tires, broom handles, rakes, chains, umbrellas, splintered shovel handles, unidentifiable machine parts, sledgehammers, hedge clippers, buckets, oily rags, deer bones and splitting mauls, as well as the old junks Jet had taken to transform for some fantastic scheme: a Volkswagen bus (the so called Incubus he'd been trying to exorcise last evening), a trailer he was going to convert into a lunch wagon, and an ice cream truck that was going to be a meat freezer on wheels, to name a few—but all the roadside wrecks along the Corgan property (now 16 to be exact) had appeared mysteriously in the night, one at a time over the past five years. Though Jude was only nine at the time, he remembered the morning of the first wreck and the wrenching brittle shout coming out of his mother when she saw it. The way she bent over the sink, as if she were going to break in half.

Then, Aster had thrown herself on Jet for comfort. "Who would do such a thing? How could they? Why? Who could be so cruel?" Most of what she'd said poured out of her mouth in a weepy fog, but Jude recalled the exact words, as if he'd understood them and knew she had spoken them. Now, she blamed Jet for getting the spell all wrong and, rather than ridding them of the vehicle as Osmena Searle had promised, brought yet another one into their overcrowded junk lot.

When it first began, the Corgans' had notified the local authorities in outrage. Sheriff Logan was sympathetic and grave, but he kept glancing skeptically back and forth between Jet's junk and the first wreck. He had respectfully declined to do anything about it. You could see he thought Jet had taken on the vehicle and then, as with everything else on the property, given up his scheme and concocted a crazy story about the car appearing suddenly, just to see if he could finagle someone else into towing it away. "Did all this other stuff just appear out of nowhere?" The Sheriff had finally summed up his point in a question.

Never one to be put off by the tactical maneuvers of authority, Jet had impulsively notified the local paper. A reporter came out faster than you could say 'car wreck'. **Mysterious Wreck Revives Family's Grief**, the headline would read with a subversive photo angle catching, not only Jet and the wreck (Aster refused to pose for the shot), but also junk piles in the background, not to mention a quote from the Sheriff's Department, saying in not so many words that the claims had been investigated and lacked credibility.

Aster had thrown the paper at Jet. "You've made us the laughing stock of the county."

Jude had picked up the paper and pointed to the photo. "Hey, there's the Incubus." Truth to tell, not a soul believed the cars had appeared out of nowhere, and the more the Corgans insisted on it, the more quickly they gained a reputation as hoaxsters so obsessed and deranged by grief they'd taken to acting out their dead son's tragedy.

In short order, the Corgans learned to shut up about it and let the vehicles pile up rather than rave pointlessly to their disbelieving neighbors. Well, of course Jet could have had Chet Atwood tow them away, but on account of pride he refused. It would be admitting they were frauds and liars. Eventually,

3

Jet had grown stubborn and optimistic and wouldn't hear of hauling the wrecks away. "Aster, these wrecks are saying something—I just don't know what yet. Someone's cursing us, but they're giving us a gift in disguise."

"Saying something! They're saying we're bigger fools than anyone could have guessed!" Aster screamed. "Fools for every bit of rubbish ever put on God's green earth. They're wrecks, Jet. They're totaled. Ugly and worthless. They don't even have engines!"

"Yeah, well," Jet had answered, "even if we have them towed away, who's to say they won't keep coming? You're just making more room for the next ones. We might as well fill up the lot and be done with it."

But a wreck coming so close to the anniversary was trouble.

Jude tried to tune out his mother's shrieks and Jet's sleepy groans of protest. Now, when a wreck showed up, they didn't cry, they fought, and then they got cold and quiet, so that Jude could barely stand to be around them. Sometimes it was like he was invisible anyway. It would always be about Kennedy. It would always be like their lives stopped that day. And who was he but a big oaf who ate and crapped and reminded them of the golden son they'd lost.

Besides being tiresome and insulting, his parents' fights distracted Jude from hitting on the right names. He closed his eyes and suddenly it came to him. He stood up at the kitchen table, picked up the chalk and triumphantly, with absolute conviction, drew large squeaky characters on the kitchen chalk board beneath No. 15 (Food Poisoning): Sweet 16. Pure genius this time. This was the only one of the wrecks to refer to Kennedy and his death. He sat back down at the table and waited for Aster to bring Jet out for their ritual look at the new addition. He knew the name would be trouble, but it was about time somebody came out and said what the curse was all about.

Aster took one long look over at the sixteenth name on the blackboard, pointed her first cigarette of the day at Jude, like she'd just as soon burn him with the glowing end of it, and said, "Young man, you are so grounded. Grounded for one—no—two weeks. Don't you have a shred of decency and feeling, making light of this whole thing from the very start? I've put up with a lot of nonsense, but this time buddy, you've crossed the line. Sweet 16. I ought to whip you good."

"I'd like to see you try," Jude said. As far back as he could remember Aster had never laid a hand on him one way or the other. Who was she to talk about feeling? It was all just talk. Love and threats. Sometimes he really wished she would just haul off. At least that would be something. She fumed and puffed on her cigarette, but she didn't bother to erase the name on the blackboard. She knew it was futile. The name was as good as set in stone. She resumed her lean against the countertop and finished her cigarette. Jet came out in his wife beater and boxers scratching his low hangers. His dark curly hair lay flat on his sleeping side, giving his head a lopsided look.

"Our first Volvo, for Pete's sake." Jet looked over at the blackboard and smiled. "You've got a way with words, don't you, Jude. I bet Kennedy would've liked that."

"Except he thought Volvos were for old hippies with no sense of style," Jude reminded him.

"Oh, Jesus, don't encourage him, Jet. Haven't you got a lick of parental sense in your entire head? I just grounded him."

"Well, un-ground him then. What's the harm in it? You got to keep a sense of humor or you go crazy in life."

Aster just broke up laughing at that one. She doubled over, her cigarette ash shaking and scattering on the kitchen floor. She was so weak with her fit, she dropped to her knees right there in her white nurse's aide pants. Jet started chuckling to himself. He'd never understood irony at all.

"Crazy?" The word came out of Aster in a wild yelp. She looked up at them from her knees trying to spit out the rest. Her eyes welled up and her mouth was stretched open, moving around her wheezing sounds. "You mean we're not crazy yet? There's crazier stuff than this? Thanks for the warning, Jet."

Only Jude understood a single word she said.

⌘　⌘　⌘

J UDE FOLDED HIS flimsy umbrella and squinted up into a fine mist. Across the road the corn was shooting up in perfect bright green rows, and beyond the field, the hills of Twin Gaps rolled lush and motionless. Spooky pockets of mist rose like the smoke of smoldering fires.

Jude stood out in front of the new wreck on Old Route 9 waiting for the school bus. Rather than walking a dignified piece down the road—as he had since the first grade, and as Kennedy had done before him—he had been standing right in front of the junk piles this whole school year. He wasn't sure if and when he had ceased to be ashamed of the prolific blight synonymous with his name, or when he decided his school mates deserved a daily full-frontal, dead-stop view of the most amazing junk piles this side of an urban landfill, but somewhere between Valentine's Day Blizzard (No. 3) and Flunking Gym (No. 14), local opinion had begun to swing in the Corgans' favor.

Aster and Jet hadn't gotten wind of it yet, and Jude wasn't about to let them in on it. For one thing, he was sure his parents would spoil whatever pleasure he derived from the growing Corgan mystique, and for another, he didn't want to jinx a good thing. He thought it might have something to do with the number of vehicles reaching a critical mass. It seemed nobody really thought Jet Corgan was crazy enough to purposely gather so many useless wrecks on his property, no matter what the rest of his yard looked like. Facts are facts. Jet didn't own a tow truck and the word would've gotten out a long time ago if he'd been taking money for other people's junks.

Jude definitely noticed the change after Lightning Strike (No. 13) late last spring, because school was almost out then too and everybody on the bus knew about Jet's close call with the lightning. Then, two days later, a wreck shows up on their lawn. The entire bus full of kids was pressed against the windows on the Corgan side of the road until the bus driver had to shout at them to get in their seats for fear they'd tip the bus right over. It must have been going around long before then, but that was the moment he realized people were talking about it.

Jude couldn't have planned a more fitting climax for the last day of school than to have a brand new wreck for them. He stood in front of the specter of the Volvo's violent end, trying on grave expressions, which wasn't difficult considering his large dark, deeply circled eyes, matching dark hair, pale complexion and full face.

The wrecks had even begun to overshadow the stigma of the junk (the real curse of Jude's existence all these years), for they were somehow inseparable from the logic of the Corgans' strange misfortune. For years he had been called "Son of Junkenstein" and had been shunned for living in a virtual trash heap, but lately something had shifted around their heaps of misery. Because, in a way, they were a human car wreck you just couldn't look away from, and maybe it was really true that misery loved company.

2.

Just-a-Moron Regional School

N O SOONER HAD Jude stepped off the bus and under the portico of Justin Morgan Regional School—a stark slab of concrete supported by neon orange columns—than the feeling of the Corgan mystique he had savored on the bus ride vanished like morning mist. For one thing, the jocks of Brimfield and Marston were clueless about it.

Brady Hunt was coming toward him now with the orange arms of his baseball jacket swinging like cocky little columns of stone. "Hey, fat boy—you, melon head." He pointed menacingly at Jude. "Ultimate Team Handball!"

Jude rolled his eyes. "Have fun."

"I will. Woofph." Brady wound his arm up and made a throwing motion, as if he were firing a ball, but his arm came close enough to suggest the threat of a punch.

Jude fought the urge to flinch. He kept walking. There was nothing worse in his whole life than first period gym class. Things had begun badly enough in the fall with soccer: standing out on 36 degree mornings wearing only gym shorts and a t-shirt, slipping and falling on the glistening, frosty grass, and his throat and lungs aching from the cold air when he ran after the ball. Then he had to wear his wet sneakers, caked with little bits of cut grass, for the rest of the day.

The second unit had been swimming and Jude had drawn the line there. Undressing in the locker room had been humiliating enough, but appearing in swim trunks at the pool every day in front of all the popular girls and muscular jocks was simply dehumanizing. He sat out the class at poolside in his street clothes and took an F for the semester.

Gym class was Jude's own daily hell, with Coach Cutler its sadistic gate-keeper, checking to make sure everybody wore a protective cup in the event of an underworld misfortune, and the other boys his tormenting demons, taking turns snapping the waistband of Jude's jock strap (127 times at last count), with every snap accompanied by a rude comment about his body or his looks. Somehow he had endured an entire year of it. Surely, Cutler wouldn't make him dress for gym, let alone subject him to the terror of Ultimate Team Handball on the last day of school. Jude was wrong.

Ultimate Team Handball was code for ultimate humiliation. The object was to pass a volley ball down the field to your teammates and eventually throw it past a goaltender into a net. When you put it like that, it sounded easy enough. Only if you caught the ball you couldn't run more than two steps before you had to throw it again. This required hand body coordination well outside Jude's skill set. It was like the worst of water polo, basketball and football all rolled into one—which made it difficult to remember exactly what the rules were. Second, if you didn't want to look like an absolute clod, you had to run like a sprinter, catch like a wide receiver, and throw the ball like a pitcher. Case closed. Usually when the ball came Jude's way he fumbled it. When he did manage to catch it, his mind went blank and he either threw it right back to his opponent (All jocks looked alike to him; why did they bother dividing them into teams?), or he dribbled it like a basketball ("Throw it, fathead; throw it!" they shouted at him). The very first time he caught the ball, before he knew about the three step rule, he'd just taken off down court with it, head down, elbows thrown out, lumbering triumphantly past the bewildered goal keeper into the net. He had no idea why they were on the gym floor laughing. They got such a kick out it, at least once a game, somebody would toss him a softy and let him go, while they chanted in unison like the guy on ESPN, "He—could—go—all—the—way!" That ritual was as close to acceptance as Jude had come, but when he started feeling like Shamu tricking for fish at Sea World, he decided enough was enough. Yesterday, when they'd tossed him the ball, he'd wacked it across the gym, as if he were serving a volleyball. They were not amused.

Brady Hunt had let Jude know, in no uncertain terms, there would be no softies and no mercy today. His teammates made him goal keeper. For twenty minutes, he flailed his arms and legs futilely to swat or kick the shots away, but no matter what he did the balls kept flying past him in a blur into the net. The only shot he stopped was when he tripped and the ball accidentally hit him in the butt and bounced up over the crossbar. "That's using your head," Jaden West said, and the whole game stopped for a laughter time-out at Jude's expense.

The boys thought that was so hilarious, they started aiming their shots at Jude, instead of trying to score. "Hey, coach they're nailing me on purpose," he complained.

"Suck it up, Corgan," Cutler barked and went back to flirting with Ms. Geischler, the big babe tennis coach.

Soon Jude's teammates were not only giving the other team easy shots at him, they were taking aim as well. Somebody got the practice balls and soon they were coming at him three and four at a time. Suddenly, they were no longer amusing but avenging themselves, for the balls were coming with such force and their faces were clenched in such cold fury, Jude began to feel not only the sting and thump of every shot, but their pure contempt for him. They were using his body—his back, butt, head and chest—like a paper target of some hated enemy. He was bigger and taller than any one of them, but each blow made him feel smaller, flatter and somehow naked. His insides felt like liquid pulp, as if he were about to melt into a puddle on the gym floor. But, something else was also rising in his stomach, something hot, like acid. As it rose up into his throat, he reached out in self-defense and, to his surprise, caught a ball incoming for his head. He spun around once like a shot-putter, flung the ball blindly back at them, and let out his loudest Junkensteinian bellow. Then, without another sound, Jude walked off the court and into the locker room.

For a moment, everything stopped. Even coach Cutler ceased his pointless flirtation with Ms. Geischler. They could stare as much as they wanted for all Jude cared. He couldn't and wouldn't go back, whether there were twenty minutes or twenty hours left in class. He got changed and went straight up to Principal Ringweld's office, where Cutler would have sent him anyway for walking out of class.

⌘　⌘　⌘

RINGWELD WAS IN an unusually cheerful mood, despite Jude's unexpected appearance in his office, as if he was bored and needed a diversion to pass the morning. He sat straight up at his desk, hands folded in front of him. He had a small, pointy nose, pinched at the top by square black glasses. His eyes appeared magnified, perpetually wide behind their thick lenses, giving him the look of a giant fish leering through aquarium glass. His toupee, which ran like a slick of black shoe polish across the top of his head, was noticeably off center. "Let me guess, yet another chapter of Jude and the Giant Jocks. What a surprise! Do please have a seat, and don't spare any of the gory details."

Jude ignored the offer and remained standing just inside the door. He never sat in the Principal's office no matter how long he had to stay there. First of all, it was impossible because the chairs were strictly first grade issue; for another thing, even if he enjoyed sitting with his knees tucked into his chin, he suspected Ringweld of playing mind games with his detainees, like some twisted FBI interrogator, and Jude was not dumb enough to fall into such an obvious trap.

"I guess I kind of *wigged* out today," Jude said, staring right at the black toupee.

Ringweld seemed oblivious to wig jokes. "What was it this time? A two fisted wedgy with a full twist? Icy hot in your underpants? Or an old fashioned jock strap catapult? Tell me it wasn't a frontal cup slingshot?"

Clearly Ringweld wanted Jude to say it was.

"They used me as target practice in Ultimate Team Handball and Coach Cutler let them."

12

"What a shame—the way all originality has gone out of bullying these days. It used to be different. We used our God-given imaginations in my day." Ringweld stared wistfully into space, as if the past were hovering just above Jude's head. "Have you ever had a bubblegum perm?"

"A what?"

"That's when the kids sitting behind you throw wads of ABC gum into your hair. At the time, you think it's only spitballs, but they stick and harden. Later you have to cut them out with a scissors, giving you permanent bad hair days. It's a rather helpless and humiliating feeling, but eventually, one that passes." Ringweld spoke as if he'd been a victim, but the strange smile on his face made Jude think he'd been on the giving rather than receiving end of many bubblegum perms.

"Eighth grade is unfortunately laced with trying rituals..."

Ringweld had said that about seventh grade last year.

"...Youthful pranks. All in good fun. We grow up and forget about these little insults. One day we'll look back at it all and realize they made us stronger..."

Jude had heard enough. As he stared at the crooked black slick at the top of Ringweld's head, his anger formed itself into words. By the time Ringweld finished, it had become a little speech. "So, we grow up," Jude said, "but they don't have to? Nothing ever happens to them. No matter how *bald*-faced they are, you just sweep it under *the rug,* until eventually there is so much nasty dirt under *the rug,* the whole *crooked* attempt to hide the *root* of a *congenital male pattern* is obvious to anyone with eyes. But, if you ask me, Mr. Ringweld, the *cover-up* is ten times more shameful than the *bald* truth."

All at once, the light dawned in Ringweld's magnified eyes. His face burned red and he reached instinctively to right his hair piece. Then, he composed himself and folded his hands on his desk again. "Very cogently and eloquently put, Mr. Corgan. I feel your pain. A very compelling extended metaphor as well; you should put it to better use in your school work next year. I trust I'll see you in September, though, I hope, less frequently under such trying circumstances."

Gym class had been so surreal, and second period Spanish had been so loud with music and shattered piñatas, that Jude almost forgot he was going to surprise Merrilee with news about the wreck. It didn't come back to him until the moment she walked into English class. All at once he felt the nightmare of his morning vanish like fog at the touch of sunlight. His entire eighth grade year would have been a total social disaster—every morning as humiliating and lonely as the year before—had he not met Merrilee Rainey in the lunch line on the very first day of school.

Merrilee had been in front of him, looking at the offerings in disbelief. She had very short, rust orange hair (recently cut because the ends still looked a little choppy), a strong, straight nose, and the most direct, stone gray eyes he'd ever seen. She wore tiny oval glasses, that looked not quite hip and not quite old fashioned, but when she looked at you, she almost always dropped her forehead and looked over, rather than through, her lenses. "What is that?" she turned to Jude and asked. He thought he remembered her from English class that morning. With the entire student body self-consciously absorbed in social jockeying, it was the first time that day he hadn't been deliberately shunned.

Jude was going to speak his reply, but, before he'd even started to answer, a little play on words came to him. He sang it to the theme from American Top Forty. "American Chop Suey." Jude picked up a spoon and spoke into it, like a microphone. "Hi, I'm Casey Casing, and welcome to our countdown. The food gets tougher to digest as the numbers get lower.

"Up a notch this week to number two is the oldest entree on our countdown. After stalling for a couple of weeks in the third slot, Beef Stroganoff moves up closer to the top. But, before we get to our new number one, Craig in Barfsville asks, 'Dear Casey, what dish holds the distinction of having been released into the cafeteria line the most times without hitting number one?'

"Well, Craig, the answer is, or course, meat loaf. Most of us came to know this dish when it first hit our charts last year smothered in gluey brown gravy, but, on its first release it never got higher than number 5. Since then it's been remixed as Shepherd's Pie; remade as meatball grinders; then pizza burgers, and most recently, where it currently sits at number 4, as Salisbury steak. Thanks for your question, Craig. Now, on with the countdown..." By the time, Jude had finished, this strange orange-haired girl was smiling like a satisfied cat and clapping discreetly. "Kudos," she said. "Thank God there's somebody in this school with a live brain. I'm Merrilee Rainey—two rr's, one l, two ee's. You're in my English, aren't you?"

Merrilee had moved to Twin Gaps two summers ago from Burlington, which meant she had a kind of mystique of her own—at least until the other kids had sized her up for better or worse. Jude had seen her in school and a few times in the village, but last year he'd had no classes with her, and so had never met her until that day in the cafeteria line. Of course, once she and Jude became friends she was pretty much stuck in his unpopular boat. Not that being a "brain" got her invited on dates, but Jude was a decided step down on the social rung. As it turned out, she could have cared less about popularity and referred to it almost daily as an oppressive form of social control. Thereafter they were unshakeable allies and had come to refer to the 3ʳᵈ period class they shared alternately as 'my English', 'your English', and sometimes 'our English' as if it were a child they sometimes wished and sometimes didn't wish to claim as their own.

Merrilee slipped into her chair in the next row and leaned over. "You look like you've been trampled by a moose? What happened?"

Jude told her the whole story.

Merrilee looked over the top of her glasses at him. "That's a welt on your neck. Are you alright?"

"Yeah. I'm fine." All the same Jude touched his neck and felt a sore swollen spot.

"You burst their inflated jock egos and defied their tyranny; for that, my dear, you were severely punished. Don't you just find martyrdom a little overrated? I recommend early release and large doses of chocolate. Look, your Mr. Campbell's reading a novel. Meanwhile we're just going to sit here and gab the period away; we might as well gab somewhere in private."

Merrilee wrote something in her notebook, tore the scrap of paper off and handed it to Jude. They went up to Campbell's desk together.

"Excuse me, our Mr. Campbell? I need to see the nurse; I think I'm breaking out." Jude pulled down the collar of his shirt to show off the giant welt.

"Oh, dear; well, by all means." Mr. Campbell wrote out a pass.

15

Merrilee added, "He's in dire need of moral support. Just look at our Jude."

Mr. Campbell looked back and forth between Jude and Merrilee and smiled faintly through his regal salt and pepper beard. He wrote out a second pass and wished them an eventful summer.

Out in the hall Jude could hardly wait to spill the beans. "You'll never guess what happened this morning."

"Another wreck appeared. A silver Volvo."

Jude stopped dead. "How did you know?"

"While you were having the stuffing knocked out of you by rampaging jocks, I was busy gathering my daily intelligence. Actually, the kids on your bus were talking about it in the hall. Your life is such an open book, I didn't even have to eavesdrop. Disgracefully easy."

Jude and Merrilee resumed their pace, turning the corner and starting down the long glassed corridor of the cafeteria wing. The rain had stopped and the sky was beginning to brighten, but the picnic tables in the courtyard were still dark from rainwater. They went into the cafeteria. They held study halls there before the lunch waves, and the 3rd period attendance had just been taken. The teacher, an easy going substitute who let anything go as long as it was quiet, was already absorbed in a magazine. Jude and Merrilee snuck over to an empty back table.

"But you didn't get the name, did you?"

Merrilee covered her face. "I'm the disgrace."

"Are you ready?" Jude opened his eyes wide and raised his eyebrows. "Sweet Sixteen."

Merrilee clapped her hands once, then looked around and put one hand over her mouth. "You didn't!" She repeated it silently to herself. "Simple, yet audacious."

"Audacious enough to get me grounded and clever enough to get me ungrounded all in a matter of minutes. At least I think I'm ungrounded. I guess I'll find out when Aster gets home."

"What? Something's wrong."

Jude looked down at his hands. They were joined at the fingertips, flexing up and down like a spider bouncing on a mirror.

"Well, don't hem and haw; spit it out."

"Tomorrow is the anniversary," Jude said, still looking at his hands. "Aster is going to be a mess. I used to wish more than anything for the cars to stop coming, because they made her cry and always reminded us of Kennedy just when it seemed we weren't thinking about him every minute of the day. But now we kind of need them, because—well—because each one kind of brings him back, closer to the time when he was still alive. I know it doesn't make sense, and don't ask me how I know Aster and Jet feel it too. They'd never admit to anything that weird, because that's pretty much what they've been accused of. The thing is, I don't want them to stop coming anymore, because now it's like a mystery, and finding out who's doing it and why keeps us going.

"Aster has her Murder-on-the-Orient-Express-Theory that everybody hates us for our junk and they are all in on it together just to drive us insane. What do you expect; Aster is paranoid and has low self-esteem. I'm partial to the lone gunman theory, while Jet changes his mind every time a new wreck arrives, each one crazier than the next—one time it was Grandmother Meades. Boy did he regret letting that little theory slip. Another time he was almost convinced he'd done it himself while sleepwalking."

Merrilee laughed. She never tired of hearing it.

Jude went on. "As stupid or paranoid as it all sounds, one theory is as good as the next, because we've never seen or heard anyone bring a single car."

There was more. About two years into the wrecks, Jude's parents got religion. (It was that or Prozac.) Believing God had cursed them for living in sin all these years, Jethro Corgan and Aster Meades started going to a local Baptist church and finally, after 18 illicit years, got hitched. But this had availed nothing. In just a few months, another mangled car appeared at the edge of their property. While God had an abiding interest in the business of salvation, he apparently was not in the salvage business. Jude had been devilishly thrilled to shatter their righteous delusions (having been dead set against all the guilt and church-going in the first place), announcing, with more than usual glee, the first, Post-Born Again wreck to grace their yard. He had christened it, Answered Prayer, just as he had taken to naming all the other junks. Begrudgingly, Jude's parents had given in to his precocious

17

sense of irony. He had a knack for naming the wrecks after famous Corgan failures, or, it seemed, the cars arrived on the heels of some sunken aspiration. Along with Answered Prayer, there was PR Disaster (The first wreck, in reference to the backfired newspaper story); Weight Watchers; Valentine's Day Blizzard (Jet letting the 4x4 run out of gas during a two day storm); Nicotine Fit; Warhol's Revenge (Jet's junk lot art installation using "borrowed" mannequins, turned into a 30 day suspended sentence for petty larceny); Science Project (Jude did not exclude his own failures from the family scrap heap); Christmas Goose (Burnt to a crisp); Weight Watchers II; Corgan Family Reunion (One of Jude's cousins fell butt first into the bonfire and the whole boozy sham ended in a caravan to the local hospital); Near Divorce (His parents still didn't think that one was so funny); Nut Cancer Scare; Lightning Strike (Jet in the shower having to be rushed soaking wet and naked to emergency); Flunking Gym and Food Poisoning.

Merrilee was in stitches holding her sides. "I'm sorry. This is supposed to be serious. It is. You guys are seriously cursed."

"Yeah, and people are starting to believe us now. Jet says the cars are telling us something, and they're a gift. But it's not enough to just say that and not know what it is. If we don't find out where they're coming from we're just going to be stuck where we've been the last five years, waiting for something to change."

Jude looked up finally. Merrilee stared over the top of her glasses at him. "You really want to find out who's behind the wrecks?"

Jude nodded. "I have to know."

"Then come to my house this afternoon—two o'clock."

3.

A Strange Development on Gemini Farm

A T GEMINI FARM, about the same time the Corgans discovered the sixteenth wreck, Jude's cousin, Junie Meades, asked his father if he could skip the last day of school.

"It's nothing but a party day. We've already taken our finals."

"Yeah, can we?" Jesse, his identical twin brother, echoed.

David and Raeanne Meades looked at each other before answering their sons.

"It's a perfect day to plant the late beans," Junie said.

While David and Raeanne hemmed and hawed, a distant rumble of machinery came to them, like the tick of a wall clock suddenly loud and crisp in the quiet of morning.

"A perfect day for what?" said 9-year-old Willa as she came down the stairs to the kitchen.

"Shhh!" Raeanne held up her hand. "Sorry, honey, we're listening."

It was indeed the sound of machinery, yet no sooner had David and Raeanne confirmed it, than a glance between them confirmed something more disconcerting than the noise itself: the awareness, like two people discovering they've had the same dream, that they'd been hearing this uneven drone for days without having acknowledged it.

19

"What in heaven's name is that?" Raeanne said.

"And where is it coming from?" David added.

"Sounds like its coming from Charbonneau's. It must be he's finally putting up that new barn he's been talking about."

"Maybe," David said. He put down his coffee cup and listened again. "Sounds a little closer." He stood up suddenly, grabbed his keys off the table and his cap from a hook on the kitchen wall. "I'd better have a look."

Jesse and Junie followed him to the door.

"Boys?" said Raeanne.

David shrugged and nodded for them to come along.

"Where are they going?" said Willa.

"They're going to help your father out today."

"Can I stay home too?"

"No honey, you have to go to school."

"It's not fair they get to stay home."

"I guess it sort of isn't; but we can't have everybody in the family playing hooky."

In a few minutes they were out beyond the berry bushes, up the slope of the orchard and over to the back pasture. The road made an S curve, turning sharply east over the crest, and then swung in a downward northerly arc around a stand of maple trees, and then east again across from Charbonneau's. The rumble, louder now and accompanied by steely claps and the hollow tumble of stony ground, was that of large earthmovers, and it was coming from just beyond the dense screen of maple trees.

David Meades stepped on the gas, careless of ruts and the speed he was gathering down the slope. When the truck rounded the curve of the screening maples, he slammed on the brakes.

The lower slope had been leveled and braced by a stone retaining wall. On the level ground two Caterpillar backhoes gouged claws full of earth, swiveling and dumping them stiffly into giant mounds. The blank backing of a sign fronted the site and a newly packed dirt road wound slowly down to the private gravel road that separated Meades and Charbonneau land.

20

For a moment, father and sons all sat silent with their mouths open. David's color drained and then flooded red, but it was the look on his face that gave Junie a terrible pit in his stomach.

"What the hell is this?" David finally spoke, and didn't even apologize like he usually did when let out one of his lame swear words.

Junie saw a hundred thoughts and questions run through his father's head, but they didn't burst out in a torrent of words, rather in a sudden stomp on the gas pedal. They flew past one of the swiveling Cats, around the retaining wall and stopped with a lurch in front of the sign, nose to nose with a red, Ram pickup.

"Stay in the truck," David told the twins. Then he got out and slammed the door. He stared at the sign, outraged by what he read, and not noticing the man in the hardhat walking toward him from the other side of the retaining wall.

There was going to be trouble. Junie looked over at his brother. Jesse nodded, opened the door and piled out on the passenger side. The twins came up quietly behind their father and read the sign. GREENWAY VENTURES INTL. INC: Future site of the Vermont Agricultural Museum and Catamount Cooperative Farming Retreat.

"Mr. Meades?" The man approached, took off his hard hat and extended his hand.

David Meades looked in disbelief at the odd little man. His head was bald—except for a close cut shadow of silver on the sides—and so large it seemed impossible the hardhat in his left hand had actually fit over his crown. His slender silver mustache arced down to meet a well-kept, shocking black, capuchin beard.

"Merlin Greenway," the man announced himself.

"You? This is a mistake. Do you not know this is private land? My land. You are to stop work immediately, do you understand? You have no right, none whatsoever. My property runs clear down to the road. If Charbonneau sold you his land, you're on the wrong plot."

Greenway held up his hand. "We don't want Charbonneau's land. You see this slope is visible from the interstate. This land is superior; indeed your operation here is just what we needed—a model for all we hope to achieve."

"Just what you needed? And who decided you could have it?"

Greenway reached inside his coat pocket and pulled out a document. He unfolded it and handed it to David. "It's a copy of the deed of transfer from Gemini Farm to the Catamount Trust."

"This isn't legal. I never signed and—" David broke off in mid-sentence. Down at the bottom of the page, beneath all the wherefores and herebys was his signature. It was dated May 1st this year. "I never—this is outright forgery and theft. You'll never get away with this. I'm calling my attorney and he'll put a stop to this so fast it will make your head spin."

"Do as you wish, Mr. Meades. But, the Catamount Cooperative Farming Retreat is a vital part of Vermont's new economic infrastructure. We know you're in debt up to your eyeballs. Barely staying afloat month to month. Farms like yours must inevitably fold. You haven't got the resources to expand, promote yourself or—for that matter—wage a protracted legal battle with the likes of my corporation. Unless you become part of a greater vision you will vanish like so many of your kind. You see, you have skills and independence that the average city dweller secretly envies. Yet in the past, you were just a pit stop on somebody's leaf peeping tour, a novelty, a fleeting respite from the high-tech, high-stress, urban world. Now, they are not just going to come to buy your maple syrup, they're going to come and make it; and you're going to teach them how."

"I'm going to show you the toe of my boot, in a minute. Are you completely insane?" David let out another long torrent of curses, ripped the deed—so that each foul word coincided with a *shhrp* of paper—and threw the pieces into Greenway's face. "This is our farm. You will never have it." He turned to get back in his truck.

"Mr. Meades?"

David stopped, but didn't turn around. He glared at the twins for getting out of the truck.

"Have you ever heard of eminent domain? You ought to familiarize yourself with the concept. When a state or municipality deems the resources, or the location itself, of a specific property essential and strategic to its best interests and to the good of the community, it may legally claim such properties. You never know just what valuable resources might be buried on your land. Of course you'd be compensated. Think about it, Mr. Meades. You and your family may be instrumental in instructing visitors to the retreat in the artful way of life you've so beautifully and precariously crafted: beekeeping, sugaring, candle making, crop production, wood sculpture, quilting, cheese making, canning and preserving…it would be such a loss for all concerned. Take my advice Mr. Meades, the sooner you come on board the better for you and your loved ones."

4.

Let Them Eat Cake

ZEPHYR LAFRANCE ERASED the blackboard with a sigh, stood for a moment in a cloud of chalk dust, as if mesmerized by the dull powdery smell of it, and then she turned and stared at the empty table tops ringed with upturned chairs. She rolled out her chair and sank down into its worn cushion. She was tired, through and through, yet something deeply melancholy about the silence after she let out class for the summer made her wish for school to begin again tomorrow.

Zephyr felt this way to one degree or another at the end of every year, because she'd failed in the one particular, impossible thing she wanted most: for all of her students to succeed—if not equally, then at least to their full capability. But capability was relative when the entire process of public education was dedicated to separating the brilliant from the dull, the curious from the complacent and the compliant from the intractable. Exceptional. Average. Poor. Failing. Labels to follow children around for life.

Sometimes, beneath all the urgent talk about improving test scores, she wondered what they really strove to impart. Cognitive skills? Decent manners? Critical thinking? Or some other more subtle and devastating knowledge? Were they merely teaching children to spit back what adults thought they should know? Wasn't it really the unwritten table of placement in the world they studied? This one a doctor; that one a writer; this one a computer engineer; that one a farmer; here a drop-out; there a criminal; here a nurse; there, one just like her teacher.

Oh, Zephyr wanted to teach them to add and write and read as much as anyone (and she probably achieved more toward that end than most), but a part of her knew she was pretending if she thought she'd given them all the same things. No matter what she did, they would not all leave her class feeling smart, confident, pretty or clever. For there was a hard magic hanging over some of them like a cloud, and she knew they were always going to live under it. She should know.

Zephyr sat up with a start and looked over at the party remnants. She'd forgotten to dispose of the cake. Along the left-hand wall, a folding cafeteria table was overspread with celebratory decay: three plastic tubs of melting ice cream (chocolate chip, strawberry and Rocky Road), two pitchers of punch, bowls of potato and nacho chips, a plate of cookies, and the hacked up cake in question. The garbage barrel at the end of the table was crammed with confetti bright plates and napkins smeared with chocolate ice cream and sugary blue frosting. The punch would go down the sink and the chips were probably turning stale already, but the ice cream could still be reconstituted in the cafeteria freezer, and the cookies could go home with somebody. Osmena Searle had assured her the blue powder she used in the frosting was safe, but she didn't want to take any chances.

Just then, Renata Bishop, the second grade teacher and Vice Principal, strode into the classroom pushing a cart. "Oh, good, Zephyr, you're still here. I'm getting some things together for Loaves and Fishes. Do you have anything left over?"

Zephyr started for the cake. "You don't want this; look at the mess those children made. I don't even think it's legal to serve leftover anything at a soup kitchen," she said, trying to get a hold under the cardboard sheet she'd set it on.

"Legal schmegal. It's perfectly fine." Renata strode in beside her and picked up a knife. "No point in wasting perfectly good cake. Just even out the edges."

"Well...really they've made such a mess out of the frosting, I'd be mortified..."

"Oh, for heaven's sake, nobody's going to care if it doesn't look like it came straight from a bakery. It's for a soup kitchen, Zephyr. They'll be glad to have it. Look and we saved them the time of having to cut it up." Renata lopped off a jagged mess with one swift sharp stroke and cut out a corner around another one. Then she sliced it up into little squares. "Ready to serve. Now, we'll just set these on a pretty plate and nobody will ever know the difference." Renata looked at her and stopped, the knife poised midair. "Are you all right, dear, you look ill?"

"I'm fine really. Just a little tired." Zephyr kept her eyes on the cake as she spoke.

"Well, I imagine you are. It looks like you had quite the party in here. This ice cream will never survive the trip."

"I was going to firm it up in the cafeteria freezer."

"Good idea." Renata Bishop bagged up the cookies, loaded the cake and ice cream onto her cart and started to wheel out of the room. "Will you be going away this summer, Zephyr?" she asked, stopping, as though she'd come here to ask about Zephyr's vacation plans all along.

"No. I'm pretty much going to stay around here. I love my garden too much," Zephyr waved her hand as if to banish the idea of luxury travel.

"It can survive without you for a few days. Well, staying home will be restful. You do look a little—tired. I can certainly understand why. Speaking of which, you should be very proud of the work you've done with Cody LaRoy. It borders on magic."

Cody LaRoy. Cody, who had brought her to the point of desperation—the only time in 17 years of teaching—and caused her to drive the steep, winding, mountain road into the Lease Lands and The Cosmos, Osmena Searle's sprawling estate.

Zephyr would be the first to admit it might have been pride that set her up for the fall in Cody's case. Although she'd had no choice but to accept the problem Ms. Finch couldn't handle, she may have overestimated her own ability to transform the boy. It had gotten to her that everything that had worked before with other students now failed miserably with Cody. If she was easy on him, he mocked her weakness; if she got tough with him, he out-toughed her. He was stubborn, psychologically savvy and hell-bent, which was a rare combination in a child, but a demon to deal with when you were faced with it. The morning he'd squeezed Zephyr's breasts, like they were a couple of old fashioned bicycle horns, was the end of the line for her. The taste of failure and tears were bitter that day, so galling, the name of Osmena Searle had just come to mind unbidden, no, actually sprang to her lips without forethought. It had been many years since she'd thought about Osmena and she wasn't even sure if she was still alive.

Zephyr had grown up aware of Osmena's presence, as if her existence were as essential to reality as her natural surroundings, an element like the water she drank and the air she breathed. She had been much more a part of Zephyr's childhood, lived in the shadow of the Lease Lands, a large tract of mountainous forest so called when the colonies still paid taxes to the King of England. She was as mysterious and unquestioned as God—part doctor, part economist, part confidant, part priestess, part counselor and part sorceress, though it wasn't perfectly clear to Zephyr how someone could fill all those roles and retain any semblance of integrity. She inspired an equally puzzling mix of respect, fear, resentment and dependency. Osmena Searle was a fact of life and a natural wonder; a whispered scandal and a source of pride; her word was gospel, yet was viewed with suspicion; her magic was law, but as hard to comprehend as the speculative, rumor driven ticker tape of Wall Street. Alternatives to her wisdom seemed questionable if not downright loopy, and yet no matter how many times Osmena was wrong, or how much trouble her guidance wrought, she never seemed to lose her credibility.

Zephyr grew up with a sense of outrage against Osmena, because, her father, Gerard LaFrance had no use for superstition, social control and economic exploitation and he had raised her to resist them wherever they raised their heads. Oddly enough, people went to Ms. Searle for magic, miracles and life guidance, but they always came back as if they'd just gone to see her about some practical matter like how to prune roses, or just to have a friendly chat. They talked about the practical things, but they never spoke in public about the matters of the heart that had drawn them to her.

Zephyr had been ashamed for giving in and glad her father hadn't lived to see the day a daughter of his went traipsing out to The Cosmos, though she told herself she was doing this for a boy on his way past the point of redemption.

It was late March, when the mountain roads were still packed with ice, and Zephyr had gotten caught in a blinding squall on her way up. The air was so thick with snow and windblown powder she'd come to a dead stop three times to figure out which way the road was going to turn. You often heard about things like this happening to other people going out to Osmena's for the first time—getting caught in some freak storm, having car trouble without a house around for miles, grown men wandering off into the woods, never to be heard from again. Oh, she'd broken out in a cold sweat all right, and then, just like that, the snow quit and the sky cleared off. She'd felt silly for being so superstitious and easily frightened, but then, the belief that brought her out on her supernatural errand could not entertain the possibilities of magic without contemplating curses as well.

Osmena had given her a strange electric blue powder, which Zephyr managed to slip into the boy's juice during recess when the children were in the gymnasium. Well, didn't his behavior start to change that very afternoon. He'd sat attentively (to his own chagrin) during Social Studies and he'd even asked a question about the Mayan temples they were studying. The next morning, he'd handed in his homework assignment, full of mistakes, but completed nonetheless! There was a minor altercation during recess, but after his second dose at lunch that day, he was as good as gold.

The change was so remarkable that within a week it was the talk of the school. "I can't believe it's the same boy," Clara Finch told her one day with begrudging admiration. "What on earth did you do with him?"

Zephyr had shrugged it off and made some lame remark about Cody adjusting to changes in his home life. Well, what credit could she take without feeling a sharp pang of guilt?

This was really why Zephyr felt so miserable about the end of the school year. For she had not solved Cody's problems or changed his circumstances one whit. She had just dimmed the outward signs with chemical magic. He still bore the scares of abuse and abandonment. That was why she had laced the cake, having no choice this time but to drug the entire class with Osmena's formula, a heavy dose in hopes of getting Cody safely through the summer. She blushed at the memory of her pandering—how she encouraged him to have a second and then a third piece.

But why did Zephyr care so much? After today he was no longer her problem. She had done her job and had gotten him through the fourth grade. Now, no matter what she wished for, it was out of her hands.

Zephyr had just finished packing up her things, when she felt as if she were being watched. She instinctively glanced out the side windows. There stood Jude Corgan, his hands cupped around his face, staring at her through the window. He was actually tapping with one hand when she turned, and it occurred to her, after feeling momentarily unnerved, that some part of her mind had registered the faint tapping and had translated this awareness into the feeling of being watched. He waved at her and she waved back.

Zephyr walked over to the heavy glass door with its latticed wire filigree and let him in. "Hi, Jude."

"Hello, Ms. LaFrance."

Jude always addressed her that way, never lapsing into Miss like the other children (and adults for that matter). This had always struck her as solicitous rather than strictly polite, as though he needed to set himself apart from others in her eyes, and he alone knew how to address her properly. That he kept coming back to visit her four years after he'd left her class, was evidence that Jude attached some particular importance to his year with her. She didn't think it was vanity on her part, because he never showed the slightest interest in any of his other former teachers. He displayed a curious formality with her as well, whereas he turned this same formality to humorous effect with his classmates. Only with them she felt he was being ironic, letting them know he wasn't being serious.

Sometimes Zephyr found him awkward to be around, though she sensed if Jude knew she felt that way, he would be wounded. On the other hand, she'd always found his original and strange mind compelling, and his pariah status had made her protective of him and secretly proud of his scholastic efforts. He was certainly not someone who drew you in with beauty, the mesmerizing kind some children possessed that acted on you like a will of its own. You really had to resist being overpowered by such children into treating them differently.

Jude's older brother Kennedy had been beautiful that way—golden haired and wild eyed. Yet, what she remembered most about him now was his sense of fairness. He had a love of justice (there was no other way to put it) and that quality gave his rough beauty a kind of majesty. He was no saint, but it was never meanness or rudeness that got him into trouble, but his runaway enthusiasms and forgetful absorption in things.

Zephyr recalled one afternoon recess in the early spring. The field where the boys played 'Kill the Guy with the Ball' was still puddled in places. She and the girls had stayed on the black top shooting underhand baskets with jelly balls, and playing hopscotch. When it was time to go in, Zephyr blew the whistle. The girls began to line up and head up the hill to their classroom door, but the boys continued playing. She blew the whistle again to no avail, so she went out onto the grass to get their attention. The swarm of boys turned and ran toward her in full pursuit of the guy with the ball. One of the smallest boys, Jimmy Servione, slipped and fell on a wet spot and slid across the soggy grass. The other boys finally noticed Zephyr and stopped running. Jimmy had gotten up but was standing apart from them now, one leg covered in a slick of grass stain, mud and wetness. One of the boys pointed and laughed. 'Hey, pig pen!" Soon they were all laughing and pointing.

Jimmy's face twisted up into a cringe of discomfort and embarrassment. He reddened and his lip began to tremble. Before Zephyr could utter a word to intervene, Kennedy, the guy with the ball, ran toward Jimmy and slid by him feet first into the same puddle. The boys were in an uproar and began to cheer. Kennedy leapt up and raised his hand up to Jimmy in preparation for a high five. Jimmy had been so close to tears it took him a moment to get it. His expression changed to surprise and then a smile. He slapped Kennedy's hand and another cheer went up. Kennedy tucked the ball under Jimmy's arm and they walked stiff legged and soggy up to the school followed by the commotion and laughter of the other boys.

All Zephyr could do was smile and shake her head. She asked Kennedy to stay for a few minutes after the final bell went off. The chorus of "Ooh, you're in Trouble!" swelled and then faded, as the children exited the side door. She asked him to come up to her desk.

"I was just wondering, Kennedy. Why did you do that today, on the playground?"

"Are you mad I did it?"

Zephyr shook her head and smiled. "I'm just curious what made you do it."

"It looked like fun."

"Did Jimmy look like he was having fun?"

Kennedy shook his head. He looked around as if trying to find an escape route. Finally, he said. "We stayed away from the puddles all recess, but if it was after school we'd all have done it on purpose. Just that Jimmy…"

"Jimmy what?"

"Didn't mean to, you know he slipped."

"Who wants to be the only one with muddy pants, right?"

"It isn't that funny then."

Zephyr squinted at Kennedy, curious at how he knew that and somewhat in awe of him. "Okay, go home and put some clean clothes on, Pig Pen." She ruffled his hair and sent him on his way. It was as if he knew instinctively, were it not for his golden looks, he would have been as unremarkable and every bit the runt of the litter Jimmy was to them.

When Zephyr had seen Jude's name on her class list, she remembered having Kennedy many years back, no less because he'd died tragically the summer before. So with Kennedy's golden image in her mind, she was quite unprepared for the sight of Jude. Even in the fourth grade, he had been much larger than the other children, which made him appear to shamble around, shoulders rounded, back hulky and his head as large as a child's football helmet, an appearance that had earned him unfortunate nicknames like "Lurch" and "Andre the Giant". But, the one nickname that had stuck harder than all the others was "Son of Junkenstein".

"I'd offer you some goodies from the party, but Mrs. Bishop's already taken them to Loaves and Fishes."

Jude shrugged. Another reason she felt awkward around him was his habit of showing up at her door and lingering with nothing whatsoever to say, a silence she felt obligated to fill.

"Actually, Jude, I'm glad you came by. Would you mind terribly helping me haul these boxes to my car?"

Jude perked up immediately. "Sure, I'd be glad to, Ms. LaFrance." He went over to the desk and lifted each of the boxes to feel their heft, and then he said, "I'll take this one, it's heavier."

⌘ ⌘ ⌘

"So, ANY BIG plans for summer?" Zephyr asked Jude, recalling Renata Bishop's compulsory question.

"Sure, I think I'll climb Everest again."

Zephyr bit for a moment, thinking he had turned his irony on her, and then she remembered the big junk heap he'd told her about and laughed. "Plant a flag up there for me."

"Actually, don't tell anybody, but I think she settled last winter and lost a foot or two."

Zephyr smiled and shut the trunk of her car. "I'll never tell."

They stood in silence behind the car.

"I guess I should be going," Jude said. His bulk looked even more awkward when it was not in motion.

"Me too. Thanks so much for your help, Jude."

Jude just stood there and she thought she'd better say something more. "School went okay this year?"

"Nothing too taxing," Jude said. "To tell you the truth, I wish sometimes I could be in your class again." He cocked his head to the side and his black hair fell across his eyes.

"Well, it's funny you should say that. Before you stopped by I had just been thinking wouldn't it be nice to have the same students every year right up to grade 8."

"That would be awesome, if it was you."

"Oh, I bet you'd get sick of me after a while and want somebody different."

33

"No way. You're the best." Jude looked down and buried his hands in his pockets.

"Jude, you just made my day," Zephyr said.

A little smile started on one side of his face.

"Can I give you a ride home?"

Jude's eyes registered alarm.

"It's the least I can do."

"Well, alright. Okay. But I have to warn you, it won't be pretty."

Jude got in and Zephyr drove. Being guardian of small minds for so long, she took extra care to mind the rules of the road. She made sure Jude was belted, kept her speed down (not that she had a heavy foot), looked very carefully both ways at the stop signs and signaled well in advance of her turns.

As Jude and Zephyr passed through the village, some children on the sidewalk caught their eyes. Zephyr noticed, not only because they were two of her students, Sally Wright and Jane Montgomery, but also because they were skipping down the sidewalk. Not just skipping, but kicking high, swinging their arms and wagging their smiling faces side to side in rhythm. Nobody skipped home from school anymore. She used to skip as a girl, but somewhere down the years since then, it had gone seriously out of fashion and had never come back in. It had so completely passed out of the collective consciousness that kids today didn't even know how it was done. She smiled and thought how nice it was to see it making a comeback. Then she noticed another one of her students, Adam Reid, blithely skipping the green. Then at Maple and Main it was Bobby Walsh and Kristen Scott skipping in unison. Finally, Jude turned to Zephyr and said in disbelief, "Are they on drugs, or what?"

5.

Nine Tenths of the Law

THE STATIC ON Chief Rinaldi's radio blasted like a bomb in the silence of the station. He started in his chair and scattered the report he was writing across his desk. He stifled a curse and reached for his belt. The volume was all the way up again. He turned it down and pressed the talk button. "This is Twin Gaps PD; come in," he said, a little surliness creeping into his voice, as if it were the dispatcher's fault the volume was always cranked up high.

"This is Crawford State Police dispatch, do you read?"

"10-4 Crawford; we read."

"We have a report of a 415 at 26 Mechanic near the corner of Mechanic and Maple. Requesting a cruiser. Let us know if you need back up."

"10-4. Unit 2 copies a 415 at 26 Mechanic."

Rinaldi snapped the radio back onto his belt and headed out the door. Tulley had been outside cleaning the windows on the cruiser, but he was in the driver seat idling on the side of the road ready to go. The chief got in beside a roll of paper towels and a bottle of Windex.

Tulley said, "26 Mechanic. Isn't that Loaves and Fishes? That's a first. Somebody must have spiked the Kool-Aid. Hope it wasn't Viagra."

Rinaldi just shot him a look. The problem with Tulley was his addiction to television crime drama. For him the great challenge of confronting crime was to come up with an appropriate and timely quip for every call. Rinaldi made it a point never to encourage such foolishness, although occasionally Tulley came up with something genuinely funny, and he had to cover his amusement.

It was a straight shot down to Main Street and over a block to Mechanic St. They were stopped at the curb outside the Loaves and Fishes in about a minute. Chief Rinaldi felt silly intervening in something like this. Armed with a pistol, a night stick, handcuffs and pepper spray on his holster, he felt a bit overdressed for the occasion.

Rinaldi opened the door and Tulley followed him inside. They were instantly engulfed in shouting and a flurry of edible projectiles; though most of the arsenal now was being applied in hand to hand combat. It was a freaking food fight!

The cafeteria tables were all knocked askew and pushed up against the walls, as if they'd been used as battering rams. In fact, a blond woman bent over one now, arms extended and her soiled hair falling across her eyes. She commandeered an assault on two fellow diners trying to protect the last of the ammunition, a partial pan of stuffed shells. "Give it up or I'll crush you both!" she threatened.

"Don't you! Don't you dare! These shells are hot. I'll dump them on your head so help me."

Other combatants moved with less tactical efficiency, rubbing handfuls of chocolate pudding and stuffed shells into each other's hair and faces; others dragged their victims as if to mop the floor with them. At this point, there was a good deal more stumbling, flailing and slipping than actual violence.

Rinaldi held out his hand to stop Tulley from charging into the fray and stood sizing up the scene. There wasn't a soul from the soup kitchen staff as far as he could see—they'd probably all run for cover—though come to think of it, everybody was so covered with food it was difficult to identify anyone. There was only one solution when you couldn't tell the perps from the vics. He put his bullhorn to his mouth and shouted, "This is the police: get down on your knees and put your hands behind your heads."

A tall boney man—naked to his food-soiled briefs, face and body primitively smeared with marinara sauce and chocolate pudding—pointed at Rinaldi and Tulley, shouted "It's the pigs," and flung a fistful of shepherd's pie at them. Tulley ducked and the sodden clump of mashies struck the Chief right in the face. He staggered back and tried to clear his eyes, but he stepped on a slick of pudding, went down twisting sideways and landed with a lusty grunt.

Tulley, still ducking, quickly wheeled and knelt down over Rinaldi. "You okay Chief?"

Rinaldi didn't move. "My elbow hurts like hell. Arrest that son-of-a-bee."

Tulley, ever the student of TV crime, reached for his radio. "Officer down at 26 Mechanic Street. I repeat officer down at 26 Mechanic," he called out in his most urgent television voice. "We need an ambulance."

Ben Tulley was at his best when he worked at law enforcement as if he were playing a sport. Once the Chief was safely out in the cruiser waiting for the ambulance, he felt instantaneously free to practice his game. For instance, if he were a contestant on a reality TV show, he might be charged with tackling and subduing as many perps as he could in two minutes. All he needed was some rope. He dashed into the kitchen, ducking at incoming pasta torpedoes and dirty pudding bombs. He went to a door on the far wall that looked like it might be either a pantry or a closet. When he opened it he came face to face with a frightened old woman holding a soup ladle up in self-defense. The woman saw the uniform, dropped the ladle and raised her hands.

"You wouldn't happen to have any rope in there?"

The woman looked a little stunned for a moment, but then her pale blue eyes lit up and she turned and scanned the shelves behind her. "I know I've seen it here. Where is it...ah, here." She grabbed an unopened, plastic bound clothesline rope and handed it to the officer.

"Thank you ma'am." Tulley took the rope, closed the woman in and took out his Swiss army knife. He slit open the plastic and cut several 3 foot lengths of rope. Then he looped them through his belt so that they hung like limp spaghetti down the side of his right leg.

Tulley was ready for action now. In his mind, the timer started. He burst through the dining room and tackled the first person he met.

⌘ ⌘ ⌘

WHEN THE CALL came over the radio that Chief Rinaldi was down, Sergeant Nolan Roderick was relaxing in his rocker, revolver in hand. Being on back-up allowed him to use his old .357 Magnum. He'd never liked the semi-automatic SigP229, neither the grip, nor the trigger weight of the VSP side arm that had been standard issue since the 90's. Now they were using the M&P.40. It was a better weapon than the Sig for sure, but it was no more than that.

Roderick spun the full barrel once and clicked it into place, but he didn't jump out of his chair and rush to put on his uniform. He reached to the oval antique table for his radio and depressed the talk button. "Officer Tulley, come in, this is Sergeant Roderick; do you read me?"

"Tulley, over. The Chief slipped and fell, possibly chocolate pudding, or shepherd's pie. Looks like a fractured arm."

There was a lot of shouting and commotion in the background, as if it was a riot, but the sergeant had heard the initial call and was listening to the dispatches with amusement. He was even more amused to hear about the Chief's accident, and took a long moment with his eyes closed to visualize the scene and imagine a whole summer ahead of him with Chief Rinaldi out of commission, with himself, perhaps, as acting chief.

"Well, put it all in your report, Officer Ben. Do you need assistance?"

There was a very long pause, in which the sergeant finally rose from his rocker, all six foot three of him, and walked down the hall to the bathroom. He went to the medicine cabinet and looked through some of the prescriptions bottles there. He found the little zingers he was looking for, popped a couple in his mouth and swallowed them without water.

"This is Officer Tulley, requesting assistance."

"Roderick copies. Responding to the scene at 13:50."

In the few minutes it took the sergeant to put on his uniform and walk over to Loaves and Fishes (he lived two blocks away), Officer Tulley had roped in the last of the combatants and was down on one knee pulling taut a perfect hitch.

Tulley had them all hog tied and lined up face down on the floor. He was covered in food, but grinning proudly over his quarry through the marinara smeared across his nose and cheeks.

"You literally tied them up, Officer Ben." Sergeant Roderick tilted his head and smiled faintly. "If anybody came in and saw this, they'd think you were taking these people hostage. You're a regular psycho. Color me impressed." He reached out impulsively to pat the young officer on the back, but caught himself in motion and gave him a stinging head slap instead. Roderick seldom missed an opportunity to inflict pain. It was its own reward. "Damn good work."

"Ow. Thank you, sir." Tulley looked no less proud, but a bit dazed and confused by the force of the sergeant's compliment. "Remind me not to do such a good job next time, sir."

"Don't be modest, OB. A job well done is its own reward. You know, we're going to need a police wagon to process this bunch. Frankly, we ought to strip them and hose them down right here. They're going to make a filthy mess of the station." There was nobody on the force in Twin Gaps who was as freakishly neat as Roderick. Now, he squinted and tilted his head as if having second thoughts. "But, throwing food is not a crime. Has anybody here actually been assaulted?"

"I don't know, Sergeant, sir. The one in briefs threw mashies at the chief, which caused him to fall."

"Damn. I guess we'll have to bring him in; but hose him off out front where we wash the cars. What about the others?"

"Breach of Peace?"

"Just issue a warning citation to the Loaves and Fishes for excessive noise in a residential area."

That was the weird thing about Roderick. He was gung-ho for prosecuting even the smallest infraction of the law, but if some circumstance came between one of his private obsessions (like the absolute cleanliness of the station) and the pursuit of justice, he might just as suddenly look for a technicality to wash his hands of the matter. As long as the perps endured some form of pain or humiliation in the course of their capture and he had the pleasure of inflicting it, he often felt deeply satisfied that justice had been served. (This tendency, and the unrelated fact of his missing right index finger, had converged in Roderick's local nickname: Nine-tenths of the Law.) It dawned on Tulley that he'd enjoyed too much satisfaction today for Roderick's liking and this may have been the reason he'd been head slapped. After all, he alone had dished out today's generous serving of law and order. By the time Roderick arrived, everybody—fallen and fractured Chief Rinaldi (since taken to the hospital) and all these people trussed in painful positions—had suffered sufficiently except for Tulley. It hadn't escaped his notice either that Roderick was calling him OB, his favorite insult.

Suddenly, Tulley remembered the woman in the closet. "We do have a witness." He ran to the pantry and retrieved the shell-shocked old woman. She walked with tentative steps and looked around cautiously, like a child coming out in the open during a game of hide and go seek.

"Ma'am. It's quite alright now. We'd just like to ask you a few questions about what happened here. Just tell us who you are and what you can remember."

"I'm Gloria Walker and I volunteer here every Wednesday and Friday. I just don't know what happened. We served the lunch meal as usual and then they just started going crazy." The woman raised her hands in perplexity and shrugged. "I wish I could be more help."

Roderick cleared his throat. "Well, do you remember when they started going crazy?"

"Let's see, dinner was almost over. People were eating their dessert and enjoying themselves. You know it was actually rather quiet. We had some apple pie and whip cream topping. Oh, and then Ms. Bishop from the elementary school brought some cookies and cake. I remember the cake went very fast and things got a little livelier. You know how it is when a room of people talking gets louder—so I came out of the kitchen to see what the buzz was all about, and they were raving about the cake and going back for seconds. Well, that's when the first trouble started. Some people were arguing over the last piece. It was very strange. We've never known people to behave like that when the food runs out. But, it wasn't just that. Soon every corner of the room had erupted in arguments. Then the food began to fly. I was afraid and hid in the pantry. Sheila Givens managed to get out in time. She must have called the police." Mrs. Walker closed her eyes and crossed her hands over her chest. "It gave me quite a fright."

"Well, everything's alright now," Officer Tulley reassured her.

Roderick shot him a cautionary glance. "Maybe not, unless we find out what set them off."

Mrs. Walker's eyes opened wide with alarm.

"Is there any more of that cake?"

"Oh, dear no, but the last piece was smeared in someone's hair. You can't miss it. The frosting was electric blue."

Roderick and Tulley went over to the row of suspects, all wiggling and moaning with tape over their mouths, and began to search their heads.

"There," Tulley pointed at a blob of blue on a blond head.

Sergeant Roderick unhooked a knife from his belt, produced a little evidence bag from his belt, cut off the blue frosted lock of hair and dropped it the bag. He stared close at the bright blue frosting, at once familiar and eerie. There was only one place he had ever seen that shade of blue before.

"We'd better have this examined ASAP." Roderick stood up and turned to leave.

"But, Sergeant Sir, what should I do with all these people?"

Roderick turned again, tilted his head and squinted. "Arrest the one who assaulted the chief. Do what you want with the rest; just don't bring them to my station."

Tulley was confused by the complete freedom and absolute restriction of Roderick's directive.

Roderick rolled his eyes. "Give them all a few spoons of castor oil and leave them tied up for a few more hours. Or...let them go. I don't care, OB." He shook the little baggie of blue frosting. "This will lead us to our culprit."

6.

Geist

THE FIRST TIME Jude stepped foot in Merrilee Rainey's house, he'd felt mesmerized. For one thing, it was a real house, not a trailer, and for another it was full of books and interesting things from different parts of the world: Irish and Russian novels, huge art books with beautiful photography, ebony sculptures and pale pottery from North Africa, tapestries from India in brown, gold and turquoise colors, oil paintings from Spain and Mexico of blocky, white-shirted peasants. Jude would not have lasted ten minutes in there, if it had been spotless and dead as a museum. In fact, it was the familiar clutter, the casual jumble of incompatible objects (however different from the stacks of cheap monthly magazines, dollar store knick-knacks and filling-station glasses cramming the Corgan trailer) that made him feel at home.

Jude felt even more at ease in the Rainey's garage, where they were meeting today. It was actually an old barn wide enough for two cars below. The hayloft had been converted to a great room with rustic barn board walls and skylights letting sun shine on the old naked beams and the painted rust red floor. In the center was a huge rug, all red, tan, black and white, patterned in dots, zigzags and native stick figures. Among the furnishings were an Ethan Allen rocker, an uncomfortable wingback chair, and a sagging couch so bolstered with multicolored pillows and quilts Jude had never seen the upholstery they covered. Opposite the couch was a huge rolling blackboard that made the loft look like the coolest classroom in the world. His favorite was an overstuffed tapestry chair with a matching ottoman. It smelled sweet and exuded clouds of dust when you patted the arms. There were cubbies and shelves on the walls stocked with board games, decks of cards, bestselling paperbacks, and collections of tins and antique gas station globes and oil cans: Sky Chief, Norseman, Phillips 66, Sinclair Dinolene, Golden Leaf, Esso. All from a time Jude's parents didn't even remember.

There was no trace of hay, yet it was both pleasant and mysterious how the musty smell of it persisted, greeted you when you first came upstairs to the loft, like the haunting of a sweet-tempered ghost. The floorboards creaked reliably, but somehow felt solid under your feet. If Jude could have lived in a room like this for the rest of his life, he was sure he could want nothing more.

Jude had no idea what to expect, but when he arrived at 2pm, Merrilee and three other girls he knew from school were sitting around the loft with open notebooks.

Merrilee stood up. "Everyone, this is Jude Corgan."

"Hi, Jude," they all said at once.

"Oh, sorry, wrong meeting." Jude pretended to retreat.

They all got it and laughed.

Merrilee began by introducing him to the other girls. Alison Hartshorne was a tiny girl with long, dark, tangled hair and a pale complexion. She was the quietest of the three. In school, she always wore knee length skirts and blouses under lacey cardigan sweaters. Sandra Duke was as direct in her manners as she was in her dress—usually a pair of faded jeans and an oversized jersey would do. Her sandy brown hair was parted in the middle and hung straight down the sides of her head. She had violet gray eyes, rimmed in an even paler shade, that were almost hypnotizing to look at. Cate Robinson was robust and solid, with short dirty blond hair and a kind of wet, raspy voice, as though she were just as likely to spit as speak when she opened her mouth.

"We call ourselves GEIST," Merrilee began, standing beside the rolling blackboard, "Which stands for Gaps Eavesdroppers & Information Surveillance Traders. It's a stretch, but what can I say, we thought of the acronym first." She flipped the board on its spindle and revealed the acronym spelled out. "And what we do is gather information—not just stupid stuff that everybody knows and couldn't give hoot about—but all the things about people we hear that we're not meant to hear. We listen to what is said, by who and when. We write it down, compare notes, and then we wait and see what is true, what is mixed-up and what is nonsense. We find out who can be relied upon and who cannot. Knowledge is power, but, you see, it does no good if what you know is rubbish. In fact, it can be your undoing. Most people are constantly trading in rubbish."

Merrilee flipped the board again to the blank side, and with chalk poised to write, began naming categories. "First, there are FACTS—verifiable statements of reality (within reason) reliably witnessed, self-evident, or experienced first-hand. Going along with this are EVENTS—things that really happened. Then there are RUMORS (stories about actions or events that can't be immediately verified)."

Here Merrilee looked up and withdrew her chalk. "A rumor may turn out to be a FACT, and it may turn out to be UNTRUE. That's the tricky part. When it is untrue, it's a good thing to know whether the rumor was a LIE (either out of malice or idle speculation), or whether it was MISCOMMUNICATION, and who was responsible for spreading it.

"Then there are LEGENDS—stories, usually about more distant events, that have a suspiciously mythical quality. MEMORIES are important sources of information about the past, but notoriously vague and corruptible over time. Finally, there are IMPRESSIONS. These are unproven feelings about people and events that are only as good as the instincts of the person who receives them."

Merrilee put down her chalk, gave the board another spin and flopped down on the rug. They all grabbed some pillows, including Jude, and joined her on the floor.

"The reason you've never seen any of us together at school, Jude, is because our group is secret," Merrilee began.

Sandra said, "Not because of some snobby private school hocus pocus, but because it works best that way. If we hung out as a group, people would start to notice us each as members of a group. We're kind of invisible now. People say things around us because they think we don't count, don't care and don't know anybody."

"Yeah, but Merrilee hangs out with me in school,"

Sandra gave him a deadpan look. "Exactly." Then she smiled.

Jude threw a pillow at her.

"Before we help you, you have to promise you won't talk to any of us in school, except Lee," Sandra said.

Merrilee added, "And you can't breathe a word about GEIST."

"Who am I going to tell?"

"Exactly," Sandra said.

"Alright. But, I have a question. If you don't talk to each other in school, how did you ever meet?" Jude asked.

Cate said, "Back in September of 7th grade, there was supposed to be a book club forming after school in the library."

"I bet the library was rocking," Jude said.

"Well, it was just the four of us."

Merrilee said, "Turns out we didn't like the same books at all."

"But we got to talking about school stuff and town people. It was kind of weird, but each of us knew about someone or something that one of us had wondered about."

Alison finally spoke up, almost apologetically. "But, in almost every case we had it wrong, or had heard completely different stories."

"So we thought wouldn't it be cool to have a club dedicated to finding out the truth about things," Cate said.

"Except, the only way it would ever work, was if nobody knew we were a group," Sandra added.

Merrilee said, "We had to be omnipresent and invisible as a ghost. Thus, the name GEIST. Anyway, enough already about us. We're here to help Jude find out who has been leaving wrecks in his yard for the past five years."

The girls looked at Jude eagerly and waited for him to speak with pens poised over their notebooks.

Jude settled uneasily on his cushion and cleared his throat. Although, lately he'd become accustomed to regaling the school bus with stories about the Corgan curse, he realized he'd kind of developed a slick, commercial version ready made for public consumption. What he was about to tell the members of GEIST was very personal, and full of impressions and feelings that he hadn't dared express to anyone, for fear he'd sound weird, at least, weirder than people thought he was already.

"Well, actually, it's even more than just finding out who's been dumping the wrecks. To find out who is to find out why, and what it all means."

"And what do you think it means?" Sandra said.

"I don't know, but I'm sure it has to do with my brother, Kennedy, and what really happened the night he died."

The members of GEIST leaned forward on their pillows in anticipation.

"I remember something from that night, but I can't prove it happened, and Aster and Jet say it didn't. I was in my room and overheard a fight between my parents and Kennedy."

"What was it about?" Merrilee asked.

"That's the problem. I couldn't hear most of it. Kennedy was shouting. I'd never heard my brother sound so angry. Aster was crying and Jet was trying to calm her down. He wasn't saying much. Mostly it was Kennedy's voice."

"Do you remember anything at all?" Alison said.

"Just one thing that Kennedy kept shouting. He said, "I want to know who?"

"That was it?" Sandra said.

Jude nodded.

"What do you suppose he meant, 'I want to know who?'" Merrilee asked. "Who did what, I wonder?"

Jude continued, closing his eyes, trying to recall an image of something he never saw, but only heard from the darkness of his room one night five years ago. "Then the door slammed, the car started and tore up the road. That's when Kennedy left. He never came back."

"Are you sure the fight definitely happened that night?" Merrilee asked.

"That's how I remember it."

"But, why would your parents say it didn't happen?"

"And how could they forget anything so important about that night?" Cate said.

Jude shrugged. "Then there were the dreams. I can't be sure, but I think I dreamed about Kennedy's death right before it happened."

47

The four girls looked at each other with knowing looks, skepticism mingled with fascination.

"Even if you did, it could be a coincidence. Everybody has nightmares about people dying," Sandra said.

"I know, and I'm not really sure that it didn't happen afterwards."

"What did your parents say about that?"

"Are you kidding? I've never told anybody about that until now. And what good would it do anyway? It doesn't change anything."

"You said, 'dreams'," Cate reminded him.

"A couple of nights after Kennedy died, I dreamed he was alive. In the dream I was asleep and he was standing over my bed. He just stood over me and said nothing."

"Cool," Sandra said.

Alison physically shivered. "How creepy."

"There is one other thing, but it doesn't really have to do with Kennedy at all. I don't think Jet is really my father."

Sandra gave him one of her you've-got-to-be-kidding looks. "Why on earth do you think that?"

"Because, Jet is a total idiot. Listen, he's such a dunce he forgot his own blood type. You know life and death stuff. Back before Kennedy died he had this school project and when he asked Jet what his blood type was he got it wrong. Aster had to remind him and we razzed him mercilessly for days. It's embarrassing. I don't look like him at all—"

"You have his dark hair and the same color eyes," said Merrilee. "Besides you get along better with your dad than with your mom, why not disown her?"

"Because, she gave birth to me. It's kind of indisputable, but the way he acts and thinks, well, you wouldn't think it was genetically possible that I was related to him."

"You mean you wish he weren't?" Sandra said.

"No, I mean—" Jude said. He shook his head and looked down at the floor.

"Well, it's not exactly hard evidence."

"I heard your dad is a really good inventor," said Alison. "He can't be that dumb."

"He isn't dumb. Just very clueless sometimes," Jude said.

Merrilee said, "And I don't know how you expect to prove it without causing a divorce."

"Okay, so forget about it already," Jude said.

"Is that everything?" Merrilee asked.

"I guess so," Jude said.

"Alright. What do we have on Jude?"

The girls began to flip through their notebooks.

"You have information about me?"

"Don't look so shocked. You're suffering under the curse du jour and it happens to be a serious topic of discussion." Merrilee looked at Jude over her glasses. "Who wants to start?"

Alison hesitantly raised her hand. "I've recorded a rumor." She looked apologetically at Jude and began to read. "Janie Wiggins said Jude is Goth and killed his brother out of jealousy and his parents have gone crazy covering it up all these years and they're behind all the wrecks in an attempt to gain sympathy."

"That's a legend, not a rumor, Alison," Sandra said.

"Oh, right. Sorry."

"Somebody actually said that?" Jude asked, incredulous.

"There's worse," Sandra said.

"I'm sure there is. Does anybody have anything remotely helpful?"

"On this past March 16, Lester Higgby was overheard at the Horse's Mouth, saying that some of the Corgan wrecks came from Atwood's Salvage," Cate read from her notebook.

"Does your father know Chet Atwood?"

"Sure, my father used to work at their garage; but they're not enemies," Jude said.

"Well, who else works there that you know?"

Jude shrugged. "Well, Les. He used to work there too."

"Isn't that just a rumor? About the wrecks? He could be mistaken, or he could be lying," Alison said.

"Wait," Sandra said, flipping through her notebook. "Personal knowledge. Les Higgby's wife Corinne left him for Chet Atwood the previous December. Lots of hard feelings there."

Sandra closed her notebook. "Perhaps, we're overlooking the obvious. Is there any possibility your father is responsible and had help from Atwood?"

"No way," Jude said.

"Can't you just call DMV and use the VINs to track the cars?"

"The VINs have all been removed. Believe me Jet's checked every one of them (except for Sweet 16)."

"Isn't it illegal to remove the VINs?" Alison asked.

"Yes. It's a way a used car dealer can hide the fact that a car's been in a serious wreck," said Cate.

"And if somebody local recognized their own vehicle, wouldn't there have been some talk about it that would point to Atwood or another auto salvage?" said Merrilee.

"If we'd been doing our job we'd know," said Sandra.

"Speaking of overlooking the obvious, if it's really a curse then there's really only one person who could be behind it," Merrilee said.

"Osmena Searle?" Jude said.

"But that still wouldn't tell us who put her up to it. Even if you went up to see her, she wouldn't tell you who did it. My father says it would be like a conflict of interest. Because even if you guessed, or figured out who was cursing you, she couldn't admit it or take the curse off, because it's paid for. All she could do is curse the people back who are cursing you. For a price. I guess she's kind of like a legislator."

"God, that could get complicated," Jude said.

"Yeah, she's got the God Problem. How can you be on everybody's side at once? I guess that's why it helps to look at every wish she grants as plain old buying and selling."

"Does she ever make mistakes?" asked Alison. "I mean, did you ever think the curse was meant for somebody else?"

Jude scowled at the suggestion. "Sixteen mistakes?"

Merrilee continued. "If you don't have money, she might do a spell for you, but you have to take one of her experimental potions." She flipped through her notebook. "Here. April 19 of last year. Reg Bagley let it slip in Samms Luncheonette that his Uncle Nels took one of her experimentals years ago. In exchange, he wouldn't have to pay off the debt on his failing farm. Fortunately, there were no nasty side effects, like unwanted body hair or bad smells. Unfortunately for Nels, she was testing out some kind of juice that makes you stupid. After a few days on this stuff, he became so senseless he didn't even know enough to look both ways while crossing traffic. Sure enough, he got run over by a truck. No debt worries for him. Some people would say that's criminal; other would say it's just business."

Through the skylights, shafts of bright sunlight suddenly streamed into the room. It was like somebody had thrown a light switch, reminding them that it was getting late.

"Anything else?" Merrilee asked.

"I have," Cate said. "Two things. October 13, last year; Blanche Turcotte and Sassy Romanov were gossiping in the launderette about the Corgans. Blanche said that Jet was on his way to being a brilliant inventor until his son died in that awful wreck. She said he was building a flying machine, but had never been the same man since. Sassy said Aster had a miscarriage by another man before she had Kennedy."

Jude felt his jaw slacken. A strange tingle washed over him, the kind of sensation that follows the illumination of secrets, but also something else. A jolt of shock that his parents harbored secrets, and there were important things about them he might not know.

The girls observed his shock with sympathy, while glancing back and forth at each other with those peculiar knowing looks.

Merrilee seemed to say what they were thinking, "It is just a rumor, but your parents are not innocent Jude—of course they're keeping secrets from you (all parents do; it's in their nature), even as we speak they're plotting to shield you from all sorts of vital information. Your parents may be holding the key to the secrets you want to unlock, but you'll never find out unless you make it your business to know."

7.

Ominous Signs

T HE NIGHT AFTER David Meades discovered the illegal development on his property, he suffered a nightmare where more and more of his farm was being transformed by bulldozers. He woke up several time, but each time he returned to sleep the dream continued. In the morning, he awoke with bloodshot eyes, a headache and the dreamland echo of land movers ringing in his ears.

Slater Knox, a well-liked local attorney, would file an injunction to stop the work on their behalf, and he'd assured David there was no exception in the state's Eminent Domain laws that allowed the condemnation of private property for a third party profiteer. Greenway's plan did not comply with those defined for public use and he was not acting on behalf of the State. Even if he were, such a transaction and use would have to be affirmed by voters at Town Meeting. Knox suspected it was an empty threat.

"Coffee?" David offered the twins.

Jesse and Junie nodded and sat down at the kitchen table. Oscar was already having a cup and eating his breakfast. On the weekends, when the twins did the morning milking, they were allowed coffee. David filled their mugs and served them scrambled eggs, toast and sausage.

Once Oscar was off to the chicken coop, and the twins were in the barn seeing to the cows, David ventured out in his truck to the building site. The sky was blank and pale, harbinger of another hot day. By the time he arrived, a buff yellow glow had appeared in the dip between two silhouetted mountains, like a skim of cream in a black bowl.

David got out of the truck and walked around the rectangular pit to inspect the work. The forms for the foundation were all in place, but the concrete had not been poured. Suddenly, the gall of Greenway's plan almost brought his breakfast burning up into his chest, and filled him with the urge to preempt legalities with some destructive force. It would be so easy to crush these forms, but blowing them to Kingdom Come was a far more satisfying fantasy.

David took a deep breath and walked back to his truck. It was too soon to even think about dismantling the site, outrageous as it was. Knox was optimistic the developer didn't have a leg to stand on, but he was scouring the law books for legal precedents and any archaic state laws and regulatory codes that Greenway might pull out of his sleeve. As far as David was concerned, it was trespassing and destruction of property plain and simple and a call to the police should have been sufficient to stop Greenway and prosecute him. The problem was Greenway possessed building permits and an apparent legal deed, while David, after a rather frantic search, seemed to have temporarily mislaid his. The back "40" was really 47 acres purchased separately from Charbonneau years after he and Raeanne bought the lower 35 from the Zengers.

David got in the truck and wound slowly up the back pasture. When he came over the crest, a honeyed strand of sunlight struck his eyes. For a moment, the land below—the orchard, the barn, the gardens and the house—disappeared and he had the sensation of teetering over a void that stretched on the sunbeam from his eyes to the horizon. A wave of vertigo made him slam on the brakes. He closed his eyes and waited for his head to clear. A red after-image of his signature floated across the amber shade behind his eyelids. He opened his eyes, flipped the visor down and descended slowly through the orchard. Once back in the shadows the familiar features of the farm reappeared.

Yet, the vision of the signature brought to the surface the most troubling and inexplicable things about all of this. Where was the deed to the back 40? And how had Greenway obtained David's signature, or, at least, something so close to his signature it might well convince a handwriting expert, probably a judge as well?

David had just reached the gardens when he saw Jesse running towards him from the barn. He stopped and rolled down the window.

Jesse came up to the truck out of breath, his tan complexion strangely flushed and his placid golden brown eyes bright with alarm. "Dad, hurry. Something's wrong with one of the cows."

The next day was the 5th anniversary of Kennedy's death and Jude knew he had to get out of dodge before things got ugly, so he'd gotten up early to head to town.

Jet was at the table slathering a half inch layer of marshmallow on his sandwich, when Jude came into the kitchen. Aster was still in bed, and she was always the first one up. All signs pointed to a real humdinger of a day.

"God, don't hog it all," Jude said.

Jet took a big bite, "Wah suh?" He offered the half-eaten sandwich to Jude. "Too muh pea buhr." He separated the bread and slathered another glob of fluff onto the sandwich.

"That's obscene; somebody arrest that man," Jude pointed at his father.

Jet burst out laughing with his mouth full. He always lost it when Jude did one of his outraged authority routines, especially if Jude caught him eating or drinking. Thank God he wasn't drinking, or he would have sprayed a nose full all over Jude. With the peanut butter, the worst he could do was choke on it.

Jet swallowed hard and cleared his throat. "You sure? There's plenty."

"Not hungry." Jude looked back once from the door. Jet was sitting there having another long cogitative chew as if oblivious to a tornado that was about to demolish his trailer. "Sorry, I can't stay, Dad."

Jet came out of his dream and looked up when Jude called him Dad. "I know you can't, son." Then he lowered his eyes and took another bite.

Old Route 9 crossed over the southern face of Catamount Peak. It used to be the only way over Catamount Peak until 30 years back when they built Route 17 through the northern gap. Being narrower and mostly gravel, it was much less traveled by through-traffic and day trippers these days. The village of Twin Gaps sat at the juncture of the gaps in the shadow of Catamount Peak. From the Corgans' trailer down to the village, OR 9 rolled gently downward like a kiddy rollercoaster, not steep enough for Jude to pick up dangerous speed going down, or to stop him cold peddling home. It became much steeper and curvier by the time you reached Atwood's Salvage a couple miles above them.

At the bottom, Jude passed over the trestle bridge that spanned the Green River and stopped before turning onto Main Street, which was Route 9A. To his left, Route 17 jutted off at a forty-five degree angle to OR 9, and Main Street, bent like a drinker's elbow, took a hard turn east toward Marston. He waited for some cars to pass and turned right toward the village.

At the heart of Twin Gaps was U Street, a broad one way trombone loop on the left of Main on the way into town. It had a center green and diagonal parking in front of the shops on either side. The U ended in the Riverside Park with its white gazebo, paved paths and big shade trees that extended to the banks of the Green River. The General Store, Samms Luncheonette and The Horse's Mouth (the local pub) were on the U. They were the best places in town for gossip. Jude and Merrilee usually ended up at Samms Luncheonette after school. Today Jude would have to solo. Merrilee was off with her parents on a literary conference in New York State for the weekend. She'd be back on Sunday night.

Jude was about to turn into the U when he spotted Officer Tulley directing traffic around an orange barrel up ahead at the mouth of Winter Street, the next street on the right. Main Street was down to one lane and the traffic was backing up to Jude as Tulley waved cars on from the other direction. A crowd of people gathered on the sidewalk at the corner of Winter Street. They were all gazing down towards Pullman's Mobil. Jude peddled over to the edge of the crowd but couldn't see anything. The air was heavy with black smoke and the smell of burning petroleum.

Jude rolled up to Officer Tulley.

"Hey, cool bike," Tulley said.

"It's the Byclops. My dad built it." Byclops was the weirdest bike in the world, built like a chopper with a small wheel in the front and a giant one in the back. A complex series of chains and gears made it pretty easy to go uphill, but God help you if one of the chains came off during an extreme shift. You needed an engineering degree or a free afternoon to put it back on again. The frame was a nearly indistinguishable blend of rust and rust-colored primer. Jude used to be embarrassed to ride it into the village, but lately, along with the curse, his Junkenstein bike had acquired gear head chic.

"No kidding. You'll let me take it for a spin sometime?"

"Hey, sure. Anytime. What's going on? Fire?"

One thing about Officer Tulley, he liked being down with the local teens and you could get a lot of information out of him if you played your cards right.

"Man. Worse. An explosion." Tulley stepped out from around the barrel. He flipped his sign around from STOP to SLOW to change the direction of the traffic flow and stepped back again. "Yeah, somebody bombed the Mobil. Probably a homemade job with household chemicals. Did the trick though. The tanks and everything—BOOM! Happened about 3:30a.m. Betz had just gone off duty and gone home for the night. Good thing. The station took a little hit from the explosion, knocked out some windows and took a few shingles off the roof. Roderick went ballistic."

"Is it still burning?"

"Except for a couple of hot spots, it's all under control; otherwise you wouldn't even be allowed this close. Luckily the tanks were almost empty; due for a filling this morning."

The Amtrak Station with its pricey tourist trap eatery had nearly escaped, but looked blackened and damaged on the far end. The police station was far enough away to be damaged from flying debris alone.

"How do you know it wasn't an accident?"

"Someone's taking credit for it."

"Like who?"

Even Officer Tulley had limits of indiscretion. He blushed a little, as if he were afraid he'd already said too much. "Can't say. Pending investigation."

Aster and Jet toasted Kennedy for about the sixth or seventh time. Somewhere between their bittersweet reminiscences the sure number was lost in a deepening haze of tears and drink. With each toast, their glasses clinked harder and the threat of breakage was a danger they seemed to be daring, even willing, on each other, as if the point of the toast were no longer their son, but the breaking point of their grave celebration.

"Ta Kennededy," Jet bumbled the words, dipped his head in disappointment at his own botched toast.

Aster giggled viciously. "Kennededy! Deady! Deady awrighty!" She slapped the table.

"Shhh. Doan mock me. Dya hear me? Doan do it. 'Ees my son too."

"Your son too! Thass rich. For the love a God Jet; just once could we get through a doggam toast without your self-pity ruinin' it. Jude's right, you don't get ionry. Ne'er did. Dense as brick. I was mockin' death and Freudian slips have a way of bein' 'ronic."

Jet only got angrier. His face was red and shiny with the sweat of the rising heat. "Wouldn't be aronic; wouldn't be deady if—"

Aster sat up from her morose giggling lean, as if suddenly pricked by a needle. "Oh, oh! If what, Jet? Go head an say't. You sonvabitch had to say't; Couldn reziss. If what?"

"Asser, no, I'dn mean it."

"Oh, you men it n'pleny. Ne'er lemme forget it. No you started say'n it; now say it!"

Jet was shaking and about to weep. He threw back the rest of his drink and swallowed through clenched teeth.

"Too muchova cowrd to say't. I'll say it then. If I'd a told Kennedy the truth. There it is Jet. All my fault. What you ahways wanna say."

Jet stood up and slammed down his glass. He started down the hall toward their bedroom as if he had good legs under him, but he lurched and jarred the table. The bottle of Jack tipped and began to dribble its dwindling contents on the plastic table cover, while the empty bottle they'd finished tumbled to the linoleum and clunked but did not shatter. Aster put up her hands beside her head and waved Jet away, her mouth open and eyes filled with tears. Jet held onto the wall and stumbled off to bed.

Aster almost lost her breath in a silent spasm of sobs, but finally when Jet was gone, the brittle cry broke through. A pillow muffled cry from Jet sounded from the bedroom like a responsive chorus.

"If only..." Aster laid her head down on the table.

"Pull ahead of the space. Yep. Signal. Okay. Now, nice and slow in reverse cut the wheel to the right."

Kennedy put his right arm over the seat and looked back at the parking space. It had been his choice to practice parallel parking right in the village on Sunday morning. Aster marveled at his confidence, not yet sixteen and parking the car with the gymnastic flare and calm he showed dismounting his bike.

"Okay, now watch your nose. Clear the fender and cut hard the other way. Inch back as far as you can. Great, you cleared the curb. Straighten the wheel and come forward just a bit, so you leave some room between both cars. Perfect."

Kennedy smiled in relief. His appearance of aplomb belied the effort and concentration it took to get it right in one try.

Aster hated to say it, but she'd been driving for 20 years and she wasn't sure she could have done much better. She looked at the side view mirror. True, he was at a bit of an angle and he'd only missed the curb by about 2 inches, but it was good enough to pass the driver's test.

"Now that we've gotten the hard part out of the way, what do you say we go for a cruise up to the Granger Falls?"

"Sounds good to me." Kennedy pulled carefully out into traffic and took a left at Mechanic Street. When they got out of the village they turned onto Route 17 and started up to Granger Falls. There were trails to the falls from the woods behind their trailer, about a two and a half mile hike. From the pull-off on Route 17 it was only about a half mile in to the falls and the trail was easy to follow.

"I've been talking to Chet. You know he's got the crusher working. He says if we can haul the junk up there, you know, in a big dump truck or something, he'll flatten it down to nothing."

"But, how are we going to get your father to let go of this stuff. We'd never hear the end of it. How much time he spent sorting the aluminum from the tin, the No.1 grade from the No.2. The money we're throwing away."

Kennedy winced and smiled crookedly. "We could get him good and drunk. That'd be easy enough. Then bind and gag him for a couple of hours. Get a backhoe and a big truck and just keep filling it and hauling it away."

Aster laughed at the thought of Jet, wiggling and moaning while they hauled away the beloved straw he would never spin into gold. "It would take more than a couple of hours. How long do plan on tying him up?"

"We'll run a hose down his leg to a jug so he can pee all he wants. I don't know. And Jude can feed him fluff and peanut butter sandwiches. That usually shuts him up."

Aster was taken in a fit and she was trying to speak. Kennedy imitated her windy mouthing, which made her laugh all the more. She finally caught her breath and was able to speak, but her face hurt from laughing and was still frozen in a smile. "Much as I'd be tempted, I don't think you father would forgive us. In fact I'm sure he'd spite us by just collecting more stuff to replace the old stuff. We're just going to have to keep working on him until he decides to get rid of it himself. It won't do any good to force him."

"But you should have a say in how things are, Mom. It isn't fair."

"I know." There were moments like this when Aster felt her son was practically an adult already. Kennedy had both hands on the wheel and was watching the road intently, making sure he was smooth around the corners and not drifting over the line. All at once she had the impulse to tell him everything. He was old enough. Grown up enough. All she had to do was look at him to know. "Kennedy—"

"Yeah?"

Where was Aster going to get the words? Her throat seemed to close up, her mouth went dry and her mind went blank. She felt her face flush hot and then freeze cold. If he was ready, why wasn't she? He looked over at her.

"What is it, Mom?"

"Nothing. Just thanks for understanding."

If only she'd found the words.

It must have been Jude's lucky day, for when he arrived at Samm's Luncheonette, old Hiram Rafferty and Dunky Lagro were in the midst of speculating about the explosion.

Dunky's eyes got a wicked glint, made all the more demonic by wild eyebrows that shot upwards like silver flames. "I coulda told you it weren't no accident."

Jude moved closer to the counter, slid into the nearest table and quietly opened his notebook.

"Anybody coulda told you that could read."

"What'd the message say?"

"Something like *the end is comin'*. A black skull and the initials VLF."

"You see it?"

"It's sprayed painted across the police station roof," Hiram said.

"The end of what?"

"Don't say."

"What's VLF?"

"More like a who."

"Sounds familiar for some reason. Lot of other strange things going on, the likes of which reminds me of when the Sokols' barn and that denist's burnt to the ground five years ago. And that boy lost it up on the gap, burned beyond recognition the same night."

Jude felt his skin prickle on the back of his neck. They were talking about Kennedy. He wrote furiously to keep up with their conversation.

"Lot of fire then. Arson sure as I'm sitting here, but they never caught no one for it," Hiram said.

"They were looking for Francy's boy at the time. Never found him."

"Never will. He were gone long 'fore then. Dead men don't talk and they don't blow things up. Got nothing to do with him far as I can see. More to do with that Greenway fella's big ideas, I can't say I blame folks for wantin' to blow things up. Don't forget who owns Pullman's now. Won't have nothin' when he's through tearing things up; less folks stop him somehoe."

Dunky persisted. "Harmon Gage got a look at a catamount just last week. I say look out when the past starts repeatin'."

61

"Ain't been catamounts here since before I was born," Hiram said. "People get all worked up over nothing. One thinks they seen a cat, then another one seen it too. 'Fore you know it everybody's uncle has one in their cow pasture."

"Took two of his cows five years ago. That weren't getting worked up over nothing."

Hiram made the sour face that was his trademark expression. As he'd aged, his head seemed to have shrunk to about the size of a medium cantaloupe, while his ears, nose and chin had taken on gigantic proportions. "Catamounts don't have nothin' to do with bombs, and then don't have nothin' to do with now. It is what it is, as my grandkids say. Folks getting fed up with flatlanders taking over."

"Suit yourself, Hiram, but som'un or somethin's got big plans for us."

Aster was at the kitchen table when Jude came in. She didn't look up but she wasn't looking at anything either. The stony trance. An empty bottle of Jack stood in front of her like someone she'd been talking to. She had one hand around her glass, resting on the table, in the other she held a cigarette with an inch long ash. Jet was nowhere to be found. Jude headed past her toward his room.

"Where have you been?"

Jude stopped. "In the village."

"In the village! I don't know why you want to ride around on that thing where the whole town can see you. Don't you know they laugh at you, the same way they laugh at your father? What do you care though? Just ride off without a word, like you can come and go as you please."

"Jet knew where I was going. Where is he?"

"Where? Down the hall in oblivion. That's his gift, his calling, his escape. He can just get away, like you."

Jude went down the hall into his parents' bedroom. Jet was out cold, face up on the bed. Jude rolled him over and set his head with his face out, just over the edge of the pillow. He went back into the kitchen.

"You didn't even turn him over."

"Did you ever think he might not want to be turned over?"

"Shut up."

62

"Don't you tell me to shut up. I tell you when to shut up, which is right now." Aster lifted her glass and raised it like she was going to throw it at Jude, and then she drank it down instead. She put down the glass and took a deep puff on her cigarette, staring straight at him all the while, stony in her eyes, bitter lines in her upper lip. Her head tipped just the slightest bit from side to side.

When Aster was like this she never called Jude by name, or even 'young man' like she did when she was angry. This was something else, as if under her hard, drunken gaze he was beneath naming.

Jude turned away and headed for his room.

"When your father wakes up why don't you ask him whose idea it was to let your brother start driving at 16. Ask him who gave him the idea it was all right for him to drive alone with only a permit. I want you to ask him, do you hear me? I'm talking to you—"

When Aster woke up tomorrow she wouldn't remember any of this, but Jude would recall every single word.

8.

A Mad Cow and a Catamount

ASTER AND JET were sleeping it off. The trailer was quiet. Jude couldn't stop thinking about the explosion and the conversation he'd overheard in the village that day. Certain things Dunky LaGro had said came back at him like an echo. He'd never heard about those mysterious fires before. 'A lot of fire then', he'd said. What did he mean? Too much fire to be a coincidence? Who was Francy's boy? And why would people think he set the fires?

By evening, when the sun lowered and the light grew thick and golden, Jude's excitement ebbed and a sinking sadness fell over him. He didn't know exactly why at first, except that his mind was less focused on unanswered questions, and more fixed on the grisly details of his brother's death. At the funeral, what Jude could remember of it, the casket had been closed because Kennedy had been burned beyond recognition in the crash. *A lot of fire then.* Hearing Hiram and Dunky talk about Kennedy's death had confirmed his absence in the world. He was dead to everybody else too, and Jude was forced to face the fact that Kennedy was never coming back, as if for the first time. He hadn't been allowed to see Kennedy's body, so a part of him still held onto his brother as a living person, perhaps away on an extended trip, existing somewhere in the world unchanged as the night he'd left, alive because people and objects remained devoted to his memory. Sixteen wrecks, each like a spirit haunting their lives.

Jude went outside and wound his way between the mounds of scrap: Everest, Pike's Peak, Kilimanjaro, Mt Washington, the Cascades in the northwest corner of the yard, (Mount St. Helen's was the blackened one that had spontaneously burst into flames one hot, July day the summer Kennedy died). Not so long ago, Jude did nothing but fantasize scenarios about getting rid of Jet's "mountains".

Once, Jude's fantasies had actually coalesced into a plan. What if they took a piece of junk every day and dropped it on somebody else's property. The question was whether there were enough properties in all of Vermont to absorb their surplus, one rusty piece at a time. The large appliances would be a hassle, but there were some stretches of gravel road where you could roll an old washer or refrigerator out every couple of hundred yards or so into a ditch without anybody being the wiser. He imagined himself with Jet, guiltily kicking large appliances down steep ravines, like a couple of serial killers dumping dead bodies along lonely interstates, while Aster kept nervous watch.

The beauty of Jude's plan was that the removal of the Corgans' legendary cache would transpire so gradually, nobody would even know it was happening. It would take months of daily trips before you'd even make a visual dent in the stuff. People were nosey by nature, but generally not that observant. Years would go by, and then one day Mr. Montagne would drive past their yard and say to his wife, "You know, their junk really isn't as unsightly as we once thought it was." Yet just a few years later, when all of the junk was gone, it would finally dawn on them that the Corgans had cleaned up their act for good. As for the recipients of Corgan generosity, they too wouldn't notice what they had inherited for many years, at which point there really would be no way to trace anything back to its source. Jude even rationalized that his father had been taking useless clutter off of people's hands for so long, that perhaps the only fair thing left to do was for everybody to return the favor by sharing in the burden of Corgan wealth. Was it too much to ask them to store one rusted tool, one mangled bicycle, a hubcap, a stacker washer/dryer, or one little twenty-five foot lunch wagon? It would be kind of like a junk tax from which nobody was exempt, and where everybody stored according to their capacity.

Right after the tenth wreck, Jude had tried out his plan on Jet. He must have still been smarting from Aster's morning reaming, because he succumbed right away to Jude's suggestion and agreed to have a go at trying to convince her. Oddly enough, as much as Aster wanted every piece of useless clutter off her property, they knew she would be the one to object to Jude's wealth redistribution plan. The remnants of her born again religion predictably came out of her. "Do you really want to do unto others, what they've done unto us?"

"But mom, there's no proof anyone has done unto us."

"Jude's right, the golden rule doesn't seem to apply here. We're just giving back to the community."

"Come on, Mom, it's just one piece of junk each. God gives no man more than he is able to bear," Jude quoted back to her.

"Giving back to the community. Quoting scripture back at me. That is what the Reverend Giddings would call outright sophistry. I guess I failed to teach you anything about right and wrong, Jude. I'm ashamed of you both. It's just not right. Besides, what if we got caught?"

"Well, fine. If you won't do anything about it, you're just as much to blame as he is," Jude accused Aster and stomped off to his room. He knew then it was hopeless. His parents would never do anything about the way things were. Jude would bide his time, and then he would leave them both and their endless piles of misery behind forever.

The shade over the Cascades felt cooler, but the air was humid and very thick with haze. Funny how the long cool spring had made an 85 degree day feel like a 100. That was the other thing about tonight that made Jude feel sad. It came back to him now so clearly, he couldn't believe he'd forgotten to mention it to Merrilee and GEIST.

Only hours before Kennedy had driven up the mountain, he and Jude had gone up through the woods to Granger Falls for a swim. Aster and Jet were at a bluegrass concert on the green in Marston and wouldn't be back until after dark.

The boys put on mosquito repellent and followed a little footpath that eventually came out onto an old logging road. You had to follow this for about two miles, then find the turn off onto another footpath that led up to the falls. At that age Jude never ventured there alone, because it was easy to miss the second path and he was afraid of getting lost. This was the back way to the falls and hardly anybody but they ever used it. Most people drove up Route 17 a couple of miles and parked their cars along a little turnoff with its own well-trodden path to the falls.

Jude and Kennedy didn't stay in the water long. It was cold, despite the heat, and the narrow gorge was air conditioned by the brook. Yet, they lingered for some time in the cool air until, miraculously sweat free, they actually began to feel chilled and the thought of going back out into the evening swelter was welcoming. They sat side by side on a smooth stone shelf overlooking the darkening pool below the falls.

Kennedy was strangely quiet. Usually when they were here alone, he told Jude stories about his own adventures in these woods when he was younger, or repeated a string of the latest jokes he'd heard, including the dirty ones, so long as Jude promised he wouldn't tell Aster. Kennedy wasn't in a joking mood. He just sat there in his cutoffs staring into the water. He was short and compact like Jet, with humpy wrestler's shoulders and a slight but chiseled chest, and had thick, wheat-colored hair. The dusty blond color along with the golden hazel eyes came from the Meades, so that he looked more like a brother than a cousin to the twins.

At first, Jude thought Kennedy was just tired. After all, he'd come in very late and slept until about two in the afternoon. But, this was not the empty quiet of somebody spacing out from too little sleep. He was thinking hard and, by the way his lips kept parting, it was obvious he had something to say.

At last Kennedy broke the silence. "It's weird how everything can change just like that, you know, Judo?"

Jude sat up intently to listen. When you were young, you got used to not being taken seriously by adults and teenagers. Kennedy wasn't like that and had treated Jude more like a peer than the much younger brother he was, yet he couldn't ever remember Kennedy talking in such a serious voice, and he had a feeling this was something hard to understand.

"What do you mean?"

"I mean, you think the world is a certain way and then one day you wake up and it's all flipped upside down. Nothing is the way you thought it was. And the people you trusted most aren't who they pretend to be."

Jude didn't understand at all. Surely, Kennedy could see that he was lost.

"What's different, Kendy? We still have all our junk. I'm me and you're you."

"Right. What else does a family need?" Kennedy smiled, reached over and put a hand on Jude's shoulder and gave it a shake. But, the pensive look returned. "You'll find out soon enough." He saw the bewildered look on Jude's face and added, "Don't worry, Judo, it doesn't affect you. I don't know what's going to happen now. But you're gonna be okay."

Kennedy's lips had gone blue and began to shiver. Goosebumps rose up everywhere on his tight smooth skin. He stood up, pulled his towel around his shoulders and looked off down the gorge. A sheer sand stone cliff defined one side, undulating along the watercourse like a brittle ribbon; a wooded slope chucked with boulders and jutting ledge bounded the other side. Dark moss clung and cliff ferns stirred on the currents of cool air above their heads. The tunnel-like feeling made it look like dusk, even though it wouldn't be dark for another hour. "There's something I have to know—a couple of things. Then we'll see." His voice had an angry edge and his eyes took on a dark flinty shine. He looked down at Jude and held out his arm. Jude took hold and his brother pulled him to his feet. "No matter what happens, Judo, you'll always be my brother, right?" He sounded so small and lost just then it seemed to Jude that Kennedy was the child looking for reassurance.

Jude nodded vigorously, as much to reassure himself as Kennedy. "Sure, Kendy. You know. Why wouldn't I be?"

Despite what had happened later that night, the quarrel and the accident, Jude hadn't thought about that conversation once over the years. Had he truly forgotten it until now, or had it just made so little sense to him then, that he hadn't connected it to the events of that night? Another memory leapt out at him, one he couldn't place exactly, except to say it must have come near the end. Somehow it was paired with the memory of the fight. He'd gone in the trailer to find Kennedy and had found him in Jet and Aster's bedroom. He was just standing there holding Jet's wallet. Jude wondered if he'd caught his brother stealing money from Jet and whether this had caused the argument he overheard. He couldn't even be sure the two things were connected, but

69

there was something about the look on Kennedy's face that made him think it was.

Jude never imagined his life would change completely too, because the things Kennedy told him that evening seemed so much a mystery. A dark emptiness had filled him that night, and an uneasy shifting feeling too. It came with the knowledge that the people he loved, and who were so much a part of his childhood happiness, had been so full of sadness.

Jude stared at the dark opening where the path led into the woods. With the rampant summer growth partially obscuring it, and the path fallen to disuse, he wondered whether he'd be able to find his way to the logging road. For some reason, he didn't care if he got lost. In fact, he had a sense that what he wanted to find was not at the falls, but much deeper in the woods. Something irresistible drew him on. He wandered to the edge of the woods, carefully pushed aside an arching whip of bramble and disappeared into the shadows.

"To be honest, it's almost certainly BSE," said Kendreth O'Hanlon. "Of course we have to wait for the results of the test, but if it's Mad Cow the whole herd will have to be destroyed. I'm sorry."

The entire Meades family—David and Raeanne, the 14 year old twins, Jesse and Junie, 17 year old Oscar and 9 year old Willa—sat around their dinner table with Slater Knox and the only large animal vet in three counties. Kendreth was a tall, solid woman with long, graying red hair, a freckled complexion and luminous silver blue eyes. While you felt instantly assured and safe in her presence, a call from Kendreth usually meant you had a very sick animal on your hands.

As soon as David arrived in the barn that morning and saw the cow staggering around in its stall, he felt a sickening lurch and then a tightening knot in his stomach. The latter had not let go in the intervening hours. In his heart, he knew the worst was happening. He also knew the minute he examined the cow, despite the number on the tag in its ear, that it was not Anabelle. This was not even one of their cows. Junie had noticed it right off, because he'd named Anabelle when she was born and had also been especially fond of her. The tag number was hers, but the markings on her face were not. It didn't take David long to figure out that somebody had made a switch, and who that somebody might be. No matter that Anabelle had lived her entire life on their farm, and that his cows were fed on grass and silage alone, he knew he couldn't prove what he suspected. Possession was nine-tenths of the law. Necessity would demand that swift action be taken no matter what they could or couldn't prove.

David shook his head and put his hands to his forehead. "I understand, but I'm telling you this is not my cow. Greenway is trying to destroy me, and he's succeeding. We'll never recover from this."

"Well, David, it's a serious crime if it's true and you'll need to get the law involved. I hear he's a pretty powerful fellow, your Mr. Greenway. I'm sure I wouldn't want to be the one standing in his path of progress." Kendreth stood up. "I'll have those results for you as soon as I can."

"If the news is bad, what happens then?"

"The same thing that happened to the Freeman's and Faillace's sheep. The government will come in and seize them. They'll be observed for a few days, destroyed and their brains will be tested. A Prionics test could save the herd, if it's found to be clean, but given an advanced full-blown case of Mad Cow with exposure—no matter how remote transmission may be under the conditions on your farm—I'm afraid the herd hasn't got a prayer."

Slater Knox said, "DNA could prove its not one of your cows, but it doesn't mean the cow can be traced to anybody else. And the government is not going to wait around for DNA results."

"Thank you for the supper, Raeanne, really," Kendreth said. "I wish it had been under better circumstances."

After Kendreth O'Hanlon left, Raeanne and Jesse started clearing dishes.

Willa said, "Daddy, do we really have to kill all the cows? They're not all mad."

"Yes, I'm afraid, if it's Mad Cow. You can't take a chance of it spreading."

"It's not fair." Willa began to cry.

"It's not even our cow," Junie said. "Can't we prove it's not?"

"It's beyond proving; it's on our farm, wearing one of our tags," David explained. "The feds are not going to believe its sabotage." It called to mind Jet and David's sister, Aster, and their predicament with the wrecks. Nobody believed them either. The difference was the Corgans had no idea who was cursing them.

The sound of Granger Falls up close drowned out just about every other noise you could imagine—bird calls, voices, footfall, thunder. It was possible to sneak up on people without being detected, just as it was possible to be snuck up on. Jude stood for a while, staring at the white cascade and listening for the rhythm of the falls. If you listened to moving water, you could hear a kind of pulse, a strong beat and a weak beat. Sometimes when he arrived there, the rush of the water was like a current that filled him with its roaring energy. At other times he was completely calmed by the sound of the water.

There wasn't a soul at the pool. In fact, there weren't any of the usual signs that people had been there recently: no beer bottles, cigarette butts, or junk food wrappers. Yet, Jude felt a presence.

Jude took off his shoes and crossed carefully over the slick stones to the other side and made his way back along the sheer cliff wall of the gorge to the well-trodden path. It continued for quite a ways above the falls. Jude decided to go up and have a look.

Once you got to the top of the falls, the path branched off. Jude followed the one that came back behind the falls. He rounded an outcrop in view of the brook again and stopped. For a moment Jude thought he saw a large animal crouched in the brook. He froze and looked harder. To his relief it was only a boy having a dunk, crouched with his face in the water and his arms bobbing at his sides. The boy stood up suddenly in the thigh deep water, his back to Jude. He wasn't wearing a stitch of clothes, but from the small of his back to the nape of his neck he was clothed in an elaborate animal tattoo.

Jude hid quickly behind the outcrop before the boy could turn around. He waited a few minutes and peaked out from behind the rock. The boy was nowhere to be seen. Jude approached cautiously, looking around and behind him, until he stood just a few feet from the water's edge.

Suddenly, the boy popped up from behind a rock. "Yoohoo!" He had pulled on some cutoffs and a black leather vest, but he was still dripping wet and barefoot.

Jude must have jumped a foot in the air, for the boy began to apologize immediately. "Sorry, there. Didn't mean to make you jump. Well, actually I did a little." The boy smiled mischievously. "Because you found me out." His head was shaved down to a thick dark shadow of hair that came to a sharp widow's peak on his forehead. He had dark brown eyes to match. Though he looked to be about eighteen and had a young man's build, the top of his head was only level with Jude's eyes.

The boy stepped forward and held out his hand. "I'm Calvin."

Jude still hadn't quite gotten over the scare. "I'm Jude."

"Must be quite a walk from where you live," Calvin said.

"Not that far." Jude was about to point and stopped. He was wary of telling a stranger where he lived. He wasn't sure if the boy was fishing for information or just making conversation. Let him think he'd come by the road. "Actually, just down the path to the road. My mom dropped me off. The pool at the falls is better you know. You can dive and swim."

"Yeah, well. I thought it would be a little more private up here."

"Sorry, I didn't know anyone was here," Jude said, which was technically true, but somehow false. "I like your tattoo."

Calvin tipped his head back and laughed. "That's good, Jude. I like your style. Did you get a good look, here." Calvin took off his vest and turned around. His entire back and neck was cloaked in a catamount, as if a big brown cat had leapt on his back and then merged with it. Peeking out from the top of Calvin's cutoffs and curling around the small of his back was the catamounts brown tail. "Look, this is great work." Calvin pulled his shorts down slightly, where the tail started just above his crack. He looked over his shoulder at it. "What an artist. Like the tail's growing right out of my spine."

"Cool," Jude said.

Calvin turned around and sat down on the rock he'd hidden behind. "It's not done yet. Thing is, I can't decide whether the arms and paws should follow my own, or whether they should come down over my chest with the claws dug into my flesh."

"That would be intense."

"You think that's a bit much, don't you?"

Jude tilted his head and nodded. "I guess it depends on your concept. Are you the catamount, or are you the prey?" Jude came closer and sat down on a smaller boulder in front of Calvin.

"That's the question, but I don't know the answer. Can I be both?"

"Dinner and diner? You'd probably end up featured in the Sunday magazine."

Calvin laughed again. Despite his dark hair and eyes, not to mention his beasty tattoo, he had a gentle face. His skin was pale and smooth and his eyelashes were thick and long like a child's. He wore the slightest smile on his lips, as if he were amused or delighted by everything in the world.

"I think you should leave it as it is. This way you're a man coming and a catamount going. It's mysterious. Like you're a changeling. You aren't and then you are."

"That's an idea. Now I've got three concepts to consider. Thanks, Jude, for narrowing things down for me." Calvin stretched out his leg and playfully pushed against Jude with his bare big toe. He reached into his pants pocket and pulled out an expensive looking nautical watch. He put it away and began wiping pine needles from his feet. He put on his socks and boots and stood up.

"Well, maybe I'll get to see it when it's done. Are you from around?" Jude asked.

"You might say that."

"Did you see that explosion this morning?"

"Not when it happened. Talk about intense." Calvin looked over his shoulder. He seemed a little restless all of a sudden. "Still, don't be surprised if there are worse things to come." He lowered his voice, "You'll have to excuse. Nature calls." He waved and disappeared around the back of some ledge rock.

Jude stood around for a while and waited. It was very quiet for several minutes.

"Calvin?" Jude called. There was no answer. A hermit thrush let out its fluty call in the stillness. Behind him, the muted waterfall rushed on. Just as Jude had sensed his presence down below the falls, he now sensed his absence. He climbed over the ledge Calvin had ducked behind. As far as he could see, there was no sign of the man coming or the catamount going.

9.

A Threat, a Promise and a Plan

THE KNOCK AT the front door stopped Zephyr cold in the midst of the Sunday morning crossword. (Thirty-six down: bureaucratic bunch, nine letters, eighth letter E). Not that she minded visitors, but she was not expecting one, and the tenor of the knock froze her—crisp, official and intrusive. She went straight to her bedroom and threw on some walking shorts and a t-shirt over her camisole and panties. The knock sounded a second time, louder and more rapid. "Oh, hold on for heaven's sake," she muttered, genuinely annoyed but also flustered, and hurried out through her sitting room to the front door.

Zephyr opened the door to two uniformed police officers and cursed under her breath. *'Just stay calm, act casual and admit nothing,'* she coached herself. She took a deep breath. It had been over a week since the cake had gone to Loaves and Fishes. A story was circulating that there had been a disturbance there the last day of school, but she'd heard nothing more, crossed her fingers and hoped that it had nothing to do with her cake.

"Zephyr LaFrance?"

"Yes?"

"I'm Sergeant Roderick, Twin Gaps PD. This is Officer Tulley. We have a warrant to search these premises."

"A warrant for what?"

The sergeant handed her the signed warrant. Then, he grabbed the handle of the screen door and pushed his way in.

"Excuse me. You have no probable cause to search my house. You'll stay right where you are."

"Miss LaFrance, we have traced a controlled substance found at Loaves and Fishes back to you. And we have reason to believe you knowingly administered it to children. Please step aside."

But there was no please in Sergeant Roderick's please at all. He was tall and very thin. His face was narrow with slightly hollow, ruddy cheeks and a slender pointy nose. His eyes were gray and evinced a calculating detachment, so no matter what the circumstance, his expression never betrayed surprise or uncertainty. For want of a better term, he was a know-it-all. His voice was calm and measured, but tight and unyielding when he responded to any challenge to his authority. Zephyr had never met him before, but she'd seen him enough around town and had heard stories about him that frankly gave her the creeps. He was rumored to enjoy inflicting physical pain and psychological torment, and was known to be vindictive and obsessive. When he went after someone he combined the calculating, time-biding patience of a snake with the vicious tenacity of a Pit Bull.

"I'm sorry; I want an attorney present to witness this search."

Roderick walked past her into the kitchen. "Feel free to call one."

Tulley rolled his eyes and gave her an apologetic look and followed Roderick into the kitchen.

The sergeant began opening cabinets, one after the other. He stopped when he found the food cabinet, and began taking things out—first the flour, then the sugar and the baking powder. "I see you do a lot of baking, Miss LaFrance."

Zephyr stood in the kitchen doorway watching him. She was sure she'd used all the powder when she baked the cake. After it had gone to Loaves and Fishes she had been fearful of this very scenario and had gone home directly to dispose of it, but she had found none. Yet, she felt a little nagging doubt. The one thing she hadn't done was take everything out of the cupboard.

Roderick stood on his tip-toes and surveyed the top shelf. He reached in and pulled something out. "Well, what do we have here?" He produced a clear plastic bag of blue powder closed off with a twist tie. There was less than an ounce left. "I personally don't like blue frosting, but then not all of them have that special kick."

Zephyr let out a pursed breath to calm her racing heart and stem the rise of color in her cheeks. "That's just some colored sugar, Sergeant. Is baking illegal now under the Patriot Act? Who's next on your list, the Betty Crocker heirs?"

Roderick lifted his chin and stared at her. He produced an evidence bag and dropped the plastic bag inside. "Well, that all depends on the secret ingredient. I don't suppose you'd serve that cake at a teachers' meeting. Well, I have what I need; we'll just run some tests on big blue and see what we have here." He took a step toward the doorway, where she stood. "You'll excuse me."

Zephyr stepped aside and let him pass. "You won't find anything," she said.

Roderick stopped, his hand on her front door, and turned around. "Actually, I've already found out some interesting things about you, Miss LaFrance. A Vermont Teacher of the Year, twice nominated, you're the pride and joy of Twin Gaps Elementary. That's why they gave you that miserable brat this year. Tough nut to crack, but Mrs. Bishop told me all about the wonders you've worked with him. Imagine if everybody knew how you really got through to Cody? That's a mighty striking shade of blue, and only one place I've ever seen it. If I were you, I'd be very careful about that kind of special education, and about the company I kept. You don't want to get in over your head with her. I know from personal experience what she can do."

Zephyr opened her mouth, but decided not to deny or confirm anything. She'd heard stories about his history with Osmena. She stared right at the hand with the missing finger. "If you want *her* so badly, you ought to go after her. But you haven't got the goods or the guts, so you pick on decent folk for kicks."

Roderick may have been seething inside, but you wouldn't know it from his expression. He smiled, bounced the evidence bag around, and said, "Decent folk like you that make her what she is? What do you suppose your commie father would have thought about you cavorting with that wicked speculator?"

Zephyr looked down at the floor. She just stared and waited for Roderick to leave.

"Just as I thought," Roderick said. He opened the screen door and stepped outside. Ben Tulley caught the handle of the screen door and turned to Zephyr. "I'm awfully sorry for this intrusion, Ms. LaFrance. When he gets a bee under his cap there's no stopping him is all." He tipped the bill of his and left.

From high above the forests of the Lease Lands, the encampment was invisible. There appeared to be nothing but a lot of very old and dense evergreens on the Eastern face of Hidden Mountain, inaccessible to vehicles (or so it appeared). For, though the hunting was rumored to be rich, the closest road was on Osmena Searle's land and few folks would dare take the risk. Beneath this evergreen haven, with its dense hemlock skirt and its tall white pines, the understory was limbed up a good fifty feet all around. The smaller trees had been cleared, so there was room for vehicles to pass.

There were four Quonset huts, two on either side of the road that divided the camp (a pair of dormitories for the men; one for supplies and the last housed two open jeeps, four ATVs, a workshop and all of their equipment). The larger trucks were kept outside. Six perimeter look-out posts in the trees commanded a clear survey of the camp and a camouflaged view of the surrounding forest. A concrete bunker had been jack-hammered into ledge and poured in concrete, an emergency shelter accessible through a trap below what appeared to be a central campfire.

Luc Dentremont surveyed it all while keeping watch in one of the lookout posts. It was on the idea of a large, well built, weatherproof deer blind. Just not comfortable enough to sleep in.

"Hello up there."

Luc peered down the hole in the floor. It was Jake Allard.

"Want some company?"

Luc threw down the rope ladder and Jake climbed up, pulling himself up through the hole by handgrips and swinging his legs to the side.

"Hooff!" Jake complained, a bit winded by his climb.

"You ought to quit smoking," Luc said.

"We ought to have quit hiding out in forts by our age, but look at us." Jake raised a dark eyebrow gravely and then smiled at his friend.

Luc offered him the bench, but Jake waved him off. They stood side by side looking out at the forest view. The sunshine was bright, the sky blue and the woodland was deepening to its richest green.

"You have something on your mind?"

"Well, now that we have everybody's attention, what will we do for an encore? People should know that when we say '*The End has Come*', that we don't mean it is the end for them."

"I doubt it would be lost on anybody whose building we blew up. And that Greenway had bought the building and then made it impossible for Pullman to keep renting it. He put a local man out of business so he could reopen it as part of his Catamount Farms chain. He has one in Marston already. I know these folks. They see Greenway's fingerprints on everything and don't think for a moment they aren't secretly glad he got paid in kind for his dirty deed. So long as nobody was hurt, it's a display of decisive anger we can afford. A strong opening shot."

"So long as Pullman isn't accused of it."

"He'd sold everything and moved out of state when Greenway shut him down. I think he'll be in the clear."

"What are people saying?"

"I had a talk with Chet—he'll give us more at the meeting—but, right now, the police think it's the work of some local no goods. The Feds are thinking homegrown terrorists. As for the VLF? The Feds questioned the Vermont Secessionists for any connection to us, but as far as anyone knows, we disappeared over 20 years ago without a trace. We don't exist."

"I hope you're right. Because when it comes to taking control of the financial machinery, you know we're going to meet a fire storm, literally, from the Feds."

"Yes, but they don't know about the skull. To them it's a threatening logo teenagers would come up with from reading too much Harry Potter."

"Harry Who?"

"Never mind. The thing is they'll see it as a general threat and nothing more. Well, they don't know what it is or what it can do. They'll be looking for technological terrorists: hackers."

"Do you think Osmena will guess that we have it?"

"If she hasn't yet, she will after the 4th of July."

"Ah, yes. More explosions."

"Only the celebratory kind."

Jake put a hand on Luc's shoulder. "Are we sure we want to tip our hand?"

"Let them feel afraid for a change. Besides, there's word about a land grab on a local farm. Could be something more than land Greenway's after. When they find out we have the skull, it will either put an end to their dirty work, or it will drive them harder to it. It depends on what they're after. We need to find out what it is."

"Did Chet tell you this?"

There was a familiar edge in the question that sent an old shiver down Luc's back.

"You lean on Chet a lot these days. I hope you are sure about him."

"I trust Chet, and we need him on the outside. He can tell us things we can't find out for ourselves."

"And he can tell others things that we would never want found out as well." Jake's hand dropped away from Luc's shoulder.

Luc lifted his own arm and put it around Jake's shoulder now. "Chet is a trusted friend. You are like family."

Jake stared off into the forest. "Like," he whispered.

Jake Allard had come to Twin Gaps when he'd been placed in foster care at age 14. A new kid at school always got a certain amount of attention at first, especially one as striking and spirited as Jake, with his dark wild hair and daring ways. Beside the mystique of being a foster kid there was also the fact that he had a chest full of hair and could grow a moustache in the 8th grade. While most boys were still embarrassed about shaving fuzz from their upper lip, Jake Allard already looked like a man among them. Yet, soon the other kids would learn that Jake wasn't easy to befriend. He smoked, cut classes when it pleased him, and had a penchant for smashing things or setting them ablaze. So, if you wanted to hang out with him, you could almost count on getting into trouble with him also. By the end of the school year his aura had darkened and the clamor to befriend him had dwindled behind a wake of scandal.

The last straw had been the keg party. Jake had been invited to a high school kegger the Friday night of Memorial Day weekend—quite a coup for an 8th grader. But things had gotten out of hand in the woods behind the school athletic field that night. A boy had been badly beaten, and it was whispered too that he'd been raped, though there were never any charges brought except for simple assault.

Jake had gone to Chet Atwood in a panic the next morning and asked him to say he'd spent the night at his house. He swore up and down he'd had nothing to do with what went on, but Chet refused to do it. He knew his parents couldn't and wouldn't verify that Jake had been there, so it would just be his word against other witnesses at the party. To Jake it was a crowning blow, a betrayal. The way he saw it, he was innocent and hadn't seen what happened, so it wasn't wrong to say he'd never been there. It could only have meant trouble for him.

Luc was on the outside of Jake's sphere then, admiring many things about him—the sense of purpose and cool he projected despite his uprooted life, and most of all the way he stood up to authority, especially when it was unjust or tyrannical. Yet, Luc had also feared for the reckless way Jake took up the mantle of rebellion and had not joined the fascinated clamor that had surrounded him. That distance was like a magnet for Jake, especially as infatuations wore off and troubles mounted, and he'd tried to draw Luc in. In fact, he'd told Luc about the party that night and asked if he wanted to go along. Luc was glad he hadn't gone.

The next morning Jake showed up at Luc's back door. He smelled of beer and wood smoke, and looked like he hadn't slept.

"Luc, I really need your help, man. Something happened in the woods last night, at the party. Something bad."

Luc stepped outside and closed the sliding door behind him.

"I had nothing to do with it, I swear. I didn't even see it happen, but some guy, I'm not even sure who, got messed up bad."

"Do you know who did it?"

"Not sure. I went off to take a piss and I tripped. I was drunk and dizzy so I just stayed down and I must have dozed off. I don't know how long, but when I got back to the campfire a lot of people had left and this guy was on the ground and he was crying and looked messed up. Nothing on but his underwear and they were ripped and dirty or bloody I couldn't tell."

Luc shook his head. "Did anyone say what happened?"

"A couple of the girls were trying to help him and ask him what happened, but he was so drunk and couldn't stop crying. You couldn't understand a thing he said."

Luc looked Jake in the eye. "And what did you do?"

Jake looked down. "I took off."

"You just left?"

"I couldn't stay, Luc. I couldn't be there, man. They're just looking for an excuse to send me packing."

"Who?"

"My fosters. Look, I know I've been trouble, but I've never hurt no one. I don't mess with people." Jake was pacing now, walking away and back again. "Help me man. Chet wouldn't. I need you to say I was here all night. I told my fosters I was staying at Chet's, but it doesn't matter. I misspoke; they misheard. I was here."

Luc saw for the first time that Jake was desperately alone and clinging to this place as if it were the edge of a precipice, and what his father told him once came back to him like a lightning bolt of truth: that a man could never lose his dignity as long as he had even one person to stand beside him, loyal to him, right or wrong, to the very end. Praise and honor and possessions could be withdrawn but a person's worth was his soul. If Luc didn't help Jake at that moment it would mean not only that he had failed to be a friend, but also that Jake had failed to make one. He couldn't have put that into words then, but he felt it in Jake's downcast eyes—the sense of failure, of somehow being undeserving of friendship and trust.

"Look, Jake, if we're going to do this, then we have to tell my dad. Tell him exactly what happened. I know my dad. If you had nothing to do with it and didn't see who did, he'll understand. He knows the system and what you're up against. I think he'll help."

As it turned out, Jake had been at Luc's house all night. That became the official story.

"You are family," Luc said.

Jake smiled distantly. "I know; I'm just tired now. I think sometimes it's too late for me. You still have family on the outside, if and when we come out of hiding. What do I have?"

Luc shook Jake's shoulder heartily with his big hand. "It's not an if, it's a when. Things are about to change and soon you're not going to have to worry about being alone. You'll find a love and a life of your own, and you'll always be part of our family. Our best days are still ahead."

Jake's smile was tinged with melancholy. "If I am impatient sometimes, Luc, it's because I don't know how much longer I can live this life."

"I promise you. We are this close." Luc put his thumb and index finger together so that the space between might accommodate a pea.

⌘   ⌘   ⌘

As Zephyr drove for the second time up to Osmena Searle's, she felt a sense of déjà vu. The first time she had been desperate, willing to do anything so long as she didn't fail with Cody LaRoy. Today, she was in pure panic over the confiscated blue powder. She broke out into a cold sweat every time she thought about the consequences of a positive test. Her name would be dragged through the newspapers and she would lose her job, maybe even her certification to teach. Worse she could end up with an absurdly long jail term and labeled for life as a child predator. She felt little better about herself when she considered she was trying to extricate herself by the very means that had gotten her into trouble in the first place: Osmena's magic.

"You said it was calming blue powder. You said it was safe. Those people went crazy," Zephyr had complained to Osmena over the telephone.

83

"I told you it was safe for children. I didn't know you were going to feed it to half of Twin Gaps," Osmena had replied tartly.

How could Zephyr put her trust again in someone who had led her down this path, and had not even decently warned her of all of its side effects? Just as she had in March, she felt recriminations from the person of her dead father. Only today she felt the pain more keenly, because the consequences were nearer and direr than she'd ever imagined, and Osmena's web was tightening around her.

Zephyr tried to deny that it was happening, telling herself that if she just straightened this mess out today she could be done with it once and for all. Lesson learned. But, many years ago, her father had described the gradual demise of one of his best and dearest friends at Osmena's hands. She couldn't remember the details, whether it had begun with some foolish speculation, or a debt, but it had gradually spiraled toward disaster just the way it was happening to her.

The mountain road curved sharply to the left, snapping Zephyr out of the crisis in her mind to one nearly at hand on the road. She braked hard at a sharp curve, almost skidding on loose gravel, before righting her car again. She pulled onto a little shoulder and turned off the engine. Zephyr got out of her car and looked around. She needed a few minutes to collect her thoughts before she met with Osmena.

The woods around, the music of the hermit thrush and the little tick, tick of its hopping in the undergrowth, recalled the camp her father owned on this very mountain. Could she have found it now even if she had the time, assuming it was still standing? If she could see it again, she thought she might be able to figure out what she ought to do. For, it was there and at her father's side that she had learned about these mountains, the natural world she loved and the world of human systems that was at times strangely like nature and at other times so clearly at odds with its mysterious workings. The human world and the natural world could both be unfair, even cruel, but in nature competition and cooperation, parasitism and symbiosis, achieved an amazing balance. Her father had showed her that a healthy system was naturally diverse and that diversity of life kept a system in balance, so that everything could thrive in the same space. In human systems where competition was overvalued, someone's profit often caused someone else's impoverishment, one man's inalienable rights meant another man's slavery, and one nation's manifest destiny meant another people's extinction.

"It's not strictly natural or necessary for anybody to suffer unduly in this world. There's enough with natural disasters and disease, and just plain mortality, without human beings adding to the misery with wars and the like. There's no good reason for it going on like this—systems so out of control they solve their problems with body counts, and renew themselves on the ashes of their victims," Gerard LaFrance had told her once, as they talked around the campfire one cool autumn evening. Her younger brother was already asleep in the cabin and she and her father were alone by the fire. Her mother had been dead almost two years by then, taken by a mysterious and deadly influenza, and she knew whenever her father talked about disease and suffering, he was thinking of her.

Well, it had all sounded so bewildering and severe back then, Zephyr sometimes wondered if her father had gotten it wrong. As a child she had never thought of the people she knew as poor, and had never encountered the adult struggle to make ends meet until she was off on her own. She lived and grew up with people who had very little, and wanted very little except to make it from week to week with enough to eat, clothes on their backs and a roof (preferably one that didn't leak) over their heads. She didn't think it strange to see people wear the same old clothes so often, duct taping an old pair of boots, or fixing up old "beaters" to eke out another winter on rough, icy roads. She never suspected that people bartered goods and services because they didn't have the cash to pay for them. To her it seemed just a friendly way of doing things.

That night was the first time her father directly warned her about Osmena. "Stay away from her," he'd said, casting his eye further up the mountain. "You wouldn't know by the way folk talk about her that a good half of her spells aren't worth a plug nickel, and the other half that work, cause so much unintended grief, you'd end up hoping you'd been one of the unlucky ones."

"Then why do people still go to her?" Zephyr asked.

Gerard LaFrance's eyes twinkled when he was about to reveal a mystery to her. Despite the darkness and the flickering shadows of firelight, Zephyr caught the glint. "Because, Zephyr, people want to believe that failed magic is better than no magic at all. To think that in a moment, in this ocean of failure and swamped dreams, they might ride the sea of change to some golden shore. But, the odds against it are staggering—with or without Osmena's help. The world is bound up in a wondrous, hard magic, and we're bound up with it. Living and figuring things out by experience. What works and what doesn't. There's nothing easy about it. It means we grow up, get old and die. It means we lose things we think we shouldn't; and yet, the life we have, this little window each of us opens to eternity is so miraculous, you know that even for all the sorrow and uncertainty of it, you wouldn't trade it for anything. And so you work for just enough justice and hope for just enough good luck (and I mean luck) to make the few people you really love as happy and secure as you can. Because everything can vanish in the twinkling of an eye. And so it's tempting to go to her when trouble comes."

"But, where does Osmena get the magic from? I mean, what gives her the right to do whatever she wants with people's lives? And why doesn't somebody stop her?"

Gerard LaFrance had been pleased with his daughter's perspicacity. "Ah, those are two questions that beg an answer. But, that's easier said than done." Her father thought for a moment, staring into the fire. It was getting late and the flames were dying down, but she didn't feel sleepy at all.

At last her father said, "If I told you she got part of her power from an old tree, you'd think it was a fairy tale. Let's just say it's something very old. Some of it comes from the power of the earth, part of it is something I don't yet understand, and the other part of her power is human. I call it, 'The Will of the World.' And that is also the reason nobody stops her. Nobody really wants to."

"Do you want to stop her?"

"That is the plan," her father answered. The glitter had gone from his eyes, and he'd stared into the fire with a deadly serious look on his face.

Zephyr shook off the dark image. She turned her back on the mesmerizing, green wood and got in her car. She carefully belted herself in and pulled back on to the road. There was one other question she had wanted to ask her father that night, but she hadn't dared, partly because she'd had nothing but the look in her father's eye to justify it. She wanted to know if Osmena had had a hand in her mother's death.

As the years passed, Zephyr became more involved with her school friends and the possibilities of the world outside of the Green Mountains. The looming figure of Osmena Searle receded into the background, as did the woods she had walked with her father and the cabin that had been such a part of every season of her childhood. Years later, after she had earned her degree and was teaching in Massachusetts, her father had fallen ill and had sold the cabin and the property to pay his medical bills. She'd come home to care for him near the end of his life, and that was how she'd ended up in Twin Gaps, back in the house she'd grown up in.

"What was the plan?" Zephyr wondered aloud as she pulled up to Osmena's gates. She had no doubt the old witch had something planned for her. It was about time she hatched one of her own.

10.

Looking for Trouble

THE HIGH FORESTS of Catamount Peak, from the south face above Old Route 9 over to the north face above Route 17, remained wild and among the oldest in the state. There were rumored to be pockets of old growth forest with giant maples and towering pines the likes of which hadn't been seen in two centuries, large buck with legendary racks, cedar bogs cloistering rare orchids, not to mention catamounts—long thought to be extinct in Vermont—haunting the high elevations like sleek, powerful ghosts. Hunters dreamed of stalking their quarry in these woods, but very few dared these days. All along the steep sides of OR 9 and Route 17 the land was posted, but not with the usual yellow and black signs nobody much paid attention to, but an inexhaustible number of hand painted signs bearing the warning: **Those who enter do so at their peril.** The signs and their message were somehow personal, and if they were not enough warning, there was a growing toll of those who dared having met with bizarre accidents or untimely death. Five hunters and six hikers had gone missing in the past 20 years. Two of them were found frozen to death. Another had been mauled by a large wild animal, causing a brief frenzy of catamount speculation. The rest of the missing had never been found. Countless others had lived to tell tales of horrific falls, freak squalls, sudden car troubles, exposure, poisonous spider bites, and they had vowed never to venture into those woods again.

It was like having a mountain top Eden just out of arms reach. Some said the land was guarded by watchers (who and what was a matter of opinion), but with Eden being such a deadly place to enter, the local folk were usually wise enough to avoid its fiery sword. Most of the casualties these days were out-of-staters.

Jet and Aster Corgan had little thought of danger as they drove up Route 17 that Sunday morning for their appointment with Osmena Searle. Among the many things Aster shouted at Jet the day the last wreck arrived was a demand that he call Osmena to complain about the spell going all wrong. This had been the first available appointment.

Jet had gotten them onto Greylock Road okay, but he was having doubts about the unmarked fork they had just taken. He was sure the correct branch ascended immediately so he veered left, but about a mile later nothing looked remotely familiar. After several miles, they were convinced they had to turn around.

"I thought you said you knew the way."

"Dagumit, I swear the fork I took went up sharp. You saw the other one."

Turn around the Corgans did and took the lower fork. After a few miles, Jet said, "This definitely isn't right."

"Oh, come on, Jet, we're going to lose the appointment if we're late. You know how she is."

Just then, they came around a corner and the roadside opened up onto a grassy slope, fronted by a broad wrought iron gate mounted on square, white granite pillars.

"This is it. How the heck? Last time, I swear this gate was on my left. Darndest thing."

Jet pulled up to the gate and waited.

"What do we do now, there's no one here. Should we beep?"

"We just wait."

In about five minutes, the gates swung slowly open. The road continued under a loose, high canopy of locust trees, underplanted with long wispy grass, naturalized clumps of chocolate brown lilies and carpets of wild azure speedwell. The morning sun slanted under the trees, lighting golden the dewy grass and burnishing the large brown lilies to the color of wine. After a half a mile, the trees suddenly broke and a wide estate opened up, the sight of which never failed to astonish anyone who had seen it for the first time.

A black gravel driveway wound its way through a dazzling lawn of velvety Irish moss. A serpentine dry stone wall crossed the road seven times in high keystone arches and each sweep of the wall retained the next tier of ground. At the curves the walls rose free in dragon back spines and descended at the horizontal to hold back the next swell of moss clad earth. In the shelter of these freestanding arcs were clustered topiary cropped in spirals, globes and plates, like carnival rides frozen in motion. The serpentines narrowed with each pass until the drive reached a cul de sac.

Jet parked the car in front of the last retaining wall. A ten foot hedge ran the length of it and screened the house from view. He and Aster got out, mounted a central stone stairway and passed through an arch cut in the shrubbery. The path immediately diverged three ways. Here began the gardens. They completely encircled the house in a series of flowing vignettes, each leading deeper in toward some new marvel, glimpsed through a portal cut into a hedge, or through a transparent screen of moor grass, or at the far end of a shaded arbor like the revelation of secrets. You heard water trickling and followed the sound. You smelled a heavenly fragrance and followed your nose. Yet, there was no direct path to the house, as if to insist you wander where your senses led you. Occasionally you rounded a hedge or a tall stand of Delphiniums and found yourself with a direct view of the house, either much closer at hand than you'd expected, or surprisingly distant yet.

After such an entrance you expected to see nothing less than a palace; instead a rambling, gray monstrosity greeted you. Yet, the fade and crack of weathering proved up close to be a stain designed to look like wear and water mark patina. The blue slate roof rolled smooth in patches under the spread of dark green moss, and yet this dereliction too appeared to be a trick of the eye, a tromp l'oeil work that left Jet and Aster second and third guessing.

"That's moss. No wait you're right it isn't."

"No I was wrong, Aster; it really is."

"No Jet, well, maybe you're right."

"Wait, no it can't be."

"Is anything real around here?"

All the gables were tipped in terracotta Maltese crosses. Along the eaves ran a mysterious lattice of skulls, flowers, rams heads and hoop snakes connected by scrollwork and abstract characters. Above the window moldings and lintels were reliefs of ravens and owls in either pose or midflight. Off the main house three rotunda wings had been added, each capped in a giant cupola. The turrets were all scalloped tile, each covering an open carousel and each encircled by a widow's walk with gray balustrades and clean white pickets.

Aster had worn a look of utter astonishment from the moment they'd emerged from the shade of the locust wood.

"Where do we go?" Aster said, turning and taking in at each turn some new source of amazement.

"This way." The answer came from behind them.

Aster and Jet turned. There stood Osmena Searle, as though she had been there all along.

Jude waited twenty minutes after Jet and Aster left to go down the hall to their bedroom, just in case one of them had forgotten something and came back. They were always leaving and returning like that, especially if they had to be some place at a certain time. Their room was neater than he'd expected (tidier than his own), but then with Aster home for the weekend, the bed was made and the clothes were picked-up. There was a load of wash tumbling loudly in the little stacker tucked into the hall closet outside of his parents' bedroom. Aster had asked him to hang it out on the line for her when it finished. Every time he put laundry out, Jude couldn't help wondering what it would be like to be a clean pair of trousers dangling over so much filth. It would be enough to frighten the laundry dry.

Jude tip-toed when he first entered the room, which was silly with no one there to hear him. Yet, it would have seemed irreverent if he'd been whistling or rifling noisily through their things. It was a matter of respect. Never mind that he was violating their privacy—something no self-respecting teenager would have tolerated in his own room.

Jude began with his father's dresser. There was nothing interesting under his clothes—just a few coins, screws and washers, and a chewed-up pencil—but the jumble there looked like a replica of their yard. The sock and underwear drawer particularly had succumbed to an advanced state of chaos. Jude couldn't resist taking out and holding up the last pair of his father's old tighty-whities, and was glad Jet had switched to boxers. They were faded gray, the elastic in the legs was stretched out and the seat was worn almost transparent.

Jude moved on to Aster's dresser with a tingle of nervousness. The top of her dresser was lined with her cosmetics and perfumes, a small jewelry box and hair brushes. He opened the top drawer and was greeted by a potpourri of roses and lavender. Aster's clothes were laid out so neatly he was afraid that to touch them was to give away his snooping. The order he found, on the other hand, excluded the presence of meaningful artifacts.

Next was the closet. There were always interesting things in closets. Jude went right for the boxes on the top shelf. One box held various papers–bills, bank statements and receipts. Another box had titles to cars, birth certificates and the deed to their property. There were two big boxes full of photographs. Jude took one box down, sat on the bed and began to look through them. He opened one envelope and there were pictures of his cousins, Jesse and Junie, and him playing on a tire-tube swing over at Gemini Farm. He saw his four-year-old self in the pictures, but he had no memory of doing any of these things. He hated seeing himself this way, especially with his blond cousins in the picture. Even at four Jude's head was too large for his body. The camera always caught him looking clumsy and disheveled, and always with a spill stain on the front of his shirt.

Jude put the photos away in disgust. There was one envelope that intrigued him. These were pictures of his parents he had never seen before. He stopped when he came to a photograph of Jet and Aster standing arm in arm in front of their trailer on a sunny late winter day. There was a yard then with matted grass and melting snow, and no piles of scrap yet, only a generalized clutter in the yard—a rusting charcoal grill, a big satellite dish, some scrap wood leaning against the side of the trailer, a wheelbarrow, some plastic buckets, and, in the upper right hand corner of the picture, the familiar fender of the Incubus. Aster was very pregnant with Kennedy and she was wearing a drop-waist maternity dress and a sweater. They were so young.

Both looked pale after the long winter, and sleepy, as if they'd just awakened from hibernation, but their smiles looked contented. Who would have taken the picture? Behind that one was a black and white picture of a man Jude didn't recognize. He was broad in the shoulders with a wild mane of blond hair, a big logger in woolens and suspenders, standing on a large stump in the woods, as if boasting over a tree he'd felled.

Jude looked up from the photo in a cold sweat. He had only an hour or two at the most and here he was wasting time on memory lane, and they weren't even his memories. He put away the pictures, closed the shoe box and brought it back to the closet. Things had to go back on the shelf exactly as he'd found them or Aster would notice. He reached up and slid the box back into place, but it wouldn't go to the wall. He pushed harder and heard a papery scrape. Jude moved the box aside, stood on his tip-toes, reached for the back of the shelf and pulled down an envelope.

It was golden with the flap tucked inside rather than sealed. Jude sat down on the bed and opened it. There was only one thing inside—a yellowed newspaper clipping. Jude unfolded it and felt a sharp stabbing pain in his chest. It was cut out of the obituary page of the Twin Gaps Beacon. *Kennedy David Corgan.* He read his brother's death notice for the first time and began to tremble. Some obituaries are long with life experiences and accomplishments. Kennedy's was shockingly brief. He was a loving son and brother, a popular student and star athlete at Justin Morgan Regional School, and he had died unexpectedly. It listed the surviving family, mentioning Jude by name, and the calling hours.

Between the obituary and a continuation of a page one story under the heading **FUGITIVE**, something had been cut out. It must have been Kennedy's picture. But, why would Aster or Jet save his obituary and cut out his picture?

The word *fires* leapt out of the last paragraph of the news story: *While there are no solid leads yet in last weekend's mysterious fires, US Deputy Adam Walker, the chief investigator of the Watters Building fire sixteen years ago, believes this double arson is similar to the one that partially destroyed a government database—which housed, among other things, state tax and criminal records. "They were carefully staged to minimize the ability of the local fire departments to respond in a timely way to the Watters Building." Dentremont, the young leader of the Vermont Liberation Front, was a chief suspect, but was never apprehended and was believed to have fled to Canada after the fires. Though similar to the Watters' fires, local authorities believe this may be merely coincidental "It's premature to raise that kind of alarm connecting an old barn fire and a dentist's office to a radical political organization, especially one nobody's heard from in over fifteen years," said Brady Denton, Twin Gaps Fire Chief.*

These were the fires Dunky LaGro and Hiram Rafferty had been talking about. Jude folded the paper and put it carefully back inside the envelope. He finished putting everything back in the closet the way he'd found it, smoothed out the bedspread with his hands and closed his parents' bedroom door.

Jude went to the kitchen and made himself a peanut butter and marshmallow sandwich. The time it took to chew and swallow a single bite tended to slow time down to a crawl, so that thoughts and questions arose and hovered in front of you. He sat at the table and looked up at the names of the wrecks he'd written over the years, as if somehow he might find an answer there. Maybe there were answers in the rest of that story about the fires. *A lot of fire then.* What if Dunky LaGro was right and the explosion had something to do with those fires five years ago—including his brother's fiery crash? He had to be careful about jumping to conclusions. If there was anything he had learned from his meeting with GEIST, it was how wild speculation could lead you far astray from the truth. He imagined Merrilee shaking her head in dismay and saying, *"Of course they'd be in the same issue of the paper because they happened on the same weekend. That's not proof they're connected in the least."* When you thought about it, what could any of it possibly have to do with the Vermont Liberation Front (he'd never even heard of them, or anybody named Dentremont, before today). The old timers had talked about Francy's boy, but they seemed to think he was dead and had nothing to do with the explosion. Then there was Calvin, the boy with the catamount tattoo, who had warned that worse things might be coming. Just who was he, really? And how would he know that?

"So I understand you had a problem with the incantation," Osmena said.

"That's the understatement of the year," Aster said.

Osmena turned a curious glance at her. "Well, let's go over everything and see if we can figure out what went wrong." She had a musical voice, but not a young voice. Sometimes it cracked or rose unexpectedly, and the timbre changed with each utterance, as if to clarify the meaning of what she said.

Aster had expected a wrinkled, hunched over crone, in drab antiquated clothing. Osmena Searle was petit and short in stature, but she was anything but drab. She wore a brightly patterned, floor-length silk caftan that dragged on the ground behind her, and a bright silk scarf tied over jet black hair. She had large, deep set hazel eyes, and when she closed them, her paper thin eyelids showed the roundness of her eyeballs. Her prominent chin and cheek bones kept her face in proportion with her aquiline nose.

Osmena turned and led them under a blooming wisteria arbor. Jet and Aster walked half a step behind on either side of her.

"So, refresh my memory. What incantation did you use?" Osmena stopped in the middle of the path.

Jet felt in his pockets and pulled out a creased and crumpled piece of paper. He read it back to her.

An uncertain look crossed her face. "Well, no. That can't be right."

"What do you mean?" Aster looked back and forth at Osmena and Jet.

"Pardon, me, Miss Searle. This is the very paper I wrote it on. It's exactly the way you dictated it."

"Let me see that." Osmena snatched the paper out of his hand. She mouthed the words silently from beginning to end. When she'd finished she put her finger to her lips, as if carefully weighing the rightness of each word she'd read. "Ah!" she exclaimed, her eyes opening wide and her finger lifting from her lips and pointing skyward. "This part here is wrong. *Remove its wicked waste beyond my fence.* May I ask, Mr. Corgan, if you even have a fence?"

Aster's mouth dropped open. Jet scratched the top of his head. "Well, no, Miss Searle."

"Well, then. You've confused the Powers that Grant. If you've no fence, where were they supposed to move it?"

"But, it's not a literal fence, it's a metaphor. The point being…" Jet hesitated, suddenly lost for words.

"The point being off our property," Aster said. "Are the Powers that Grant completely stupid? Don't they know how metaphors work?"

Osmena waved a hand at them, "Metaphors are for those who can't afford magic. Magic is for those who can't abide the empty conceit of metaphors."

Jet and Aster just looked at each other in amazement. "Well, ma'am. Can't you just tell us how to fix the spell to the liking of the Powers that Grant? Something like, we paid you, now just get rid of the gosh darn bus?"

Osmena began walking again. "Well, you paid for an economy spell, and as you know, they are not foolproof."

"What do you mean not foolproof?" Aster said, her voice rising dangerously close to a shout.

"Are you saying we're fools?" Jet asked.

Aster shook her head disparagingly at her husband. "No, Jet, she means she knowingly sells incantations that don't work."

Osmena led them through another arch cut into a hedge and turned left. "Not spells that don't work. Spells that may not always work." They walked single file down a flagstone path between two towering Arbor Vitae walls, whose sole purpose may well have been to induce an attack of claustrophobia. The pungent, slightly sour incense of juniper filled the air. "Now for ten dollars a word I can guarantee your wretched bus will disappear in a puff of smoke."

Aster wanted to reach out, grab Osmena's skinny neck and throttle her until her eyes popped out of her head.

Jet cleared his throat. "Well, Miss Searle, we wondered—seeing it didn't work—if we might get, you know, a refund?"

Thankfully they emerged from the confining alley onto a charming stone terrace with planters of tropical flowers and a view to the house. "Oh, heavens, we don't give refunds. Imagine if we gave refunds for every spell that didn't work; it would just take the magic out of things for those whose spells really did work—those who paid the price for a proper incantation."

"But, what if we can't afford a 'proper' incantation?" Aster said.

Osmena sat down at an elegant wrought iron table, set with a tea service for two, and lifted her arms in a shrug. Beside her place setting lay a scroll tied with a leather string. Osmena picked it up and handed the scroll to Jet. "Now, we may be able to work out something agreeable to all parties."

Jet looked suspiciously at the scroll in his hand. Osmena tapped it with one finger. "I hear you are quite the inventor, quite a builder of mechanical gizmos. This is a blueprint for a machine."

Aster crossed her arms impatiently. "Jet, let's go."

"What kind of machine?" asked Jet.

"Well, it hasn't got a name."

"Then what does it do?"

"Jet, she's asking you to build another piece of junk to add to our collection. She's laughing at you."

"You really should have left this disagreeable woman home. It's bad energy for my plants." Osmena looked right at Aster and curled her lip in disgust. Then she turned to Jet. "Have a look at the plans and see if it's something you'd be interested in building. We could do a lot for you."

"I don't know, Miss Searle."

"Well, it won't do any harm to have a look."

"But you haven't told me what it does."

Osmena reached for the teapot and poured both cups, but she didn't offer them any, or ask them to sit down. She tilted her head as she spooned in sugar and stirred her tea. "People have wasted a good deal of time and cleverness speculating about time travel, boggling their minds with paradox. But, the past, you see, is dead—as worthless as chaff separated from grain: it is carried away in the wind and never seen again. The grain—fruit of the present—is all that remains to bear witness to it. Now, the future is about potential. That's something worthwhile, but it can't be reached without a process, or a mechanism of action. Yet, in the mind all this potential exists, all these dreams and possibilities are waiting to take flight. Have you ever wondered, Mr. Corgan, what stands between a thought and actuality? Have a look at the blueprint and let me know what you think."

11.

By Hook or by Crook

N O SOONER HAD the Corgans exited the far end of Osmena's terrace, than her tea guest entered along the daunting hedgerow alley.

"Cream or lemon?"

Zephyr LaFrance waited a few paces from the table. She hadn't expected to be received for tea like an honored guest, especially given Osmena's impatient and brusque tone during their brief conversation yesterday.

"Oh, please sit down my dear and make yourself at home."

Zephyr pulled out the chair and sat down opposite Osmena. She shifted in her seat trying to find the right posture, though she knew no matter how she sat, she would feel just as vulnerable and trapped as a trout caught on a hook. She chose to sit forward.

"Lemon, please," Zephyr said softly.

Osmena passed her a little plate of lemon wedges and tilted her head in her peculiar leading way. "No need for you to act as if we're strangers. I knew your father quite well, his father too. There's no reason we can't be friends."

"My father was not your friend."

"Well, I never said that, my dear. I said I knew him and who do we know better in the whole world than our enemies? There is a kind of bond, you know, that links enemies as inextricably as friends. Yet, there comes a time when even enemies find themselves on the same side."

Zephyr nodded vaguely, took a sip of her tea and admired the flowers on the terrace with a twinge of envy. A pair of juncos kept flying in and out amongst the lime-washed planters, their tail feathers opening and closing like black and white striped fans. The sun rose above the hedgerow and out beyond its edge, shifting the line of shade and pale sunlight across Zephyr's legs and her side of the table, enveloping her suddenly in a sticky balm of heat.

"I myself have an unpleasant history with Sergeant Roderick," Osmena continued, "so I am not unsympathetic with your plight."

"I just wondered if there wasn't some way to neutralize the powder before he tests it."

Osmena set down her tea cup and emphatically clapped her palms together. "Now, that would make a real fool out of him wouldn't it? I must say, your mind for this kind of thing is not unlike my own, much as you'd like to deny it." Osmena smiled, closing her eyelids and nodding slowly. "There is a spell for turning calming blue powder into carbon, but it is rather expensive." Osmena lifted her chin and turned her head side to side.

"How expensive?"

Osmena raised her teacup and swished the remnants around. "Well, if I had to say, it could cost as much as $5,000.00."

"$5,000! Why so much? I only paid $250.00 for the blue powder."

Osmena made a snobbish face. "Well, my dear, it is not a simple thing to change the physical properties of matter. These things are not easily, or cheaply, done."

For the first time Zephyr raised her voice. "Well, I can't see why. You made the powder, didn't you?"

"There's the thing. That powder was developed and produced right here. It didn't come about from a spell. It is made from naturally occurring substances. I can't just make its physical properties vanish. A spell of this kind requires a special magic."

Zephyr shook her head. "I don't know, Osmena. It just seems kind of arbitrary to me. I mean where do you come up with a figure like that? What does it actually cost you to say a few words?"

"Well, it would cost me nothing to say, I'm sorry it can't be done. But really, Zephyr, do we have to argue over the price? You'll pay an attorney far more than that to defend you. Try asking him to turn calming blue powder to carbon, why don't you dear? I'm more intrigued by the fact that you believe I can change the chemical composition of calming blue powder by reciting an incantation. The fact that Gerard LaFrance's daughter *believes*. Of course you do, because the blue powder did exactly what it was supposed to. Have you considered that I had no need of any magic stronger than a pharmacist's to help you cure Cody LaRoy? But, now you are asking for something along the lines of a miracle. Miracles take real power and the bearing of energy upon matter. It must come from somewhere and at some cost. Or things tend to lose their true value. Do you see?"

Zephyr picked up a paper napkin from the table and dabbed her forehead. The heat and humidity was rising quickly. With it, she felt herself wilting, slumping in her chair. Her head felt clouded and she couldn't keep her train of thought. For, she was just about to reply, when she realized she didn't know what she wanted to say, whether she had planned to argue further or offer some other suggestion. In her confusion, she fell silent. The juncos had taken cover from the heat and the background of bird song had hushed. The only music now was the rubber band buzz of hummingbirds darting among the planters of dangling red and violet fuchsias.

Osmena shrugged. She seemed not to mind the heat at all. Her brow did not betray even the slightest shine of sweat. "I can make your troubles with Sergeant Roderick go away better than any attorney, but there is something you must do for me."

Zephyr sat up in her chair. "What is that?"

"First, let's get you out of the sun, my dear; you're looking absolutely peaked."

The intercom phone rang in the kitchen and Oliver Stemple (addressed simply as Stemple these days) had to race in from the pantry to grab it on the third ring. More than three rings were unacceptable. "Yes, Madam. A hydrating beverage? In the parlor? Did Ms. LaFrance not enjoy her tea? I see, yes. Right away." He replaced the receiver. Madam's lemonade was known to put a parched guest in a better state in no time. He opened a glass cupboard and one of the tall lemonade glasses fell and shattered on the floor. "Good gracious. Esmie!" She could be so careless cramming the glasses into the cabinet instead of taking the time to rearrange them so they'd fit properly. That is what happened when you didn't mind your work. "Esmie!" He listened for the sound of her small hurried steps, but there was only silence. He sighed loudly. There wasn't time to find her. Madam would be expecting lemonade in the parlor in a matter of minutes. He went to a wall cupboard and bent for the dustpan and sweeper. A bit of carving on the inside of the cabinet caught his eye as he reached.

O. S. WAS HERE. Under it was a crude carving of a woman in a stiff trailing triangular dress wearing Osmena's trademark scarf. Facing her was a large threatening moth with battle sharp feet and large eyes. OSMENA VS MEGA GYPSY MOTH was carved underneath that.

Seeing it there for the first time, Stemple stood breathless, as if at some lost enchantment. It was Orest's handiwork. Despite being punished repeatedly for scratching Madam's furniture, he continued his woodcraft undeterred in obscure surfaces (literally in the closet), hell bent on making his presence permanent in a way his life there would ever deny him. Perhaps Oliver was the first to gaze at his brother's crude memorial. How well he remembered the gypsy moths that summer, and how they relished Madam's vexation when they attacked her ornamental trees. They imitated her shrieks and rants for a whole week in private nightly pageants, often wrapping towels around their heads in imitation of Osmena's scarves. Their glee was short lived. She tolerated the voracious larvae for only so long—believing at first they were a passing nuisance—and then with one crushing incantation, she put an end to their feasting forever.

Stemple wondered what other remnants and relics of their childhood were scrawled on closet and cabinet doors throughout the house, as Orest had a penchant for disappearing. There was one evening when he could not be found anywhere. Dark was coming and their parents were frantic. Osmena was perturbed she had to halt production on a batch of formula to have the servant's comb the house and grounds for him, even into the woods. When he appeared in the midst of their searching, unaware of the commotion he had caused, Osmena was furious. She demanded his immediate punishment, and prescribed a whipping with a strap to be executed in her presence by their father. For all anybody knew, Orest had been hiding all along in a cabinet, like this one, absorbed in his carving and captions. Oh, brother, are you hiding yet?

The phone rang again. Stemple came out of his reverie with a start and grabbed the receiver. "No Madam, I have not forgotten. There was an accident in the kitchen—some broken glass. Very sorry to keep Ms. LaFrance waiting. I'm on my way."

⌘ ⌘ ⌘

THERE WASN'T MUCH to go on, a spray painted warning on the police station roof: *The End has Come* and the image of a skull beside it, and the initials VLF. Sergeant Roderick had no luck on the internet. The Vermont Liberation Front, was so far underground all that remained of them was their myth. It made him wonder if there had ever been anything to them at all. On the scale of real world possibility, they were somewhere between the existence of Sasquatch and wild catamounts roaming the Green Mountains.

As far as anybody knew, the VLF had disappeared over twenty years ago with Luc Dentremont after the Watters' fire. The only information Roderick found on them were newspaper articles, the most recent a good five years old, and a little founding fathers kind of tribute to them on the Vermont Secessionist website. For his money, they were gone, dead and doomed as their ideas. He smelled something rotten much nearer at hand: homegrown, trouble-making punks who'd bitten off more than they could chew.

Roderick slowly cruised down Main Street keeping an eye out for any signs of the variety in question. The church crowds had gone home, the sun was high and hot and most of Twin Gaps village had taken on the scorching stillness of Sunday noon in high summer.

A hot day like this would find the locals down at the river taking a dip. Roderick turned right at the trestle bridge and followed the road down to the riverside. He parked his cruiser right in the middle of the narrow dirt road about fifty yards from the swimming hole, so they wouldn't hear his approach. He walked the rest of the way. Just up ahead was a 4x4 Tracker. As he approached the car, he stopped and listened. There was splashing and male voices, but he couldn't see who or how many through the undergrowth of shrubs and ostrich ferns. Just as well. They couldn't see him either. The windows of the Tracker were down, so Roderick didn't even have to open the car door. He produced a little plastic baggie of a certain notorious weed, opened the glove compartment and nestled the baggie under a pile of road maps and receipts. A little extra leverage never hurt.

When Roderick arrived at the river, the boys, four in all, were sitting on an old fallen tree, smoking and drinking beer. He knew them all. Ashley Withers. Dale Preswich. Mark LaVallee. Tony Africano.

At twenty, Withers had a DUI, drug possession and simple assault on his record. Preswich and Africano were partners in one of the stupidest crimes in Twin Gaps history—breaking into the Justin Morgan Regional School gym to shoot baskets one Saturday night. LaVallee was just clueless and unlucky, always in the wrong place at the wrong time with the wrong people.

Withers heard Roderick's footfall on the river stones and turned his head and cursed. They all put down their beer bottles at once.

They were underage and all drinking alcohol, and presumably Africano would be driving away in his Tracker after having a few beers. Tsk. Tsk. Roderick wouldn't even need the wacky weed.

"Hey, Sergeant Roderick," Dale Preswich waved.

Good boys, play it cool, thought Roderick.

"Hello, boys."

"You thirsty? Want some beer?" LaVallee asked.

"Idiot," Withers said, shooting LaVallee a deadly look.

"Nope. No drinking on the job, but you boys go ahead."

Not a one of them even thought about reaching for a beer.

Roderick stood over them. He put one foot up on the gray driftwood log. "But maybe you boys can help me out."

"Yeah, sure, anything, Sergeant Roderick," Preswich said.

"That explosion at the Mobil station was a pretty severe stunt," Roderick said.

"Yeah, awesome," LaVallee said.

Africano kicked him in the foot.

"If there's anything you boys would like to share...Mr. LaVallee. Maybe you've talked to someone else who thinks blowing out windows in my station is awesome?"

Withers and Preswich stood up and put on their t-shirts. Africano said, "Yeah, like I've really gotta get ready for work. You guys coming?" He reached for his shirt and Roderick put his foot firmly down on it.

"You feel like taking a breathalyzer before you take the wheel? I can arrange for you to be really late for work."

"Oh, man." Africano looked down at his feet, then back up at Roderick. "We don't know anything about that."

"Friday night and nobody in your skeleton crew saw anything suspicious in the village?"

"How are we supposed to know suspicious? We're suspicious," Withers said.

"Good point, Detective Withers."

For a moment they laughed, thinking Roderick was lightening up, and then just like that he stepped over to Withers and jacked him up by his shirt front until his feet were dangling in the air. "The next one of you with an opinion is coming with me to the station." He set Withers down on top of the log and gave it good kick. The boy reeled and fell backward, his arms flailing and his mouth open wide in stunned surprise.

Withers fell hard on his hands and seat. He rolled onto his side and groaned.

"That's police brutality," said Mark LaVallee.

"No, he was drinking and horsing around and fell, isn't that right Mr. Withers?"

The other three looked down at Withers. He nodded with a grimace. "Yeah, right; fell." He then rolled onto his back and just lay there looking up at the sky and trying to get his wind back.

"There's this guy," Preswich began, "new to the area. We've hung out with him a few times. He gets us smokes and beer, because his old man is loaded."

"What about him?"

"He's been saying some weird stuff about Vermont succeeding from the United States."

"You mean seceding?"

"Whatever. So Friday night we were just hanging around at the gazebo, when he says something big is going down in the village. We asked him what he meant, but he wouldn't say. He just kept saying, it was going to be huge; awesome, he said."

"Does this guy have a name?"

"Man, he told us, but I don't remember," said Africano.

"Well, how old is he and what does he look like? You'd remember if he had a face to go with his name?"

LaVallee smiled. "Yeah, like you can't miss him. Dude's got an awesome tat."

"Tat?"

"Tattoo," Africano said. "He's got a panther on his back."

"And if I happen to run across him with his shirt on how will I know him?"

"He's like our age. He's got a buzz cut."

"So do you, and you." Roderick pointed at Preswich and Africano. "What do you think about random strip searches for hidden tattoos?"

The boys went white with fear and their eyes opened wide.

"Just joking boys. Have a nice day."

Roderick left them, three standing and one wisely staying down for the count.

"Hey, dude," LaVallee called out to Withers, "He jacked you up good!"

"Thanks for coming," said Calvin, when Ederyck Gannon arrived at the pool above the falls. He'd met Ederyck (everyone just called him EG) at the VLF gathering in the woods a couple of weeks ago. He was the only one who seemed close to Calvin's age, or at least that was the impression he got. He couldn't be sure, because EG always wore a mask, and there was something also about his voice that sounded like a mask. When he thought about it, the name Ederyck Gannon seemed like a disguise too. Maybe he couldn't give his real name. They'd gotten to talking after the meeting and Calvin had suggested they go for a swim at the falls sometime, since he was new in the area, didn't really know anybody, and had a lot of time and not much to do this summer. EG had said on the spot, "Two weeks from tomorrow, around 1 o'clock, if it ain't raining."

Calvin thought EG would take the mask off here, but he even went in the water wearing it. It seemed odd that he was completely naked except for the strange mask.

The water was cold, but Calvin and EG stayed in for a few minutes, swimming and treading, before climbing up on smooth sun dappled outcrops. The freshness of the water always made Calvin's chest feel alive and electric.

"Did something happen to you? That you have to wear a mask?"

EG sat with both knees tucked and his arms wrapped around his legs. "Everybody asks."

"Sorry. I didn't want to be rude, or worse predictable, but—"

"Yeah, it's pretty bad. I'd feel worse for anybody who had to look at me than I do for myself. I can still imagine how I used to look and I don't have to see it in everybody's faces that I don't. I'm not so vain I have to try to prove to everyone I'm not."

"The rest of you. It's not scarred at all. What happened?"

"An accident. I don't like to talk about it though."

"Before you joined the VLF?"

EG looked up as if surprised at the question, but he didn't answer it.

Calvin prodded him. "What kind of a name is Ederyck? Sounds like you made it up."

EG said nothing again and looked away, as if, even with the mask on, he needed to avert his face.

"Hey, I understand about the mask and all. I won't mind if you take it off."

"But I do. The only time I don't wear it is at night, but I always wear it when I'm around people." EG leaned sideways off his rock and slipped into the water again like a frog taking cover. He flipped over and assumed a semi back float. "So how'd you meet up with Chet?"

"I ran into him in town. He overheard me talking about trying to have some custom work done on my Harley Knucklehead Chopper. It's a 1947

107

rebuilt, but I wasn't happy with the seat. He said he might be able to help me out. So I went up there one time and we got to talking. He'd go on a lot about this guy Greenway, and then got to talking about things in the world; you know, money, and how things run and what was wrong with Greenway's plans. I'd heard of the guy and I said I didn't think what he was doing was so bad."

EG laughed. "You must a got Chet going good."

"He gave me an earful. It wasn't like he was telling me what I should know, but he opened my eyes about things I'd never thought about and had taken for granted. We argued some. I could understand and agree with a lot of what he said, but I said that what he wanted was impossible, because people, even poor people, don't seem to accept or get who they are. He agreed that was part of it. Then he said there were other men who believed they could change things, and what's more, he said, 'we', we have the means to do it. If I wanted, he'd take me to hear what these guys had to say, but I'd have to go blindfolded."

"What do you think about it?"

"Well, I gathered something big was going down from what was said at the meeting, and when that gas station blew, it wasn't hard to put two and two together."

"And what if it were true?"

Calvin stepped over some stones to the bank and started putting on his clothes. "I don't know. It's a little scary, but it's also kind of exciting. Like anything could happen now."

⌘ ⌘ ⌘

"TAKE ONE DROPPER of this each night before bed," Osmena held the little brown bottle up for Zephyr to see. They stood in Ms. Searle's crowded apothecary. The walls were lined from floor to ceiling with shelves full of colorful pills and potions in bottles and jars, each labeled and cata- logued according to its use rather than by some Latin based chemical name.

It was a miracle she could find anything in there. The potion she held out for Zephyr came from a box on the central table where all the latest formulas were displayed.

"What does it do?" Zephyr asked with a mix of suspicion and fear.

"You mustn't worry my dear. It's a sleep aid I've been working on."

"But I don't have any trouble sleeping."

"You have nightmares, don't you?"

Zephyr's face overspread with shivers and her eyes began to mist with tears. How in the world could Osmena know about her nightmares? There was one recurring dream that had cropped up again this summer after an absence of many years. It hadn't come back to her for such a long time, she'd almost stopped thinking about it. Then one night about a month ago, it recurred again, almost unchanged.

In the dream, Zephyr was on her way to the hospital to give birth. She always began at the wheel of a car, with a recollection of having been at her father's old cabin, but soon found herself trying to negotiate a very bumpy country road on a bicycle—an old bone shaker of all things. Eventually, she ended up on foot, trying to hitch a ride on Old Route 9. The labor pains worsened and her legs became so heavy she could hardly put one in front of the other. Just when she had reached the point of desperation, and feared she'd have to deliver alone on the roadside, a car pulled up and a man with short black hair and neat black beard offered her a ride. She thought she knew him, but couldn't recall a name. He always said the same thing with the same peculiar smile, as if to allay her fears about riding with a stranger. "He's sent me for you Miss, please get in." Never once did she ask or understand who exactly 'He' was. By the time she got into the car, it had become a hospital bed. She suddenly came-to, as if she'd been unconscious, and discovered that she'd already delivered the child. She searched up and down corridors looking for her baby, calling for help, but nobody came to her aid. At last she turned down a long gray corridor and followed the muffled sound of a child crying. It came from a room at the end of the corridor. When she entered the room she was surprised to see a much younger version of herself cradling the baby.

"May I see my baby," she asked herself.

Zephyr's younger self began to loosen the swaddle of blankets. "He takes after his father, don't you agree?"

Zephyr leaned forward. Under the blankets, something wriggled, but it wasn't a baby. For, it was covered in wet silky fur. Then she would awaken, covered with sweat yet shivering cold with the terror of what she had seen. Since that night, she'd had the dream twice more.

"This will help nightmares?" Zephyr asked.

Osmena pressed the bottle into Zephyr's hands. "This should get rid of your bad dreams. Just leave Sergeant Roderick to me."

12.

Missing Pieces

"HERE IT IS." The receptionist at th3e Beacon took the flat dusty black volume down from the upper shelf and climbed down the ladder with it. She set it on the table in front of Merrilee and Jude. "Good luck with your research project. It isn't often we get students spending their summer days at study." She stood over them for a moment smiling.

"Thank you so much," Merrilee said, smiling back.

"Any time, dear. Just call me when you are finished with it." The receptionist turned and left them alone in the dusty back room. Sunlight streamed in through the high windows and motes of dust turned slowly in the beams above their heads. Jude fought the urge to sneeze.

The books were the size of a newspaper unfolded. They carefully turned the yellowed pages to the issue they were looking for. There was the story about the Sokol fire and the dentist's office on the front page. Jude and Merrilee bent over the story: SUSPECTED ARSON CLAIMS BARN AND OFFICE (Investigator Seeks Fugitive).

The who, what, when and where was rather ho-hum. Most of the front page dealt with the local angle—the Sokols losing their barn and the impact on Dr. Lane, the owner of the business destroyed by the other fire. The why was more interesting. The chief investigator, Adam Walker, had only become suspicious of the connection between these and the Watters' fires after reading the account himself in the Sunday paper. So, when the weekly Beacon went to press on Tuesday night, all that was known was that Sokols' barn had been the first alarm, and nobody thought the sequence of the fires might be a clue as to why they were set.

"It's an interesting theory, but he's only going on a hunch—there's no evidence at all. The fire chief wasn't impressed," Merrilee said.

"I mean, what would the VLF care about a falling-down barn and a dentist's office? Not like they're strategic targets. If you'd seen the Sokols' old barn you'd know what I mean. People were always talking about how close it was to falling down."

"The only thing is that both fires were set and that doesn't happen every night in Twin Gaps. If Walker's theory was right then the target was the dentist's office."

"And why would somebody burn down a dentist's office?" Jude asked.

Merrilee said, "Revenge for a painful root canal?"

"Very funny."

"How about the dentist? Did they suspect him of setting his own place on fire to collect insurance?"

"I don't know, but he retired and moved to Florida. My brother broke a tooth once and went to have it filled there. I'd never been to him."

Jude turned to the obituary page. There was Kennedy's notice and the rest of the story on the fires, but the picture that had been cut out at home was not a picture of his brother, rather the fugitive, Luc Dentremont.

Jude looked closer at the slightly grainy image. "Jeezum crow. There's a photo of that guy in my parent's closet."

"Your parents knew Luc Dentremont?"

Jude shrugged. "I guess they did. I mean he was local; it's a small town."

"You should ask them, just to see what they say and how they react." Merrilee looked over the top of her glasses and smiled slyly.

"Yeah and how would I have even heard of Luc Dentremont; they might guess I'd been snooping in their room."

"Just say you heard some talk about him related to the explosion."

"But, I didn't. I told you Dunky and Hiram were talking about somebody they called Francy's boy. They said he was dead."

"Well, we ought to find out who he was too." Merrilee went back to the fire. "Did they ever find out who set those fires?"

"Dunky and Hiram said they hadn't."

"We should look at the rest of the issues from that summer and see if there were any follow-up stories. We can't just take their word for it, can we?"

Slater Knox had viewed the sealed documents: the notarized transfer of deed from David and Raeanne and the Gemini Trust to The Catamount Trust and Greenway International, Inc. When the Meades' continued searches failed to find their rightful deed to the property, Knox began to question whether the Meades were crazy. For, nearly all the evidence was in Greenway's favor and the last conversation they'd had left the Meades with a deep sinking feeling of dread at the impending court date.

"What you are talking about is a conspiracy to commit fraud involving many people, from town employees, attorneys, bank officials and a notary public. Where is your proof of that?"

"Will all these people testify for Greenway?" David said.

"Possibly. And if they do? What are you going to say?"

"What about the money? No money ever changed hands. We owned it outright so we would have gotten a check. The bank will show that no such transaction ever took place."

"Are you sure?"

"Well, yes."

"That's one good thing. But you'd better get a copy of all the deposits on every bank account you have since the sale date."

Jesse had only heard his father's end of the conversation, but he knew it wasn't good when the phone slammed down and his father walked out of the house and slammed the kitchen door on his way out for good measure.

Junie came out of the bathroom and saw the look on his brother's face.

"What happened?"

"Dad and the lawyer. It's not good. It's like we can't even prove our land is our land. I think the lawyer might be starting to have doubts."

The twins headed outside. It was dry and hot so they decided to finish painting the garden shed. It was all scraped and ready. They wanted to have it done on time for Jude's 4th of July visit. It was only Tuesday, and with the two of them they'd have one coat on today, the second coat on tomorrow. There was plenty else to do. They'd pull the pea plants up for the last pick and get the rows ready for late broccoli and fall cabbage. Willa was inside with their mother cleaning house and changing the bedding.

Up close the chalky smell of the old paint dust was rising with faint cedar where the shakes were scraped to bare wood. Oscar was in the pasture. The drone of the bailer and the sweet fragrance of sun dried hay traveled on the breeze from beyond the orchard. Their father had taken off down the driveway in their dark blue pick-up leaving behind a wake of gray dust that drifted in a bank slowly past them.

Jesse went inside the shed for the paint. He didn't come out right away and Junie was getting hot and impatient waiting in the sun. He stripped off his shirt and tucked it in his back pocket. "What's taking you so long?"

"Can't find a key in here." Jesse rummaged around in the drawers of the potting shelf. "Wait. There it is, on the floor."

Junie thought he'd be out in a few seconds, but once again the delay went on. He went to the doorway and looked in. Jesse was sitting on the concrete floor under the tall potting bench. He had the paint can key in his hand, but wore a strange expression on his face.

"What is it, now?"

"This." Jesse laid his hand on some bags stacked on a small wooden pallet, compost by the look of it. "It's ammonium nitrate."

"So?"

"Junie, we don't use commercial fertilizers. I mean, that's what ammonium nitrate is."

"So what are you saying? We're not organic?"

"No, I wish. I mean I don't, but it's also used to make explosives. Isn't that what McVeigh used in Oklahoma City?"

Junie got down on his knees and crawled under the bench beside Jesse and looked at the bags. "Yeah. So what's that got to do with us?"

Jesse looked at his brother and cast an eye up and back as if indicating something distant.

"Pullman's Mobil."

"No way, Jesse. There's got to be another explanation. It takes more than just ammonium nitrate. This doesn't mean anything at all."

"Who wants to go first?" Merrilee looked around at the other members of GEIST.

Hay scent and amber sunlight filled the Rainey's loft that Wednesday evening when the meeting convened. They were not huddled on the floor but seated on the furniture, belying the urgency of their meeting: Merrilee in the overstuffed chair, her feet on the Ottoman; Cate stretched out on the couch; Sandra sitting straight up in the wing back chair, and Alison nervously tipping in the rocking chair.

Alison raised her hand, like a student self-conscious about volunteering an answer.

"I was supposed to find something out about this Calvin person." Before Merrilee could look down over her glasses, Alison corrected herself. "Well, somebody who calls himself Calvin. It'd be easier if we had a last name, but...so obviously none of us have seen him in school, and the only Calvin registered at JMRS is our very own Calvin Wheaton, definitely not mysterious, tattooed or sexy. Jude wasn't sure of his age, but he might not even be in school anymore."

"What about the Green Mountain Tech?" said Sandra.

"Well, they're out for summer, and unless he's from around here, he's likely to have gone home. If he's a student there staying for the summer then he has to be working and staying somewhere in the community. So, since Monday afternoon I've been scouting shops, businesses, restaurants and garages, just to see if he might be working locally and so far no sign of him. And without a full name we can't even do an internet birth search. So we're sunk there. But, you know, he's a teenager right, and so I went down to the skateboard park. I was jumping rope—"

"Jumping rope?" The girls all chimed in at once.

"I know it was lame, but I don't own a skateboard and lame is kind of disarming; so I just sort of stopped after getting tangled up in the rope and watched them skateboard. I acted impressed, even though most of them weren't very good. So, I overheard Mark LaVallee this morning talking about the guy with the tattoo—he said Sergeant Roderick was interested in finding him. Something to do with the explosion. They kind of clammed up, because I was there. So I decided I should go see Sergeant Roderick."

The Twin Gaps police station was a two story ochre yellow monstrosity. The three picture window panels of the front offices had once been the bays of the town's original fire station. The square louvered cupola still housed the old fire whistle that used to sound at noon each day. The blinds were always down on the windows, and Alison felt a bit intrusive stepping inside with no official business to transact. You stepped into a corridor with a half door at the junction of a crossing hallway. It blocked access to the offices on either side. Straight ahead was the open door to the processing room. All she could see was the end of a conference table and a machine that did god knows what. To her left just inside the door was a bulletin board with reminders of meetings, *Don't drink and drive* and *Click it or Ticket* posters tacked to crumbling cork.

Alison stood at the counter for a full minute before Sergeant Roderick noticed her from the office look-through.

"May I help you, Miss?" Roderick said with almost too much politeness.

"There's something you should know," Alison said.

Sergeant Roderick stood up and walked over to the half door. He towered over her. A cold little smile flattened his thin lips and made them appear purple under the fluorescent lights. "And that means there's something you do know?"

If Roderick was making fun of her, Alison was going to make him own it. She'd waited most of the afternoon in the village for him to return from his beat and she had steeled herself for this. Being blunt and confrontational wasn't easy for her, but she'd seen Merrilee and Sandra in action enough to channel them when she needed to.

"Does that surprise you?"

"Frankly, yes, it does."

"Well, then, I guess I don't know anything after all about that boy with the weird tattoo you've been looking for."

"How do you know about him?" Roderick's tone changed. It was full of genuine interest. He leaned over the half door towards her. "Have you seen him?"

"It so happens that a friend of mine did see him. The whole tattoo as well."

"Yes, I know about the tattoo." Roderick squinted at her with his cold gray eyes.

"Maybe where you can find him. He swims up at Granger Falls."

"Anything else you know?" Roderick was getting impatient with her.

"I guess not." Alison looked up at the ceiling as if trying to think of something else, then she turned her back and said. "Just his name. But then I suppose you already know that."

Roderick practically tripped opening and stepping through the half door to keep her from walking out of the station. "You know his name?"

Alison smiled up at him. "Guess you didn't know. Just a first name, sorry. He calls himself Calvin."

"Is there any chance I can talk to your friend?"

"He doesn't know I'm here. I'll have to ask him, but I think that's really all he knows. As far as I know."

Sandra reached across to Alison and extended a high five. "Kudos," Merrilee chimed in. Cate made an invisible notch in the air with her finger. "Alison 1; Roderick 0."

"At least we know that nobody knows any more about Calvin than we do. We're going to need a sighting and some direct surveillance," Merrilee said. She turned to Cate. "What did you find out about the fires?"

Cate opened her notebook. She'd lost the page and now she was flipping back and forth muttering under her breath. She threw the notebook on the floor. "I can tell you just as well. The fires got mentioned twice more. A follow-up piece two weeks after the original story and once more in September. Neither Sokol, nor the dentist was charged. I guess they suspected the Sokols burned the barn down, but the accelerant used wasn't anywhere on their premises. And they didn't carry any insurance on the barn. No means or motive. They investigated Dr. Lane too. He was just about to retire and was in the process of selling his practice; the last thing he wanted was to burn down the office and lose his equipment. It so happens, Dr. Lane still summers up here, so I went to see him this morning."

Dr. Lane lived on the hill above the village in an old Victorian right on Main St. "You're a little young to be doing investigative reporting," he joked, when she told him what she'd come to talk about. "But that's taking initiative," he said emphatically. "Not a lot of young people these days are taking initiative like that." He led her to a sun room that looked more modern than the rest of the house. It was all white rattan furniture on a gray slate floor. There were plants everywhere. Several ferns hung from the beams in a ceiling of tinted UV sensitive glass panels. A rubber tree and a giant palm towered in opposite corners by the windows out of direct sunlight. There were lemon trees along the windows, bright with fruit; several showy orchids on a lattice iron table, and bougainvillea hanging down from skyboxes, their hot pink blossoms giving off the heavy sweet smell of tropical places.

Dr. Lane and Cate sat at a small oval table, iron like the one that held the orchids. "Sorry I can't offer you more than water; my wife Ellie's had a bit of arrhythmia and they've kept her for a night or two in the hospital."

"Was this a bad time?"

"Not at all. They're running some tests on her this morning; if all goes well she'll be coming home today. But that won't be for a few hours. So tell me what I can tell you?" Dr. Lane had snow white hair and a beard to match. He had lively blue-gray eyes, with a skeptical glint, that may have been intentional—the way one eyebrow was slightly cocked higher than the other.

"Well, when your office burned down did you ever have suspicions about who might have done it?"

"I recall the police asking me that, but then I was also investigated as a possible suspect. I had no idea who would want to burn my office down, or destroy my business. A malicious fire bug who hated drilling and Novocain needles?"

"And the Sokols' barn? Did you think it was related?"

Dr. Lane frowned and grabbed at his chin. "I didn't think so, because then there would have to be a reason for it, you see? I just assumed for a while that it was somebody who got thrills from setting things alight and watching the commotion that ensued. But then, more than a year later, I received a huge envelope of cash in my mailbox. And it hadn't come through the post office. It had been hand delivered."

"Do you mind if I ask how much it was?"

"That's a girl! Well, I won't tell you the exact amount but it was a tidy sum."

"Was there a note with it?"

"Yes, but only these words: *Fire damage; sorry, no choice.*"

"What does that mean? They couldn't help themselves?"

"Pyromania perhaps, but in my gut I felt it was something else. A strange shiver passed through me when I read it."

"Because that person was still right here among us."

"Yes, but something more. It had to have been done with a purpose, by a person with means and a conscience. Somebody who thought they had a very good reason. But I've never had the slightest clue what that reason could have been."

Sandra said, "What if it wasn't the person who did it but a guilty parent or someone who knew who did do it?"

"Who would want their own child to get in trouble? And of course it would take time to get that kind of money together," Merrilee said.

"Meanwhile the investigation grows cold and nobody is snooping around Dr. Lane's finances by then."

"Would the VLF have that kind of money?" Cate asked.

"Why would they waste good money on Dr. Lane, or bother burning down his office in the first place?"

"Well, there could have been records there; maybe Luc Dentremont's," said Merrilee. "Maybe you should have asked Dr. Lane if he ever had such a patient."

"Yeah, but why wait more than 15 years after you go missing to lift your dental records, and why not just break in and steal them," said Alison. "Besides, wouldn't the Feds have gotten a hold of them when he became a wanted fugitive?"

"I don't know. But Jude said Dr. Lane was pretty old school. At the time of the fire, he hadn't converted to a computerized system. It was just old fashioned files."

"Or it could have been Gerard LaFrance's records," said Sandra.

"Who?" The others asked in chorus.

"That would be Francy's boy, according to Hiram Rafferty and Dunky LaGro," Sandra said. "But when I asked about Luc Dentremont?"

"Don't know any feller by that name," Hiram said.

"Don, you got anything stronger to jog Hiram's memory?" Dunky started ribbing him.

"Nothing wrong with my memory at all." Hiram's upper lip got flat and prim.

Don Samms was smiling down, leaning on the counter with both arms and his sleeves rolled up to his elbows. The luncheonette's counter was a long thick slab of rough cut maple that had been hand sanded and varnished to a high, syrup-colored gloss. Behind him the blackboard announced the day's specials in multicolored colored chalk. "Then you'll remember we don't have a license to serve liquor here."

"You too?" Hiram waved a hand at Don. "He were the one who said it; don't look at me."

Hiram and Dunky always arrived ahead of the lunch crowd and sat on the same two stools at the counter. It was a good thing Sandra didn't have to compete for their attention the way things were going. She tried to steer them back to the subject.

"But Luc Dentremont was the leader of the VLF. They had his picture in the paper. After the Sokol fire and Dr. Lane's burned down."

Dunky and Hiram looked at each other. "If you say so," Dunky answered.

"VLF. What'd that stand fer?"

"The Vermont Liberation Front."

"Can't believe everything you read," Dunky said, winking at Hiram.

"Fedral Gumment call 'em that?"

"They always got the dots connected for you don't they," said Dunky. "Neat way to make a man guilty ain't it, and fix public opinion. For all we know they made up Luc Dentremont. One of their own most likely. When the time's right they'll come up with a dead body and say, here's Luc Dentremont, master mind of the Watters' fire and leader of the VLF."

"And who'er you to be asking so many questions?"

"Jenny Duke's girl, Sandra."

"Oh, why dint you say. How's your mom these days?"

"She's fine."

"You got those eyes like her."

Sandra was about to lose patience altogether with them both, when Dunky said: "Now if you're talking about Francy's boy, he were wanted for that Watters' fire too."

"Who is Francy's boy?"

"Why Gerard LaFrance, the younger. You know his sister teaches at the school, don't ya?"

"Zephyr's brother?"

"The very same. But he's been gone since those days too," Hiram said.

"And you think he's dead?"

"Who's been telling you what I think?"

"Some people think Hiram's dead to look at him," Dunky elbowed his old friend.

Hiram swatted his arm away. "Matter of fact good money's on sad news there, but nobody knows for sure."

"But the government wasn't after him."

"Gumment's like God; works in mysterious ways," Hiram said.

"Maybe you ought to ask Zephyr there. She oughta know best where her brother went."

"But there was something very strange about Ms. LaFrance. She kept staring through the screen door like she was in a trance. It was weird. And she knows me, but she wouldn't ask me in."

"Do you think she was drunk or something?" Cate said.

"Do you think she had a man in there?" Alison said.

"I don't think so to either. Ms. LaFrance didn't sound or smell like she'd been drinking and I didn't get the impression there was anybody else there.

No other cars or anything. But there was something weird about her voice. The tone of it was—different. Almost like somebody talking in their sleep. Anyway, I told her I heard the old timers talking about the explosion and they'd mentioned Gerard LaFrance. And she said, 'How could he blow up the Mobil. My father's been dead 11 years.' Then she said, "Oh, if you mean my brother, I think my father knows about that too." She started to laugh and the next thing you know she just closed the door in my face and left me standing there."

Calvin had just put his helmet on, revved up his chopper, and was about to pull out of the Cumby's when a tap on the shoulder startled him. He put his feet down and turned his head. It was one of the local guys he'd hung out with a few times. Ashley Withers. He liked the way people's names either seemed to suit them or didn't. That was how he remembered them. If you'd tried to guess Ashley's name by the look of him—eyes slit at the ends, nose and chin kind of sharp—you'd have come up with something more dangerous, like Derrick or Dirk. That made him think of Ederyck Gannon, who also didn't seem to match his name.

"Hey dude. What's up?"

"Just gassing up for the holiday weekend. Big party on the 4th."

"Awesome, dude. I just thought you should know there's a policeman in town, Sergeant Roderick, and he's out for your ass and I mean literally. Like he's gonna strip search you, dude, to find your tattoo."

"Wait. How does he even know about my tattoo?"

Ashley coughed, a loose asthmatic cough, and laughed through the tail end of it as if the cough itself were funny. "He was leaning on us heavy. Caught us drinking at the river. He had us busted, but we fed him some shit about a guy with a tattoo and he let us go."

"You mean you fed me to him."

"We didn't tell him your name, dude."

"And you know it? Ashley, dude?"

Ashley looked down and his face turned red. "Like, what is it, dude?"

"So you can tell him next time he catches you at something?"

"I wouldn't play you like that, dude. I'm just warning you; like maybe you'd want to get out of town for the weekend. Trying to do you a solid, is all." Ashley cleared his throat. "Hey, man, you think I could borrow a few bucks; I'm out of smokes and I'm freaking from nicky fits, if you know what I mean. Just be careful what you say about that explosion and stuff; Roderick's a bad ass." Ashley's hand came out of his pocket and his fingers were down at his hip, slightly parted to receive, but discreet enough so he wouldn't be embarrassed if Calvin refused.

Calvin handed him a ten. "Thanks for the warning."

"Hey, thanks for the smokes, dude. I owe you one."

Merrilee's assignment was to investigate the Corgan wrecks, but she alone had come empty-handed to the GEIST meeting yesterday. It was true her assignment was by far the most difficult, and it was also true she'd spent a good deal of time thinking about the wrecks from the standpoint of motive and opportunity. Like a crime. To do that she'd had to see the wrecks as simply malevolent. It was hard to argue any other theory. She was at least convinced that whoever brought the wrecks (assuming they arrived by natural agencies) would have wanted to travel the least possible distance, and there was simply no getting around the proximity of Atwood's Auto and Salvage. But once you made that leap, the notion of motive didn't make much sense.

Merrilee wrote out the names of the cars in the order of their arrival:

1. Kia Optima
2. Ford Escort
3. Nissan Sentra
4. Nissan Altima
5. Ford Escort
6. Dodge Caravan
7. Toyota Yaris
8. Toyota Camry
9. Dodge Omni
10. Renault Clio

11. Geo Metro
12. Honda Accord
13. Dodge Neon
14. Lexis IS
15. Isuzu Rodeo
16. Volvo C70

Jude had said Kennedy hated Escorts, but so what? The last Escort to appear was wreck No. 5. If that was more than a coincidence, then whoever started the game seemed to have let it drop. And there were two Nissan's and then later on two Toyota's and then eventually three Dodge's. Were they random, or a pattern? Even with the VINS removed, surely if these had been local wrecks, somebody would have recognized one of their cars by now and given the game away. Yet, in five years there were little more than rumors about Atwood.

Jude also said that each wreck arrived around the time of some family misfortune, but given how frequently the Corgans were in crisis mode, it might have been no more than a coincidence. Merrilee had always been a little resistant to that interpretation, even while she fell into fits of laughter at Jude's litany of woes. It was too conveniently magical for her liking. This all left her back at square one.

Merrilee slammed her notebook shut and marched into her father's office. Except for the two corner windows, it was wall to wall, floor to ceiling with overstuffed bookshelves. There was even a shelf above the door. The room smelled of the sweet dusty decay of books, and always, even though there was nothing in the waste basket but paper, of some overripe fruit that could never be explained.

"Dad, there's something wrong with the car," Merrilee said looking over the top of her glasses.

"There is?" Mr. Rainey put down his pen and looked up from the article he was writing. He still wrote his drafts in long hand despite her frequent attempts to modernize him. His hair was getting too long. Like hers it was stiff when it was short, but when it got longer it would rise then sort of collapse in curling waves under the weight of the lengthening ends, and the few strands of gray weaving in would become more prominent.

"Yes, it's making a strange noise."

"When did you hear that?"

"Yesterday, today, tomorrow. Can we get an appointment to have Chet Atwood take a look at it?"

"Atwood!? Good god. What exactly are you up to?"

Merrilee sat down in the chair beside the desk where her father's students sat for conferences. She was looking down over her glasses and he was looking down over his. It was what they called a Rainey Standoff. The first one to blink usually had to do something they didn't want to.

"I'm helping Jude find out who's behind all the wrecks on his property."

"But should we really be wasting a busy mechanic's time over an imaginary noise?"

"Is there any greater cause than helping a friend in need?" Mr. Rainey was done for, because she was quoting his own words back at him.

"And what exactly will you be doing while I make chit chat and Mr. Atwood listens for a noise that doesn't exist?"

"I just want to have a look around. Make the call and get an appointment. Today or tomorrow at the latest. And get a haircut."

Mr. Rainey shook his head and rolled his eyes.

Something had set the dogs off again. Merrilee jumped at the sound. Sweat started on the palms of her hands. Chet Atwood was a nice enough guy, but the two junk yard dogs he kept tied on a run next to the garage were scary. They ran back and forth and barked at any sign of motion, from cars pulling in, to squirrels moving in the trees. It gave her shivers and set her on edge. You knew if they ever broke loose from the run you were as good as bitten, maybe mauled. She imagined that her snooping had been detected and Chet had let the dogs loose to hunt her down. T.V. nonsense, she told herself and shook the vision out of her mind.

Merrilee had managed to wander away while Chet drove the car into the garage and put it on the lift. Off to the right of the main bay were two bays not in use. In front of it he parked cars waiting to be picked up, or worked on. The junks started opposite them in a single row. It curved around to the left and became two, then three, rows with alley ways between wide enough for a tow truck to get through. Soon, she was safely out of view and followed the curve behind the garage bays. There it became a sea—four rows of wreckage, rust and wasteland weeds. Wild strawberry vines had overtaken many of the older cars and the air was ripe with the smell of the wild fruit. She crushed a berry stepping through the creepers and a strong whiff of their winey juice reached her. Purple bramble canes also grew between the junks, crisscrossing and poking out of broken windows. Narrow clumps of bluestem grass and rabbit's foot clover carpeted the sand in places. Stands of early goldenrod cropped up here and there, just forming their green white buds.

A weathered stockade fence bounded the yard at the rear. It was half covered in vines and a few planks had broken off high and gapped the fence like chipped or missing teeth. The mountain forest reared up behind it.

It was hot and very still among the wrecks and junks. The ground was dry, with patches of sand and yellow-orange clay, and darker veins of mineral iron bleeding to the surface. You could almost hear the soil bake and smell the weeds heating up like kitchen seasonings in a skillet. Sun glinted off the dirty old windshields. The web shattered glass flashed like sudden signals. Merrilee stood for a moment, closed her eyes and listened. She became aware of a kind of winching sound, a creak, like the wind in old tree branches, but it was virtually still. It was coming from behind the stockade fence.

It stopped. Merrilee wound her way to the last row of vehicles along the fence. Crrreeeak. There it was again. Up close it sounded like prying. She went over to the section of fence where she'd heard it. But there was no way to approach, or see over the fence, unless she walked over the top of the cars. There was no passage in between except through an impossible gauntlet of brier and itchy weeds.

The car directly in front of the noise had no front fender and a shattered windshield, so she wasn't going over that one. The one beside it was better, a small sedan that would be easy to mount. It was heavily rusted and covered in strawberry vines. Merrilee stepped up on the bumper and then kneeled and crawled up the hood, feeling the fine prickers sting her hands. She pulled herself up over the windshield and slid along the roof, trying not to cave the metal loudly and give herself away. Creeaak!

"Ouch!" A man's voice interjected on the other side of the fence.

Merrilee stopped and held her breath for a moment, and then when the prying sound started again, she walked down the rear windshield on her hands and slid down to the trunk on her knees. She got as close to the fence as she could, stood up carefully, and reached for two solid looking stockade pickets. She then stepped up and wedged her toes into the gap of a broken picket. She looked over the top and to her right.

There was a blond man, strongly built, wearing only blue jeans, and gleaming with sweat. He crouched with his back to her and he was prying the front driver's side fender of a small red car, where it was badly bent over the wheel. The car's hood was open and the engine block hung suspended on chains from a thick tree branch. The chain looped over the branch and down around the base of the tree's trunk held taut there with a come-along. An ATV sat parked beside the car in the tracks of a logging trail that ran up into the woods.

The man's arms and hands were black with grease and so were his jeans. He had a gold chain around his neck and a black hat in his back pocket. He muttered encouragement to the fender as he yanked and pulled on the pry bar. Beside his shoulder on the front door panel was the logo. Even with the chrome coat chipped, a letter broken off and a lot of rust, she could make it out. Escort.

Merrilee's right toe began to slip and she arched her foot higher to get a better toehold, but as her weight shifted, the fence leaned slightly forward with a creak of its own. The man stood up and turned at the noise. A necklace of slender metal tags caught the sun in movement as he stood. The glint of it struck Merrilee's eyes. In the blinding moment, the man reached to his back pocket, and pulled a black mask down over his surprised, grease streaked face. He dropped the pry bar, hopped onto the ATV and roared away in a cloud of dust into the forest.

13.

The Curse on Gemini Farm

E VERY SUMMER SINCE Jude could remember, he'd spent the 4th of July holiday at his Uncle David's and Aunt Raeanne's farm across town. It was a ritual on the morning he left to raise all manner of objections and complaints to Aster to avoid going. "Do you know they've never even heard of *Lucky Charms* there? Raeanne makes her own cereal out of bark and twigs and ¾ inch stone. It's your fault if I break a tooth."

Aster sat at the kitchen table, smoking and leafing through a copy of *Woman's World.* She tried to look like she wasn't paying a bit of attention, but from time to time Jude saw her biting her lip. Jet was within earshot tinkering with the vacuum cleaner, so Jude made sure he'd hear the next part. "I hope you know you're sending me to a place where marshmallow fluff is banned. Oh, and another thing, Jesse and Junie always swim naked in the pond. Aren't you afraid I might come home a naturist?"

No response. "And if they think they're going to wake me up at 4 a.m. to milk the cows, they've got another thing coming."

Aster put her magazine down. All of a sudden she got a furious look in her eyes and pointed her cigarette at him. "Your poor Aunt and Uncle have just had every head of cattle on their farm slaughtered. Some horrible man is trying to steal their land out from under them. That is no laughing matter, do you hear me? You don't have any idea how hard they work to keep their farm going. You can't even keep your socks in pairs, let alone keep track of a barn full of cattle. Well, fine then. You just won't go. You can stay here and keep the junk piles company."

Jude must have gone a bit too far this time, because he'd never expected Aster to call the whole thing off. He actually loved going to his cousins', despite all his complaining, and began to search around immediately for a way out of his predicament. He felt mean and foolish for complaining about anything on Gemini Farm, especially since his cousins were kind to him, and his uncle and aunt always made such an effort to please him and include him in everything—and not just after Kennedy died. They had always treated him that way. When it came right down to it, he objected just to be difficult to Aster and Jet. For, if nothing else, Gemini Farm reminded him how much he envied his cousins. They had each other and a beautiful place that seemed to define them and make them complete. All he and his parents had was loss and sadness as deep as their piles of scrap and as long as the string of wrecks that lined their yard. He could barely stand to look at Aster reading her cheap, tissue paper magazine, and Jet buying time on another ruined machine, without feeling sad for them and sorry for himself. He just wanted to shout back at Aster, "You want the truth—I wish they were my family!", but he knew once he said it, he could never take it back. So to spite them, and out of pity for them, he complained about the yearly trip and all the things he secretly loved about it. For, the unspoken part of their ritual was how secretly pleased Aster was that Jude showed a preference for anything about their cursed existence.

"Okay, if you don't want me to go," Jude said.

"Young man, you—are—going."

Jude hadn't been there half an hour before he noticed the change in the atmosphere at Gemini Farm. Everything looked the same—the house, the gardens, the orchard, the barn, and his cousins for that matter—as fresh and beautiful as ever under the bright July sun. Except for the absence of the cows, which had a way of going about their business without gathering much notice anyway, you wouldn't have guessed that Gemini Farm was on the brink of ruin. In spite of everything Aster had said last night, Jude had no idea how bad things were for the Meades until he saw his Uncle David's face: the care-worn look in his eyes, the stoop in his shoulders that suddenly reminded him of Aster. He was tall like his sister, but lanky and loose in the shoulders, where she was tensed and hunched over. He had tarnished loose blond curls and brown eyes that always seemed to shine with warmth. Today they looked dark in hue and blank, as though he were in shock. He gave Jude a hug as usual, and his smile was as kind as ever, but his greeting sounded tired and strained. It was enough to make Jude feel he was imposing on them at the worst possible time. He decided to help as much as possible with the daily chores—feeding the chickens, cleaning stalls, weeding and watering the garden, helping Raeanne in the house.

"Have you had breakfast, Jude?" Aunt Raeanne said.

Jude nodded. "Do you have any weeding to do?"

His aunt and uncle looked at each other.

"Have we got weeds? You don't know what you're getting yourself into," Raeanne said. "You might want to get a start now though, before the heat comes up."

Jude and the twins tackled the weeding and then decided to have a dip in the pond to cool off. While Jude felt larger and more awkward every day, his cousins appeared more beautiful each time he saw them. As summer wore on, their dusty blond hair bleached lighter, their skin grew cocoa brown, while their sleepy, gold flecked, hazel eyes stood out more vibrantly. In body they were lithe and naturally graceful, like pixies in *A Midsummer Night's Dream*. Yet, they seemed utterly unaffected by their beauty and always looked admiringly at Jude's dark eyes and hair. It seemed preposterous to Jude, and yet around them he didn't feel self-conscious in a swim suit the way he had in gym class.

The boys stretched out on their towels in the shade of a sycamore, still wet and pleasantly cool. Junie and Jesse told Jude everything that had happened since the last day of school. The latest disaster involved a fungus that had struck their honeybees and killed most of the young larvae in the hives. It had gotten to the point that every day they woke up expecting some new disaster to await them.

"Dad said it's like Biblical plagues," Jesse said, "Just one thing after another until we just give up everything to Greenway."

Jude wanted to say, 'It's just like us waiting for another wreck,' but he realized the Corgan wrecks, however cruel, were only a symbol of their loss. The only physical consequence was having no place for company to park. Not that anyone was clamoring to visit. Maybe they weren't so cursed after all.

The twins told Jude that the injunction to stop Greenway's project had been upheld that morning. Before Jude arrived, they'd all gone out to the back 40 and watched as Greenway cleared his machinery off their land. But, it wasn't over. Slater Knox, their attorney, explained the injunction was temporary and a hearing was set for the last week in August to determine the legality of the alleged sale of the back 40—and whether Greenways transfer of deed was legit.

Greenway's hocus pocus was baffling. For, already the Town Clerk and Zoning Board had clammed-up and certain documents had been legally sealed by the Court until the hearing, leaving the Meades with no answers to their basic questions. The biggest question of all was whether they'd even have a farm left by late August the way things were going.

Junie rolled over on his side and rested his head on his hand. He looked beyond Jude over to his brother. The way they seemed to read each other's expressions, reminded Jude of the way he could make out Aster when she was incoherent and nobody else could, only what the twins did seemed way more mysterious to him.

Jesse sat up and said, "Jude, did you notice anything different about our father?"

"He looks sad—and worried. I felt bad about coming; I don't want to be a bother or anything."

"You're not," Jesse said. "He wants you here. In fact, he's glad you're here. We needed somebody to break the spell around here."

Junie looked at his identical twin with impatience. Jesse gave him a helpless look back.

"Alright, I'll say it then." Junie turned to Jude. "We're worried about dad."

"Worried?"

"We think he did—might do something."

"Like what?"

The twins looked at each other again. This time Jesse shook his head. "We don't know," he said.

"We do know, but you're too afraid to say it," Junie said.

Jesse hopped up and stormed off toward the house.

"What are you so mad about; it was you who thought of it," Junie called after his brother.

Jesse kept on going and didn't even look back.

If Jude was needed here to break the spell of gloom and tension that hung over Gemini Farm, so far he had to have been a major disappointment.

The cool feeling of the swim had vanished by the time Jude reached the porch and the first prickles of sweat began to rise on his skin again. He went in through the kitchen, took a glass from the dish drainer and filled it with water from the tap. The house felt empty. Jesse was nowhere to be found, and Junie had headed for the barn to find his father. Aunt Raeanne also seemed to be absent. There was nothing but the whir of fans in the sitting room. He took his glass with him and plunked himself down on the couch right in front of the window fan.

Jude closed his eyes and let the fan cool his sweat. The next thing he knew, he was awakened by the sound of voices by the front door. He couldn't have been asleep long, because his head was clear and he hadn't started dreaming. He lay there and listened. Aunt Raeanne was talking with someone, but the other voice, a man's, was too faint to identify. It was impossible to pick up what they were saying with the fan going full blast, so Jude got up and crossed to the other doorway that led to the mudroom. He stayed out of view against the wall and listened.

"Like you say, Ma'am, if we don't raise our voices in protest and stand together, they'll just keep taking over everything until there is nothing left for us at all." It was a young man's voice, and there was a familiar lilt to it, but Jude couldn't place it.

Raeanne said, "People don't understand that if it happened to us, it could happen to them as well."

"It truly could. I guess it comes down to how much people are willing to take before they fight back. Like that explosion a couple of weeks ago. Don't be surprised if worse things than that are coming."

Jude felt a little shiver of recognition go down his spine. If only he could be sure.

"Things couldn't get much worse around here," Aunt Raeanne said.

"Well, I hope not, but you wait and see what happens if they get their way. There you go. I appreciate your taking the time to help us out. Our goal is five thousand signatures, every voting adult in the county, and then we march on the State House. Maybe, you'll join us then."

"Maybe so," Aunt Raeanne said.

"Good day, Ma'am."

As the goodbyes were said, Jude crept back across the room and leaned over the couch and looked out the window down the side of the house to the front door. He got there just as the young man was turning around to leave. He recognized the dark, buzzed head of the mysterious Calvin he'd met above Granger Falls.

⌘ ⌘ ⌘

GREENWAY'S RED TRUCK was parked outside when Junie arrived at the barn. His stomach lurched. He stood outside for a moment. Greenway's cold, sharp voice greeted him before he even entered the barn. He moved down the side of the tractor, stopped and crouched behind the big front tire and listened.

"Your day in court is coming, but if you're expecting vindication you have another thing coming. By then it will probably be too late. Your business is losing value by the day. No cattle, no bees, and who knows what next? What if something happens to your chickens? Your fruit trees? Your gardens? You're not exactly having a good run of luck."

"I don't know how you did all of this, but I know it was you."

"People will be wondering how safe your products are. They already are. It wouldn't take much more to have the State in here to shut you down. You need to consider us as an option, while you still have an offer."

"What offer is that? You took the back forty without paying us a cent. But how could you pay us when we weren't even asked to sell? I mean, where's the money you supposedly paid for that? We don't have it, because it never happened."

"Are you trying to convince me or yourself?"

"We only have to convince the court. But for the sake of assuming your aren't a liar, what is the offer? How much do you want for the land? Including the house?"

"You can continue to live in the house and draw a decent salary. The house is yours. We need you and want you here. This all depends on you. You and what you know are the main attraction."

"No offer as I suspected. You'll just *let* us live on our own land. Salaried tenants—as some agricultural side show for your rich, high-wire urbanites to patronize. That isn't going to happen. I can tell you now, I'll set fire to everything before I let that happen. Mark my words on it."

"I have every intention of paying you fair market value for your land, but if you keep resisting the inevitable you'll end up with nothing."

"If you're going to take it anyway why do you need me to agree? Why do you need to offer us anything? No, this is just another intimidation tactic. Those documents of yours won't stand up in court, and you know it."

"So you hope, but there are greater things at stake than your precious farm, and greater laws in force."

"Whose laws? Yours?"

"It is the will of the world." Greenway let out a cold, sharp laugh. "Do you know what that is, Mr. Meades? Let me tell you. When you have only riches, you may wake up one day and find they are gone; but when you have power and riches you will always wake up the next day with more of both. And you sir, have neither."

Junie gritted his teeth. The muscles in his neck tightened. He broke into a sweat. He wanted nothing more than to leap from his hiding place and take Greenway down. Kill him. Yes, kill him. Was Jesse right after all? He could understand why his father might resort to blowing something up. The sound of Greenway's voice, cold and disdainful as the day they'd met him on the back forty, was enough to throw a Buddhist monk into a flying rage.

There was a long pause, then Junie's father said, "Well, then, we have nothing to lose by fighting you. Believe me, you'll have to take it all by force, and when you do, every camera in the state will be trained on you."

"Are you sure of that? Do you know how many media outlets I own?"

Footsteps sounded on the other side of the tractor, as if Greenway had turned to leave the barn. Then they stopped. "In times like these, Mr. Meades, it's best to know who your friends are before you bet the farm on them."

Jesse heard the kick and purr when he opened the mail box at the end of their driveway. There was an older boy, maybe Oscar's age, trying to start a gleaming chopper—all black and chrome. From the house you could just see a bit of the road before it went on past, because there was a row of spruce trees on either side of the driveway that screened the view of passing cars. The motorcycle was up against the spruces to the right of the mailbox. The boy looked up and waved at Jesse. He sat on the bike and waited as Jesse came over to have a look.

"You need some help?"

"Oh, no. She's fine."

"You looking for someone?"

"I was just up at the house. Your house?"

Jesse nodded.

"My petition." The boy reached back for a clipboard bungeed to the sissy bar. "It's to stop Greenway's development. Your mom? Sweet lady. She signed it."

"Cool. He's after our farm you know."

"Yeah, your mom was saying. I'm really sorry about that. Hey, I'm Calvin." The boy stuck out his hand. When Jesse went to take it, Calvin took the power grip of an arm wrestler, and then slid the grip away to curl his fingers around the tips of Jesse's fingers.

Jesse smiled and blushed in the presence of Calvin's informal handshake. "Jesse." He walked around the chopper looking at all the details—the staggered drag pipes, the sissy bar with its black leather pad and chrome studs, the short curved handlebars with dog bone risers, and the chrome shocks coiled in black springs.

"A rebuilt 1947 Knucklehead Chopper. You want to get on and go for a ride?"

Calvin had a kind of smiling expression that made Jesse unsure if he were being totally serious.

"Really?"

"Yeah, really. Come on."

"I'd love to, but my mother would have a fit. I'd have to ask and I know what she'd say and…"

"I know. You don't know me, but I promise I won't go fast and I'll be super careful. We won't be long. Nobody will even know you're gone."

Calvin raised his eyebrows in a hopeful plea. He gripped the handlebars in earnest, gave the starter a kick and brought the engine to life. "You can wear my helmet. What do you say?"

Jesse felt a strange thrill in his chest and a goose of fear in his gut. Why not? Just for a few minutes. Free as the wind. Free from the tension and gloom around here. Why shouldn't I?

"Okay."

Jesse took the black helmet, put it on and climbed on the chopper.

"Just hold onto my waist and lean when I lean. Okay?"

"Got it."

Junie was in a state of turmoil and confusion. After Greenway left he'd retreated from the barn unnoticed. He didn't want to see what he was feeling reflected in his father's face. He went inside the house to look for Jesse, but his mother said he'd gone out to get the mail.

Jesse alone would understand what he was feeling, because he'd already sensed their father's state of mind and the danger of the situation. Something he hadn't wanted to see.

Junie reached the end of the driveway and heard the roar of a motorcycle. He stepped around the spruce hedge to see Jesse on the back of a chopper being driven away by an older boy. Even helmeted he knew it was Jesse by his build and his clothes. Before he could call out, or get their attention, the bike eased off the shoulder and disappeared around the bend in the road.

Raeanne had made a huge fruit salad and a platter of sandwiches for dinner, yet the atmosphere around the dinner table was anything but relaxed and casual. David made no mention of Greenway's unexpected visit. Junie said nothing for his part, because he wasn't supposed to have heard it. If his father wasn't talking about it, how could he? Raeanne was mum about her visitor and the petition she'd signed to stop Greenway. Even though it was cheering news, it seemed almost cruel to present a powerless local petition as a cause for optimism, or a sign that their circumstances were about to change. Jude was surprised Aunt Raeanne kept it to herself, and while he would have loved to drop Calvin's name, the fact that he'd been eavesdropping made for an embarrassing disclosure anyway. Jesse could have mentioned Calvin as well, but only at the risk of revealing his forbidden ride and his mother's omission, or—with the mailbox empty upon his return—tempting whoever may have discovered his absence to reveal that as well. Junie could have enlightened them all on the nature of Jesse's absence and the contents of the daily mail, but, being torn between anger at his brother's secret liberty and the need to confide in him, he was again silenced. Nor did the twins dare to ask what the bags of ammonium nitrate were doing in the garden shed. It was all an intricate web. Each silence suspended another thread of silence and connected all the others.

There was only the sound of chewing and swallowing and the scrape of spoons. Jude made such a loud gulp swallowing that everybody forgot their manners and stared at him for a moment. He was about to launch into a self-conscious monologue about the disastrous supper Jet had made once when Aster stayed overnight at the hospital during a snow storm: sweet potato, peanut butter and marshmallow fluff casserole topped with bacon. He was saved from further embarrassment by Willa, who had napped through all the secrets.

"Why isn't anybody talking?"

Oscar, who'd been gone the whole day, said, "Yeah, like, who did you kill this afternoon and where is the body buried?" Nobody said a word in reply.

Had the Meades broken the silence, one and all, it would have brought more than one troubling mystery to light. They might have wondered about the simultaneous arrival of Greenway and the signature-seeking Calvin on the farm. Oscar might have revealed that the bags of ammonium nitrate had been loaded in their truck by mistake, and with the haying to be done he hadn't had time to return them until today. They all might have talked about how scared and angry they were feeling, talked about how much they'd like to blow something up, or kill someone. Instead, they left the table and drifted farther apart in silence.

Sometimes it was safer to say dangerous things than to keep them inside. It was an outlet that released you from actually doing them, like the logic of a rocker valve on a pressure cooker that let off steam. When it started rocking, you minded it to keep the turmoil underneath from blowing up.

On Saturday morning, Jude awoke to the unexpected sound of rain. He heard the trickling in the gutters first and then the steady rushing sound it made as it lashed the rooftop. The air coming in the window was pleasantly cool and the whole room, musty from the humidity only last night, smelled as if it had been washed clean by the rain as well.

Jude got dressed and went down the hall to the kitchen. The smell of real percolated coffee and warm toast greeted him. Aunt Raeanne, Oscar, Willa and the twins were already gathered around the table. "Where's Uncle David?" Jude asked.

"He's not feeling too well," Raeanne said. "He did morning chores and went back to bed. It's going to rain all day; good day for him to catch up on his rest."

The twins glanced at each other and then at Jude.

It did rain all day and rained so hard there was nothing to do but stay indoors. Willa, the twins and Jude played crazy eights for a while, but that grew boring after a couple of hours. Jude fell asleep reading a popular vampire book he found on the shelf in his room and woke up hours later from a strange dream. For a moment he was filled with impossible hope—a light in his head and chest he couldn't name—and then the dream came back to him. Kennedy was both dead and alive. That is, he existed in some sub-region of the Corgan wrecks, but it wasn't as easy as just lifting up a hood and finding him. It made no sense, but instead of just walking out of the trailer to where the wrecks lined their frontage, he'd had to undertake an unfamiliar journey on the Byclops. Unfamiliar for sure, but they were supposed to be the Corgan wrecks. It only made sense that Jude knew where they were. Yet, he was peddling along a gravel road at a very high speed with no idea where he was going, basically winging it as hemlocks whipped past, and making turns without thinking and taking forks without knowing. Then the road became a corridor and the Byclops was gone. He'd started out in daylight, but at that point it was dusk and he was glad he'd arrived before dark. The hallway came to a staircase lit by a single bulb in a ceiling socket. He made it down with some smooth escalator motion and found himself in a morning world again. The wrecks lined the road along their property, only there were far more than sixteen and their trailer looked a lot more like the Meades' farm house than their doublewide.

The confusing part was that having made it here, Jude couldn't find Kennedy after all; and only then recalled an earlier part of the dream in which Kennedy himself directed him here. He could almost remember having seen him, yet Jude could only be sure of his voice.

"All the hoods have to be open, Judo, or you won't find me. I can't open them from in here. You need the key."

"What key?" Jude asked, in a sudden panic.

"I gave it to you, remember?"

"But I don't remember; I don't know what you mean."

"You have the key, Judo. Remember me."

Jude woke up and a shiver took hold of him, a kind of crawling on his neck and face. A mist gathered at the corners of his eyes. If only it were as easy as turning a key and having an answer appear before him. Soon the waking world took hold of him and the farther the dream receded from him the more nonsensical it seemed.

⌘ ⌘ ⌘

Perhaps Jude's nap that day had been providential. For, if he hadn't slept so much in the afternoon, he would not have been awake in the wee hours of the morning to see his Uncle David go out to the garden shed.

Jude wasn't sure whether it was the sound outside his window that woke him up, or whether he'd woken up just moments before, but he sat up in bed the minute he heard it. The rain had long since stopped. The air was cool, misty and very still. Water released, like a brief shower, at the slight stir of a breeze and broke the silence of the night. Jude looked out the window beside his bed. The sky must have cleared because the moon was out and illumined the lawn beyond the maple tree outside his window. He saw a man cross the lawn, but the lower branches of the tree obscured his head and shoulders.

Jude froze cold at the thought of a saboteur out doing who knows what damage to the farm, but when the figure got farther away he recognized his uncle's lanky form and long elastic stride. He was heading toward the garden shed.

Jude didn't know what took hold of him then—whether he was channeling GEIST, thinking about what his cousins wouldn't tell him at the pond, or whether the heaviness of warning in his stomach drove him to it—but he decided to follow his uncle and spy on him. He tugged on his sneakers, climbed over the bed and very carefully lifted the screen latches. It wasn't easy going through windows when you were his size and shape. He positioned himself on all fours, back to the window and placed his hands and head down on the mattress. Then, he stretched one leg at a time back through the window, until both shins were resting on the sill. He hoisted himself up on his arms, as he would in a wheel barrel race, and walked on his hands backwards. By the time his hips were balanced on the sill, he reached back with his hands and pushed off on the sill, slowly letting himself down until his feet were firmly on the ground. He lifted his head too soon on the way out and whacked it on the sash. He saw a bolt of light behind his eyes and winced through the pain in silence.

By this time, Uncle David had closed himself inside the shed. A thread of light shone under the door and shadows darkened the line of light whenever he moved. Jude circled around to the back of the shed. He'd noticed knot holes in the wood yesterday when he was putting away the rake and hoe. Some were large enough to see through. Sure enough, a narrow ray of light, like a projector beam in a theater, shone through the back wall of the shed. Jude quietly approached the hole. Inside he heard his uncle at work in the shed.

Jude put his eye to the hole and watched at an angle as Uncle David put a key into a padlock on a small metal tool chest. He opened the lid, but Jude couldn't see what was in the box. First, his uncle lifted a small cardboard box out and then he removed something wrapped in a felt bank sack. In the moment it took his uncle to remove the object, Jude had already fancied it must be some priceless heirloom he was reluctantly selling to save the farm. Then he saw the nickel shine of a revolver emerge under the sickly yellow of a bug light. His uncle flicked back the hammer and released the cylinder. He opened the box, removed six bullets and loaded the chambers. Then, he clicked the cylinder back in place and put the revolver in the inside breast pocket of his vest. He drew the gun quickly and pointed, as if he were going to shoot it. He did this over and over again—put the gun away, drew it and pointed in a different direction each time. The last time he seemed to point the gun right at the knot hole, as if he were aiming purposely at Jude.

Jude froze and held his breath. His entire body from head to toe broke out in a hot and cold prickly sweat. Uncle David had only used the knot hole as a target. Jude could tell from his face and his movements that he was unaware of being watched. He set the gun down quietly, carefully put the box of bullets and the empty bank sack back in the tool chest and locked it up. Finally, he put the revolver in the inside breast pocket of the vest again, turned to leave and flicked off the shed light on his way out.

Jude was unable to sleep after what he'd seen. He lay awake, tossing and turning, trying to banish the image of Uncle David taking aim at the knothole. Finally, he couldn't stand it any longer, tiptoed upstairs and quietly let himself into his cousins' room. It was still dark, but first light would be coming soon, and they'd be getting up to start their chores anyway.

Jude knelt beside Jesse's bed. "Hey, wake-up." Jesse didn't stir at first. From across the room Junie said, "Is that you Jude?"

"I have to talk to you guys, now," Jude said.

Jesse had come around at the sound of his brother's voice. "What's the matter?"

Junie came over and sat down on the edge of the bed. Jesse was sitting up now, while Jude was still at the bedside on his knees between them. "Listen, your dad keeps all the guns in the cabinet right?"

"Yeah, of course. And they're all locked up. Why?"

"Because I just saw him out in the garden shed practicing his aim with a gun he keeps hidden in an old tool box, which was also locked."

"What do you mean you saw him in the garden shed?"

"What gun? Are you sure you weren't dreaming?"

"I mean, I woke up and saw him outside my window and followed him there. I watched him through a knot hole. Don't you think it's strange he'd just get up in the middle of the night to load and practice drawing a gun he keeps locked outside the house?"

"Yeah, it's about as strange as someone getting on the back of a motor-cycle with a total stranger," Junie said, letting his earlier anger at Jesse resurface.

"Really?" Jesse said. "So what are you going to do, tell mom and dad? Rat me out?"

"Yeah well maybe I should."

"I was only gone ten minutes, you—"

"Shhh. You guys are going to wake the whole house."

The twins fell silent. In the darkness of their room Jude couldn't make out their expressions, but the silence felt stony.

"So all of the guns you have in the cabinet are registered right?"

"Yeah, of course," Junie said.

"So you don't know anything about this gun?"

"What did it look like?"

"It was a nickel plated revolver with a dark grip. Not more than six inches long."

The twins shook their heads and after a moment raised their eyes and looked at each other, as if the static of their anger had cleared and they finally got what Jude was saying.

"If you were going to shoot somebody, you wouldn't use a gun that could be connected to you right?" Junie said.

"Exactly," Jude said.

Junie said, "I was coming out to tell you, when you took off today, and then everything was so strange at dinner I couldn't."

"Tell me what?" Jesse said.

"Greenway was in our barn today. I went in to see Dad when we came back from the pond. Greenway's truck was there and he must have come over from the back forty. He wants everything but the house and Dad said he'd burn it all to ashes first. It was terrible, and if Dad felt anything near what I was feeling, he'd definitely be thinking about killing Greenway."

"Maybe he's just preparing for trouble, in case Greenway tries to take our house or something," said Jesse. "He'd have a right to defend us, but I don't think he'd go out and shoot him just like that."

"You thought he blew up the Mobil station."

"What?" said Jude.

"Jesse found some ammonium nitrate bags in the shed too, and since we don't use commercial fertilizers he got this wild idea about our dad making explosives."

"Well, that guy that came to the door with the petition, Calvin? I think he knows something about the Mobil. I met him at Granger Falls two weeks ago. If he's out to stop Greenway, maybe he's with the VLF or something. The thing is, your dad had nothing to do with the explosion, I'm sure of it; but I don't think he was practicing to defend you guys. The way he was pulling that gun out of hiding and taking aim, it looked to me like an ambush."

"Great, our Dad's not a terrorist, just an assassin in training."

14.

Fireworks

O N SUNDAY EVENING, Aster and Jet came out to the farm for a cookout, and then the Meades and Corgans all went to Twin Gaps Fair Grounds to see the fireworks. Merrilee was going to be there too and she'd agreed to meet Jude behind the Grand Stand at 7:30.

The rain had cleared the air, and the 4th, turned out perfect. The evening air was warm and the fairgrounds basked in a thick golden light. A steady breeze pushed around the smell of hay, French fries, barbequed chicken, cigarette smoke and beer. The grandstand stood at the south end of the great rectangular field. Beneath it, a stage and a platform were set up for live music and dancing. You could hear intermittent voices testing the PA system and the hot microphone in the grandstand ringing loud enough to make anyone near a speaker cringe. The midway took up the middle of the field with food booths and "games of skill". The carnival rides were between the bleachers at the north end of the fairgrounds, big machines in primary colors, whirring and wheeling to the distorted tinkling of calliope music.

Jude met Merrilee as they'd arranged. If she hadn't been looking down over her glasses at him, he might not have recognized her, because the overgrown my-brother-cut-my-dolly's-hair-off look had been traded in for a sleek chin-length bob and a rich henna tint.

"I like it. It's definitely you."

"Well, I made my father get a haircut yesterday and realized I really needed one too. Listen, I'm starved." Merrilee changed the subject at the prompting of her growling stomach.

"Don't your parents feed you?"

"I told them I'd have supper here. It's not often I get to indulge in greasy fried dough and gooey cheesy pizza."

"Your parents actually let you come here alone with all these redneck boys running around."

"They know I'm meeting you, plus Alison and Sandra are going to be here tonight. In case I can't get a ride with you I can sneak a clandestine ride with one of them after dark. And I have a cell phone if I need to call home." Merrilee produced a sleek silver device from her pocket. "Actually, I have two of them. One for you, in case we need to do some surveillance."

"Cool. You better show me how to use it. I'm from the low tech side of the tracks."

"Here." Merrilee pressed a button and it popped open. "Just press 2 and hit 'talk'. That automatically dials my cell number. Press 3 for Sandra and 4 for Alison. We'd press one to ring you. And here's the *piece de resistance*: it's a camera and video phone." She pressed another button and panned the phone. "See? So, I can snap a pic and send it to you and vice versa in a matter of seconds. It's got two way live video as well. We can chat face to face or see what we might be videotaping at any given moment. It's sort of a must for GEIST since we can't be seen in public together. For that you hit this button. Takes a few seconds and—"

Jet and Merrilee were looking at their phones and seeing each other on their screens. "Testing. One two three testing," they droned in unison.

At the midway, they stopped at a pizza booth and Merrilee bought herself a big floppy pepperoni slice. She folded it and devoured several, gooey, cheesy bites.

While Merrilee ate, Jude relayed the goings on at the farm, including the surprise visits from Calvin and Greenway, and about his uncle and the mystery gun. Merrilee then gave Jude the highlights of the last GEIST meeting, climaxing with her own discovery at Atwood's on Friday.

"The thing is, I should have been looking at his face, but the flash of that strange necklace blinded me, like a choker with a bunch of skinny dog tags

146

on it, and then he had the mask on so fast and was gone. But the weirdest thing of all was that it was an Escort, and the engine had been taken out."

"And none of our wrecks have engines. Do you think Chet knows about it?"

"I don't know. It was beyond the fence, but where else would it have come from and how else would it get to the other side? Do you think we should confront him?"

Jude shrugged. "Um, let me think about it. Listen, I've got to find everybody and stay close to things."

⌘ ⌘ ⌘

AFTER THEY SEPARATED, Jude went to look for the Meades and his parents, but he walked the entire length of the fair and didn't catch a glimpse of any of them. They said they were going down to the carnival rides so that Willa could go on a few before the fireworks. The fairgrounds were quickly filling up with people. Soon it would be nearly impossible to find anyone, unless you prearranged a meeting place, or, come to think of it, unless you were carrying a camera phone.

Jude was just about to call Merrilee to ask her if she'd seen his family, when a voice over the intercom called for everybody's attention. He moved closer to a timber with a mounted speaker.

"...and welcome to our 4th of July celebration. Not only are we fortunate to have such perfect weather, but we are very pleased to present Wild Man Ethan's Band, and what promises to be the biggest, most colorful fireworks display in Twin Gaps' history. In acknowledgement of that, I want you all to extend a warm welcome to the man who is responsible for donating this state of the art show tonight. Let's hear a big round of applause for Mr. Merlin Greenway."

The moment Jude heard the name, the back of his neck prickled and a tingle rode the length of his spine. He immediately headed back up the midway toward the grandstand. He flipped open the phone and pushed two. The phone rang once and Merrilee answered in a whisper.

"Jude?"

"Yeah, why are you whispering?"

"I'm *indisposed* ; on account of pepperoni, if you know what I mean. Anybody could be listening outside the door."

"East or west side of the field?" Jude asked.

"West."

"I'm on the other side. Look, get to the grandstand as soon as you can. Merlin Greenway is just about to make his speech."

⌘ ⌘ ⌘

As soon as Merlin Greenway was announced, a change came over the entire Meades' family. Raeanne looked at David; the twins glanced at each other and then looked down at their feet; Willa looked like she was about to cry. Oscar might have booed, if he hadn't stayed home to keep an eye on things at the farm.

Jet stood up on his tip-toes to see over the crowd to the podium microphone. "That's the little S.O.B.? No kidding."

"Jet, not in front of the children," Aster said.

"It's only an acronym, for Pete's sake."

Aster threw an elbow into his ribs.

Raeanne said, "Maybe we shouldn't stay around for this." She looked at David, trying to gage his temper.

"It's alright, Rae. Stay and listen to every word he says. I'm going to the car to get my vest. I feel a little chilly."

"I'll go with you," Junie offered.

"No, stay here and listen," David said. It was not a request.

David headed to the east side of the grounds toward the parking lot. Junie kept an eye on him as he wound his way against the movement of the crowd, and with everybody fixed on Greenway he took off after him. In a few seconds he too was swallowed up in a swarm of fairgoers. Raeanne turned around, but the thought came to her too late. "David, you didn't bring your vest," she said.

"Oh, well," Aster said. She came over to her sister-in-law and whispered, "He probably just needed an excuse to get away."

Raeanne nodded and looked around at the faces in the crowd. The farmers squinted and muttered. Dunky LaGro and Hiram Rafferty stood side by side, arms folded, wearing their most skeptical expressions. The applause for Greenway had been sparse at best, but there were some in the crowd who were not as sentimental about cows as they were about paved roads and long term employment. They looked up admiringly at the one man capable of dragging Vermont kicking and screaming into the 21st century.

Evening was settling into dusk, but the emerging lights over the grandstand created the strange illusion of simultaneous morning and twilight. The entire fairgrounds were dawning with this thrilling and unnatural light.

Greenway adjusted the microphone down to his diminutive height and looked out with the same steely squint of the farmers. His balding head seemed unnaturally large for his body.

"I know I'm not the most popular man with some of you right now, and that's alright. In time, I'll prove I'm not the enemy. The enemy in your midst is a lack of opportunity and economic growth. Vermont's children are leaving the state faster than you can raise them, because they know the life and opportunity they desire lies elsewhere. But that is the price of holding onto the past, without creating a provision for the future. Deep in all our hearts, we want Vermont to be a place of the future, not merely a past that is doomed to collapse and die."

Somebody in the crowd shouted, "Let us die then," followed by another voice, "Who asked for your help anyway?" and then, "Thief!"

A cheer went up, followed by a shush of disapproval. An opposing voice said, "Let the man speak."

Greenway chuckled nervously into his fist. "The problem is, we may disagree on how to get there. One thing is certain. It won't happen without change. The problem we face is how to take what is best and most distinctive in Vermont's past and transform it in the presence of new technologies and a modern infrastructure. Wouldn't it be grand to preserve a rural way of life, without preserving the poverty and joblessness? Wouldn't life be charmed if we could keep both our villages and our young people in Vermont? Wouldn't we feel blessed to grow an economy that is sensitive to the environment and the demands of the market? This is my vision—the vision of Catamount Estates. In ten to fifteen years I see Vermont poised to offer its citizens and its visitors the best of both worlds: a rural kingdom, with a unique landscape and distinctive traditions, that also accesses state of the art technology, new infrastructure and renewable energy; a place people come to experience the possibility of life at a rural pace with all of the stimulating qualities of urban life. In fact creating an alternative to the clutter and chaos of cities, and avoiding the impersonal sameness of suburbia."

Greenway didn't gesture with his hands at all during his speech. He leaned in close to the microphone and turned his head slowly from side to side, and up and down, so that he appeared to take note of every face in the crowd. "Look, I've gone on long enough tonight, but what you want to know is what it's going to mean for all of you. It's going to mean more and better paying jobs; stronger communities and schools; a flood of investment capital into the state and unprecedented business opportunities in service, small industries and boutique farms, the likes of which will take Vermont from the margins to the vanguard of our culture. Thank you, and enjoy the show."

Jude arrived at the edges of the crowd in time to hear the end of Greenway's speech, but he couldn't get close enough to see what he really looked like. Then the man sat down and was lost behind the milling crowd. Jude's parents and the Meades were nowhere to be found either. Some of the people began to filter down toward the east bleachers to find seats for the fireworks. Others flanked the west side of the grounds and set up lawn chairs and laid blankets; for the platform was always staged, by special arrangement, behind a line of trees in Neely's hay field on that side of the fair. The minutes dragged as the sky darkened and the chatter grew louder, more restless and expectant. Small children ran past, shrieking and waving yellow and green florescent wands at each other like warring fireflies. Jude searched for familiar faces amidst the crowd through shifting bands of artificial light and shadows. He turned around like a lost child, not knowing where to go and what to do next.

"What's taking Daddy so long?" Willa asked, tugging on her mother's blouse. They all stood around in a group shrugging and looking indecisive—Raeanne, Jesse, Willa, Jet and Aster.

"He knows where to meet us doesn't he, Mom?" asked Jesse.

"He knows we always watch from the bleachers. Why don't we just head over there," Raeanne said.

"What if he comes back and doesn't find us?" Willa said.

"He's probably on his way to the bleachers," Junie returned suddenly, out of breath. He leaned over to Jesse and whispered, "I lost him. The parking lot filled up. By the time I found our car, he was gone."

Raeanne cast a look of concern at her son, but her voice showed no trace of it. "Maybe he had to use the toilet. You know how the lines can be."

"Why don't I stay here in case he does come back," Jet volunteered.

"Do you mind?" Raeanne said.

"Go on," Jet winked and waved them off. "If he doesn't show by the start of the fireworks, I'll join you in the bleachers."

Jesse said, "I think I'll stay here and keep Uncle Jet company."

Jude pressed two on the cell phone and got a busy signal. After three tries he gave up and headed for the bleachers to find everybody. Just then, a very loud maroon went off, signaling the start of the show. The crowd roared and hooted in anticipation—a loud cheer on the near side of the field and another fainter cheer rising from the distant bleachers. Then the first firework whistled through the air, a white star and a faint smoky trail that disappeared as it climbed. A gold chrysanthemum filled the sky and lit up the fair with spidery shimmers, crackling faintly as it spread and turning red at the end. Jude mocked the collective gasp with his own exaggerated 'Whoooh', yet as the light dissolved and the shimmers turned to smoke, he felt that melancholy empty feeling that always followed the finale. Whether it was chintzy or spectacular, you somehow always felt cheated, reminded that everything had an end.

The chrysanthemum was followed by an impressive opening barrage that featured splintering comets, salutes, waterfalls, crowns and Jupiter rings, all hazed over in white glitter. After it subsided, Jude turned and walked resolutely toward the bleachers. If he kept staying for one more, he'd end up watching the whole display alone. He passed through the midway, stopping only once and turning too late after a heart stopping gasp to see the faint traces of three ascending willows. Jude walked faster. He came around the corner of the duck shoot at the end of the midway and ran headlong into Ms. LaFrance. From the way they hit, shoulder into shoulder, she should have taken the worst of it, but it was Jude who spun sideways. "Oh, sorry Ms. LaFrance," he began to apologize. She turned for a moment, stared at him as if she'd never seen him before in her life and said, "Why don't you watch where you're going." Then she turned and walked quickly away. "Ms. LaFrance? It's me, Jude," he called after her, but she didn't look back.

When Jude arrived at the bleachers, he picked out Junie and then Willa waving wildly at him—for she had spotted him first. He waved back. They were about seven rows up. Jude climbed the stairs and slid onto the end of the bench beside Junie. He looked down the row.

"Where's Uncle David?"

"We sort of lost him," Junie said.

"He went to the car to get a jacket and hasn't come back," Willa said.

"Did anybody go out to the car to look for him?"

"I went. He wasn't there."

"Did you hear Greenway?" Jude asked.

"The way he talks you'd never know it was the same man I heard in our barn."

Raeanne said, "He was never in our barn, Junie."

"Yes, he was. The same day that boy came with the petition. Dad didn't tell you?"

Raeanne was suddenly quiet. Aster looked confused.

"Come on," Junie said to Jude. "Let's go find him." They began to climb down the bleachers.

"Jude Corgan where are you going?"

"To find Uncle David."

Aster was about to object, when Raeanne said, "Maybe they should go find him."

Jude and Junie split up at the midway to cover more ground. Junie went to the left, Jude took the right alley. Once alone, Jude pressed two on the cell phone. This time he got through. "Where are you?"

"Look," Merrilee said. She'd sent a picture of herself on the West side of the field.

"Have you seen my Uncle David?"

"No, why?"

"We haven't seen him since Greenway spoke."

"Have you guys checked the port-o-lets? The lines are pretty long."

"Get over to the Grandstand and keep an eye out for him, okay? Hey, where are Alison and Sandra?"

Merrilee said, "Sandra's somewhere in the Midway. You'll see her soon. Alison is by the grandstand."

"Thanks. Talk to you. Bye."

Jude pressed three and Sandra picked up. "Hey, Jude, what's up?"

"We're looking for my Uncle."

"You mean this guy?"

"You see him?"

"Look at your phone."

The image was kind of dark, but just then a rapid succession of fireworks went up and there in the fire flash was Uncle David coming up the center alley of the Midway, his back to them in the photo. Jude recognized his blond curls and the tan vest he was wearing. The one he wore in the garden shed last night.

"Where's he heading?" Jude asked Sandra.

"Up the Midway toward the Grandstand."

Jude cut her off and pressed four.

"Hello?"

"Listen Alison, it's Jude. My Uncle David's coming your way up the center of the Midway. He's tall and wearing a tan leather vest. He's got a gun in his inside vest pocket; we think he's going to shoot Greenway."

"You're joking right?"

"I'm deadly serious. He's coming toward the Grandstand."

"Which side is the pocket on?"

Jude had to think for a minute. Then he remembered. His uncle had reached across his chest with his right hand. "His left side. Just stop him and get the gun. We're on our way."

Alison was just about to ask how, when she saw the tall tan-vested figure of David Meades coming toward her, head down walking with purpose toward the rostrum. She looked around for something, anything to create a diversion. Beside her a woman had set down a soda on the ring toss counter. Alison reached for it.

"Hey, that's my soda," the woman said.

"No, it's mine," Alison said. "Yours is over there." She pointed down the counter. In the split second it took for the woman to turn her head, Alison stepped back right into the path of David Meades. His leg caught hers and down she went, the soda cup flying out of her hand. He lurched over her but didn't fall himself.

"Oh my god, I'm sorry. Are you alright?"

Alison stayed down on the ground. "I think so, but my ankle hurts."

"Do you think you can walk?"

"I don't know."

The woman with the soda said, "Serve's you right for trying to steal my drink. She tried to steal my drink."

David raised an eyebrow at the woman, and then recovered his manners. "Here, let's get you on your feet. We'll see if you can stand."

David reached down for her hands and lifted her. As Alison came to a stand, she suddenly lurched into him as if losing her balance. She leaned on him heavily with her left hand and reached ever so lightly with her deft right hand into the inside of his vest.

"Steady there," David said, putting his arm around her shoulder.

Alison felt the cold metal of the gun and the texture of the hand grip. She had her thumb and baby finger on it spread and ready to lift like a pickpocket. Suddenly another report blasted. David jumped. She lost her grip and her chance to get the gun.

"I guess you're okay," David said.

"We'll, I don't know..." Alison hobbled a little and turned in appeal. David Meades was past her. Operation Fagan had failed. Alison opened her phone and pressed one.

The fireworks were coming faster now, great metallic showers of gold, green and purple melting into smoke and embers, anticipating the grand finale. David Meades moved quietly in the shadows of the Grand Stand's scaffolding. He felt his way along in the dark, weaving between the iron bars. The metal smell and grimy feel of rust was on his hands. Up ahead the row of seated dignitaries lit up in the flash glow, Greenway's large bald head in the center seat flashing green and gold before it disappeared.

Jude was out of breath by the time he reached the platform. He jumped up and down to see above the crowd and through the instrumental clutter of Wild Man Ethan's Band. He saw the row of VIP's at the back of the rostrum, but couldn't tell where Greenway sat because they'd turned their seats along the curving stage to watch the show and all he caught were glimpses of heads in profile. His Uncle was nowhere to be scene. Jude looked into the shadows of the scaffolding and felt a shiver go down his back. He'd never make it through there if he tried. The only way in was to crawl behind the band and the VIP's on hands and knees. He was too big. He'd knock everything over and cause a scene. Just then, Junie, Alison and Merrilee arrived from different directions.

Greenway would never know his own fireworks display had been the perfect cover for his murder. David Meades waited in the shadows near the edge of the knee high platform, directly behind Greenway's chair. All he had to do was step and aim. The noise was constant now and the light was bright, kaleidoscopic and uneven. Greenway clapped and nodded at the blinding array of red Strobes, gold Waterfalls and purple Dahlias, over white effervescent candles. This was it. Total sound. The Grand Finale. David Meades stepped forward and took aim over a crossbar at Greenway's head.

Jesse crawled on hands and knees in the narrow rim of the platform behind the mikes and speakers and now along the row of chairs. He tried, as he crawled, to see his father in the shadows, but the changing light of the fireworks alternately blinded him or left behind a wake of dancing spots. There was barely room to lift his head.

This was the final barrage. A great firework went up and rose like a crown higher than all the rest. A giant American flag glittered to a huge roar, and it shimmered an instant longer than all the others before it. Just then Jesse saw the arm, jutting out of the shadows. He was two chairs away. The gun was pointed at Greenway's head. "Dad! No!" he called out, but a concussion maroon swallowed his voice.

A second more was all David needed. Above the hard maroons, a shell whistled up into the sky and another soon after. Greenway's held tilted up. David's finger stuttered on the trigger. Something huge and golden broke. Cheers turned suddenly to gasps. A great gold ring encircled the fading shimmer of the American flag and then a diagonal line rippled down across the circle in the universal symbol of prohibition. David aimed the gun again, but a hand reached out and rested on his. A familiar touch. He looked down and saw his son. David lowered the revolver and Jesse took it from him.

The final report sounded, and Merlin Greenway got to his feet, unaware that his life had nearly ended. A splinter flash of green bloomed outward in a dahlia then contracted and reformed for but a second. A death head appeared and vanished with the speed of a subliminal message. Many wondered if they'd actually seen it. Merlin Greenway had never been more certain of anything in all his life.

PART II

15.

The Cosmos by Night

O SMENA SEARLE'S ESTATE, The Cosmos, was named for its beguiling design: the appearance from above of a spiral galaxy. The gardens came alive at dusk with the unnatural glow of phosphorescent light. Only then did the cosmic design take full effect. To stare down at it on a dark, moonless night was to be ushered near something so vast it could never be approached and appear like this as a whole. It was to telescope the universe. Take God's view. Flowers of every shape and size levitated above their darkened foliage in electric shades that seemed to dissolve the substance of flower petals and transform each into a radiant star.

If the fireworks in town had been dazzling, the gardens at The Cosmos were no less than mesmerizing. For, on 4th of July night, a grand fete was held for Ms. Searle's wealthiest clients. The visual effect and the intoxicating, night fragrances acted like strong drink, so that if some displayed signs of odd behavior by the end of the evening—amorously staggering about the garden, adopting repetitive mannerisms, conversing entirely in sharp, insectile clicks, or scandalously licking a bit of sauce from someone else's finger—it was neither solely due to Osmena's champagne, nor was it a cause for shame to be thus observed, rather all part of a mind-altering, high everybody had come to imbibe. Everybody on the guest list, that is.

For Osmena's servants it was another story. Anybody who had ever worked on the estate was either a "recruit", delivered from foreign lands by

Ms. Searle's clients, a conscripted trespasser—hikers and hunters who had taken the wrong turn, motorists who had been stranded in bad weather—or a lifer born there (after one or both parents had shared one of the former fates). Stemple was among the first generation to be born there some forty years ago. His father had been one rather intoxicated and bellicose logger with an eye for one of Osmena's trees, and his mother had been recruited after emigrating from Poland. He had never lived and breathed beyond the confines of Osmena's land, nor did he imagine he ever would. Unlike the guests, who were free to come and go, Stemple was no longer dazzled by The Cosmos. For, every detail of the place that awed and amazed the privileged visitor was for him just one of an endless list of painstaking duties that must be done if, when and how Madam directed.

Stemple, for his part, was in a disenchanted mood, because instead of being allowed an already brief night's sleep after the tiring party, Osmena was demanding a full night's schedule of harvest, extraction and formulation for a new experimental to commence forthwith and posthaste. It involved Datisca, Digitalis, Dendranthema, Delphinium, Dianthus, Deschampsia, Dictamnus, Darmera and Datura among others.

So while Osmena's honored guests settled into their quarters for luxurious sleep, Stemple and his fellow servants could be seen in the gardens laboring under its peculiar light, tweezers and shears in hand, baskets at the ready for the collection of petiole and petal, stem and stamen, bud and bract. All along the garden's spiral pattern, they moved deliberately from plant to plant, some following the spiral out, some following it in, like comets in slow advance across a galaxy. They bent over some luminous blue, green or violet blooms, cutting here or plucking there, like thieves making off with the stars of heaven. The removal of bracts and petioles caused some lights to merely wane, while new buds opened and their lights waxed, setting the whole garden to perpetual twinkling. Before long the baskets filled and the workers handed them off in exchange for empty ones. From there the plant materials went down into the laboratory for extraction. Above the whisper tread of feet on dewy grass, Hilton, the head gardener, raised his sharp tenor to supervise the harvest.

It was just past midnight when Stemple heard the distant hum. He thought it was a passing plane at first, but soon recognized the clop of chopper blades, and then saw a blinking red light in the mountain pass. He knew his night had just become more complicated.

Stemple immediately sprang into action, striding across the south lawn and winding quickly by the shortest route through the gardens to the house. He went to the control room, flicked on the helipad lights and headed for the kitchen to alert the chef to prepare a snack for Mr. Greenway (this was mandatory even if it went untouched). Then he flagged down a servant to deliver the news of Mr. Greenway's arrival to Osmena, and dispatched a housekeeper to double check his suite. Stemple saw to the parlor and the preparation of tea himself.

Osmena entered from her apartment moments after Stemple arrived with the tea service and minutes before Mr. Greenway entered from the hall. "What would I do without you, Stemple?" Osmena stood beside the piano with one hand on the ebony lid, like an old chanteuse moved to reprise a sentimental tune.

"Madam is too kind and shall never be without my service."

"And I should never *want* to be. What is it with these new recruits? They take years now what it took you weeks to learn as a boy this high." Osmena leveled a hand just above her waist.

"Madam forgets my many years of preparation and I think she forgets my many youthful errors."

"Those I'm inclined to attribute solely to Orest, if memory serves me well." Osmena lifted her chin and stared at him. The large gold hoops in her ears rocked back and forth.

"If Madam will forgive me, I am always her servant, if not a servant of memory." Stemple bowed and turned to leave.

"Ah, Stemple! There is one more thing."

Stemple turned again. "Yes, Madam?"

"Take these to the East Carousel Suite." From a deep pocket in her caftan, she withdrew two narrow wooden casks each no larger than a box for a perfume bottle. "I can't believe I've been carrying them all night. The Generalissimo's English was so charming I completely forgot to pass them on to him."

Stemple came forward and stretched out his hand. Osmena held the one in her left hand up. "This one is called Fresuma (freedom to consume); 1 part per billion in the water supply, but make sure it is taken with this." Osmena held up the box in her right hand. "Deludol: for reinforcing unsupportable assertions. Two parts per billion. There's enough to last a major city for a year. Tell the Generalissimo there's more where that came from, but, also tell him, if they are not taken in conjunction his people will never accept a military coup as a democratic revolution, or the ability to shop endlessly as absolute proof of one. It's tasteless in water which makes it ideal for mass consumption." Osmena stopped and put her finger to her lips. Her eyebrows arched. "On second thought, tell him nothing. He'll either figure it out himself or..." She waved a hand through the air, like the flap of butterfly wings, setting in motion some unforeseen event in the Generalissimo's homeland. "One has to keep El Presidente happy too."

Mr. Greenway entered and Osmena looked up with a smile. "That will be all Stemple." She saw the look on Merlin's face and knew that something was wrong.

Stemple looked at the two small casks in his hands, as if there were a choice to be made. He stood outside the parlor with the door shut behind him, and listened to the murmurs of Osmena and Mr. Greenway. The more Osmena said things like, "What would I do without you, Stemple?" the more he got the feeling she didn't trust him in the least. Like tonight when she mentioned Orest to see if he had known about and aided his brother's escape five years ago, and would yet give something away. It was also a warning not to attempt anything so foolish himself.

Yet, it was strange she should mention Orest just moments before Mr. Greenway entered with that frozen look on his face—an expression he hadn't seen there since the night Orest vanished. Stemple started down the hall and climbed the stairs. In the dim light of the second floor landing, he met Esmie coming from Mr. Greenway's room. He nodded at her and continued up to the third floor. It had been no secret to him that Orest wanted to escape The Cosmos in the very worst way (who didn't?), but escapes were not that common or successful. There were no fences or barricades to keep the servants in, yet there were unseen forces in these mountains, fearful enough to keep all but the most determined from straying. There were said to be beasts of the wild endowed by Osmena with cunning and deadly intent. Orest had known the odds of escape, and had probably been wise to keep his own counsel. When he disappeared that night, it was all Stemple could do to hide his terror and bewilderment. The speculation amongst the servants was that Orest had never made it off the estate alive, or that his "escape" was just the official story to cover up a more sinister fate. Stemple never believed either of those theories, indeed he resisted them with all his might. Others had attempted to escape before and they were always returned alive—often bloody and beaten—but alive all the same. He took heart from this.

The only hint of trouble had arisen two days before Orest disappeared. He got into the chef's liquor that evening and became quite drunk. He'd acted like he knew something he wasn't telling. Stemple warned him to keep his voice down. If Osmena found out there'd be trouble for him. He'd said, "Her? I know her secret. And this house is going to fall if it ever gets out." The next night he overheard the end of an argument between Orest and Osmena.

"I've looked at it from the carousel, Orest. If you had spaced them as I directed I'd be seeing Gemini in the garden. There was no Gemini last night. It's all off kilter."

Where Stemple stood in the hall he saw them reflected in the parlor mirror—Osmena's back and Orest facing her. He knew by his brother's expression it was only going to get worse.

"I put them exactly where Madam directed, according to the dimensions of the bed you approved. There's something wrong with your calculation. Take a look at it again and—"

"There was no mistake. That is your department, Orest Stemple, but perhaps it will be the last I let you make. I want it done again and if it isn't right, you'll be digging ditches and cleaning toilets until you are an old man. And you had better well be careful. Those plants came all the way from a private collection in Milano—they cannot be replaced. But you can. Do I make myself clear?"

Orest gritted his teeth so hard the words almost didn't come out of his mouth. "Yes, Madam."

"I didn't hear you."

"Yes, Madam. It will be done this evening, Madam."

Orest had turned suddenly, walked out into the hall, and almost crashed into Stemple. Their eyes met for an instant. Orest knew he'd heard it all and walked past him without speaking.

That evening instead of transplanting the rare Mediterranean spurges, Orest's last act as head gardener was to cut them to ribbons and turn them over roots up in the flower bed. There was no turning back then, and there seemed no question at the time why Orest had fled.

Stemple reached the door of the suite and put up his hand to knock. He got an idea and continued down the hall. He opened the servant's door to the widow's walk that went all the way around the large cupola with its carousel of terrestrial beasts—an evolutionary ring moving from the dinosaurs to pre-historic mammals and finally to the familiarity of domestic beasts of burden. He walked along the balustrade and looked down. The garden bed Orest had marred in revenge, glowed with the familiar pattern of Gemini—the twins—perfectly placed. His brother's replacement, Hilton, had gotten it right, but only years later.

Stemple shook his head as a new thought occurred to him. Had Orest really made a mistake, or had he laid the plants out wrong on purpose? If his brother had another motive for leaving, possession of a secret that could bring Osmena down, then all the fuss over the spurges may well have been a ruse, a noisy fight and a big mess in the garden, so that when he got away they'd never suspect what he'd found and taken with him. What could it have been? And had he lived to share it?"

"They have the skull," Merlin said, pacing back and forth in the parlor.

"Who do you mean by they?" Osmena said. "We have the skull." She was on the settee pouring chamomile.

"We had it. Has anybody checked inside the tree lately?" Merlin stopped pacing and stared at Osmena.

"Merlin, what in heaven's name happened to put you in such a state?"

"During the fireworks. The finale. Out of nowhere the prohibition symbol appeared around the American flag. It caused the entire crowd to gasp and will probably have Homeland Security investigating me as an agitator or a terrorist. And then, right there in the sky for a second—a skull."

"Extraordinary."

"There's only one possible way they could have produced those fireworks from my display. The message to us was loud and clear: they have the skull and they know how to use it. And the message to the locals, who seem to sense I'm the target of the explosion, is that we are no longer in control."

Osmena sat up pin straight and set down her tea cup. Her face now registered the same frozen shock as Merlin's. "You keep saying they. But who is this VLF really? After the explosion it was clear somebody had it in for us. But that skull seemed a generic threat like something a teenager would think of to scare people."

"You thought that. I wasn't so convinced."

"No, and you may be right. Gerard LaFrance knew about the tree, but not the skull. Did he tell his children? It's a powerful secret after all. I'm guessing he would have tried to shield Zephyr from any knowledge that could endanger her. Dentremont is another story. Calvin has verified the existence of this group and Dentremont as their leader. He's met with them on the Lease Lands (a little too close for comfort I'm afraid) so there's little denying it. Yet, when Calvin said they had the power to act, who wouldn't have thought guns and explosives, since they seem fond of using them? But, you see, this has me thinking about Zephyr and how useful she may be."

Merlin sat down in the armchair across from Osmena, as if all the nervous energy had drained out of him, and he was suddenly tired. He rubbed the bald crown of his head in perplexity. "How so?"

"I have her taking one of my experimentals in payment for my services, but now I see a greater purpose; the way her present course may help us get the skull back."

Greenway was distracted, still puzzling over how they managed to access the tree. "You can't stumble on that tree without sinking to your death in that bog first; but to reach it through the canopy supposes prior knowledge of the skull and previous unsuccessful attempts. A map or key. Only somebody on the inside could get hold of a map. Only an insider would even know about the skull or how to wield its power. There's no other way."

"Somebody here? We haven't had an escape in many years, and we all know very well why Orest left. He defied me and was going to spend the rest of his days in drudgery. I don't trust Stemple completely, but he hasn't got the stomach for rebellion." Osmena saw the troubled look in Merlin's eyes, as he stared into his cold, untasted tea. "You don't mean?" she said. He met her stare and didn't blink. "Now Merlin, Calvin may have his peculiarities, but he's a Greenway through and through."

"Well, somebody is responsible for this, and that means nobody is above suspicion."

16.

A Pact

THERE WAS SOMETHING at the back of Jude's mind that had bothered him all morning. He awoke with the unsettled feeling left behind by a dream you can't remember. All that's left is the feeling that something important has escaped you, but you don't know what it is. There was nothing spookier than some dream dropping casual hints that you were heading into deep shit without your waders—so casual it didn't even bother to wake you up to remember it. He tried to chalk it up to the near disaster at the fireworks last night—how close Uncle David had come to killing a man—but, then, why hadn't he woken up relieved?

Jude was at loose ends because Merrilee was off to see her favorite, world-travelling, archeologist aunt on Grand Isle.

Aster had noticed him moping. "You can manage without her for a few days. I mean, you're not Siamese twins."

"That's conjoined twins, Mom. Only clueless racists say Siamese anymore."

"Young man, I am not racist."

"Just clueless."

"Excuse me! Listen, she's smack in the middle of a lake and they'd all be swimming and you are terrified of water, which you'll recall is why you failed swimming last year."

"I didn't want to go with her. You are clueless. And besides, I failed swimming because I never went in the pool."

"Because you panic in the deep end, you said."

"I lied. I wouldn't swim because I look like a white whale in swim trunks."

"Vanity is no excuse for missing gym, young man, and if I'd known it then, you would have been so grounded your feet would have stuck to the floor." Fortunately, even Aster didn't believe in retroactive grounding.

Jude took off on the Byclops in case she changed her mind. He peddled around the village, weaving serpentines around the congested blocks, catching glimpses into the small back yards—laundry unfurling in the breeze, wafting the smell of detergent sunshine to the street; scattered toys fading in the sun; a trampoline waiting, as if to catch something fallen from the sky; scarlet bee balm and orange lilies clashing in the sunlight, or mountain blues glowing under a slant of late morning shade; a woman pushing a lawnmower around the circle of an inflatable blue kiddy pool, the kind of engine hum that filled a summer day in the village the way cricket chirping filled a late summer night.

Before Jude knew it, he had circled back to Winter Street and peddled slowly past the charred remains of the Mobil station. The cordon of yellow tape drooped and fluttered imperfectly along the perimeter of orange barrels, a flimsiness that assumed respect for the law. **THE END HAS COME** and the black skull were still visible on the neutral tan shingling of the Police Station roof next door. There were still fanning soot patterns on the pale yellow shakes, but a glass company van was parked out front and the blown out window was being replaced under Sergeant Roderick's watchful eye.

Winter Street was a dead end that ran along the railroad tracks and quit in a weedy wasteland—bluestem grass, spurge, wood rush, curly dock, lady's thumb and Queen Anne's lace and a lot of stuff that would end up being goldenrod in the fall. Jude rode up the last mowed bit of bank and then along the railroad bed a quarter mile to where Hooper Mill Road met Green Street. Green Street Extension jutted to the right. This was the north edge of the village. Jude put his feet down on the pavement. Ms. LaFrance lived at the end of the extension. Jude had known this since the time she'd been his teacher in the 4th grade, but he'd only dared go far enough to see it, because you couldn't casually ride by it as if you were just passing it on your way home. That was the thing about dead ends in Vermont. There were so many of them: back roads that ended at a house, or ended up being somebody's driveway. To turn around at one, to go to one even, was to draw attention to yourself. You either looked nosey, lost or suspicious: checking out the houses; taking a non-existent shortcut over the mountain, or planning a break-in. Jude never wanted to be seen there like some desperate, dead end student stalker who was still stuck in the 4th grade. Get over it already. But, for better or worse, Ms. LaFrance would always remind him of the year after Kennedy's death and how she had been there (in a way she never knew, still didn't know) like a strong hand extended to someone stuck in a grave-sized pit. Maybe he held on to that feeling because he'd never been able to put it into words, or because he still needed that hand, and Jet and Aster were too clueless to offer it. Why should he have to explain something so basic to his parents?

But last night something had happened; Jude recalled it now. It shook him out of his old comforting daydream that the strong, yet gentle, hand of Ms. LaFrance was still outstretched like a promise. He had spoken to her at the fairgrounds and she had walked right past him as if she didn't know him. There was something else. The look on her face was one he had never seen there before: a hard determined stare and a thin-lipped frown. The very thing that compelled him now to ride up to her house and knock on her door—the need for assurance that he had imagined the mask he'd seen—also gave him butterflies and sweaty palms. What if she came to the door with that same look upon her face?

Jude rode up the extension, slowing for a moment, when Ms. LaFrance's house came into view, before peddling on to the house. It was buff yellow with sky blue shutters, no more than a cottage. A terracotta brick walk led to the front door. Mounds of lavender, salvia, bellflowers and coreopsis spilled onto the bricks from either side in shades of purple, blue and yellow. Bright Irish moss flowed like liquid emeralds in the cracks between the bricks. The front door, painted the same light blue as the shutters, was shaded by an arbor, swamped with deep green wisteria. On either side of the door, the rolling pattern of flowers and color continued the length of the house. A dark hedge row bordered the far edge of the lawn and nearly hid the driveway from Jude's vantage. Ms. LaFrance's car was there, visible through an arch cut into the hedge. A bluestone walk led through the arch, down along the side of the house to the back yard. Jude rode around the hedge and parked the Byclops beside Ms. LaFrance's car.

Faintly, Jude heard a hiss, a familiar spit and gurgle from the back yard. He might not have to knock at the door at all. He passed through the hedge and down the side of the house.

The backyard was all beds of flowers, islands and curved borders that extended from the edge of a brick patio by way of three wide curving paths out to the edge of a wood. They began as brick, then trailed off to narrower dirt foot paths edged by more emerald moss. The moss seemed to be advancing from the wood toward the brick, as if the green tendrils of the forest might soon engulf not only the bricks, but the patio and the house as well. Only the beds of bright, thrilling flowers and dense clipped shrubs floated safely upon canals of rising green. It reminded him of a courtyard from long ago, like an artist's recreation of the gardens of Babylon you'd see in National Geographic.

A green hose led out from the house along the central path, and Ms. LaFrance stood at the other end of its length watering plants in the only area that looked new and incomplete: a shrubbery that fronted the edge of the wood.

Jude lifted the hose and gave it a tug and a snake like ripple. Ms. LaFrance straightened and turned around at the sudden tension. Jude waved. She stood for a moment, looked up from under the curving brim of her canvas hat, as if she couldn't figure out who he was, as if anybody who knew him could mistake him even at this distance. Then she waved back. "Jude." She dropped the hose and walked over to him, wiping her hands on her tan overalls.

Jude felt relieved at the sound of his name, but didn't know what he was going to say.

"Jude, what brings you here?" Ms. LaFrance took off her hat and set it on a wrought iron patio table with an umbrella—the only bit of shade on the patio.

"I don't know. I was riding in town. Nothing to do." Jude shoved his hands in his pockets and looked around at the gardens. "This place is wicked cool. You wouldn't even know all this is here."

"I like it that way."

Jude couldn't even imagine what it would be like to live in such a place. "There's no junk," he said.

"Oh well, there used to be, when I first moved here. Are you thirsty, Jude? I'm parched. Lemonade? Ginger ale? Water?"

"Ginger ale's fine. Please."

"Okay. I'll be right out."

Ms. LaFrance came back with a tray and two tall glasses fogged up with condensation. One lemonade and one ginger ale.

"Sit down, Jude. What's on your mind? Are you okay?"

"Yeah. Sure. I'm okay."

"You don't look okay."

"No? You know, Ms. LaFrance, what it looks like when you first see the garden back here? It looks like the wild is coming out of the woods and over-taking the bricks in the paths."

Ms. LaFrance took a sip of lemonade and touched the glass to her fore-head for a moment. She looked curiously at Jude. "It's meant to look that way, but, you know, you're the only person who's ever gotten that. Everybody else asks me when I'm going to scrape up the moss and finish bricking the paths." She tilted her head and laughed.

Jude shrugged. "It was pretty obvious to me." He blushed suddenly and looked down. "I don't mean obvious in a bad way, Ms. LaFrance, but I mean that's what it looked like to me straight off. It's just I could see what you meant. It's pretty cool."

"Zephyr. Call me Zephyr, we're not in school anymore Jude, are we?"

Jude shook his head, but he wasn't sure he could bring the word Zephyr out of his mouth.

Ms. LaFrance looked concerned again. "So, Jude, are you going to tell me why you came to see me today?"

⌘ ⌘ ⌘

ASTER SAT AT the table leafing through a magazine and having a smoke. She carefully ripped out a recipe for a summer picnic lunch—both hands on the magazine, lips around her cigarette and eyes blinking at the cigarette smoke—but when she tried to envision all of them sitting on a blanket, or at a table in some state park, she just wadded up the paper in a ball and flung it into the sink. It would never happen. Why couldn't something simple and elegant and nice ever happen to her? Jude would argue about being seen in public anywhere with them, about what they were eating, where they were going, and Jet? Well, Jet would take so long to find something presentable to wear out of the house—anything that wasn't greasy, ripped or stained with food (and that was from his clean clothes)—that by the time he got himself together and presentable, or managed to tear himself away from whatever machine he was building out behind the Incubus, the skies would have clouded up and the best part of the day would be gone.

Jet was in about the worst possible state a man could fall into: he was a derelict dreamer. Always working from what was already ruined and almost always letting flights of fancy wipe out any practical good that might come of one of his inventions. It had gone on for so long and she'd thought about his ways for so many years, she'd finally put her finger on his problem. He was fatally committed to two things in his life: complexity and failure, with the former usually bringing about the latter. Aster's mother would have added a third and fourth: laziness and Captain Morgan.

"Jet, why do you have to make everything so darned complicated," Aster had said one day after a torrential rain of curses and slamming metal summoned her outside. Jet was putting together the impossible wheels within wheels of gears and chains on the Byclops.

"That song. That song from church, you know?" Jet looked up at her crazed as a demon and sweating, hands and face smeared black with grease. "Ezekiel saw the wheels; way up in the middle of the air..."

Aster just about died laughing, lost her breath and had to hold onto the side of the Incubus to keep from falling over. "You're trying to reinterpret Ezekiel's wheels as bicycle gears? Now, I know, Jet Corgan, you have finally lost it."

"Ha, ha. You say that every time."

"Well, Jet. If you want to do Ezekiel's Wheels, make a sculpture. God knows you've got enough metal around here to make a thousand sculptures."

"I ain't no artist. Jeezum crow. Anybody can make a series of wheels and weld 'em together or hang 'em on a mobile, but they'd just be dead wheels. The magic of it is that these wheels are on a working thing. They look strange and all, impossible even, but they work and they take you someplace. It's going to be something to marvel at."

Aster looked up and listened. She'd sent Jet out this morning to weed-whack around the junk piles and the wrecks, and for a long time the sound of the weed-whacker droned and whined in the background of her morning. Now everything was quiet. She got up and went outside. The string trimmer was on the ground outside the door, but Jet was nowhere to be found.

⌘   ⌘   ⌘

THE HEAT OF the Incubus got inside Jet's head. The smell of machine oil and summer was like the sap of memory. One moment he was looking at the plans Miss Searle had given him and the next he was back when Kennedy was alive. The day he'd unveiled the Byclops to him. The memory came back to him every so often, and when it did he imagined it in some way other than how it actually went. At least he'd start out with his fantasy, but reality would always come butting in. In the fantasy, he'd have it covered with a tarp and then unveil the shining, otherworldly machine with the skillful snap of a magician. What had happened was his impatience for Kennedy to see it. Jet stood behind Kennedy and covered his eyes. He then walked him out back. The Byclops wasn't covered, and Jet hadn't even waited to have it painted. A little voice told him that was a mistake.

"What is it, Dad? What's the big surprise?" Kennedy kept his hands out in front of him, for fear he'd crash into something.

"Oh, you'll see," Jet whispered in his left ear.

"Dad, you're hands smell like grease, let me cover my own eyes."

"Wait, we're almost there. Okay. Ready?"

Jet pulled his hands away and spread his arms with a flourish.

"What's that?"

It wasn't the tone Jet expected. He came around to see the expression on Kennedy's face.

Jet held his smile, like a used car salesman, but it was straining under the weight of Kennedy's disappointment.

"It's a bicycle of course. The most amazing two-wheeled machine ever built. The only one of its kind in the world."

"Thank God for that," Kennedy said.

"You don't like it? I made it for you, son."

"I appreciate it and all, Dad, but it's, like, not really me. It's like a jumble of rust and stuff."

"Look, that's just the primer. I know I should have painted it first. Just wait. I talked with Chet and he's going to do some detailing on the frame. We were thinking black, red flames and maybe some white striping."

"It's different, but definitely not me."

"What do you mean, not you?" Jet should have known better than to ask. It was painfully obvious what he meant. You don't know me, what I like, who I am. And who you are and what you make is definitely not for me. But now he'd have to hear it.

"I mean. I'm not going to ride it. You think I'm going to be seen on that thing? It's just plain weird. Look at it. Maybe when I was twelve, but I'm almost sixteen. You think I want to ride into the village like a clown bringing along a whole circus everywhere I go. I'll be driving soon and getting a job this summer. No offense, Dad, but I'd rather have a car."

Jet never bothered to have it painted. He abandoned it, and didn't mention it again, because it hurt too much to believe in a thing rejected by the one it had been built for. It was the failure that stayed with him all these years—knowing the last thing he'd done for Kennedy had turned out wrong—and he kept replaying it, fantasizing a different ending, because he couldn't understand how the product of so much thought, effort and love could make them both so unhappy.

⌘　⌘　⌘

A STER CALLED OUT to Jet once and got no answer. She picked her way between two merging junk heaps and stepped over landmines of rusty metal and chicken wire out to the Incubus. She knocked on the door. "Jet?"

"Yea-uh?"

Aster opened the door and climbed in. It smelled of machine oil and metal filings, and was musty with summer heat.

Jet sat at a work bench over rolled out sheets of thin blueprint paper. He took a bandana from his back pocket, dabbed his eyes and mopped his forehead. "Hot box in here."

"What's that?"

"Oh, you know." Jet got a little red in the face.

"What?"

"Just those papers Miss Searle gave me when we went out there last. I'd almost forgotten about them."

"Well, you'd better forget about them. I'm not going to have you wasting even more of your time on some crazy invention for her. What has she done for us?" Aster came up behind him all the same to take a look. The first sheet diagrammed the construction of some kind of frame or seat. Jet lifted the sheet and carefully smoothed out the curl of the second page, which looked like an electrical box or panel that included computer chips. It continued on the third page. The fourth page diagramed some type of headgear, a bowl shaped cap with electrical leads, and micro thin needles protruding from the inside of the cap.

"Jeezum crow."

"It looks like a cross between a crown of thorns and an electric chair. Oh, I can see it now. You build it and get to be the first to try it out and zap. No more Jet. You'd have to be a total fool to even think about building this."

Jet revealed the last sheet. It was all detailed specifications for the materials.

"Silicon microchips. Micro thin titanium rods. Solid gold wire. I hope she's supplying the materials."

"Does it say what it's for?"

"No. There's no name or description of what it's supposed to be. Do you remember what she said when she gave it to me? Damned if I know what she were talking about. Well wait. There was something written on the outside of the roll." Jet turned the last sheet over and spread it out with his hands. There was just one short phrase in elegant black cursive: **To sleep, perchance to dream…**

"That sounds familiar."

"Sounds creepy to me."

"I suppose Jude would know where it's from." Jet gathered the sheets, rolled them up again and tied them with a piece of string. "Well, I'm more of a mechanical guy than an electronics guy, but…"

"But nothing, Jet Corgan."

⌘ ⌘ ⌘

Z EPHYR HOPED THE blank look on her face was not too revealing. She shook her head. "Jude, I'm sorry but I don't remember seeing you at the fairgrounds last night."

"You don't? It's not like you could miss me. I bumped into you."

"Really?" Zephyr felt her color rising. She hoped Jude thought it was embarrassment, but in truth it was alarm.

"You must have had something on your mind."

"I guess so. Come on, let's take a walk around the gardens."

Jude and Zephyr started on the right hand path, following the gentle undulations of the hedge row border—a sheltering mass of cottage garden annuals for the feet of tender vines and climbing roses, which reached and clung to the dark arborvitae like the tentacles of bright octopi to the sides of a great aquarium—then wound their way back down the broad central path. It divided and merged three times around asymmetrical perennial beds. These were all rolling mounds of hot orange, desert blue, with sprays of white and dots of plummy red, and a few bright green boxwoods clipped into sharp steeples, like churches in a rural landscape. They paused here and there, when Jude asked about a plant, or Zephyr pointed out an unusual flower or leaf. The far path went around the back side of a long bed they'd passed in their wending and weaving down the center. It featured three high-pruned honey locusts spreading dappled shade like umbrellaed gondoliers standing over shaggy blond heads of golden forest grass and nodding chocolate lilies. It ended, like the other beds, at the foot of the unfinished shrubbery.

"Right here where this path and the others meet there'll be a shrubbery running crosswise like a wall, and instead of paths, or arches, cutting through the shrubbery to the woods, there'll be three parallel shrubberies coming down from it, clipped in descending waves. They will intersect and cross through the wall, so that from the house it will look like waves of green are bursting through the wall of shrubbery and pouring out of the forest at the head of each path."

"Awesome. So it'll be like floating gardens."

"Yes, Jude! I think then people will start to see it. But you saw it anyway, and that it's both the forest moving in, and a kind of flood, like water."

"How did you come up with that?"

"During the June flood some years ago, I had a dream about looking out the back window and seeing waves of water, not blue water, but emerald green water coming out of the woods in great streams, though they weren't roiled and turbid, but clear and deep as if the water were traveling along an invisible channel. There was so much water, but it never seemed to reach the house and for some reason I was not afraid, just mesmerized by the beauty of it. That's when I came up with the idea and the design. So I guess you could call it a dreamscape."

In the silence that followed, Zephyr suddenly felt the urge to tell Jude everything. She could never tell another adult because, when it had to do with children, even the most trusted friend might decide to turn her in for what she'd done with the blue powder, no matter what her motive, while an adolescent—well, nobody understood better the need for secrets—would also understand about breaking rules and laws and being irresponsible. Yet, she felt a qualm, knowing how much Jude admired her, that she was putting him in an awkward situation, even taking advantage of his desire to be her friend. Then, in the next instant, it seemed this was not what she was feeling or meaning to do at all. It was a concern imposed on her by the standards of her profession. What she really felt was that Jude deserved to be treated like an adult, yet was all the better a confidant for having the heart of a child. He alone had intuited her garden design in a spontaneous insightful moment. In fact, it was she who was going out on a limb to trust Jude. It was she who needed his insight again, the honesty she felt in him.

Zephyr felt the sun burning her arms and shoulders, while the morning breeze had stilled and the birds had gone quiet. The entire garden was so soundless when she shifted her weight she could hear the slight grate of a pebble against the sole of her shoe.

"Jude, are you sure it was me you saw in the midway last night? Absolutely sure, no doubt in your mind whatsoever?"

"Yes, Ms—I mean yes, Zephyr. I couldn't mistake you for anybody else."

Zephyr took a deep breath and said, "I don't remember even going to the fairgrounds last night; I don't remember you or the fireworks. It's like my memory of last evening is a complete blank. I don't know where I was, or when I came home. I just woke up this morning feeling like I'd been somewhere, as though all I'd really forgotten was a very long dream."

"But how could you forget being there?"

"Well, there's something I have to tell you."

Zephyr told Jude everything, as they sat in the shade of the umbrella. About Cody, Osmena and the blue powder, about Sergeant Roderick and the experimental she was taking.

"You have to stop taking it," Jude blurted out when she was finished. "You don't know what it could be doing to you. My friend, Merrilee, told me about a man who took one of those things and was so out of it he stepped right in front of truck and—"

"I know, Jude. I know." Zephyr smiled at him. Her green eyes were warmed by flecks of gold, and the fine lines around her eyes crinkled. "But what choice do I have? If I don't take it, I'll never be able to teach again and I might have to go to jail for a long time."

"Jail? How can they put you in jail?" Jude wanted to be strong—the way he'd wanted to act like an adult, barely nine years old, that night at the falls when Kennedy confided in him—and ended up fighting the sting of tears instead. Yet, there was also a kind of fire in his chest, and that was what came out of him. "You can't let her control you like that. I mean, how can she tell if you stop taking it? You can pretend. Can she really see through walls?"

"I don't know, Jude. She could be bluffing. Intimidating me. She's been known to do that too, but if I stop, I take a big chance that she'll find out and then Roderick will come after me. You see, my father had a long, bitter history with Osmena. Many years ago she took hundreds of acres of his land that abutted her property. There was something on it she wanted badly and she wouldn't stop until she had it. I don't know, but I think she's the reason my mother got sick and died."

"But, if that's true, why would you go to her?"

"I never knew if it was true; my father never said it. It was just something I felt as a child. I went to Osmena because I knew she had the power to help me, and because I was too proud to accept that I couldn't do anything with Cody LaRoy. I thought I had the right to my pride. What I did is not anything that a doctor couldn't have done with a prescription; it's just that his mother refused to let anyone drug her child and she told the school to just deal with him. I met with her. She deals with him by not dealing with him. Jude, I made a big mistake, maybe the biggest of my life. One way or the other, things may never be the same for me again."

Jude shook his head. "Don't say that. You can stop it; maybe there's a way. Besides what if she's destroying your mind? I mean, you can't even remember where you were or what you did last night. What if that happens when you're trying to teach? They'll think you're crazy and put you away. It freaked me out; imagine a bunch of fourth graders? You'll end up locked away in a nut house instead of jail."

"So you think it's a trap?"

"Do you trust her?"

Zephyr shook her head.

"Well then you have to stop."

Zephyr sat for a while looking straight ahead. "Okay. That's it."

"You'll stop? Today?"

"Yes."

"Promise?"

"Yes." Zephyr extended her hand on the table; Jude covered it with his to seal their pact.

17.

The Day the Caterpillars Died

C ALVIN HAD WAY too much to drink at his aunt's party last night. Too
much was an understatement, if you considered he was forbidden by his
father to drink at all. But the people there—diplomats, politicians, entrepre-
neurs, scientists, scholars, doctors, with only a few A list actors who really
could be considered party people—all seemed caught up in the night's high
spirits, so that to resist it seemed unsociable and rude. Aunt Mena had stood
behind him at the mirror straightening his bow tie, and said, "You could
have seduced the serpent in Eden." He was dressed in white linen shirt and
pants, with a platinum silk vest and bow tie. His hair was freshly buzzed to
a dark, tight crop. "Remember, a good host never says, 'No'. Now be a good
host and have a good time."

It was Calvin who had been seduced that night, by several flutes of spar-
kling, golden champagne and a famous Hollywood actress who tempted
him, dared him, to take his first sip.

"You know I'm only 17," Calvin told her with that faint ever present smile
on his lips.

Her eyes sparkled bright, like the champagne. "No you're not. Really?
But who's going to know if you have a glass or two."

"Two?" Calvin looked around. His father was rubbing shoulders with
the locals in Twin Gaps for the annual 4th fireworks to win approval for his
development plans, but there was no such thing as being unobserved at The

Cosmos. His aunt had people everywhere with an eye on somebody ready to report all goings on. Who needed cameras when you had dozens of spies at your disposal? He took a sip and looked around again.

"If you really want to feel the rush, you can't take baby sips. Come on. Tip it back and put it down."

"Is it proper etiquette to guzzle champagne?" Calvin put two fingers to his lips, as if to seal them, and looked dubiously at the flute. Then he remembered his aunt's parting advice and raised the flute with a sigh and obeyed, all the warm bubbles churning in his throat and prickling hot in his chest on the way down. He drained the narrow flute. His eye watered and opened wide. In that instant he felt strangely free, and thrillingly alive, the way he did when he plunged into the pool at Granger Falls.

"Now, take another and let's go for a walk around the gardens."

Since there were tables of champagne flutes waiting in the gardens on up lit glass tables, like beacons of liquid light, he had a third champagne in the course of their walking, after which he was quite giddy and a bit unsteady. By the fourth flute, they found a bench behind an arborvitae hedge and sat down.

"I don't think I should have had that last one," Calvin giggled and leaned against her bare, toned, Hollywood arm and looked into her famous face in disbelief.

"Well," she said quietly, as if divulging a confidence, "you never really know you've had enough until you've had one too many."

Calvin smiled admiringly at her wisdom, and another fountain of giggles floated out of him.

"God you are so—"

The actress didn't finish her thought, but leaned over instead and kissed the smile on his lips. There were more kisses and Calvin remembered showing her his tattoo, which required removing most of his clothing. He remembered the rest of his clothing coming off, but didn't remember them ever going back on. He awoke with a giant headache, alone and naked in his bed, but he didn't know when or how he had gotten there.

There was a knock on the bedroom door. "Mister Calvin?"

"Come in Stemple." Calvin brought himself slowly to a sit in the dim curtained room. The walls of the room spun around him. He closed his eyes and braced with his hands against the mattress.

Stemple carried a tray bearing a glass of cloudy liquid to the bedside. "Your father wishes to see you; I suggest you drink this."

"My father's here?"

"He came in last night. Rather urgently. Drink all of it. You'll feel better. You don't want him seeing you in—a state."

Calvin took the glass and drank.

"Shower, dress and be in the parlor in 15 minutes."

⌘ ⌘ ⌘

"THERE YOU ARE." Merlin Greenway sat forward, an impatient edge to his posture.

Calvin sat down across from his father in a matching high-backed chair, a bit forward to mirror his father's attitude. That stuff Stemple gave him really worked. His headache had receded to a vague web of tension at the back of his skull. He had looked like himself in the mirror—his color was good, his eyes clear if a little subdued in their expression.

"What's going on? Stemple told me you got in late last night."

"They have the skull."

Calvin sat back in his chair as though thrust by gravity. "The VLF? What—how do you know?"

"They used the skull to change the fireworks last night and send us a little message. And there's only one way they could have done that."

"Has anybody checked the tree?"

"We've sent a reconnaissance today."

"But how did they even know about it?"

"Orest. He's still alive."

"But that was five years ago. Why would they wait so long to take the skull if they've known all this time?"

"Making a plan; putting things in place; what a wise person would do with so much power at hand. Trying to figure out how to use it. Or, they just found out about it from an infiltrator."

"Do you think it might be Stemple?"

"It would have to be somebody who comes and goes."

Greenway stared at his son. Calvin reddened under his gaze.

"There's something I need you to do."

Calvin looked up without speaking.

"If they have the skull, then all we have is the tree; and so we must find the spring before anything else happens."

"What spring?"

"We'll move immediately on Gemini Farm, but if we don't succeed in taking it, you'll have to find the spring."

"What do you need with their spring water?"

Greenway raised both eyebrows significantly. "It's *the* spring; not their spring."

Calvin's mouth opened.

"As long as we had the skull we could bide our time and keep the spring a secret. But the truth is the tree is damaged and—"

"You're going to take their farm for a spring you aren't sure is even there? Dad, I don't have anything against these people."

Greenway stared fiercely at his son.

"Okay, but how am I supposed to find it? There are probably dozens of springs on their land."

"Well, there's one good thing about not knowing where it is. The VLF doesn't know it either. We have a hand drawn map of their land. It's old and faint. There should be remains of an old foundation in their woodlot. And the spring is near it. It is marked with a stone, the Zenger seal; it looks like this."

Merlin took a yellowed paper out of his pocket and unfolded it. Calvin came over to have a look. It was not the map, but an enlarged image of a circular seal: a decorative hoop snake around the edge and a broad tree with a river flowing under it.

"The seal will be buried by now."

"I can't just go digging all over their wood lot. Doesn't the map tell where it is?"

"It doesn't, on purpose; there's only a legend." Merlin pointed to the script below the image. *Four stones square in a wood were placed; and from whose heart were equal spaced; a well spring lost should 'ere be found; whereon you tread is holy ground; blessed and long is the life of he; who builds upon eternity.*

"You are friends with the boy now. He might lead you to it without even knowing what it is or what he's done."

"And then what?"

"For now, you bring the water to us."

"Greenway has set his sights on a farm in Twin Gaps," said Chet Atwood. He'd come early that morning over Catamount Gap to the Granger Wood Trail—one of the oldest logging roads in the Green Mountains, and one everybody knew to be impassable by vehicle. It spanned the western back of Catamount Peak (Osmena's land) north to south. Or so it had, but few knew that it also branched to the west and traversed a shallow pass to the less grand but more isolated Hidden Mountain. About a mile in, if you made it that far on wheels, you'd be stopped by a thirty foot high deadfall that blocked further passage. From either Old Route 9 or the newer Route 17 you couldn't see Hidden Mountain on the approach, at least not until you were over the mountain and down in the valley on the other side in Middlefield, and even then from straight on it had a way of looking like the back side of Catamount Peak. Hidden Mountain was an ideal place to hide.

"Whose farm?" said Luc Dentremont. He, Jake, Chet Atwood and Jasper Landreaux sat in the back room of the concrete bunker. The ceiling was low and the walls were bare. A generator's hum was always in the background, keeping the two wall fixtures somewhat unsteadily aglow.

"David and Raeanne Meades. Gemini Farm it's called."

"I know them and they have no connection to Greenway and probably wouldn't play ball with him. So, if he is intent on taking their land, then there's something on it he really wants."

"It might be a good time to see if we can do more than send threatening messages," said Jake Allard.

"Do we even know how to stop him if we had a mind to?" Jasper Landreaux said, his sad blue eyes opening wide for a moment.

"Well, that was pretty fancy work with them fireworks last night," said Chet.

"Because we knew he was putting on the fireworks and we could focus on them."

Luc and his men had been working around the clock for the past two weeks trying to figure out just how the skull worked and how to wield its magic. They'd had many failures and a few successes. But it seemed that where they'd succeeded had been in conjuring tricks like the fireworks last night.

Luc had wondered from the outset what it meant to possess it. How had Osmena wielded its power when it was kept miles away in the hollow of a tree? Even now did she possess its magic while it was technically in their hands? Did she still have a connection to its magic that they could never hope to achieve? Or had the tree been the means by which she controlled it? Surely, Osmena knew the incantation and could recite it from memory any time, yet she had either been unaware or unable to interrupt their 4th of July designs.

At first, nobody had a clue how to use it, until EG picked up the parchment with the map and reminded them of some writing along the edge that appeared to be an incantation: *Say to the skull, 'if I am he; heir to the everlasting tree; I bend the practice of my will; to wield the curse for good or ill.*

Luc himself had recited the lines, taken on the curse, and from that time on things had begun to happen, but only when he spoke in rhyming lines. It would not work for anybody who had not recited the legend first, and you had to recite it anew before each incantation.

Control was the main problem. There were just some things it wouldn't do. They wanted to see if they could recite an incantation that would prevent another person from ever using the skull again, with Osmena in mind. So, Luc had worked on a spell to keep Jasper from using it, yet once in Jasper's hands again, the skull responded to him as it had before. A greater problem was that things didn't always come out as they'd intended. Any vagueness in the language, as to their meaning, came out in unpredictable and unforeseeable results. If you did not shade your meaning the right way, it invariably came out wrong.

A spell used to change the color of a hen's feathers blue, made it melancholy and unable to lay eggs. And once a thing went wrong, it was darned near impossible to put things back the way they were. They tried to cheer up the hen with another incantation and made her so nervous and excited she ran about until she dropped dead of exhaustion. They knew then the skull was nothing to be trifled with, and they understood why sometimes even Osmena's incantations failed. The thing literally had a mind of its own—it was a fickle but fearless interpreter of the human will.

"You've got to find out how he means to do it first, or we'll never find the right words. I want details."

"And you'd better find out pretty darn fast," Jasper said.

"That means I'm going to have to see it happening and you know what."

"Of course, we'll have to call you on a cell phone; there's no other way. Borrow a friend's, somebody you trust and who is also above suspicion, and we'll have someone out on RT 17 close enough to reach us in a hurry, but far enough away so they can't trace us here."

"And even then you're going to have to come up with something fancy fast to stop him," said Chet.

Breakfast was over and as planned, Jesse stayed in the kitchen with his mother after his dad, Junie and Oscar went out to do morning chores. Junie and he had talked it over last night and decided it was best if Jesse broke the news. What happened after that was music his father would have to face.

"Mom?"

Raeanne jumped at the sink and turned around, surprised to see Jesse lingering at the breakfast table, so quiet she'd not even noticed he'd stayed behind when the others went out.

"What is it, Jesse?" Raeanne dried her hands on her apron and came over to the table.

"Something happened last night. I mean almost happened. You'd better sit down."

Raeanne pulled out a chair and sat, not taking her eyes off Jesse for a moment.

Jesse brought his hand up from under the table and laid a small nickel plated revolver gently down on the gingham table cloth. "Last night when Dad disappeared at the fairgrounds, he'd gone to get this."

Raeanne appeared confused. "We found that in a tool box in the Zenger's old barn when we first moved here. I haven't seen that in about fifteen years. What was your father doing with it?"

"He—he was about to shoot Merlin Greenway with it last night, but we figured it out, thanks to Jude, and we stopped him."

Raeanne brought both hands down to her stomach, as if she were going to be sick. She leaned forward and then sat back, bringing both hands to her temples. She sat like that with her eyes closed for several seconds, unable to speak.

"But it's going to be okay, Mom. Nothing happened and nobody saw him."

Raeanne let her hands drop down flat onto the table, as if she needed to hold herself steady. "Oh, Jesse. It's not okay. Jude figured it out? And you didn't tell me? What is wrong with your father? What is wrong with all of you?"

"We wanted to tell you last night. You sensed something. I know you did when we couldn't find Dad. It's just with Jet and Aster there, and Willa besides, we really couldn't. And we didn't have any time to lose. I just barely stopped him, Mom."

Raeanne closed her eyes again and nodded. "I know you did what you thought was best, but you should have told me, no matter what. I mean, what if you hadn't stopped him? Jesse, I don't know what got into your father's head. If he was feeling this way, he should have told me."

"He didn't tell any of us. He thought it was the only way to stop Greenway."

"But even if it was; what would have happened to us if he'd been caught? To him if he'd succeeded? Listen to me, Jesse. We're still here. We haven't lost the battle yet, and it's way too soon to give up our faith in who we are and what we stand for to resort to murder."

"I know that Mom. We're the ones who stopped him."

"How did Jude know?"

"He was awake the other night and saw Dad go out to the shed. I guess he followed him out and watched him through a knot hole. Dad loaded the gun and put it in his vest pocket. It's just the way Dad's been the past week, and when he said he was going back for his vest, when none of us had seen him take it with him. We got worried and tracked him down."

"Well, God bless your cousin's overdeveloped sense of curiosity. But right now I need to think, and then I'm going to have a talk with your father."

Junie went out to the chicken coop to gather the eggs. His entrance stirred some gentle clucking and raised some heads. It was dim still so he tugged on the pull chain. He stopped at the sight of two chickens on the floor over by the water pan. The way they lay there, claws stiff, he was certain they were dead. He thought he should find out for sure, and then he remembered the cows. He dared not touch them. The sick and sinking feeling flooded his gut. Maybe his father had seen this coming; maybe he'd known there would be no end to it until Greenway took everything. He tugged the light chain again and left the coop without gathering a single egg.

On the way back to the house, Junie heard the sound of engines faintly, then drawing closer. He went along the farmer's porch and peeked around the corner to see a green SUV with a state seal pulling a livestock trailer and two state police cruisers turning off the main road and coming up their winding driveway. Junie ran as fast as he could back to the coop.

Chet Atwood had set up a blind in a small stand of trees just beyond the Meades' apple orchard, and watched through binoculars in camouflage fatigues. It was the State. Department of Agriculture with some police escort. Chet knew about the mad cow incident and Greenway's strong arm tactics, now he was seeing it first-hand. Luc was right. Greenway was moving fast to shut them down. But this was not what he'd been sent here to stop. This would bring them to their knees, and then Greenway would swoop in and pounce.

David, Raeanne and one of the twins arrived from the barn; the other twin (Chet could hardly tell them apart face to face let alone from here) had run like a wild horse back to one of the outbuildings. Then the state inspector and the troopers got out of their vehicles. The inspector shook David's hand and started to gesture.

"Jim Taggart, Department of Agriculture."

"What can we do for you?"

"We're conducting a random inspection of your farm. Normally you'd be notified before a state certification, but you are on our list for a random inspection because of the recent incident at your farm."

"At this hour?" David ran his hands through his hair. "We're kind of in the middle of morning chores."

"I understand and I'm sorry for the hour. The schedule is rather full and I'm due out of state by mid-afternoon."

Jim Taggart raised his clipboard and said, "Well, if I can get started, I'll be out of your way that much sooner." Taggart looked down at his clipboard, pen poised. "Shall we begin in the chicken coop?" he said, without looking up.

⌘   ⌘   ⌘

RAEANNE TURNED TO Troopers Mars and Dunston, "How about I fix you some breakfast? Coffee? Jimmy? I bet you haven't had any breakfast." Jimmy Dunston had grown up right down the road.

Dunston and Mars, both of whom had been startled out of bed for this unscheduled assignment, looked at each other and then back at Raeanne. They wore their hats so low on their brow you could hardly tell that both also had a trace of sleep in their eyes. "Sure." "Yeah, okay."

"Come on in. You both look like you could use some good strong coffee."

"Well, everything looks fine," said Jim Taggart, glumly. "Just fine." He looked around the yard one last time, as if perchance to catch a glimpse of something amiss.

"Thank you," David said, wiping a trace of sweat from his forehead with the back of his arm. Raeanne, Jesse and Willa came out of the house and stood behind David on the porch and watched as the caravan rolled reluctantly away. Oscar was already gone to his job at the feed store.

"That were no random inspection," said David, in his best imitation of an old Vermont farmer. "When he said let's start in the chicken coop, the hairs on my neck just about stood up. I held my breath when we went inside expecting to find—"

"This?" Junie came around the back of the porch holding a burlap sack open like a kid on Halloween waiting for a treat. David looked down into it. Raeanne and Jesse came over next. "I was just coming back to tell you when I heard the vehicles. I knew this was what they were meant to find, just like the cow, so I went back, took them away and hid."

"How much do you want to bet they'd test positive for bird flu. Was the lock broken on the coop?"

"No, and none of those birds looked sick yesterday."

"None of them were sick. He's just switched them out somehow. A matter of seconds one way or the other and they'd have found those birds first and shut us down. He was going to shut us down this time."

A look came over his face, dark and blank. An angry tremor shook his chin.

"But we stopped him, Dad," Junie said.

"We can't stop him, Junie. I could have stopped him."

"David Meades! You had better thank your stars you did not. And you had better get it out of your head once and for all," Raeanne scolded.

"Get what out of his head, Mama?" Willa asked.

A rumble from beyond the orchard prevented her answer. A red truck came over from the back pasture and down the road through the orchard. A greater rumble came behind it. First one, then another giant yellow bulldozer lumbered over the crest of the hill and down behind the truck.

The Meades' family just stood and watched, as if they all knew who it was and what was going to happen, but, as in a dream, they were frozen and unable to move or speak.

The red truck stopped ten yards from their porch and Greenway got out. The giant bulldozers flanked his truck, puffing diesel and heat into the cool morning air. The men in the glass enclosed cabs were helmeted and stared impassively through dark sunglasses.

"Jeezum crow!" Chet Atwood fumbled his binoculars. He reached into his pocket for his cell phone, flipped it open and hit call. It picked up on the first ring. "He's coming with bulldozers. Two big Cats. And you'd better hurry it up or I have a feeling there won't be much left standing." Greenway's inspector left empty handed, but he was not taking 'no' for an answer. This was wrath, pure and simple, coming down on the Meades and their house.

"For the last time, I'm offering you $700,000 for the house. That's three times what it's worth."

"The farm is worth double that," said David Meades. He, Raeanne, the twins and Willa stood in front of the porch like a slender and ridiculous line of defenders against the giant machines.

"The land is already mine. The fruits of your many labors lost when you refused to sell."

"That's news to me."

"That train's come and gone, and neither you nor your small time lawyer can do a thing about it. For all we know it may come to light that you are a terrorist, perhaps connected to that explosion, and eventually what the government seizes it will sell, and when it does I'll be the highest bidder. You see, Mr. Meades, there are so many ways you can lose, and only one way you can win. That is to deal."

"No deal, Greenway. We're just supposed to walk away from what we've built and trust that you'll buy us out, when you claim our land already without a penny of compensation? You are going to have to take it; you are going to have to act on your claims, over our dead bodies."

The Meades all joined hands without a word and shuffled their feet as if trying to find firm footing.

"You are an evil man, and somebody should stop you," Raeanne shouted. Her face colored red suddenly, from both outrage and shame, as the urge to go for that nickel-plated revolver took hold of her.

"I am a reasonable man, who won't take 'no' for an answer."

"But we've done nothing to you," Raeanne protested.

Greenway stepped out of the sun and into the house's shadow. His dark capuchin beard, with its trimmed precision, and the razorback rim of his eyebrows bristled with alertness. "On the contrary, you've committed the unpardonable sin. You have what I want and need."

"Then I guess you'll have to take it."

"Have it your way, then." Greenway walked back to the bumper of his truck and lifted his hand in a signal.

The gullet burp of the diesel engines started and smoothed out into a steady rumble. The diesel pipes hissed in tandem as the big Cats rolled slowly forward. The Meades looked at each other and held tighter to each other's hands. To their own amazement they remained, frozen again in something like a dream, palms sweating, feet shifting. The Cats rolled past Greenway's truck. The massive blades glinted in the sun, then went cool silver in the shade.

Suddenly, the machines began to shake. The wheels spun in place. The drivers were trying to shift, looking at their consoles. The more they gunned the engine the more violently the big Cats shook. The engines at the rear began to smoke and shriek—an unbearable whining and grinding. The Meades stepped back onto their porch and covered their ears. Greenway and his truck were right between the engines. He retreated to his truck and backed up in haste.

Two loud bangs erupted, followed by the sound of clanging, flying parts and the whip- snap of broken belts. Then the engines went silent, except for a faint hiss of steam, and a tick, tick, tick. Greenway honked. The drivers remained in their ruined machines. Greenway laid on the horn again. From behind, the drivers appeared to sit motionless, and then one, followed by the other, fell forward onto his steering wheel. Greenway got out of his truck and approached the cab of the bulldozer on his right. "Roger?" He hoisted himself up by the hand grip, leaned into the window, and felt the driver's neck. He was dead. In the other bulldozer it was just the same. It was no accident, but in the media, and as far as local opinion was concerned, that is exactly how it must appear.

18.

Under Suspicion

ZEPHYR HAD ONE phone call to make, and while that call should've been to her attorney, she knew Osmena could do what her attorney couldn't: make all of this disappear.

The experimental would've done the trick, but last week Zephyr stopped taking it at Jude's urging, and this, she assumed, was the cause of her arrest. Osmena had assured her the lab results would come back negative, but, according to Roderick, the blue powder was a perfect match for the substance in the frosting found at Loaves and Fishes. The powder may have been no more than clever pharmacology, but knowing she'd stopped taking the experimental was something else altogether. Zephyr had underestimated Osmena. Her father had warned her long ago, but even he had been vague about what Osmena could do. What she grew up hearing more often than not was her father's philosophical disagreement with Ms. Searle, and stories of how she destroyed lives with the power she wielded.

Now, Zephyr was doubly stuck in her predicament. Not only did she stand to lose her freedom and her livelihood, but the indignity also came at the expense of her world view. The trap into which she'd fallen, and the means of escape, led her further away from the path of independent skepticism that had guided her life and deeper into an unfamiliar wood of belief and dependence on a power she didn't understand or trust. She was indeed standing upon a dangerous cliff, or, perhaps, already over the edge and watching herself fall in slow motion.

The holding cell, as indeed the Crawford State Police Barracks, had a stark new look. A metal plated slab attached to the wall was the only thing to sit on besides the floor. The cell was cinder block and concrete and the disarming buff yellow walls were designed either to induce calm, or a craving for cheddar cheese. It was also windowless, with fluorescent inset panels in the ceiling, so it was impossible to gage the passing of time. When they came to let Zephyr make her phone call, she glimpsed a clock through the Plexiglas panel of the processing office. She was incredulous that she'd been there for just under an hour. She would have sworn it was more than two. As she picked up the receiver and began to dial, she imagined the drag of days passed behind bars, the clank of heavy doors marking the hours in a bleak state prison, and her hand shook at the stirrings of her unwelcomed, new found faith: Osmena.

"The man told us to do it," Ashley Withers said.

"Yeah, but bare ass? Can't we wait till he comes out and puts his clothes on. I don't need to see his junk," Mark LaVallee said.

Calvin stuck his toe into the water, then dove into the pool below Granger Falls. All Withers and LaVallee had to do was come down the bank and swipe his clothes and roust him.

"Well, you're going to have to. That's our advantage; he's not going anywhere without his clothes. For two-fifty, who the hell cares about his junk."

"You said it was fifty each."

"Yeah, well that was four way, but between the two of us."

"But it's just two of us now, so ain't that a hundred twenty-five each then?"

"No, a hundred. I said two hundred total. Get the wax out of your ears. Hey, you got to admit that's some awesome ink on his back. That's worth a close up ain't it? Come on, let's roll."

Withers and LaVallee bounded down the bank shouting and whooping with their arms beating up and down like the flying monkeys in Oz.

Calvin turned in the water at the sound. Withers picked up the shorts and shirt and began whipping them around like propellers. He tossed the shirt to LaVallee. They waved and taunted.

"Hey Calvin, panther boy, come on out."

Calvin swam over to the rock he'd just dove off and draped his forearms over it. "Hey, guys, what's up?" He smiled up at them. "Water's great, you should come in."

"No, you should come out. Tell us about those explosives you used on the Mobil Station. Tell us what you're going to do next, big man. Maybe we'd like to blow something up too," LaVallee said.

Calvin propelled back into the pool and floated away without a word.

Withers rushed over to the edge and got down on all fours on the rock and shouted after Calvin. "You think you can wait us out. I know how cold that water is, panther boy, and you can freeze your nuts off in there if you want, but we'll just wait. Hey, maybe we should call Roderick and complain about the naked freak exposing himself at the falls."

Calvin drifted over. "What's this all about? I'm not bothering you."

"Blowing things up, that's like nothing, huh?"

"I had nothing to with that."

"Yeah, well, Roderick's on our ass again thinking it's one of us. So you know what? We decided we're going to haul your ass, tattoo and all, down to the station to have a little talk with the Sarge to straighten things out once and for all."

"I'm not going anywhere with you."

"Oh, yeah? Well, how about we call Roderick out here and just split. He's a crazy bastard. I mean, just your bare ass, Sarge and his gun. Isn't he supposed to have, like, the biggest schlong in the state?" Withers looked over at LaVallee. They started doing mock measurements with their hands, until a fit of laughter took them.

"I'm just saying, is all."

Withers shrugged at LaVallee and stood up. They balled up the shirt and shorts and stuffed them into Calvin's boots. Withers tied the laces together and slung the boots over his shoulder. "So we're leaving with your clothes; you can go with us in them, or—"

Withers swatted at a cloud of deer flies buzzing around his head. "—or you're stuck here until dark with the deer flies and mosquitoes. These woods are dark at night, man; better watch out for that broken glass around the head of the path by that old campfire; wouldn't want you to cut your feet or anything."

Calvin stroked calmly to the edge of the pool and hoisted himself up on the rock. He stood up and spread his arms. "Okay. I guess you got me."

"Jeezum crow," said LaVallee.

⌘　⌘　⌘

"YE-UH? CAN I help you?" Chet Atwood asked, emerging through the open bay. He wiped his greasy hands on a gray shop towel. "Don't look old enough to drive, and I don't fix bikes."

Merrilee smiled at his joke. "Maybe you remember me from a couple of weeks ago. My father brought his car in for you to look at?"

Chet thought for a moment, as if looking back at pictures stored inside his head. He was a typical Vermont guy—a big husky build, a careless beard and hair not particularly styled or combed. His was dark, parted down the middle, and fell almost to his shoulders, like a 1970's mountain man. He also used the wide, loose Vermont vowels, as if he were trying to stretch his o's and u's.

"Ye-uh. I remember. Weren't nothing wrong with his car, if I recall."

"Dad was so relieved. I tried to tell him it was nothing."

"I'm sure you did." Chet squinted suspiciously at her.

"But I noticed while I was walking around that there was a red Ford Escort on the other side of that fence out back."

"Did you, now? You see through fences?"

"Just over them. The thing is, I'm a good friend of Jude Corgan's and I'm sure you know about all the wrecks on their frontage."

"Who don't?" Chet said. He started wiping his hands on the towel again.

"Right? I saw the engine block was hoisted up, and, well, all the Corgan wrecks are missing engines too, and I couldn't help wonder if, you know, maybe that car was going to somehow end up at the Corgans'. It's just that I saw a man there prying the fender off the wheel—"

"You get a look at him?" Chet tossed the towel away towards a grease-spotted cardboard barrel in the corner of the bay.

"That's the thing. I didn't really see his face."

Chet's eyebrows dropped, as if he were relieved.

"He didn't want me to see him because he put on a mask and took off into the woods. I was just thinking that maybe you ought to know about it in case something was going on with some of the junks here, maybe that you didn't know about. Not that the Corgans think you had anything to do with those wrecks." Merrilee looked over the top of her glasses at him.

Chet's eyebrows shot up again.

"Those are just rumors, but they know better."

"Don't know anything about that, or anybody prying fenders, but I can tell you we took the engine out of it because it were still good; but that car went through the crusher last week. Be my guest if you want to take a look behind the fence; search all the bays too."

"If you don't mind."

Chet took her on a guided tour. They looked over the fence, around the yard and in all the bays. No red Escort.

"And you don't know who that might have been monkeying around with that car?"

Chet stuck out his lower lip and shook his head.

Merrilee got back on her bike. "Well, thank you. I just wanted to be sure. It seemed so strange."

"Okay. Well, sorry I can't tell you more."

Merrilee circled away from the bay, then put her feet down and stopped the bike. "All the Corgan wrecks had their VINS removed too, which is illegal, and of course you wouldn't have done anything illegal."

"So, Calvin, is it? Calvin what?"

"Calvin Hobbs."

"Sounds familiar. You have any ID?"

"No, sir. I was swimming at the falls."

"You drive there?"

"I got a ride."

"You say you're 17. Where do you live?"

"Twin Gaps."

"Address?"

"Trout Brook Hill. Sorry, I'm new to town and I haven't memorized the number."

"I bet. Still in school?"

"I home school, sir."

Roderick didn't really like the overly earnest tone of the 'sirs', and he didn't like the placid sweetness of his face. That was one thing you could never trust if you saw it in an adolescent. It was in itself a form of deception belying the nature of the beast. He had the sudden urge to taser the look off his face and cane the truth out of his tattooed back. Instead he sucked on a hard candy with cold ferocity. He had Calvin beside his desk in his office within arm's reach. In the processing room he'd have to sit across the wide table and that would never do.

Roderick mustered all the condescension he could to counter the earnest 'sirs'. "So Calvin, do you want to share with me some of the things you've been saying around town. Because if you've got some valuable information and you don't disclose it, that could make you an accessory to a crime. You know that don't you?"

Roderick stood up for effect to tower over the seated boy. Calvin looked up, eyebrows raised a little, giving him an ever more innocent expression, a kind of pure curiosity. Intolerable! Roderick reached for the taser and zapped him on the shoulder. Calvin cried out and flopped out of the chair onto the floor. He rolled on his side and rocked, paralyzed and gasping. "God, I—didn't—you didn't give me a chance."

"Hide and seek at the waterfall is over. It's truth or consequences now. So why don't you spill what you know, or else."

"Okay." Calvin tried to raise his hand to ward off another jolt but it just flopped across his stomach.

Roderick sat down in his chair, but he didn't put the taser away. "I'm waiting. The next one will be harder."

"It was the VLF."

Roderick pointed the taser. "The VLF is taking credit for it; tell me something I don't know before I fry you within an inch of crisp."

Calvin turned his big eyes on, which only made him more worthy of another jolt than anything at this point.

"I know somebody who is in the VLF. He's been talking. I went with him into the woods where they meet."

"A name."

"They don't go by their real names. I swear."

That was it! The earnestness of petty criminals was galling. Roderick struck like a cobra and zapped his neck. Calvin's eyes rolled back, his arms and legs flew out to his sides, like an Electro Convulsive Therapy patient without restraints, spittle oozing out of his mouth. His eyes fluttered for a while, then he finally began to feel his body again, control his eyes and mouth. He couldn't have gotten up if he'd wanted to, so he just lay there on his back looking up at the ceiling and breathing shallowly. Eventually, he could move his lips and tongue again to speak.

"I went with him to the clearing in the woods to see a meeting. They have a camp somewhere. The clearing is just a place where some of the members on the outside can meet without being traced to it. But if you knew the woods, I bet you could follow them."

"Did you ever try?"

"No."

"How do they get to the clearing?"

"I don't know. Four wheelers, something. I was escorted blindfolded coming and going out of the woods so I couldn't see who went where. I heard water though."

"This VLF contact you have; do you know where he lives?"

Calvin shook his head. "He's local."

"Could you identify him in a lineup?"

"Yes."

"Do you know where he hangs out?"

"I could find him."

"Is that a yes?"

Roderick reached out with the taser for Calvin's thigh.

"Yes, I will find him for you. Please."

Please! Please! Oh, that was beyond the pale. More than he could take. In his book, that was asking for another jolt.

Roderick zapped his thigh. Calvin's wavering, electrified vocals rang out, and a wet spot darkened the front of his shorts, spreading like a spilled drink absorbed into a paper towel. Tulley walked into the station, craned his head into Roderick's office to follow the sound, and stopped dead at the sight of the young man convulsing on the floor with a wet crotch. Roderick sat with the taser still poised and looked up at Tulley. He put a finger to his lips. Tulley turned around and quickly ducked across the hall into his office. He sat down, reached into the top drawer for his IPod, and plugged in his headphones.

"Until I can verify who you are, Calvin Hobbs, we're going to have to hold you down at the police barracks in Crawford. Overnight. Maybe more. You never know how a sleepless night will jar your memory."

Roderick put away his taser. He motioned for Calvin to get up. Calvin didn't move. Roderick came across the hall. "Tulley?"

Tulley stood up and turned as if he'd been utterly oblivious to Roderick's presence. "When he's feeling better, cuff this young man and escort him to the state barracks for an overnight."

19.

Strange Discoveries

ERRILEE FOLDED THE newspaper when Jude found her in the reference room of the library. She bit her lip, as if she were literally holding back her words. Jude sat down opposite her.

"What?"

"Brace yourself." Merrilee turned the newspaper around and pushed it over to him.

TEACHER FACES CHILD ENDANGERMENT CHARGES

Jude blanched white. He saw Zephyr's name in the first paragraph and turned the paper over.

"What. Aren't you going to read it?"

Jude didn't say anything. He looked down and his hands were doing their bouncing spider thing on the library table. "I know about it," he whispered.

"How?"

"After you went to your aunt's, I went over to see her."

Merrilee looked puzzled. Her nose wrinkled as if she were sniffing something strange and malodorous.

"The night of the fireworks, when she acted so strange, like she didn't know me? I knew something was wrong. It's not like her. So I went over to see her and she confessed everything to me. She got the blue powder from Osmena, and now she's taking an experimental to make the trouble go away. I wasn't supposed to tell a soul about it, so you can't, absolutely can't, tell anyone. Not even GEIST. Promise?"

"Promise. Cross my heart, hope to eat rat poison and die an agonizing death. Nobody can know. You'd be a material witness, if it came out you heard her confess to the crime. God, she was weird like that when Sandra went to see her too. Now we know why."

"It's my fault she got arrested. I told Zephyr to stop taking the experimental and she did, and Osmena must have found out and gone back on her promise."

Merrilee looked appalled and at the same time impressed. "It's Zephyr now?"

Jude scowled back.

"You see the trouble you get into when I'm not around? You're actually getting far too good at this—finding trouble. I'm not saying I wouldn't have done the same thing. I mean, there's no telling what the experimental might have done to Ms. LaFrance, and you were right to tell her to stop. She didn't have to do it if she didn't think it was the right thing to do. Still, she might not be convicted of anything. Can't she just say she thought it was blue sugar crystals? That it must have been tampered with in the store? There have been instances. I mean, is Osmena going to publicly contradict her and expose herself? I doubt it. They have no way to trace this substance to a source unless she tells them. So where did she even get it? It's not like she has a chemistry lab at her house. All they have is this baggy of blue powder, she might have purchased innocently at the grocery store. With her reputation and a good attorney I doubt there'd be a jury in the state who would convict her."

"Maybe, but sometimes, once you're accused of a thing, it can stick to you forever, or at least for a very long time, and she might lose her job." Jude could see Merrilee didn't really understand about reputation. In her head, she knew what could happen when you were accused, innocent or not, but she had the luxury to live above the possibility. Her parents were well off, had respected careers and a beautiful home. And so in people's minds they sort of stood for those things. Merrilee didn't know what it was like to be connected with something ugly, the way he was, inseparable from it in people's minds and memories.

"Jude, I'm really sorry about Ms. LaFrance, but isn't your fault. You were concerned and you took a risk in saying something, and maybe you changed the outcome of things, or maybe it really won't make a difference. It may all work out no matter what you did. If we carried around the weight of everything adults messed up in the world, we'd never get out of bed in the morning."

"But we have to live with it too. And aren't we almost adults? Doesn't anything we do matter? It's like, the only thing we're expected to do well in is school, sports and the youth turkey hunt. How lame is that? And when you read about somebody our age doing anything else, it's usually bad—shooting somebody's cat or vandalizing property."

Merrilee sensed it was time to change the mood. Jude was about to get gloomy and sorry for himself. "Well, we are doing something aren't we? Do you think Brady Hunt even has an opinion about the explosion other than that it was loud and awesome."

"Ack!" Jude held up his fingers in the shape of a cross. "Don't mention that cretin in my presence."

"Well, you should feel lucky you weren't born with a scoreboard for a brain and a personality to match. So, anyway, I found out some interesting things."

Merrilee told him about her encounter with Chet Atwood.

"So you confronted him?"

"Well, almost, but not quite. I hinted that maybe, unbeknownst to him, somebody might be planning to haul that wreck to your place. I know one thing is for sure. He got nervous when I mentioned seeing that man prying at the fender, and he seemed almost relieved when I said I didn't get a good look at him."

"I just can't believe Chet would have done that to us."

"He seemed taken aback when I said he was rumored to have done it. I also couldn't help wondering if that man I saw was part of the 'we' that took the engine out of the car. I mean, what total stranger is going to come out of the woods and start doing body work for the fun of it on some piece of junk that obviously wasn't going anywhere."

"So you don't believe him?"

"It doesn't make any sense. He didn't even seem concerned that somebody was nosing around his junkyard doing whatever to one of his cars. But, the car was gone and it's not in your yard, so it would seem he's telling the truth. Unless the man I saw warned Chet and they got rid of the car to avoid discovery."

Jude sat for a moment pondering in silence.

"On the Osmena front," Merrilee said, "I found an old *Vermont Magazine* article from about 20 years ago. For somebody so well known, her name doesn't often make it into print."

"I guess she doesn't need or want too much attention given what she does."

"Exactly. So why even be interviewed for the piece? I mean, they could do a story without her say so, but she had to have approved it because there are quotes from her and pictures of her gardens, even one of her. In the piece, there's no mention of magic, spells, potions, or experimentals. Nobody with anything bad to say about her. There's no hint of a dark side at all. She just comes across as a kind of colorful character, sharing bits of wit and wisdom."

"So? It's like *Vermont Magazine* not *Rolling Stone*."

"I know, but there's a similar piece in the *Beacon*'s first anniversary issue from forty-four years ago. And she doesn't look a whole lot different in that picture than she did in the later piece."

"Yeah, but *Vermont Magazine* could have used an older photo. Maybe she wouldn't let them use a current one."

Merrilee was staring hard over the top of her glasses now. "But she looked like she was at least 60 in the *Beacon* piece. So, even if she's a few years younger than she looks, that still puts her at about 100 today. Is she even still alive?"

"What do you mean, alive? My parents went to see her. They bought the spell from her. Zephyr bought the powder from her."

Merrilee put her elbows on the table and rested her face in her hands.

"What are you thinking?" Jude said.

"Or they bought if from somebody who says she's Osmena."

Jude blew her a raspberry. "No way." The librarian stuck her head in the doorway and put her fingers to her lips.

"Why not?"

"It's too convoluted."

"What if it's a relative. A daughter and Osmena Searle is just a brand name. The original is always the best. Why settle for watered down magic. You see?"

"How long could they get away with that? There's got to be people around old enough to remember her as a young woman at least."

"Right. You couldn't get away with it beyond a human lifespan, but with mixed up chronology and fuzzy memories maybe 100 or 110 years tops. Look, there's so much information coming at us every day, the average person can't keep track of what happened and when; ten or twenty years past is so much information ago, it might as well be 100 years. Having something new is more important than sticking with things long enough to find out what's true. It takes time, right? Like what happened the night your brother died. So, if you were a reporter, you couldn't stay at it long enough to get to the bottom of things. There has to be an official version to wrap things up. You know, to move on. And sometimes it comes out more like myth than fact.

"So Osmena's just a myth?"

"She's real enough, whoever or how many she is, but logically the myth of her wouldn't stand up to close examination. She doesn't appear in public by design; maybe via a rare magazine or newspaper profile when she needs a dose of good PR, or to stay in the public consciousness. But, how many people have actually seen her?"

"A lot of people."

"Okay. Your parents have seen her this year, but have they ever before seen her in their lives?"

"Not that I know of."

"So once in forty some years. Conceivably they could live into their 80's and never see her again, and if she looks sixty to them now; it's reasonable they could still believe she was alive for the rest of their lives. See how it could work?"

"Did they say how old she was in the stories?"

"The VM writer asked her, but she said 'a lady never reveals her age.'"

"That's what birth records are for."

Jude and Merrilee went online at the state archives and requested every record that would contain Searle's from 1760 forward—births, deaths and marriages, but there was no telling how long they'd have to wait to get them back. They checked out two books—*The History of Twin Gaps vol. 1* and *vol. II*—and went back to the loft at Merrilee's to read.

Roderick didn't like Greenway pushing him to investigate the VLF, but with the federal investigation going nowhere at present, having Greenway behind his rogue inquiries gave it a stamp of moral authority. It helped seeing it all as part of the same thing. Greenway's property and his place of work. He had a harder time convincing himself the VLF, if they existed, was anything more than a bunch of fairies prancing naked in the woods around a sacred circle. Whoever these people might be, they weren't hiding their politics behind airy fairy nonsense. These were men of action like him.

Roderick leaned back in his chair and smiled. It was far more satisfying to recall how he'd leaned on Withers and his friends by the river and how little it had taken to get them to do his work for him, bringing him the kid who was boasting knowledge of the explosion. Ha! Perfection. A textbook demonstration of psychological control: how the malleable and weak shrank in the presence of authority, complied at the pressure point of fear. All with only a modicum of force. Calvin had required the disorienting threat of unpredictable and sudden violence against anything but clear direct answers. No eye contact. No vagaries. No pleading. Masterful! Even if it wasn't necessary, and all the information turned out to be false, unmitigated cruelty in the service of truth was its own reward.

Either way it was a win for Roderick. In the absence of proof, he could continue to run his show his way, and if the boy coughed up a name or led him to the VLF, he'd take maximum credit, then step back and let the Feds swoop in for the kill.

Zephyr looked up at the opening click and slam of the cell block door. Footsteps neared but she heard no voices. Could it be Osmena already? She went across the cell to see. No. A young man in handcuffs walked ahead of Trooper Mars.

"Stop," Mars ordered. He unlocked the cell across from Zephyr, told the boy to step inside and closed the door behind him. "Now hands through the slot."

The boy turned and slid his hands through a horizontal slot in the door. Trooper Mars unlocked the handcuffs and hitched them to his belt.

Mars left and the boy remained at the door across from Zephyr. He watched her for a while before finally greeting her. "Hi."

"Hello."

The boy, a young man really, was pleasing in his features and in build as strongly formed as a man, yet without the knotty density that came from years of country labor. There was also something childlike in his eyes and mouth that made it difficult to guess his age, something in the mystery of him that drew her in. He tilted his head and the light caught the matte path of dried tears on his cheeks. Zephyr couldn't help notice the wetness on his pants front.

"Are you okay?"

"Yeah, I'm better."

"Better than what?"

"Better than being tasered by that psycho, Roderick."

"He did that to you?"

"My leg and shoulder are still numb, but I'm okay."

"I'm so sorry."

"That's okay. I'm Calvin."

"Zephyr."

Calvin looked down and smiled. "I know who you are."

"I know. It's in all the papers."

"Not because of that." Calvin looked up. "What do you know about the VLF?"

"The Vermont Liberation Front?" Zephyr shrugged. "Not much more than anybody else."

"You see, I've been to one of their meetings, in the woods. They're real. Roderick's after them and now I've got to give him a name, or I'm literally toast. I mean, I suppose I should, right? They're blowing up things. Do you think I should? Do you think it's wrong?"

"To turn the someone in?"

"To blow up things."

"I've been wondering that myself. I don't feel much like judging these days. I don't feel I know the answers."

"But what is it supposed to mean when you blow up something like that? If you want to do good, maybe don't start by blowing something up. Don't they know people are going to be afraid?"

"Do you think people are afraid?"

"That's just it. They're not. It's like secretly they all want to blow something up themselves. It's like, so long as nobody got hurt, they're glad."

"Why would people be glad about it?"

"Maybe because of who it targets."

"Who is that?"

"Greenway."

"Well, a lot of people aren't happy about what he plans to do."

"Would you stop him if you could?"

Zephyr opened her mouth to speak and stopped. She got the feeling he wanted something from her, but she didn't know what he was after. "You said you knew who I was, but not from the newspapers, didn't you?"

Calvin nodded. "Your father was a secessionist, wasn't he?"

Zephyr nodded. "That was a long time ago."

"But it's still alive. I mean, I was there in the woods and I saw their leader."

Zephyr stood up tall. "You did?"

"I did." Calvin stared distantly, as if remembering it. "He was magnificent. All that wild blond hair. I wanted to believe him. I did. But I know they're behind the explosion."

"Calvin. I think a group like that wants things to change. It's to get people's attention. I don't think they're especially fond of explosions. I know my father was not destructive and I'm sure their leader feels the same way." Just speaking of him in the present made Zephyr's heart race with hope.

"You seem pretty sure, but you said you didn't know much about them before."

Zephyr looked closely at him, but all she could discern was his sincerity. "Well, maybe you should just wait and see what comes of it before you decide whether it's a good or a bad thing."

"But I have to decide, very soon, whether to turn this guy in."

"Well, my father always used to say, if in doubt, don't. You have to figure out what you believe in. From what I know, the VLF wants Vermont to separate from the United States. Some people would call that treason. Other people believe our government is more oppressive now than England was before the Revolution; so if the conscience of the people is still free, it's their right to oppose tyranny. I think the VLF wants local people to have control of their own lives again, but not just so anybody can do any old thing they please. But so people are freed from having to be selfish in order to survive. So people can learn to live interdependently. Governments have control over things, and as a result they also have responsibilities. If that control shifts to the people, responsibility falls on the community to care for itself and its members. But, what would happen and what would it all mean if it ever came to pass? I can't even guess how people would behave without the government watching over them, and I'm not sure exactly how I feel about it."

"Do you think they're really going to do that? Okay. So even if they didn't harm anyone and all they did was make a mess and cost a very rich man a little money (and how much, really, with the insurance money he's going to get?). How does it change anything?"

"Maybe it doesn't, but it makes people start to think, maybe things don't have to stay the way they are, and maybe they don't have to go Merlin Greenway's way either."

Jude and Merrilee had been lying on the floor pillows slogging through the books for almost two hours. They weren't sweeping accounts, but anecdotal histories about families and remembrances of winter storms and spring floods. Some of the stories were amusing and they'd stop to read them aloud from time to time, but it was beginning to look like there would be nothing about Osmena.

Jude rolled over onto his back. "I don't think I can take much more of Volume 1."

"Me either." Merrilee put down her book and looked up through the skylight.

"Jeez. You'd think Osmena would have cured somebody's cow or nursed somebody back to health or won a blue ribbon at the fair."

"I know, but let's keep looking. Just another half hour."

"Okay, but it's starting to put me to sleep."

"We should've stopped for a cafe mocha or something."

Jude and Merrilee settled down again to reading and for a while there was hardly a sound in the loft except the occasional scrape of a turning page.

Jude looked over at Merrilee. "What if the opposite were true? I mean, say you're right about her being a kind of myth, but what if the myth is that she's been around for such a long time, but she really hasn't? What if she wants to make it seem like she's part of the fabric of things? I mean, after all this reading, it's like she wasn't here at all."

Merrilee sat up. "I hadn't thought of that, but you may be right."

"Think about it." Jude sat up too. "Usually those pieces about old local folks brag about how many generations their families have lived there. Did it say that anywhere?"

"It was pretty blank about the past. It kind of assumed her fixture status, but there was nothing about where she came from, or even if she was born in Vermont."

"Why don't we skip to the end and work back."

Merrilee flipped to the last page and began to read. "This is weird, reading backwards forwards." About her fourth page in, she tapped the book with her index finger. "Here: '*It was a busy year for Miss Osmena Searle. After a trip abroad to Europe of several weeks, she returned to work on her conservation plans by purchasing 1,200 acres of Twin Gaps mountain woodlands, which she has placed in a trust. As usual her gardens were splendid and her cut flower arrangement and orchids won first prize at the garden show.*'"

"That's it?"

"Well, it's something. The Beacon story also talked about conservation as her great passion, and that she'd succeeded in obtaining land from all of her abutters. All we have to do is find the properties she owns at the town clerks and trace back the transfer of the deeds to her. I think they list where the buyer came from and when. If the point was not letting on that she hasn't been here as long people think, then her first purchase was probably small so it wouldn't be noticed."

"Or bought under a different name."

"But what about her appearance? How do we explain that she hasn't changed much in the past 40 something years and that nobody comments on it?"

Jude thought about it. "I'm sure she cooks up spells for herself. Hey, what if she really does look old, but she makes it so people see her as unchanged?"

It was Merrilee's turn to be skeptical. "Talk about convoluted."

The men were all jubilant when Luc's incantation succeeded in putting a halt to Greenway's machinery. It meant they could stop him and his plans, but more than this, they had the power to master and frustrate the technology that would soon be brought to bear against them. Make no mistake, they had a lot to learn, and there were still several things that must be done, things that needed proving before they dared declare Vermont a free republic. There was a greater concern than whether they could simply master and destroy things, but whether they had the skill, or even the capacity, to prevent human casualties in the process. Only not all of Luc's peers seemed to share it.

For what had happened at Gemini Farm was not the singular triumph they made it out to be. Chet Atwood had confirmed that both of the men driving the Caterpillars at the farm that day had died also when the machines broke down, and he'd been quite shaken by it. He'd come to Luc privately with the news, even before the general announcement of their success had been made to the compound. His hands trembled and there was a tremor in voice.

"That wasn't supposed to happen. For God's sake! What went wrong?"

Luc could only shake his head. He'd had to produce the incantation in haste and perhaps had been too careless of his words.

"Man, when I signed on for this, Luc, it weren't to become a killer. I mean, what if something else had gone wrong and that whole innocent family had died right there on their front porch? Do you know where we'd be? Do you know what that would make us? Devils like the government with their collateral damage. That's what. I'm going to tell you; that skull's an evil thing."

Luc recalled with pangs of regret that he had indeed used the word 'die' in his incantation and wondered, as the pangs worsened into panic, if he had caused their deaths. Was it even possible to be that true with language? To perfect the will in words, so as to guide all possible ways a spell would work upon the world?

Luc could barely breathe, and went to the wide door of the hut to take in the air. Nobody else had stirred. In the summer, they were up at dawn and always stopped to rest in the heat of the day and then resumed their work until dark. He looked back into the hut. EG and some of the others were still asleep in their bunks.

Luc wanted to believe that along with achieving a desired end, there must also be a way of lessening harm to the greatest degree, yet the death of those two drivers sobered him like a cold slap. He shuddered with dread to think that death was part and parcel of the skull's unrivaled force. The recited words that sealed him to the skull in sovereignty came back to him with their dire portent: *Say to the skull, 'if I am he; heir to the everlasting tree; I bend the practice of my will; to wield the curse for good or ill.*

Perhaps it was enough to wrest the skull from Osmena's grasp. Even now, Luc did not know for sure whether his claim upon its will had wholly mitigated hers. She had wielded its power from a distance all along. But, proximity was in his favor. There were signs afoot that she and Greenway were desperate without it, and unable to anticipate and foil his aims. Might the skull only serve one master, or owe its fealty to one immediate and present voice?

Deep down Luc believed he must destroy it: that such power as it granted was too corrupting, and vast enough to overwhelm a sea of good intentions. What would happen to him, his place and their untried republic, if he should grow in his conviction and make it known?

20.

Alliances

ZEPHYR AND OSMENA rode in silence in the back of Miss Searle's Bentley, through town and then up Route 17 though Catamount Gap. The day passed in stark splashes of shade and sun, dimmed through darkened glass with the diurnal pall of a solar eclipse.

"You said this would go away if I took the experimental," Zephyr said at last.

Miss Searle glanced out of the corner of her eye at Zephyr. "That I did, with the proviso that you must not stop until the entire course was finished. So it stands to reason that you stopped."

"It's just that I was feeling so strange, and sometimes had no memory of where I'd been or what I'd done. You never told me it would do that."

"If I told you what it was supposed to do, it would have ruined the experiment."

Osmena's critical gaze at Zephyr changed to one of keen curiosity. "But if you had no memory of things, how did you find out you'd been anywhere? Somebody told you?"

Zephyr nodded. "I had been at the fairgrounds for the fireworks and didn't remember anything."

"Excellent. Interesting. And what else did it do?"

"Well, I guess it sort of changed my personality. I appeared not to be myself."

"Did you talk to people under the experimental?"

"I don't know. I walked right by somebody I knew, as if I had no idea who they were. I don't know if I was even aware of anybody around me."

"But you weren't bumping into things?"

"Not that I know of."

"Wonderful."

"Wonderful?"

"Yes, like an induced sleepwalking. A person might walk or drive or do a number of complex activities—all while being in a completely unconscious state and upon waking also have no memory of it."

"It doesn't feel wonderful to me."

"Well, at least that's something. But you've stopped it now, and we were oh so close to the observation stage."

"Observation stage?"

"Yes. Once the drug had reached a certain level in your system, you would have been observed to measure its potential, but you've spoiled the experiment. No matter now." Osmena tipped her head side to side as if rolling an idea around. Then she turned her gaze on Zephyr again. Her papery eyelids closed and opened once.

"It happens I have something new for you, something better that I've been working on. I can only say that you will be conscious this time, and that you will be questing."

"Questing?"

"To find out if the experimental works, you will be given a task to complete, and it will be revealed to you in due course—so that not only the quest but the conception itself will arise in your consciousness. But, Ms. LaFrance, don't even think about backing out of this one, if you value your freedom and ever want to teach again. I'm giving you one more chance; if you fail, I guarantee it will be your last. Agreed?"

Zephyr looked out the window at the glass-darkened, soundless, sheen of the day. "Agreed."

"Good. We shall begin today."

Calvin returned to The Cosmos after his release from the police barracks. He came in through the servant's entrance to the big industrial kitchen.

216

It still felt unexpected in such a rambling old mansion—all steel and soapstone with rows of copper bottomed pots and utensils hanging above its great prepping island.

Merlin Greenway, his father, had lunch waiting in the alcove where they often dined when they stayed with Aunt Osmena. Calvin came in and stood behind a chair across from him.

"You could have come for me yourself."

Merlin Greenway folded his newspaper carefully along the crease and set it down on the chair beside him. "I could not have."

"Aunty came down to pick up a stranger, but you send George to come for me."

"I can't afford to be seen having anything to do with you. I thought you understood that was the whole point. And Roderick certainly mustn't find out that Osmena and I are related. He is out for revenge, so we can't afford to have him nosing around here and pointing the Feds our way. He just needed a push in the VLF's direction, and you were the bait. By the way, I hope you were convincing."

"Convincing?" Calvin echoed the word and looked away through the glass doorway out to the tropical garden patio. "He doesn't want to believe me, but if I come up with a name, give him someone from the VLF, he'll bite."

"Eventually you'll give him Atwood, or that peculiar masked man. What did you call him?"

"Ederyck Gannon."

"Yes, then Roderick will go to the Feds, and it won't be long before they're all found out."

Calvin nodded, but continued to look through the glass.

"But the timing has to be right. We can't have the Feds swooping in until we get the skull back. That would be a disaster. Right now it'd be just your word about Atwood. You'll have to lead Roderick to a meeting so he can witness it himself."

Greenway shook his head and laughed, a deep but rapid report that sounded in his chest, like an underground tremor that was felt rather than heard.

"What?"

"Roderick thinks it was his tactics that got those local boys to haul you in. My five hundred dollars was more like it. Sit down; you must be hungry."

Calvin sat down. He pushed the bowl of chilled cucumber soup aside.

Greenway ate his soup with rigorous attention, between giant bites of cucumber sandwiches, as though consumption required the same single-mindedness he reserved for drafting a blueprint, or devising a development plan. He seemed indifferent to Calvin's lack of appetite. When he finished, he wiped his mouth on his napkin and looked up at his son again.

"So what did Ms. LaFrance have to say? What does she know about the VLF?"

Calvin picked up the spoon at his place and tapped it on the napkin absently. "I don't think she knows anything of them, but she seems to know a lot about them. She didn't condemn the explosion when I brought it up. She practically defended them."

"Well, of course she's a sympathizer. Her old man was one of them. What about Dentremont? Did she react?"

"I didn't mention him by name. I said I'd seen their leader and I described him. She stood up straight, got really intent, hoping I'd say something more, but she wouldn't ask directly for information about him, or admit she knew him."

"She didn't trust you,"

"I didn't have a lot of time."

"You made her suspicious and she clammed up."

"Dad I—"

"Well, she knows he's alive now and she might try to find out where they're meeting."

"I did the best I could."

"You did what you do. You're transparent and people see right through you." Greenway folded his hands as if closing a book and gazed narrowly at Calvin.

"Transparent? Maybe I am. You seem to see right through me to whatever you want. I got the Meades' signatures you needed; how come they didn't see through me if I'm so transparent?"

"Because they are just like you. Zephyr LaFrance may be a grade school teacher, but she's no unsophisticated country girl. If she's half as savvy as her father, she'd smell you a mile off. You're disarming, but you're inexperienced when it comes to talking to someone like her."

Calvin gripped the napkin and stood up, kicking his chair out behind him. "Well I got some experience at the police station, alright. That sick cop you fed me to played taser tag with my body. I was on the floor paralyzed, wetting myself and waiting for him to decide if I'd said the wrong thing so he could give me another jolt. But, you know, you can go yourself next time. You take it next time, because I'm over it." Calvin threw the napkin into his soup.

"Calvin." Greenway stood up and came over and put his hand around the back of his son's neck. Calvin tossed his head, but his father's hand remained, a firm and reassuring massage on the back of his neck, the way he would to rub the scruff to calm one of the big cats. He looked Calvin in the eye. "I didn't know he was going to do that to you. No. I wouldn't ever do that to you."

Calvin nodded, gazing back at his father for a moment and then looking down at the floor.

"You're good around the Meades; that's where you should be, and that's where I need you most. Take that boy out on your bike; be his best buddy and find out where that spring is. Because if we don't get the skull back, we are going to need the water. Your aunt especially."

⌘ ⌘ ⌘

O SMENA RECLINED ON a chaise in the shade after she'd finished with Zephyr and sent her home. She was strangely fatigued. The humidity and heat seemed to increase each day. By afternoon, she was listless and in need of a nap. She must have dozed in her chair. For she had closed her eyes to concentrate on the skull—to see if, against long odds, she might yet tap its power to reinforce the potent formula she'd given Zephyr—and the next thing she knew she heard Merlin calling her.

Osmena removed her sunglasses and raised her arm to show she was not asleep. There was another lounge beside her, and when Merlin arrived he sat sideways in it leaning forward. He studied her with uncertainty. "Are you ill?"

"I'm quite well; just enjoying an afternoon rest."

"I'm glad you can."

"Trouble with Calvin?"

Merlin shook his head. "Nothing really. I'm more concerned about the skull."

"Yes, quite a setback at the farm last week." Osmena motioned to her brother. "Sit back in the chair Merlin and reflect with me."

Merlin made a gruff noise and reluctantly assumed a reclining position beside her.

"You mustn't worry. We are going to get the skull back. Zephyr is our secret weapon."

"You keep saying that, but we can't trust her to do our bidding for us, or our cause. She's in full sympathy with the VLF."

"Well, we'd expect no less of Gerard LaFrance's daughter would we? But it is not about trust anymore, dear brother. Each time she comes to me, she's deeper in, the way a fly becomes more entangled the more it struggles to extricate itself from a spider's web. What she has embarked upon today cannot be reversed by the sentimental meddling of that peculiar Corgan boy, or anybody else. For, what she will do for us shall be of her own will. She will be ours by assumption, body and soul. Our desires will become her desires, and so the conscience of her father will not infect her thinking. Like any good assassin, the self she embodies will be for her a useful mask, and her knowledge of these woods will be the key. Much of it used to be her family's property. As far as I know her father's old cabin is still there, rotting away in the forest."

"Now that would be a tall order under any circumstance. Is she capable? Are you sure any of this will work without the skull."

"The skull controls the will of the world—people and systems and the objects made by man—things we no longer control, I'm afraid. My incantations are useless. I now know why that spell I gave the Corgans failed.

At the time, I was puzzled by it, but of course one never lets on. I said they got the wording wrong. I'd rather appear a capricious scoundrel than a sorceress who no longer had power over her words. It's why the results of the tests on the blue powder came back positive. Fortunately for me, Zephyr admitted to having stopped taking the experimental. So now she thinks I can see through walls. Ha! Ha! That will keep her from going back on her word again. Only, now I'll have to use ordinary means to make her legal trouble go away. I have a contact who can make the evidence disappear without magic.

"Yet, we still have the tree. The tree controls the things of the earth, and all my formulas come from it. My blue powder worked and my experimental worked before she stopped taking it. I haven't tested this one yet, but with any luck—"

"Luck? Has it come to that, Osmena?"

"It's an expression, Merlin. Oh, they were all quite cross with me and terrified of Hilton the night of the party. But the distillation of that night's long work became my Assumption Formula. Well, they took us by surprise all right, staying out of sight all this time. The VLF: a bit of folklore and local mythology that sensible people dismiss as hype at best, if not downright fiction. They took a page out of our book, you might say."

Osmena raised her head and looked at her brother. "But we will strike back swiftly in the night, from a most unlikely source at that. When we do, Luc Dentremont will disappear forever and the skull will be ours again"

The first order of business was naming Jude an honorary member of GEIST. When the girls clapped for him, he blushed and clowned and bowed, but he was deeply pleased by their unanimous approval. He'd never belonged to anything in his life, not a club, a team, or even an informal group of friends at school, but this seemed right because he felt his heart swell and knew it was the truth. He did belong. Something had happened on the night of the 4th, when they had come together on a moment's notice to stop a terrible thing from happening. Not only had they succeeded without drawing attention to themselves, but they knew from then on, in matters of life and death, they could depend on each other. That was real. It was one thing to sit around a room and share information and speculate about the truth of things; it was another thing to use what you knew and to go out into the world and change things for the better, or at least, keep things from getting worse.

"Speech! Speech!"

"You'll regret it, trust me. Merrilee's a lot better at speeches than I am. She makes at least one at every meeting."

Merrilee raised a pillow and flung it at Jude, end over end, like a big harmless Chinese star. "So that's the thanks I get for nominating you."

Jude sat down under a hail of pillows and boos. "That's one way to get out of giving a speech."

"Weasel," said Sandra.

"Chicken," said Cate.

Merrilee gaveled the meeting with three hard knocks on the floor.

"So, Jude and I have been digging into Osmena Searle's past without much success. This got Jude thinking that Miss Searle had not really been here as long as she'd like everyone to think."

Merrilee pointed to the History of Twin Gaps books on the floor. "Other than two relatively recent features on her, *Vermont Magazine* from 20 years ago and *The Beacon,* 44 years ago, there isn't a lot of public information about her. The thing is, she looks to be in her 50's or 60's in the *Beacon* photo, so if she's still alive—and we have plenty of current sightings—how old might she be? We didn't find much either in the local histories we found at the library, except the purchase of some major acreage for conservation about 35 years ago. What we really wanted to know was when did she first purchase land in Vermont, or had it been in her family for two hundred years? Then I kept reading and found one other reference to her."

Merrilee looked at Jude to register his surprise.

"A mention of the *old Searle place* from the year 1919. That suggests an earlier arrival."

"So I went to the town clerk's like you asked," said Cate. She opened her notebook. "The land her house is on was bought from Cyrus Rafferty about 60 years ago, around 30 acres. Not anytime close to 1919. All the pieces she's bought since then used to be owned by Dentremont, Rafferty, Granger, Smith, Robichaud, Landreaux, Preston and Atwood. Basically everybody who abutted her 30 acres and then some. The biggest piece was the 1,200 acre tract she bought from Dentremont on the back side of Catamount Peak. That's the big one you read about in the history. All told she owns 3,000 acres."

"Who's the Dentremont?" asked Merrilee.

"The J Dentremont Trust."

"What about LaFrance?" Jude asked. "Zephyr said Osmena took her father's land because she wanted something on it."

"There wasn't any land there owned by LaFrance, not then or now."

"But how can that be?" Jude asked.

"Well, maybe Ms. LaFrance got it mixed up. How long ago did it happen?"

"I don't know. I think when she was a girl, because it was right around the time her mother died."

"And who is J Dentremont? And is that Dentremont related to the VLF fugitive Luc?" said Merrilee.

"There's still a pretty big piece of Dentremont land that runs from the end of Osmena's down to the Eastern face of Hidden Mountain. It's also in trust."

"Battle of the conservationists," said Sandra.

"Yeah, and guess who's winning?" said Cate.

"Did it say where Osmena came from?" asked Merrilee, looking at her notes.

"Get this. Greenwich, England." Cate closed her notebook with a satisfied thump.

"She's not from Vermont. I guess we don't have to wait for the results of the birth search," Jude said.

"Not necessarily." Merrilee sat forward with her face in her hands. "She could have been born here and lived overseas for a while. The book did say she travelled to Europe. Maybe she still keeps a place there. She's rich enough."

"But she never owned land here until 60 years ago," said Cate.

"Jet and Aster didn't say she had an English accent. They didn't say she had a Vermont accent either," said Jude.

"She's a witch," said Alison. "Do witches even have accents? For that matter she can probably look any age she wants to."

"If you believe she's a witch," said Merrilee.

"Well, what else would you call somebody who casts spells and sells potions?"

"But people don't actually call her a witch," Sandra said.

Merrilee was ready to move on. "Item 3. The skull. It appeared on the police station roof after the explosion and again in a green firework on the 4th. Did anybody find anything out about it?"

"It's not a logo or the symbol of the VLF. That's a big tree against the backdrop of a mountain," said Sandra.

"Well, what is it then?"

"A threat, like the skull and crossbones on a pirate ship," said Jude.

"What are people saying?" Merrilee said.

"You saw the flag in the circle with the slash through it," Alison said.

21.

A Changing World

"**N**O IFS, ANDS or buts this time. Whatever end were coming has come. You know 'bout all the machinery going dead? Don't every piece of truck and bulldozer conk out at the same time without some mighty big help from somewhere." Dunky LaGro raised a finger to heaven, and then poked it down on the lunch counter to bring home his point.

Hiram Rafferty took to a laughing fit. "Imagine the whole Catamount project come to a stop, just like that. Imagine Greenway's face? Like the hand of God saying, 'Oh no you don't.'"

Dunky winked with sly satisfaction. "Yup, if God spoke sign language. It's Francy's boy givin' 'em the what for, you know. Coming back to set things right. I knew it, he weren't dead."

"You knew. You know nothing except about what you hear."

"Not being found don't make a man dead. Supposed to be that God is dead too; people say it. So take your pick when it comes to who shut down those machines. About now, Greenway wants whoever done it dead."

"Yup. Maybe, but it ain't all about Greenway," Hiram said.

Mrs. Samms set their coffees on the counter and leaned toward them on her elbows. "I'll say. There's big trouble for some folks. Why Becky Gage—"

"Becky Cadaret," Don Samms corrected her from the store room.

"She'll always be Becky Gage to me, and given the number of times she's been married and divorced I don't know why she bothers to change her name."

Hiram and Dunky chuckled and rocked in their stools.

"Well, Becky works at the bank, and she says something's gotten into the computers and everything is all a big mess. The accounts are all wrong."

"Is why I ain't ever put my money in the bank. Can't trust 'em," Hiram said.

"You ain't ever had much piss to put in that pot."

"Dunky!" Mrs. Samms pointed a finger at him. "It'll be on the news by tonight I bet, but you shush about it for now. I don't want Becky in any trouble."

"Can't trust computers neither," Hiram said.

"Couldn't use one if you had a mind to." Dunky was grinning and riding him hard.

"Will you feed him something, Dodie, to shut him up?"

"I'm telling you it ain't like the computers crashed." Dodie Samms leaned in closer and whispered, "The money is changing hands. People who can hardly rub two cents together have thousands in their accounts, but folks with money ain't so lucky. Oh, it's going to be a mess when it comes out."

Hiram shook his head. "It ain't right to steal from a man 'cause he's rich."

"Rich man's way of stealin' is called tax law. Poor man's way is just called a crime."

"Well, I know Francy and Francy never stole from nobody. That weren't his way."

Dunky pointed a knobby finger at him. "You never had much use for Francy when he was living; but if it wasn't for him and his like, people like me would still be workin' factory six days a week, 12 hours a day, with no benefits, no vacation, and could be fired on the spot if we so much as complained about a broke machine."

Hiram made his sourest face. With his little oblong head and gap toothed gums he looked like a lemon sucking itself. He waved a hand at Dunky. "On a farm you work 14 hours a day, 7 days a week and you don't get no vacation."

"Ain't the same and you know it. You get some rest in winter and at least no one can fire you. Trouble is you been walking in cow pies so long you can't smell what's rotten in the world. Never could. About time there was a little evening-up for folks around here. And you'd think so too about now if you had any sense. Getting riches like Greenway's got riches requires a kind of stealing. Just look at that farm he were after. What if it were your land?"

"I'd shoot him dead between the eyes if he took what were mine. But, he offered to pay those folk for it," Hiram said.

"They ain't obliged to sell, no matter what he offered."

"For what I hear he offered I sure as hell would've sold. You heard him talk. Some sense to what he says, even with his flatlander ways. Wouldn't be no factories or jobs without rich folk. Nothing in the world would get done neither."

"Nothing, if all that needed done was screwing folk."

"Darn it Jet," Aster muttered under her breath. The gas gage was courting empty. "You were going to put gas in when you went to the parts store yesterday." She had to go around the corner on Route 17 just beyond the village because the Mobil was nothing but blackened debris.

Gas prices were going through the roof again. Aster pulled up to the pump and reached inside her purse for her wallet. She had all of two dollars in cash. Two dollars' worth wouldn't get her home and back to work again tomorrow. That clutch of money trouble grabbed her right in the middle of her gut and in her chest. It made her sick in the stomach and sweaty with panic all at once. She couldn't put it on the bank card without checking the account first, so she drove back to U Street and went in to the ATM. She stuck her card in, punched the code, chose balance inquiry and held her breath. The machine rumbled and hummed—chicka-chicka-chicka-chicka-zip. Out came the little white ticket upside down. How discreet banks were when it came to giving you bad news. She inhaled and turned the slip over. Then she screamed.

⌘ ⌘ ⌘

S TEMPLE FOUND HIMSELF listening in on conversations with greater frequency since the trouble on the 4th, as if his powers of hearing had increased five-fold at the spur of necessity, like an evolutionary response. A domestic heard and saw many things he wasn't supposed to in the execution of his duties, especially when, like himself, he was confined to the small world of an estate. Mr. Greenway—here with Calvin for an unusually long visit—was clearly agitated, and, well, if he used the word 'helpless' aloud to describe his present state, no doubt he would have been horsewhipped by Hilton on the spot and demoted to cleaning toilets. When it came to Osmena, if the word 'frail', the most apt for her appearance of late, had escaped his lips, even in a tone of sympathy, he'd just as quickly be confined to a catamount cage on bread and water rations for a week.

Stemple heard mentions of water, a complete stoppage of work on the Catamount Estates and a setback at Gemini Farm, but the mood of anxiety and intimations of trouble left Stemple frustrated, because he had no knowledge of their substance.

Then there was Mister Calvin, butting heads with his father over who knows what. It was a mercy Stemple had found Calvin after the party—passed out and naked in the grass beside a starlet—before Mr. Greenway arrived, or things might be worse. The boy did everything Mr. Greenway asked of him, but he simply could not help his open and spontaneous nature.

Stemple thought of Orest at that age, risking Osmena's wrath by leaving his post at more than one of her parties to pursue his latest love or lust, and how, when Osmena finally caught him at it, she did not chastise him, but then began to use him in that capacity on occasions when she required a seduction to get her way. Orest didn't know for a long time that it had been a punishment, because of the privileges it granted him, but when being intimate often meant being false, it taught his soul to be untrue. How could he blame Orest for wanting to be free of it?

Stemple tried not to think so much of his brother. It didn't matter how different they were, how differently corrupted their souls—Orest from the misuse of his affection; Oliver from the complete deprivation of its use—the farther in opposite directions their deformities led them in Osmena's service, the more they'd relied upon each other. It was the one real intimacy either of them knew, the only antidote for the poison she'd forced on them, and the bond that allowed brother to forgive brother for possessing in surfeit the virtue the other wholly lacked.

Yet, Orest had left him here, cut the cord that kept his lonely soul afloat in the spiral of Osmena's design—the beautiful, beguiling and deathly Cosmos. He used to call out in his head and implore his brother, *Why didn't you take me! Come back for me! Come back for me!*

In the beginning, when Orest was not apprehended and returned, there was a time when Stemple felt thrilled at his brother's brave act and knew he would return for him one day. Of course he'd had to escape, find help on the outside to liberate them. Six months passed, then a year, then three, and still he cried out for Orest in his heart. By then hope had turned to despair, and admiration to anger. The one who had been there with him his whole life, brother, confidant, friend, had left him alone in Osmena's grip forever. Where once there'd been pleas, now there were recriminations in his head. *Did you not care for a soul but your own? What about me? All of us here against our wills? How can you consider yourself at liberty until I am also free?*

Even if Orest had escaped into the world, there was no guarantee he'd been safe there either. Anything could have happened to him. Yet, the silence surrounding his name and his escape had always been a sign to Stemple of Osmena and Merlin's defeat. No rumor of his demise had ever reached his ear, and there wasn't any story, if it was circulating among the servants, that didn't eventually reach him. No, that silence was an admission. The look on Hilton's face that night had been proof. His air of smug efficiency was jarred by the clenching of his jaw. His eyes were wild with confusion, his body drenched in the sweat of futile exertion.

Then, life went on at the Cosmos as if Orest had never existed. Only Osmena had not forgotten. Her pointed remarks on the night of the party indicated her mistrust, concealed in compliments. If only Stemple knew what lay behind all the whispers and snippets he heard. He dared not think it, but even now a flicker of hope almost too dim and too intangible to grasp stirred in him.

⌘　⌘　⌘

J ESSE AND CALVIN peeled off their shirts. They stood on the dock in their shorts for a minute looking down at the water.

"Is it cold?"

"It isn't warm," said Jesse. "But it's not Granger Falls either."

"I've been there. It's cold but I love that place."

"Ready?"

Calvin looked around, squinting into the reflected brightness of the water and smiling. "Is it okay if I go in skinny?"

"Yeah, sure. Junie and I always swim that way—unless Willa's around. I just didn't think—"

"I know. But, it's one of my favorite things."

"Mine too."

"Water feels like silk."

"Feels free."

The boys dropped their shorts and kicked them away.

"Ready? Count of three. One. Two. Three."

Jesse and Calvin dove in, disappeared and then resurfaced in bright liquid gleams, for a moment more water than flesh, like sprites forming at the touch of air. They swam a few times across the length of the pond to get warm and then hovered in the middle together treading.

"I love water," said Calvin. "How it feels, tastes, looks. We have to drink it, but we can't breathe it. It's so common and still a mystery. We need it to live, and yet it's dangerous. If I could I'd live in the water, I think I would. But something warmer than this."

Jesse laughed. "Come on, let's warm up on the dock."

Calvin pulled himself out of the water first and Jesse saw the full tattoo on his back.

"Wow. How long did that take to do?"

Calvin looked over his shoulder at his back and then down at Jesse. "Too many hours; and it's not finished." He hoisted himself up to a sit, pulled one knee in, and let his free leg dangle over the edge of the dock in the water. Jesse got out and sat beside him with both feet gently stirring the pond. "At least, I'm not sure if it's finished. Somebody told me I should leave it as it is. I'm thinking about it."

Jesse looked out across the water. "I don't usually like tattoos to be honest; most of them look like people bumped up against the funny pages and it came off on them. All the color. Yours looks natural like a second skin." He leaned back and closer to Calvin to inspect the details. "The different colors in the catamount's fur are amazing. I've never seen a tattoo that looked so real. The tail looks like you could reach out and grab it."

"If you could, it wouldn't hurt as much as the tattoo did. The closest thing to Trompe l'oeil in tattoo art. Painful in every detail. But maybe that's what I am: a masochist."

Jesse looked at him, puzzled. "A what?"

Calvin raised his eyebrows, as if about to explain, then let them fall and shook his head. "Nothing. Just daddy issues." The faint musing smile returned. "You guys have a spring or a drilled well?"

"Both. Why?"

"I told you I love water. I'm a connoisseur and I'm thirsty. Lead me to it."

"Sure. But let's take another dip first. I'm getting hot again already."

Jude came out of his room when he heard Aster's yelp in the kitchen. She was holding up a white slip of paper and running in circles around the kitchen.

"If you're going to pee or have puppies the bathroom's free actually."

Aster stopped running and pointed at him. "Normally you'd be grounded for a smart remark like that, but I'm so happy I'm just going to let it slide today."

Aster yelped again. "Where's your father?"

"Out behind the Incubus working on the next great mode of transportation, where else?"

Aster took her white stub and danced out the door.

"This ought to be good." Jude followed her.

Jet was sweating, covered with grease and stripped to his boxers. He looked up at Aster's latest spontaneous yelp. "Aster, what the? Jude? Is she having seizures?"

Jude pointed at his ear and drew circles. Usually when Aster found Jet working in a state of precarious undress, as Grandmother Meades called it, there was hell to pay for the bad example he set. Although around here— with all the cussing, smoking, drinking, futile tinkering, pathological junk collecting and now consulting with witches going on—it was damn, sorry, darn near impossible to tell if a good example ever got set.

Aster looked about ready to burst, and, as there wasn't much room to move, she jumped up and down in place like a game show contestant.

"Aw, you ain't gone and got the spirit again have you?" Jet said.

Aster shook her head.

"Well, spit it out woman."

Jude stepped up from behind and snatched the slip from Aster's jubilant grasp.

"Don't you dare!" Aster turned around and grabbed the slip away so fast Jude almost fell backward into the Incubus. "This is my good news young man, and you are not going to spoil it!"

Aster turned back to Jet and flourished the slip. "There's almost two thousand dollars in our bank account. I paid the bills last week and nearly every one of them has already hit. There's no way there should be that much. There's never that much."

"Well, I'll be. Do you suppose it's a mistake?"

"Of course it's a mistake."

Jude ventured a step forward. "Is anybody here going to take the moral high ground and tell the bank, or do I have to call?"

"Young man, you pick up a phone to call that bank and you will be so grounded your friends will have to come visit you in the cemetery."

"Now that's grounded," said Jet. "Jude, don't vex your mother."

"It's a joke. Jeeze. Well, if you're hell bent on spending it, shouldn't you, like, go buy some food before somebody notices?"

"I already did, the groceries are in the car; and gas, a full tank. I bought milk and cheese and fresh vegetables—and steaks for a cook out Jet, rib eye steaks, and some for the freezer. But there I was in the store and I heard a couple of other ladies talking about it too. Something's going on with all the money. It's a mistake, but it's not an accident. A Robin Hood effect. That's what the woman called it."

⌘ ⌘ ⌘

S TEMPLE BROUGHT OSMENA'S afternoon tea into the parlor. Until today she'd been taking it outside in the tropical garden—her exotic patio of rarities that went outside from mid-June to late-August—but she'd complained of feeling sapped by the humidity and wanted to revive herself in the air conditioned parlor. In all his life, he'd never seen her so much as grow moist with perspiration on her forehead, be it in a trying situation, or on the hottest day of summer. He couldn't help the sudden magnanimity he felt toward her, which was overcompensation for his pleasure at her frailty.

"Is Madam certain she does not want iced tea this afternoon?"

"High tea is high tea, Stemple. If you bring me iced tea it will be the last tea you serve. Now, pour and go away you foolish man."

"It's just that Madam's color is—"

"Is what?"

"Madam is rather pale."

"It's the yellow in my caftan; it washes me out. I am perfectly fine."

"Of course. I see my mistake. Madam's color is fine. Forgive me." Stemple poured her tea and backed away deferentially. "If Madam needs anything at all."

"Stemple?"

"Yes, Madam?"

"When your brother—left, did he ever mention the reason?"

A trap. "Madam, if I had known my brother had plans to leave I would have done everything in my power to dissuade him."

"Yes, of course, Stemple. I meant did he say anything before he left that, in retrospect, might have been telling? Or suspicious?"

"Madam knows what my brother did to the garden, and how he must have feared your just displeasure."

"But, if he were unhappy with anything, surely he would have mentioned it to you."

Stemple stood holding the tray, perfectly still and silent, as if he'd been asked to stand guard rather than called upon to answer a question.

"You needn't fear to answer," Osmena said.

"My brother, Madam," said Stemple with a slight bow to her, "if I may be frank, was not happy with the way his affections were—used. He didn't need to say it. I saw it in him. But, that was five years ago. Why does Madam ask me this today? Is something wrong?"

Osmena's expression turned poisonous.

"Yes. Somebody has vandalized all the machinery at Mr. Greenway's project site."

"What would I know about such things, Madam?"

"You know your brother. Given his penchant for destruction, I can't help wondering if he is somehow behind this. If you know anything of his where-abouts, or his designs, now is the time to speak."

Stemple cleared his throat several times for fear the thrill rising in it would come leaping out in laughter. "Madam knows my brother's disappear-ance has been a great sorrow to me. It is I who have wished, often, to ask if you know of his whereabouts."

"I see."

A hard rapping on the door startled Stemple and nearly caused him to drop his tray.

"Yes?"

"Hilton, Madam; may I come in?"

"Come in, yes; break down the door, no."

Stemple moved aside as Hilton strode in.

"Madam, all de carousels are broken now and—"

Osmena held up her hand to stop Hilton. "Stemple, you may go."

Jesse and Calvin were still wet and dripping on the farmer's porch when Junie came out of the house. Jesse's hair was water dark and slick. Calvin's buzz had a silky seal's gloss. Their arms and chests were all goose flesh, and they wore sleepy, wistful looks from the afternoon sun warming their bodies after the cold swim. But their shorts were only patchy wet.

Junie turned his back on them and stood on the edge of the porch, rock-ing on the balls of his feet.

"Water was great, man," Calvin said. "You should have come in with us."

"You didn't ask me," Junie said. He held onto the post and looked back over his shoulder. "Just like you took Jesse for a ride on your motorcycle and didn't ask me."

The screen door opened with a creak and Raeanne came out just in time to hear the remark. Junie turned around, his mouth ajar. Jesse stood up. Calvin sat forward in his chair, forearms on his thighs, head down.

"What is this, about a ride on a motorcycle? Jesse?"

Calvin stood up. "After you signed the petition, Mrs. Meades, I took Jesse for a quick ride on my chopper. It was my fault. I'm the one who asked him. I'm older and should have known better. He wore my helmet and I was super careful. It'll never happen again."

Strangely, Raeanne didn't feel that upset about what Jesse had done, but she was exasperated at how she'd had to find out. She threw up her hands. "Why is it that everybody around here seems hell bent on keeping secrets." She picked up the laundry basket beside the porch door and marched off across the lawn to the clothes line.

"I can't believe you told," Jesse started in on Junie. "What is wrong with you?"

"What's wrong with me? How can you even ask that? How can you act like you don't know?"

"We'll deal with the broken carousels in due course, Hilton. They are just symptoms of our problem. I want you to think back very carefully to the night Orest disappeared. There is something we missed. Gerard LaFrance most certainly knew about the tree, but he knew nothing of the skull. And the only way that any-body could have learned about it and could have come prepared to take it was with the aid of an insider. Tell me, Hilton, how many people know about the skull?"

"Mr. Greenway, you, Mister Calvin and me."

"And Calvin was only told after he turned sixteen."

"Madam, you cannot think that I—"

"I think nothing of the kind. Orest is the only one to have escaped from here, and everybody thinks he left because of what he did to the garden. But, what if he found out about the skull?"

"Madam, I never let de words pass my lips."

"There is the map and the legend."

"Madam, only you and Mr. Greenway know where it is kept."

"So he or I would have had to tell."

"Madam, what are you saying?"

Osmena made no reply. She held up her hand as if to collect her thoughts, but she knew the answer already. There had been a solstice party that year—smaller and more intimate than her party on the 4th. As sunset neared, all her guests, herself included, had partaken of an elixir she'd prepared to heighten the experience. It was not something she ever did—indulge in her own chemical solutions—but the air was so mild and fragrant, the sky so soft and limitless in its reach, that she succumbed to the vague desire for something she barely apprehended, the kind of thing that summoned people to her door even at their own peril and great cost.

The elixir not only made Osmena feel euphoric, but also amorous. When she saw Orest with some guests touring the gardens, the vague desire fixed powerfully on him. What Stemple said this afternoon brought it all back to her, and brought with it the truth that in casting him all those years as an object of desire for others, she had both satisfied and removed him as the object of her own affection: he pleased others at her command. But that night all would change.

Osmena had called Orest away from the guests and in to the parlor. They sat side by side at the piano. She played soft, tentative chords. He unconsciously fingered a melody to follow her, but it fell into dissonance and he stopped.

"A good host never says, 'no'," Osmena had reminded him.

"On one condition."

"You are not in a place to name conditions."

Orest got up from the bench and walked around the piano and faced her. "Sometimes you ask too much of me."

"Is it so much to ask?"

"I've done everything you've ever asked."

A chord was quietly reverberating. She took her foot off the pedal and it stopped. "What is it then? Your condition?"

"Take Lethex, so you will not remember it when it's done."

"Dear poor Orest. What is the point of doing a thing, if you can't recall its pleasure?"

"It is a thing that exists only in the pure present, and then exists no more. It is better for me not to think of it; better for you should you repeat it; it would always feel like the first time."

Osmena had checked the label of the bottle Orest retrieved from the apothecary, and she'd watched him add it to each glass of wine. Had she gotten more than she bargained for that night? She had been too willing to believe in his vulnerability—her power over him—to doubt his motive, and failed to recognize the opportunity she'd presented him. Yet, he'd returned so quickly she'd neither suspected him of mischief, nor believed him capable of thinking so quickly. Perhaps he'd plotted his revenge long before and had seized the chance she'd unwittingly given him. In any event, they had both partaken of it, so Osmena had foreseen no danger.

Osmena tried to recall it as it was, not as she had now come to envision it. There was something. What? Orest had added the drops to one glass of wine. And then? A sneeze. Orest sneezed. As it overtook him, he capped the bottle so not to spill it, and then reached into his left trouser pocket for a tissue, but he couldn't get there in time for the second sneeze. He turned his head into his right sleeve. This time the right hand went down into his pants pocket and found the tissue. He blew his nose and put the tissue back in his pocket. The bottle was in his left hand, but he had never transferred it from his right hand. He unscrewed it and added the drops to the second glass of wine. His glass. He drank from it quickly, as if to obliterate as much of the night as possible, but what he'd really done was mark the glass as his. Then, he came around to the piano bench and handed her the other glass. He raised it and said, "Have you ever played a game called Truth or Dare?" They clinked glasses and sipped. "To truth or dare then," she'd said. The last thing she remembered was the touch of his hand and his kiss on her lips before she drank.

A Judas kiss. Now Osmena understood what Orest meant by truth or dare, and what he'd done. He had pulled off a switch and she'd been none the wiser. How cunning and ingenious to slip something (perhaps Veritas formula?) in with the Lethex. So she would reveal the secret of her power and its location and then forget she'd ever told him. The second bottle, that spiked his glass, would have been nothing except water.

"That snake. That Judas," Osmena said at last.

"Madam?"

"Tell me again what happened when you came upon that accident in the Gap."

"It was a dreadful hot night, Madam. De forest as thick and still as a jungle. De cats were on his scent, but I had no way to know how far ahead he was. Den I saw light trough de trees. I made de cats stay and I went closer. It was fire, Madam, and when I got to de roads edge I saw it was a car wrecked into a tree dat was on fire. Standing off from it was two men with yellow hair."

"Yellow hair? Blonde you mean?"

"Yes, Madam. Deir car was faced de other way like dey had come upon it. I stayed hid. De one man made a call on de cell phone. De younger one was crying. Den I saw dere was a body in de burning car. A terrible sight, Madam. And den dey got in deir car and drove down de mountain toward de village.

"I went to get de cats and came back with dem to de road, but dey would not go on. At first I tought dey were afraid of de fire, but den I knew de trail of his scent had ended. He had hitched a ride to get away."

"Do you think they were hiding him? The two men?"

"Madam, I do not think it possible. Deir car was an open Jeep. Even in de fire light I could see de interior. And people act a certain way when dey are aware of another presence. Dey did not look back to de car, Madam. Not once."

"That wreck. Why is that familiar? The Corgan boy, of course. I had to listen to the whole tale when they came for a spell. Peculiar, sorrowful people. They keep cropping up these days like plug nickels in your purse when you need change at a toll booth."

"What do you suppose caused de boy to crash?"

"Well, you know something jumped out of the woods at him, a deer or moose, or—"

Osmena set down her tea. "Orest?"

22.

Present Dangers

A NOTHER FLASH OF lightning pierced the window and lit the walls of Jude's room, but it was soundless heat lightning. He wished it would rain to cool things down and wash away the dust. Even with the fan blowing on him, he was damp with sweat, restless and unable to sleep. In the night stillness, smells came over him, familiar and yet so strange that he was forced to notice them. The sharp, sour smell of the wood's edge, ripening grass, like spices, the watery air and everything it touched in his room—bed sheets, paper, the metallic dirt smell of his blue jeans draped on a chair, the sweat on his upper lip, the oily potato chip smell of his nose, as if he, too, were dispersing into the night air—all of it became part of what was now, and then, in a flash like déjà vu, part of the past. What was it he remembered? A night like this the summer before Kennedy died.

That night there were real storms rolling down the valleys. It was so hot the Corgans had cooked out and just stayed out long past dark, as if daring and waiting for some rain to cool them down.

Jet and Kennedy had cleared space at the top of the driveway and rolled out a big square of indoor outdoor carpeting, like a makeshift lawn, and had set up chairs and a long table on the space. Jude remembered how nice it felt to walk around barefoot in that square of green without fear of broken glass or rusty nails for once.

Supper was over, but there was still a faint glow and wavering of heat coming off the grill. The torches around them burned citronella and the warm lemony smell of it washed over them like a protective field, now and then mixing with barbequed rib fat when a bit would drip and sizzle in the coals. Jet and Aster had stuck to soda that night, and they were feeling pretty good without the Captain in those days.

It was so hot the Corgans all stripped down to boxers. Even Aster just had on a pair of Jet's boxers worn with a camisole. Jude hadn't felt self-conscious either then, as he hadn't gone from being "husky" to outright "fat".

Kennedy had a six string guitar and knew some chords, and so they'd sung some corny campfire songs and railroad ditties until they were pretty silly and just about hoarse.

Jet picked up the Coleman lantern and started shining it around on their boxer fronts and imitating Grandmother Meades. "Now you all put some clothes on."

Aster laughed. "Oh, Jet, stop that." But she didn't mean it as anything but encouragement for him to go on.

"I come over and this is how you greet your Grandma? In a state of precarious undress?"

That was Grandma Meades' favorite condemnation of inappropriate attire.

Aster took to a laughing fit, cackling like a loon, but soon she lost her breath and was gasping like an asthmatic.

Kennedy popped up out of his chair with the guitar strapped on, like he'd gotten a hot idea, and started to strum in a fast-walking, locomotive rhythm. He began to talk-sing some lyrics.

"Their whole yard is a pig sty; a blight I must confess; what makes it worse, and the neighbors curse is precarious undress.

"Jet's hanging out of his underwear; oh, who can bear to watch; before you know it, oh my God; he's scratching 'round his crotch.

"Precarious undress; precarious undress; so come on join the family in this god forsaken mess."

"Whooh!" Aster slapped her knee and then began to clap in rhythm.

Jet danced over to the grill, grabbed the spatula and metal lid and began to drum in time. Kennedy kept strumming the chord sequence, but he looked stuck on the next lyric.

Jet held up a finger and began a new verse in Grandmother Meades' voice.

"*I can't believe my daughter; married in the Corgan clan; uncouth, uncut, uncultured; is he beast or is he man?*

"*It's bad enough they're dirty, poor and just plain old depressed; bad enough that we're related, but precarious undress?*

Jet and Kennedy sang the chorus together this time, with Jude and Aster clapping and laughing along.

Kennedy slowed the tempo down and shushed their clapping and drumming. Jet held up his hand, as if a verse was forming, and then he nodded when it came.

"*In the end of days, we'll change our ways; clean up our sinful mess, and God in all his wisdom will rapture up the rest.*"

"Uh—"

Now Jet was stuck. Kennedy picked up the thread.

"*No butt crack shows, or cleavage lows; goodbye open flies and bare white thighs.*"

Kennedy stilled the guitar and the music stopped. Then he started up at the faster tempo and finished the verse. "*But they're here to stay, in the present day of precarious undress.*

"*Precarious undress; precarious undress; so come on join the family in this god forsaken mess; precarious undress; precarious undress; we've nothing left to lose but clothes; we're nearly naked to our toes; this all or nothing really blows; precarious undress.*"

Kennedy changed up the chords and finished with a square dance rhythm. He motioned for Jet to put down his drums and Jude to stand up with them. He turned his back to Aster and they did the same.

"*So grab your waistband, round you go; and moon your mamma, down they go; one, two, three, four—precarious undress.*"

A clatter of metal interrupted Jude's reverie. Somebody or something was outside coming toward the trailer. He sat up in bed. Outside his room he heard footsteps in the hall. A line of light appeared under his door. Jet and Aster must have heard it too.

Jude got up, pulled on his pants and went out to the kitchen.

Jet was dressed, holding a flashlight in one hand, a rifle in the other. Aster was in a camisole and boxer shorts.

"Something's out there. You stay in here with your mother."

Jet went out. Jude and Aster paid no attention. They followed him out the door and stood on the metal steps, staring out into the dark.

There was another clatter, farther away. Jet shined the light, but the beam only went so far in the darkness. Then a flash of lightning lit up the night, just long enough for them to see a masked man running away into the woods beyond the Cascades.

Jet ran off after him.

"Jet, you'll kill yourself. He's already gone."

It was too late. In a moment, all Jude and Aster could see of Jet was the beam of the flashlight bouncing off the junk heaps before it disappeared into the woods. The rifle fired once and Aster jumped. Jude almost fell off the step.

"Jesus, Jet!"

"Taking the Lord's name in vain will get you nowhere."

"Hush your smart mouth for once. This is serious."

Aster and Jude waited in the quiet for what seemed a long time. Then the beam flashed out of the woods at them, steady now and growing brighter as Jet approached. He shined the light up at the trailer and saw them standing on the steps.

"Couldn't see who it was, so I fired a shot up in the air just to scare the wits out of 'em."

"You scared the wits out of us, is more like it," Aster said.

"I thought I told you to stay inside? Don't anybody listen to a man around here?"

"Depends on the man," Aster and Jude said at the same time. They looked at each other and then back at Jet.

"You're a thankless lot. I'm going back to bed."

⌘ ⌘ ⌘

THREE MEN RODE slowly in a truck through the pass of Hidden Mountain to the old logging road on the back side of Catamount Peak. They were on their way to meet up with a supply truck.

Jake Allard drove, Gus Penrod sat on the passenger side, and Pascal Dupre sat in between.

"You heard him say it. When he puts everything right he wants to destroy the skull, all because two of Greenway's puppets died trying to bulldoze the home of a decent family. I only wish Greenway had been in the seat of a bulldozer that day."

"It ain't right." Gus Penrod shook his head. "He can't be trusted and we're right to act while there's still time."

"As if you can put something right once and for all and it's going to stay that way without the power there to back it up," Pascal said.

"But he won't listen to sense." Allard banged the steering wheel with his hand. "He thinks he won't need the skull once people see how good things are."

"People will have nothing to say about it when the Feds swoop in to take everything away. And then it will all have been for nothing. You think they'll stand for people being free?"

"Or untaxed? Unwatched? Unlicensed?" Pascal added.

"Don't forget uncensored," Allard said.

"And without the skull they'll be unprotected too."

The deadfall was up ahead. Jake stopped the truck. He looked at his watch, waited one more minute and then unclipped a remote control device from the truck visor. He pointed it and clicked a button. There was an underground rumble and a steady hissing sound. The dead fall rose a foot above the ground. The rising hum quit, and then the big hydraulic lift stopped. Jake hit another button and now the entire deadfall—a massive and masterful carpentry of chaos by design—moved en masse and swung open like a gate on jointed arms. Chet Atwood was there with the supply truck. Jake drove out and stopped beside him.

Atwood had been quiet at the meeting where Luc announced his plan to eventually destroy the skull, but word was, it had been Chet's influence—his reaction to Greenway's men dying—that had caught Luc's ear and swayed him to succumb to fear. It was just as it had been back in their school days. When the going got tough, Chet Atwood got scared, but unlike then—while Gerard LaFrance yet lived—he'd succeeded in poisoning Luc with his fear.

Jake leaned out the window. "Be careful on your way down the mountain."

"Ye-uh? What's going on?"

"Squirrels. If one darts across the road you might have to swerve into a tree to avoid it."

Chet turned his head and stared ahead for a moment. Then he turned again to Jake, and spit out the open window. "Is that all?"

Jake didn't answer but grabbed the door handle and climbed down from the drivers' seat, stepping just wide of where Chet had spit and waited. Chet got down and had no choice but to step where he had spit, or once more look like a man possessed of petty fears.

The men switched trucks in a matter of seconds. Chet drove the empty truck away. Allard drove in, closed the deadfall behind him and started back to the compound with the supplies.

"So who is with Luc on this?" Penrod said.

"Landreaux, EG, Sokol, and Atwood, but Chet won't be a problem or any of the guys on the outside. After the meeting they'll just go their way. A lot of the men agree with us. Eventually Luc will see it's the only way. After we put things right our way."

"What if he doesn't come around?" said Pascal.

"Right now he's afraid of ending up like Osmena—using power to keep power rather than using it to do good. That's why we trust him, because we know he wants what's best, but even to presume to know what's best assumes the kind of power he wants to avoid. And this isn't the time to second guess what we've planned for so long, or to pass up the chance we have. It'll never come again." Allard tightened his grip on the steering wheel. "I'm split in two. I've known Luc since we were boys and have been through thick and thin with him, but how can I betray our principles in favor of the man? It's not his to decide for all of us. Where's the liberty in that? It should've gone to a vote as I wanted, but I'm not an equal—a foster brother yet, who, when real decisions are to be made, should be lucky to be included at all. How has anything changed?"

"What if we can't get the skull?" said Penrod.

Allard said, "I've prepared an incantation to neutralize Osmena. She and Greenway will be as harmless against us as one of their bowing servants, but

I need the chance to lay my hands on the skull early Saturday, so that our purpose will be set in motion even before the meeting."

"What are they doing down in the wood lot anyway?" said Junie.

Raeanne didn't miss a beat snapping green beans when she looked across the kitchen table at her son. "Calvin's interested in water and they're trying to find a spring with Haggai Zenger's dowsing rods; the ones we found in the old barn when we first moved here."

"It seems weird to me. Why doesn't he go find water in his own yard? And dowsing is a lot of bunk anyway. I read that the way you have to hold the rod tires out the muscles in your hands and causes a downward jerk, eventually. And just about anywhere you dig in Vermont, you'll find water."

"But it's just for fun, don't you think? Something to do on a hot day."

"This is something to do on a hot day."

Raeanne stopped snapping. "Are you upset they didn't ask you?"

Junie looked down at the bean in his hand. "They never ask me."

"You know, you and your brother are going to have families of your own someday. You aren't always going to be together and do everything together, even as close you are."

"It just feels..." Junie swallowed. "Did I do something wrong? That Jesse doesn't want to hang around with me?"

"Of course not. When you and Jesse are together you have a way of making other people disappear."

Junie looked up at his mother, not sure what she meant by it.

"I mean, you have a way of communicating and being together that sometimes excludes other people. Not in a bad or rude way. It's just a measure of how close you are. Jesse maybe doesn't know how to be with you and Calvin without excluding Calvin. He might not even have thought about it the way I'm saying it. It could be he sensed it, like judging whether a stream is too wide for you to jump across."

"So I'm excluded."

"Maybe for now, but it'll all work out in time. It might speed things up if you talk to him about it."

Junie shook his head. "I think it's Calvin who doesn't want me around. I mean, why did he choose Jesse and not me? We look just the same."

"Look the same is right; but you are not the same, never have been and never will be. Maybe this is the first step in finding that out. More than likely it was just circumstance; they met first and hit it off. Calvin seems perfectly nice. He's certainly been very polite to you."

"Yeah. So polite it—"

Raeanne squinted, trying to recall an impression she'd had but couldn't quite express before. "So polite it has almost the opposite effect?"

"Exactly."

Calvin looked over his shoulder, but Jesse was up ahead of him now about fifty yards to the left and still intent on his stick. Calvin had chosen to walk along the old cellar hole. He carried the stick as he was told, but he was focused on the legend his father had shown him in the parlor and on the landscape where it was hidden, not on the rod in his hands. He'd been here in the woods with Jesse twice before and had yet to find the likeness in the clue: *Four square stones in a wood were placed; and from whose heart were equal spaced; a well spring lost should 'ere be found; whereon you tread is holy ground; blessed and long is the life of he; who builds upon eternity* For all he knew the markers had long been knocked down and buried like the ornate seal.

Calvin was tired of walking around in circles looking for what was lost and long gone, if it had ever existed at all. He walked over to the cellar hole. It was built between two berms, and the walls built against the berms were the only two intact. The parallel side walls, where the mounds sloped away, had stood free above ground, and so had come down most likely when the old house had been demolished. Most of the stone must have been hauled away and reused, because there were only a few large mossy stones half buried by the decay of the seasons and half heaved by frost.

Calvin climbed the berm and walked the edge of the wall toe to heal to measure it. Just about 24 feet. He then came back to the middle. The berm walls made it easier to imagine the basic footprint. It looked like a twenty-four foot square. Four square. Four walls. Four corners. Four stones...*in a wood were placed...and from whose heart were equal spaced.* Who built his house in a perfect square? A man who loved symmetry. A man who built upon eternity. Calvin looked down at the center of the cellar hole and pointed his forked dowsing stick. He heard a voice, but didn't turn or heed it. A moment later there was Jesse standing on the berm beside him.

"Hey, water witch, did you find anything?"

Calvin handed Jesse his dowsing stick. "Nothing happened."

"Junie always says dowsing is a lot of bunk."

"Sorry. Kind of a waste of time, huh?" Calvin said.

"It's alright. I've always wanted to see if it really worked."

⌘   ⌘   ⌘

WHAT COULD BE duller than a hot summer afternoon in Twin Gaps? Nothing, it seemed, if you asked Ben Tulley and Nolan Roderick on that last day of July that summer. It was as if the heat had restrained even the incorrigible from venturing out to do mischief. Technically, you could always find something amiss: speeders in the twenty-five mile an hour school zone (even though school was out); an expired emissions sticker; even better, a DWT (driving while texting). This was precisely what the day had reduced them to, each on opposite sides of the village, at corresponding points of speed reduction. Yet, everybody seemed to be on the up and up. Stickers up to date, plenty of cell phones in use, but no texting, and speeds in a reasonable range.

Sergeant Roderick was so confounded he'd stooped to talking with Officer Ben on his cell phone to bemoan the lack of traffic violations. Well, talking 'to' Officer Ben was more like it. With the dismissal of the charges against Zephyr LaFrance on his mind, it was even easier than usual to ignore Tulley's occasional comments. The evidence—both the frosting from the crime scene and the blue powder from her house—had been lost. Lost! (As if he'd just misplaced his finger when he lost it.) The evidence was thought to have been left where a cleaning person had mistakenly disposed of it. It didn't matter what the story was, he knew Osmena was behind it, as surely as she'd been the one to post Zephyr's bail. Not even a sleepless night at a county jail for her. It was over before they'd even had time to transfer her.

Roderick felt his attention melting in the heat, and swallowed up by the growing ache in his lower back. Each passing day brought him closer to the boiling point about Osmena, but he had Greenway shouting in his other ear about the VLF. He wanted to bring Osmena down, and also knew that whatever favor she'd done for Zephyr had a hefty price attached. So, he was torn between his plan to expose the VLF and his desire to keep an eye on Zephyr, get close enough to read that price tag, and catch Osmena at something nefarious. He wanted to put the cuffs on her so tight she'd lose permanent feeling in her boney hands.

Officer Ben finally sensed Roderick's distraction. "You're upset about that evidence, I bet. It ain't the first time they've lost stuff over there."

"If you believe that."

"Sergeant Sir, why do you want Ms. LaFrance to get in so much trouble? She's a really nice lady. It's seems like all she did was help that boy pass the fourth grade."

"Well, she broke the law and she didn't do it alone."

"Who helped her then, sir? No one else was charged."

"You think Ms. LaFrance is a first class chemist as well as everybody's favorite teacher? Only one person could have helped her. That's who I want. But if we don't get Zephyr, we don't get Osmena."

"There's a rumor, sir, that's how you lost your finger. Some deal you made with Osmena gone wrong."

That was all Roderick could take. He pulled out and headed into the village. "Sir, are you there?" He was not going to complain about what he got in the bargain, but then it wasn't easy getting along without one of his fingers, living with that maddening sensation: the illusion of feeling where there was only thin air. What he would never get over was being gotten over on by that vindictive old witch. No matter how long ago it was, the incantation lingered in his memory: *The measure of a man though it is given him at birth; is not revealed in time until he gains his height and girth; but rather than exert his will upon a limb or joint, reciting this enlarges it, though after he may miss the point.*

Roderick was going to get Osmena, if he did nothing else. First things first, though. Today, a head slap for Tulley. "Sir, are you there?" Then, on Saturday, young Calvin would pass by the station in the evening and lead him to where the VLF was meeting in the woods.

⌘ ⌘ ⌘

JUDE HEARD THE shots before he'd reached Zephyr's house, but he thought they must have been coming from the woods. By the time he'd parked his bike there was no doubt they were coming from her back yard. He knew Ms. LaFrance didn't own guns. She'd said it once in class. He stopped at the corner of the house and peered around in case the shots were coming his way. She was standing at the edge of the brick patio, aiming a handgun out across the gardens toward her new shrubbery. It looked like she was just shooting off into the woods, until Jude saw the bird feeder hanging from a wrought iron shepherd's crook. Even from this far away Jude could see the bright yellow flash of a gold finch. Zephyr fired. Jude jumped. He must have blinked too, because when he opened his eyes there were yellow feathers drifting to the ground, but no finch. Zephyr waited, staring straight ahead, the handgun down at her side. Then a flash of blue alighted on the feeder. Zephyr raised the gun. Jude's mouth fell open. *The bluebird of happiness too?*

Zephyr whipped around, still aiming the gun. "Who's there?"

"It's me, Jude."

Zephyr lowered the gun. Something about the sharp timber in her voice made Jude come into the open with his hands raised.

"Jude you can put your hands down for heaven's sake. Well, don't just stand there, come and sit down."

Jude came over to the table, where they'd sat together more than three weeks ago and made a pact. Zephyr put the gun in a belt holster. "Do you want some lemonade?"

First you're going to shoot me, now it's lemonade?

"No thanks, I'm not thirsty."

249

"You've got to be thirsty on such a hot day."

"What's with the gun? You said you didn't own one."

Zephyr pulled out a chair and sat down across from Jude. "I know. It's everything going on lately. I don't feel safe, Jude. Even with the charges dropped, that crazy Sergeant Roderick is kind of obsessed with it, and there might be people who don't like what I did."

"What were you shooting at?"

"Just a target back there behind the shrubbery. I'm afraid I need more practice. My father taught me to shoot as a girl, but I haven't even held a gun since those days. You can't be too careful, though."

No, especially if you're a gold finch or a bluebird.

"But you're okay with Osmena and everything?"

"That's all over, thank goodness. Turns out that experimental worked just the way she wanted it to, and she found out what she needed to know. I just want to put all that behind me now with school only a month away."

"We did some checking, about Osmena's land."

"We?"

"Merrilee and I. But we couldn't find anywhere that part of Osmena's land had ever been owned by a LaFrance."

"My father couldn't keep up with the taxes on a lot of his property, so he sold it to her conservancy."

"Yeah, I read about that too, but there's no LaFrance there either. I just thought 'sold' was Osmena speak for 'stole.'"

Zephyr laughed. "Jude where did you get the idea that Osmena stole the land from us?"

"From you."

"Oh Jude, you must have misunderstood me. It wasn't like that. And it was such a long time ago. Why does it matter now?"

"I was just trying to find out what I could about her, you know, to try and help if I could."

"That's very sweet, but I say let bygones be bygones. How about that lemonade, now?" Zephyr stood up and laid a hand on Jude's shoulder. Her grip had such masculine force, Jude almost twitched at the pressure, as though she couldn't measure her own strength. Through his t-shirt he felt the chill of her palm on his skin, still cool from gun metal.

"Something is really wrong. Ms. LaFrance was out in the back yard picking off bluebirds." Jude was leading Merrilee on a tour of the 'mountains' while Jet started the charcoal, but his heart wasn't in it. Her eyes had lit up with horrified fascination at the scale of dereliction, but she was underwhelmed by his presentation.

"I'm trying to be a good tourist, Jude, but—"

"It was like a mask. The same person, the same expression, but something missing. Just things she would never say; the way she said them. I don't know. It was weird. And when she touched my shoulder, like it was meant to be gentle, but it was an iron grip. Like she couldn't tell the difference."

"That's creepy."

"I got out of there as fast as I could. I mean, it's worse than before, because then when the drug wore off she was herself, now she's wearing her 'self' like a disguise. And it was like she and Osmena were cool. Oh, and get this. Now she says Osmena never stole the land from her father. They sold it to her."

"And what is she doing using songbirds as target practice? What is she practicing for?

Jude and Merrilee circled around and started back to the trailer.

"Do you really think it's hackers who've done all this with the money?"

Merrilee shook her head. "I wanted to think that at first, but it's too widespread. I mean government, banks, and private investment companies. My parents aren't rich, but they're doing pretty well. They can both retire comfortably at 62, and I can pretty much go to school wherever I choose. Well, at least I could before all this. We're not broke or anything, but they've lost about a third of what they had in their investments and retirement accounts overnight. I wasn't sure how they'd react, but they've been really cool about it. In fact, I think they're relieved that it's happened, because sometimes they felt guilty about having so much, and they can see that whoever is behind it is actually doing something to help people who don't have much."

"Like us."

Merrilee smiled. "But is it the VLF? Is there a VLF? And who are they if they exist?"

"Calvin knows something. He was talking like he knew about the explosion."

"But didn't he say things 'worse' than this were coming? If he is with the VLF, he wouldn't put it that way, would he? We don't really know who he is."

"Yeah, but he was up at my cousins getting signatures to stop Greenway."

"Yeah, but for whom? I mean, if you wanted to get as many signatures as possible wouldn't you go where the most people were? GEIST has done a little checking into it and we haven't heard of anybody else signing such a petition."

"What made you do that?"

"We discuss everything you've told me and we write it down. It's just that most times you can't get at the truth if you take everything at face value. So we didn't. And that's what we found out. But there's a missing piece. Like why did Calvin want your aunt's signature and apparently nobody else's? I mean, didn't your uncle have some issue with his signature on Greenway's deed? Think about it."

Jude shook his head. "Man, you guys are good."

Merrilee and Jude arrived back at the trailer. Jude and Jet had managed to move one of the newer small mountains of aluminum scrap—giving Mt. St. Helen a badly needed facelift—to make a place for that old square of indoor outdoor carpeting they used for cookouts.

"What are you two whispering about?" Aster said. She held her neon green, plastic cup of coke and Captain Morgan like a socialite, rocking it back and forth as she swung her wrist.

Merrilee said, "The VLF. What do you think about them?"

Aster swirled her cup around and made shifty faces.

"I mean you've got to be a big fan right about now, and you must have known their leader, Luc Dentremont, before he disappeared."

Jude elbowed Merrilee.

Aster took a very long sip of her coke and Captain (as if anybody thought it was just soda), covering her expression for several seconds. "Mmm," Aster said. She held up a finger. "I just remembered, I have to take those strawberries out of the freezer to thaw." She turned and hurried off into the trailer.

"What are you doing?" Jude said.

"It's called the direct approach. I have a hunch. Be right back."

Aster was leaning with the small of her back against the kitchen sink, smoking, when Merrilee came in. She was so lost in thought she didn't even look up for several seconds. When she did, she looked resigned rather than evasive.

"You knew Luc Dentremont, didn't you, back then?"

Aster blew out a long trail of smoke. Merrilee stood by the kitchen table with one hand on a chair back.

"The summer before I got pregnant with Kennedy, Jet and I had a big fight and broke up. I saw Luc a few times late that summer and early fall. It was nothing serious. God help me I was still hung up on Jet." Aster took a long draw on her cigarette.

"Serious enough that you still keep a picture of him in your closet."

Aster pointed the cigarette at Merrilee. "Did you put Jude up to snooping? He's too trusting to do that on his own. He's like Jet that way. I guess I didn't even know I still had his picture."

"And then the Watters' fire happened," Merrilee steered her back.

"I knew he was into something, but I wasn't sure what until the day he disappeared. I was kind of scared of his politics; you know his beliefs. It all seemed so extreme, even changing his name when he turned 18."

"Changing his name?"

"To Dentremont. It was his mother's maiden name. Everybody knew him as Gerard LaFrance, Jr. It had to do with all that land that had been in his mother's family and how he was going to get it back from Osmena Searle. I guess it was some kind of statement. Anyway, by the fall Jet and I were talking and back together again. Luc was just gone, and nobody knew where he'd gone to."

Merrilee stood stunned, a strange thrill caught in her throat as another piece of the puzzle fell into place. For a minute she couldn't think of what to say. "And now, if he's alive and behind all this?" she managed finally.

"Thanks for the barbeque, I guess. There might be nothing more to it than that."

Jet had just put the steaks in the middle of the grill with tongs, and arranged the ears of corn around the edges, when Merrilee and Aster emerged from the trailer.

"Hey, I have something to show you," Jet said. "The first and only vehicle of its kind is finally complete."

"Whoopdy-doo!" Jude said, and Aster made big circles with her index finger in the air.

Jet led them around the back of the Incubus. The new vehicle was covered with a tarp.

"It's a mower, a tractor and a passenger vehicle all in one." Jet flung off the tarp with a flourish.

"You forgot to mention that it's ugly too."

"Yet, so practical," said Merrilee, nudging Jude with her elbow.

It was a lawn tractor with huge, knobby chained wheels and an unusually high clearance, welded to a small flatbed platform—six wheels in all. Instead of seats in the flat bed, there were three triangulated metal posts—two in the front one in the center rear—and large iron ring grips for holding on.

"It's four-wheel drive. With the mower carriage up you can clear a 12 inch rock in your path and roll right over small branches without getting hung up."

Jet bent over and pointed down to the carriage where the blades were housed. "Beastly blades. Snaps inch and half diameter branches like wishbones. Meant for the field and off road, trails and such. Mows to eight inches, so you don't hit the small stones you can't see in a field.

Head lamp for night driving with protective cage in case you clip a bird. Oh, and the poles in the flatbed can be removed if you need to haul. There's a place to hitch straps for securing your load."

"It's brilliant," Merrilee said.

"But does it work?" said Aster.

Jet looked down and scratched his head. "Course it works. We'll test it out after we eat."

The smell of cooking steak drifted over them. Burning steak.

Merrilee tossed her pillow aside and sat up in bed. She had tried for the umpteenth time to clear her mind, relax and go to sleep, but the questions kept turning over in her head. She'd told Jude about Aster knowing Luc Dentremont and how he had changed his name from LaFrance. Francy's boy, Zephyr's brother, and Luc Dentremont, VLF leader, were one and the same. Yet, if Osmena had acquired the land unlawfully, why was Zephyr denying it now? Merrilee turned on the bedside lamp and went to her desk. She turned the lamp on there as well and opened her notebook. She flipped to her notes from the GEIST meeting on the last day of school. She found the reference to Aster's rumored miscarriage by another man. She only wished she knew the exact days or weeks Aster had been seeing Luc.

"Think Merrilee. What do you really know?" she said. Again she turned to her notebook to Cate's conversation with Dr. Lane. The note had said: *Fire damage; Sorry, no choice.*

Cate had made copies of the two follow-up articles on the fire, but Merrilee had only skimmed them. She recalled Cate couldn't find her place in the notebook that day and had tossed it on the floor, so she hadn't actually read from her notes, which were always very detailed and precise, but had instead recited the relevant facts from memory. Memory was notoriously fallible.

Merrilee read over the pieces. There were just a couple of lines in an odd place in the last piece: a fact that had been missing from the original *Beacon* story, probably because the investigation required it be withheld. What had pointed Walker in the VLF's direction was the Sokol barn. Turns out Goran Sokol's son Ivan was thought to have been involved with the VLF and was also a wanted fugitive in connection with the Watters' fire. In Walker's mind, there was the VLF connection. The Sokols. But without evidence they'd set either fire, he could never make a case, or come up with a compelling motive for the VLF to risk exposure for a meaningless double arson. It made no sense. So why go through such an elaborate arson scheme when you could break a window and steal a file?

23.

A Devil in the Bargain

T HE FIRST WEEKEND of August marked the height of summer. The early corn was coming in and tomatoes were on the verge of ripening. Ask anyone what the summer was like and they'd tell you by what happened to their corn and tomatoes more times than not. Too wet for the tomatoes; not enough heat for the corn. Just two years ago the late blight about got everybody's tomatoes, while the cool just stunted the corn so awful the fields looked like shabby, threadbare rugs rolled out along the roadsides.

When that happened all that was left was to vie for who had the worst corn, tomato and pestilence stories. Harmon Gage could be heard trying to outdo Dunky LaGro and Hiram Rafferty at the Luncheonette. "Weren't enough beer in VT to drown all them slugs." "Every tomato plant turned black as night." "At least your potatoes didn't rot too." "My corn weren't worth feeding to a pig."

But from the vantage of a banner year like this one, the Twin Gaps Farmers' Market would be abuzz with optimism and heavy with bounty on the first Saturday in August.

Buoyed by their recent windfall, the Corgans ventured down to farmers' market the morning after their celebratory cookout. Jude rode in the bed of the truck with the Byclops. He planned on meeting Merrilee there and would need to bike home after Jet and Aster were done with their marketing.

Jet caught sight of Les Higgby straight off and went to talk machines with him. Aster was in her glory, walking with her head high and her shoulders back, looking more relaxed than Jude had ever seen her. The sullen stoop of her morning moods was gone. It was as if she had forgotten how much fun shopping could be when it was stoked with the possibility of purchase. Everybody else seemed in exceptionally good spirits too, and you didn't have to strain your ears to hear people talk about the sudden turn in fortune, wide-eyed with wonder about the cause, and skeptical yet about how long it would last.

"You're going to scrape your nose on a cloud if you hold it any higher," Jude said to Aster.

Aster stopped and shielded her eyes from the sun to look at him. "Is it too much for your mean little heart to let me enjoy a single living day on earth without some smart mouth attempt to burst my bubble? I'm not acting proud, I'm just enjoying myself for once. You've no idea how hard I've worked to keep everything together; and if you had you'd be glad for me. Just get out of my sight, Jude, before I ground you for life."

"Mom, come on. It's just a—"

Aster walked away and left him there. Jude felt the blood drain away from his face, and felt the wiggling of guilt and regret in his stomach, but he tried to shrug it off. "Okay, if you insist."

Jude crossed to the other side and walked down the row of vendors keeping an eye out for Merrilee, but he didn't see her. Farmers' market could be boring if you weren't buying, or in on the local gossip, so, not having benefited personally from the wealth redistribution yet, he decided to dawdle by all the tables, pretending to look at things while listening to people talk. This turned out to be maddening, because everybody was talking money and nobody was making sense. It'd be one thing if they had a clue about what was going on, but it was just a lot of stupid speculation. Sure it was the VLF, a group nobody knew about, and who hadn't taken official credit for it yet. Sure it was Osmena Searle, who wouldn't even give a refund for a spell that didn't work. Sure it was a sign the Lord was coming and the world was going to end. A little money shifting to the poor was a sign of the Apocalypse? Better end it all before things got too equal.

Jeezum crow. If only Merrilee were here for that one. She'd have launched into one of her speeches.

The row on Jude's side of the market ended in shade, so he made for it. He sat in the grass on a little swell next to the last booth. It was just an old woman in sunglasses and a colorful dress—all blue and green and purple, and a purple scarf on her head. He didn't recognize her and it seemed nobody was stopping at her booth. There were handmade wooden cases on her table displaying bottles, probably fragrances or herbal tinctures. She must have sensed him watching her, because she turned her head and looked right at him.

"Do you always wear your sunglasses in the shade?"

The woman smiled. "I'm a woman of mystery."

Jude looked at her a while longer. "You're her, aren't you?"

"You're sharp, aren't you? Yes, I am she. Always remember to use 'she' when referring to the subject of a sentence. It's not a crime to use my name you know, Mr. Corgan."

"How do you know me?"

"Oh, I have my eye on you."

"That's not exactly comforting."

"Come now." Osmena waved her hand as if shooing a cloud of flies. "You can't believe everything you hear. I bet people say a lot of things about you that aren't true. It's never easy being an object of either scorn or envy, is it?"

"But I know what you did to Ms. LaFrance."

"Ms. LaFrance is out of trouble thanks to me."

"She got into trouble because of you in the first place."

"Ah, not true. She got into trouble because the meddling Vice Principal high-jacked her cake and gave it to adults. I warned her of the paradoxical effect. All an unfortunate accident. I neither foresaw, nor intended it."

Jude was so mad he stood up to keep from shaking. "But you took advantage of her once she got in trouble."

"I asked her to do me a favor and she agreed. No harm has come to her."

"She pointed a gun at me the other day. I know you're doing something to her."

259

"Jude, isn't it? Jude come sit down close to me. We may as well talk like adults. I brought an extra chair today in case I had some company. Quite providential, don't you think?"

Jude hesitated for a moment, then ducked under her sky blue canopy and sat down, yet he couldn't help thinking about a famous line of verse: *Come into my parlor, said the spider to the fly.*

⌘   ⌘   ⌘

"A RE YOU ADA Landreaux?" Merrilee asked the old woman who sold pies at the market.

Ada Landreaux held her hand up to her ear and Merrilee repeated it a little louder.

"Yes, I am."

"Hi, I'm Merrilee Rainey."

"Well, nice to meet you Merrilee."

"I just finished reading your History of Twin Gaps volume II."

Ada Landreaux smiled and nodded. "Very good."

"I'm so glad I ran into you, because I have a question."

"What would you like to know?"

"There's a passage that makes reference to the old Searle place from 1919."

Ada Landreaux looked like she'd been flash-frozen.

"But there's no record of her or anyone by the name of Searle owning land in Twin Gaps that far back."

"That bit's made up," Ada whispered. "I remember well when she came here. You're quite a remarkable girl to have figured that out; but if you're looking into Osmena Searle's past, you had also best be careful of her."

"I don't understand; if it's made up why did you write it?"

"I didn't. It's not in the original volume II. It was her doing. Adding it to the second edition that came out for the town bicentennial."

"But who let her do that?"

"The Historical Society. She didn't dare ask me. But I suspect it involved a rather sizeable contribution to the historical preservation fund, and it seemed such a small thing, an offhand reference to connect her name to a place she wouldn't come to own for decades. To me it was like changing history. You see?"

"Yes, but didn't you say anything?"

Ada Landreaux lowered her voice again. "I was warned to stay out of it."

"Right now, Zephyr is afraid," Osmena explained.

"Of what, bluebirds?"

"Afraid that people have the wrong idea about her, and may try to harm her."

"She told me that."

"But you didn't believe her? Don't worry, she'll be herself again in no time. I'm what you'd call an aspirational thinker, Jude. I see potential. Zephyr sees herself, and I suppose you do too, only as a teacher of children; but I see her knowledge of these woodlands, her fortitude and determination, as qualities that might be used for another purpose entirely."

"That's what I'm afraid of."

"Now your father for instance, underneath the grease and dirty clothes, is a very talented and attractive man with absolutely no prospects."

"Because he's a screw up."

Osmena smiled conspiratorially and patted Jude's arm. "Now, now. I think you're too hard on your father. He has no prospects because he isn't well connected and has very limited resources. You can have all the talent in the world and still be applying your genius in complete obscurity behind an old VW bus without the right opportunities. He's a bit rough around the edges, but I wouldnt have asked him to build a revolutionary machine for me if I thought he was a screw up."

"What machine?"

"I see he hasn't told you. Well, now that you know perhaps you could put in a word to your father; persuade him to begin without delay. I understand from Ms. LaFrance you can be quite persuasive when you want to be. Your mother, I'm afraid, will oppose anything to do with me."

"Well, you stiffed them on the spell; what do you expect?"

"I expect I can make things happen for your father beyond his wildest dreams."

"Well, maybe you're too late. Maybe nobody needs you anymore. Look around. I mean, I don't see anybody lining up to try your latest experimental."

Osmena removed her sunglasses at last. Her large hazel eyes had a faint gold ring around the iris that made them blaze. "But you do need me, Jude. You want to know what happened the night your brother died and why, don't you?"

Jude stared back in disbelief.

"And I have answers. I'm the only one who can help you."

"Then help me. Why does everything have to be a bargain with you? Money and favors. Buy and sell. Can't you ever just do something because it's the right thing to do?"

"Must we cheapen the fair exchange of commerce with sentiment, Jude? The right thing is un-American. When two mutually interested parties get something in exchange for something given, it's a clean transaction. No endless obligation. No guilt. Nobody needs to grovel to a benefactor, or nod at the philanthropist when she passes. No. A man wants to pay up and be a man about it. He wants to owe nobody."

"Yeah, in theory, but a man also wants to get what he paid for, and you cheated us. Tough luck for us, since magic spells aren't exactly regulated by the FTC."

"I was in a rather awkward position you see; I didn't know at the time that I no longer had the power to cast spells that altered the material world. The VLF had stolen the skull."

"The black skull? You mean it's real?"

"Powerfully real. It can control many things if you know how to use it, but it was gone and I was just as dismayed as your parents, believe me. But I certainly couldn't let on that I had no explanation for my failure. It would have been bad for business."

"But what about your experimentals? They still work."

"You don't miss a trick, do you? Oh, I do like you, Jude. Yes, my potions work because their power derives from a different source. But you see, I've entrusted you with sensitive information; I've made myself quite vulnerable to you, and so now you must trust me. I need your cooperation, and I've given you an incentive to cooperate. Come to my house today. There's much more we have to discuss about the future and your brother."

"I can't. How can I? There's no way."

Osmena went to her display case of potions and took a small bottle of liquid and pressed it into Jude's hands. "This will give you the energy to ride up the mountain to The Cosmos."

"But, how can I? I don't even know the way."

"Take it one hour before you are to ride; you'll know the way."

"But—"

"Your brother, Jude."

⌘ ⌘ ⌘

"WHAT IS SHE doing here?" Ada Landreaux grabbed her cane and stood up.

"Who?" Merrilee said.

"The one we've been talking about. There!"

Merrilee turned around and followed the line of Ada's finger. So there Osmena was at last, so tiny standing beside Jude and shaking his hand, dressed in the bright flowing caftan of a fortune teller.

"Hey, that's my friend Jude."

"Your friend, you say? He's in great danger, Merrilee. Quickly."

Ada Landreaux came out from around her table, cane in hand and walked across the grass toward Jude and Osmena.

"But how do I know it's going to do what you say it will? How do I know it won't kill me, or make me forget everything you've told me?"

Osmena smiled at him admiringly. "You'll just have to trust me."

"Trust you. Trust you!" Jude was fuming again. It always played out to her advantage. He had to trust her, take some crazy-eyed, wild man potion before he'd find out a thing about Kennedy, or the machine she wanted Jet to build. But this might be his only chance to help Zephyr and get the answers he'd been seeking.

"Yes, trust me."

"On one condition. You'll tell me the truth about Zephyr. Everything or no deal.""I'll tell you everything, but you mustn't tell a soul about our arrangement."

Jude grasped the bottle and stuck it in his pants pocket.

An old woman with a cane was bearing down on them with Merrilee sheepishly a step behind.

"You old devil." Ada raised her cane and pointed it at Osmena. "You have no business here."

Osmena lifted her chin. "It's a free market."

"Young man, you'll stay far clear of her if you know what's best."

Merrilee gave Jude a what's-going-on look. Jude shrugged.

"Maybe it's you who should mind your own business." Osmena leaned over her table of wares and waved a hand as if to dismiss the old woman.

Ada Landreaux took a step back as if knocked by a blow. She tried to steady herself with her cane, but it was too late. Her left ankle turned and then she crumpled and fell on the grass with a groan. People came running over from across the lane and from the next booth.

"Are you alright, Ada?"

"Does it hurt?"

"Can you move?"

Jude turned and left Osmena alone under her sky blue canopy. He stood around the others waiting to see if Ada Landreaux was okay.

"Somebody call an ambulance."

"No. No. No," Ada Landreaux said, more embarrassed by all the fuss than she was injured by the fall. "I'm fine, just give me a hand getting up."

The Johnson's, from the next booth, supported her under each arm and lifted her up, held on until she was steady on her feet.

"Are you sure you don't want to go to the hospital?"

"I'm fine. Nothing hurts. Thank you all very much."

"Be careful, my dear," said Osmena. "We can't afford to lose one of our historic treasures."

Calvin had never been inside Osmena's vault before, but when she took him there and opened the massive one foot thick door, he was surprised to find a room more like a museum than a narrow bank vault lined with shelves. The reason nobody but Osmena and his father were allowed inside was that the treasures and objects kept there were either very well known, or not believed to exist at all.

Calvin had come home from the Meades with a sick feeling in his gut. The tension he had caused between the twins and his discovery of the location of the spring had left him uneasy and ashamed of his role in the demise of their farm. He had an idea the spring had healing powers of some kind. He'd known about the skull also, and that it was very powerful, yet he felt he'd been largely shielded from the true nature of these objects—the tree, the skull and now the spring—and had been asked to act without knowing what exactly he was obtaining and protecting.

So today Calvin had asked Osmena directly about the skull and where it came from. She'd replied by taking him down to the vault. Osmena stood by the door and watched as he walked slowly around the room in awe.

"What's this, Aunty?" Calvin stopped in front of a gold angel. It kneeled in profile and stretched its left wing out in front of its body, as if covering or sheltering something.

"All that remains of the Ark of the Covenant. One of the covering Cherubim."

"It really existed?"

"Yes, whether or not the God it represented did, the objects of belief persist."

"Wouldn't he have to exist for the skull to be what it is?"

Osmena tilted her head and smiled.

There were crown jewels adorned with the orthodox cross, Islamic icons from the first millennium, ancient papyrus under glass, even small stone tablets engraved with images and glyphs.

"Those scrolls were saved by a scribe from the burning Alexandria library."

"Wow." Calvin turned around and looked at her. "Why didn't you keep the skull down here? Wouldn't it have been safer?"

Osmena walked over to where he was. "Not as it turned out. You see, the only map of the skull's whereabouts and the incantation that unlocks its power was kept here and somehow that was breached. Inside the tree, the skull had even greater power. Nobody could have discovered it accidentally because an innocent hunter or hiker would have perished in the bog before ever reaching the tree. So long as nobody got into this vault or learned of the skull's existence, it was safest held within the tree."

"What exactly does the skull have power to do? It's just..."

Osmena rested a hand on her nephew's shoulder. "You are worried about the Meades family? Put your mind at ease. They will not be harmed, Calvin. But without the skull, something has happened to me. I have been so connected to its power for so long, it's as if its absence is draining me."

"How can that be? It's just an object, like these things."

"Would that it were, but it is something older than any of these things; something directly marked by divinity. You might say it is my own object of belief. When I understood how it could protect its bearer, I finally understood God. I had seen his face by the mark he'd left in the skull. I knew God, the real god, was the god of developers and murderers too. Our god. But until we have it back, I require that water. By finding it, my dear Calvin, you have given me the ultimate gift."

Calvin blinked and a tear fell to the floor. He turned away and looked toward the far end of the room. Three open sarcophagi in glass were lined up side by side. They were the full mummified remains of three people. Calvin walked around them in horror and open mouthed fascination. The coarse embalming clothes, the blackened desiccated flesh, the shrunken brittle arms and skulls and human hair.

"Egyptian royalty," Osmena said.

It was like flying. Jude had never felt anything like it. There was sweat and exertion, but no pain or fatigue, only boundless energy. The steeper the grades and the tighter the curves, the greater his intensity rose to meet them. Downhill was pure exhilaration. Roller coaster screams of joy and terror came out of him in spontaneous whoops as he careened around a curve at impossible speed. His balance and control were Tour de France caliber. His body felt weightless and invincible. And just as Osmena predicted, he recognized the turns in a flash of intuition, as if controlled by intercellular GPS.

When Jude rolled up to the iron gates between the giant granite pillars, he was almost sad his wild ride was finished, as if it had not been the means to something but the ends. The gates opened in and closed behind him. He rode through a grove of locust trees with a grassy floor, bright with filtered sunshine, like a room with an invisible light source.

At the end of the wood, an emerald green lawn opened up in front of him. It rose in terraces by a serpentine dragon's back stone wall—free standing in its curves and retained at each terraced rise. Seven times it crossed the road in broad, high arches. Dark green constellations of topiary dotted every curve—all spheres, disks and spirals. The way the serpentine tightened drew the eye like a hypnotic pendulum toward the mysterious galaxy of gardens and the cupolas of the house in the distance. The draw of it was like the sway of a cobra.

Jude decided to make a more subtle entrance. He parked the Byclops against a tree and continued on foot under the cover of the wood toward The Cosmos.

It felt like Jude would never make it to the house. He'd managed to enter from the wood through the outer bands of the garden—through cutout arches in the shrubbery, around arbors, anything that kept him out of open view. The effect of the drug was wearing off, because the heat was sapping him. His shirt and pants were soaked with sweat and he was painfully dry in the throat with thirst.

Jude glimpsed the house and knew he was close, but he didn't have a plan and he wasn't sure what good it would do even if he managed to reach the house undetected. If he was discovered wandering, he would just say he'd become lost in the maze of the gardens and was looking for somebody to direct him. But sometimes when you found yourself where you weren't supposed to be, there was always a chance...

Jude stopped at the sound of voices. They were coming from the other side of a yew hedge. He got down on all fours and crawled along its straight edge to where a small weeping tree broke the stiffness of the yew with its graceful canopy. There was a gap between the yew and where the weeping tree was pruned. He crawled under it with the greatest care not to brush or move the branches with his bulk. It would be hard to see him from either side now, unless he stirred the tree.

The voices were familiar, but only after Jude had settled on his knees, and the pounding of his heart had stopped echoing in his ears, could he focus on the words.

"The cats are ready."

"Good. The Meades will be barricaded in their house, and we can just roll the truck in and pump out the water from the spring, during the night."

"Promise me that nothing is going to happen to them. Does Hilton know that?"

"They should be completely safe, unless they try something really foolish."

"Is the water really what you say it is, dad?"

Jude craned his head back and forth to catch a glimpse of the speakers through the overlapping leaves, but all he could make out were their forms. It was two men sitting at a table on a small outdoor terrace. Jude lifted a leaf so he could see their faces. He would never have guessed it. They were familiar voices, even if he'd only heard them once or twice. It was Calvin, the boy with the catamount tattoo, who'd also gone collecting signatures against the man he'd just called dad: Merlin Greenway. It had been a set-up to get Aunt Raeanne's signature on a piece of paper. How long before had Calvin come to the house, with longer hair, maybe, and some other worthy cause, to get Uncle David's John Hancock? Long enough so nobody would make the connection, or remember Calvin. It had to be. Because there was no other way Greenway could've had signed sale documents. It also meant that Osmena was in on Greenway's attempt to steal Gemini Farm.

"That map and the legend were from the journal of Melchizedek Zenger. There were eye witness accounts, documentation. Haggai Zenger, his grandfather, lived to be 153. He built the house on top of the well to protect it."

"Then why isn't he still alive?"

"Nobody knows."

"Is Aunty going to be alright?"

"Better than ever when we get that water. She's taking a rest. That market took it out of her, but she said she had some business there that couldn't wait. She says her visitor is coming, but it looks to me like he's going to be a no show."

Jude iced over in sweat. He had to get away and warn his cousins, warn his father about Osmena's machine. He'd been a fool to come here. A fool to trust her.

Jude crawled out from under the weeping tree and hid behind the yew hedge. Now he had to get back to the woods unnoticed. He started to retrace his steps back along the hedge and came face to face with a short dark haired man. "Jude?"

Jude wanted to run but his body froze. He nodded.

"Miss Searle is waiting for you."

⌘　⌘　⌘

"OH, EVERYBODY GETS lost in here. Either on the way, or in the gardens." Osmena had taken Jude to an air conditioned parlor, where a servant, the one who'd found him in the garden, set down a large tray with a pitcher of lemonade and a plate of chicken salad sandwiches. Jude drank his lemonade in a long, remarkable chug, so that before the servant even made it to the door, Osmena called him back. "Stemple, pour Mr. Corgan another lemonade, please."

"Yes, Madam." Stemple poured and caught Jude's eye for a moment.

There was something in the servant's look—concern, curiosity, sympathy—as if in recognition of a circumstance he knew well but did not envy. It lasted two seconds. Then Stemple stood straight and bowed with his impassive face intact again.

"Even with a little help from our friends, it's still a grueling ride. Have a sandwich. It will help your body recover."

Jude took another sip of lemonade, but he didn't take a sandwich. He was hungry in a strange, sick way, as often happens when a bodily response like hunger got crossed up with an emotion like fear. It was all happening in his gut and the fear was winning. There was no way he could eat.

"I'm curious what you make of all the recent changes."

"It's pretty cool I guess. It's not like anybody knows what's happening."

Osmena tapped a spot on the table. "I'll tell you what's happening Jude. Misguided people, who have no idea how human nature works and how the world operates, are about to plunge our state into a very dark time. Not only are they pitting us against the Federal Government, but they are attempting to master powers they do not understand."

Jude finished his lemonade. "I don't know. They're doing a pretty good job so far. You were at the market today, and I know you're not deaf." He thought of Aster, happy and relaxed for the first time since he could remember. It wasn't that they had so much money. Two thousand dollars was nothing, but it meant that for a week, two weeks, a month or however long it lasted, they would have enough, and enough was enough to lift a great weight off his mother's back. He felt even worse now for trying to douse her happiness.

Osmena stood up next to the piano. "Come take a walk with me. I want to show you something."

Jude followed Osmena out of the parlor and down a long hall. At the end they reached a door. Osmena opened it and turned on a light switch. They stared into a wide spiral stairwell. "You think it's going well right now," she said, leading the way, "but what happens a year from now, five years, however long it takes, when everybody has had enough for so long, without having to do anything for it. Just waiting for that bump; or just quitting their jobs and deciding they can get along on what the powers that grant so graciously provide. Where is the bump going to come from, when people lose their incentive and the economy dies with it?"

Jude laughed. "People aren't going to quit their jobs if they like them. Aster likes being a nurse's aide because she gets to help people and it gives her purpose. It gets her out of junk land four days a week too."

"And the jobs nobody wants to do? Dishwasher and field hand?"

"Well, you could start paying dishwashers and field hands more money, and start paying executives less."

"Don't be absurd. Jobs that make people money pay more money. It's as simple as that."

"Did they take a pay cut when they lost everybody's money? I don't think so."

Osmena sniffed with disapproval. "I see your red-headed friend has filled you up with all of her nonsense."

"You don't have to be a genius to know what's fair and what isn't."

Jude and Osmena reached the bottom of the stairs at last and stepped out onto a broad corridor.

"We must be like way underground. What is this place?"

"Kind of a shelter, or a bunker you might say."

"Plan on being bombed any time soon?"

"It pays to be prepared." Osmena smirked and waved Jude forward. On either side of the corridor were rooms divided from each other by concrete walls, but open to the passage. Each room was furnished with a bed, a chair, a desk, a toilet and a sink.

"You're not big on privacy, are you?" Jude had a dream once that he had to use the bathroom really bad, but all the toilets in the public john were out in the open without stalls.

"I'm big on aspiration, Jude. Yes, don't sigh. Soon everything will succumb to stagnation. There'll be no urgency to invent; or advance technology; no reason to finish that novel or painting. Eventually depending on 'enough' will sap the culture and the economy of its drive. The only happiness in the world is in the quest for happiness."

"Well, you seem to have more than enough of everything around here, including servants to fetch and pour your tea and lemonade. It doesn't seem to have sapped your aspiration. Or does that only happen to lazy, poor people with no connections and resources."

"But, Jude, I want your father to have more than enough. If he works for me, he'll be compensated generously beyond belief. All the best materials, a state of the art shop to work in. Your lives will never be the same."

271

"And you want to do this because?"

"Because your father has a rare kind of conceptual and mechanical genius, and talent like his should be rewarded. But I need your father's help right away."

"To build your machine?"

"Yes. You can take your chances with the VLF—for all we know about them—and what little they can give you until the world they're making crashes and you're left with nothing, or you can hitch your star to The Cosmos and to me. I'm a proven entity."

"The VLF wants to help everybody."

"But I have chosen you; and now the choice is yours."

"Why didn't you just make an offer to my father. Why is it my choice?"

"Because he hasn't committed to it; he needs a greater incentive."

"Look. I've come all this way and you haven't told me anything I want to know. For one thing, what are we doing down here?" The knot in Jude's stomach kept tightening.

"Patience, we're getting to that."

"You promise and never deliver. You just keep taking more and putting people off." Jude stopped in the middle of the corridor. "I want to know what's going on with Zephyr right now, or I'm not going another step."

Osmena turned to face him. "Very well then. I'll tell you. Zephyr is going to get the skull back for me tonight. She agreed of her own volition to take a second experimental. In some ways it's a bit like the one you took today, only she'll be directed to the skull the way you were to The Cosmos. But her formula has a killer kick to it."

Jude stared back in silence.

"All that target practice hasn't been for nothing. Tonight she will assassinate Luc Dentremont, and, if necessary, anybody who gets in her way."

"That's her brother! Is that what you call her great potential? Turning her into a killer?"

At that moment Osmena could have turned Jude into a killer too. The fear had burned off with the rising rage. It was up in his throat and threatening to overwhelm his brain. It would take nothing to wring her skinny neck. He lunged for her, but somebody very strong grabbed him from behind and threw him across the hall into one of the rooms. Jude stumbled and fell to the floor. He heard a metal crash. He looked up from his tumble to see a grid of iron bars lower from the ceiling, turning the open room into an instant cell.

Jude flung himself at the bars and shook them. Solid steel. He called her every name in the book, enough curses in a string to ground him until the age of 36.

Osmena had recovered her composure and stood facing Jude. His assailant stood beside her in wonderment with his hands on his hips, as if looking at a wild caged animal.

"You insisted on knowing, so I told you the truth. But now that you know, I can't let you leave until Zephyr's work is finished and your father agrees to build my machine. I'm sorry, but I can't risk your interference tonight."

24.

Into the Forest

MERRILEE KNEW IN her gut Jude hadn't told her everything, even though she'd grilled him after they left the farmers market that morning.

"What on earth were you talking to her about? I mean you must have known it was her."

"The subject came up. Turns out she gave my dad some blueprint for a machine when they went up to see her. She wants me to help convince him to build it for her. That's all."

"Well, that's news to me. You might have mentioned something that important." Merrilee had given him a stony stare.

"Yeah, if I'd known. You know parents and secrets. Jet didn't tell me anything about it."

"You don't think it's that Mowercar thing?"

"Uh uh."

"Well, what is it?"

"She didn't say. But she says it'll be worth a lot to us if we help her."

"Famous last words. You know she can't be trusted."

"Yeah, I know."

"Well, what did you tell her?"

"I told her I'd think about it."

"More like you should tell your father not to build it."

"Aster already did apparently."

"Well, at least somebody in your family has some sense. Don't you think it's weird she's approached you? It's not like your parents weren't at the market too."

Jude shrugged and said, "How else are we going to find out what she's up to?" That was how they'd left things.

Now, Merrilee wished she'd asked Jude exactly what he meant by that. The more she thought about it the more it nagged at her. In her mind's eye, she saw something change hands between Jude and Osmena at the Farmer's Market. Was she imagining it?

If Jude was entertaining some kind of involvement with Osmena, if he'd become that desperate, it was due partly to Merrilee's slowness in finding answers. Despite her digging and prying and speculating, she'd been unable to put all the tantalizing pieces together. She flipped through her notebooks again in search of something she'd overlooked. She seemed so close to the source of the wrecks with her discovery of the Escort at Atwood's, and the man prying at the fender, but the evidence was gone and Atwood had given away nothing. If only she'd gotten a good look at the man's face. The bright flash of the necklace came to mind. What was it made of, a string of long narrow metal tags, like a weird charm necklace.

Merrilee returned to the notes from the last day of school once more. Somebody had mentioned a rumor about Aster, and then she looked again at some of the things Jude told them.

Merrilee then laid out the copies of the articles on the fires from five years ago and finally Merrilee flipped forward to the day before she'd gone out to Atwood's and the sheet where she'd written the names of the wrecks.

1. Kia Optima
2. Ford Escort
3. Nissan Sentra
4. Nissan Altima
5. Ford Escort
6. Dodge Caravan
7. Toyota Yaris
8. Toyota Camry

9. Dodge Omni
10. Renault Clio
11. Geo Metro
12. Honda Accord
13. Dodge Neon
14. Lexis IS
15. Isuzu Rodeo
16. Volvo C70

What was it Jet Corgan once said? That the wrecks were a gift. It was easy to scoff at Jet's optimism as so much wishful thinking, but what if somebody had been trying to tell the Corgans something?

Merrilee began to look at the letters, looking for patterns and words. She started and stopped several times. It seemed hopeless. There was nothing. Even a straight up acrostic was nonsense. There were two noticeable patterns that grabbed her attention. The two Fords sandwiched around Nissans and the two Dodges wrapped around Toyotas. Beyond that there was nothing.

Merrilee wondered if it was something about the vehicles themselves, something on them physically they'd overlooked. Jude had walked her past the entire row of them the night before, but he'd been so preoccupied with Zephyr he hadn't really given her the most thorough tour. She sat down at her desk again, deeper than ever in confusion. No sooner had she set her eyes back to the page than she saw something, a flash, a momentary recognition, and then the insight vanished.

"Just in time; the water's boiling," said Raeanne. Oscar had come from the field with fresh corn, and, in seconds, he and the twins had shucked a dozen ears. Corn was never better than when you brought it straight from the field and put it right into the pot. Raeanne quickly lowered the ears into her giant canner with tongs and set the timer. David was manning the grill and Willa was setting the table. The smell of barbecue's tangy sear came through the kitchen window and brought with it a sense of the rightness of things.

The nightmare of the last six weeks, if you went by the smell and look of things on the farm, might never have happened at all, except for the reminders they bore within themselves, things the familiar smells of a summer night could not erase. Like the loss of the cattle, the frightening change in David, and the inexplicable and eerie deaths of the bulldozer operators right in front of their eyes. How strange it had been one moment to stand terrified, hand in hand, as two giant earth movers bore down on them and their home, and then to witness a miracle, sudden impossible salvation and its chilling aftermath. It all happened so fast they barely understood the 'what' or 'how' of two machines breaking down catastrophically at once, but when the noise and smoke had cleared they sensed that something more than luck and poor engine maintenance had been at work. At the very least somebody had sabotaged Greenway's vehicles (somebody powerful was on their side), but the dead men in the cabs had been harder to fathom. Just how had they died? David thought perhaps they'd been electrocuted. Raeanne didn't think so. She'd been staring one of them in the eye (well, looking into his dark sunglasses), a mother's last defense against a heartless destroyer, and she had witnessed no commotion or spasm in the driver until the moment of the machine's last sputter, when he slumped forward over the wheel. Had they been meant to die? It haunted her.

At times, Greenway's power had been so uncanny, it seemed to defy nature to their utter detriment, and yet some opposition had acted with such divine speed and deadly power, they could not help but wonder and tremble in the aftermath that such force should prevail on their behalf.

The timer startled Raeanne. She lifted the basket out of the boiling water, feeling the hot cloud of steam on every pore of her face and set the ears on a large platter. She covered them with foil and went outside.

David saw Raeanne and held up one finger. Oscar, Willa and the twins saw her too and eagerly took their places around the picnic table.

"Butter it while it's hot." Raeanne set the platter down and each of the Meades' children held up a plate. She looked up at David and dropped the tongs.

A catamount, like something in a dream, was slinking across the lawn behind David. It would advance, then crouch and wait.

"David. Slowly turn your head and look behind you."

The kids all looked in that direction too and saw the catamount at the same moment their father turned his head.

"All of you in the house, now. Don't run just walk slowly."

The entire family got up and walked as calmly as they could toward the back door.

"There's another one," Junie said. The cat was advancing from the other side of the picnic table as if to bar escape.

Merrilee's cell phone rang.

"Hello."

"Hi, Merrilee? This is Mrs. Corgan, Jude's mom. Is Jude there with you?"

"No. He left here hours ago. You mean he hasn't been home?"

"No. Hours you say? Like when?"

"Like two o'clock."

"Did he say he was going somewhere?"

The nagging feeling was back, but now it felt like a sickening weight on Merrilee's stomach. "Not that I know of."

"Oh dear."

There was silence, and, in that gap, Merrilee could hear the mounting fear of a mother who had already lost one son on a steep mountain curve.

"But where would he go, Merrilee?"

Merrilee thought for a minute. "Maybe he went to see Ms. LaFrance."

"Why would he go there?"

"He's been kind of concerned about her since all her troubles—she was his favorite teacher and everything. I'll ride my bike over and see if he's there."

"Would you?"

"Sure."

"Let us know if he's there, okay?"

Merrilee went to get her bike in the garage below the loft. An older boy passed her house. He wore no shirt and the moment he crossed the street, turning his back to her, she saw the tattoo. It was Calvin.

Merrilee was on her bike and phoning Sandra. "Jude never went home today after he left me. His mom is worried, so I'm heading over to see if he's at Ms. LaFrance's house. There's something weird with her. She pointed a gun at him last week. And you'll never guess, it looks like our tattooed Calvin is heading the same way."

"I'm on my way. I'll call Cate and Alison and tell them to head there."

Zephyr let the curtain fall back in place when the tattooed boy walked by. That was the signal. She had the rifle assembly in its canvass knap on her back and a loaded pistol in her belt. She was heading for the back door when she heard a knock out front. This better not be Jude. She opened the door. The next worst thing: his best friend, Merrilee.

"Hi, Merrilee; you caught me heading out the door, I'm afraid."

"I was just wondering if Jude had been here."

"No, I haven't seen him since last week."

"It's just he never went home and his mother is worried."

"Well, Jude's a big boy; I'm sure he's alright. I hate to be in such a rush, but I really do have to go." Zephyr closed the door on Merrilee.

Merrilee stood there for a moment with her mouth open. She phoned the Corgans back. "Hello?"

"No sign of him at Ms. LaFrance's. There's something you guys should know. Jude was talking with Osmena Searle today after you left the market. Jude said she asked him to convince Mr. Corgan to build some machine for her. I don't know where he is, but it's possible it has something to do with her. One other thing."

"Yes, Merrilee?"

"Something I have to ask you."

"Okay."

"Jude told me on the night Kennedy died he overheard a fight between you and Jet and Kennedy, but he also told me you said it never happened."

There was silence on the other end.

"Mrs. Corgan?"

"It never happened like that. I mean, it didn't happen the night he died. We came back late from a concert and the boys were in bed. The next thing we knew—"

"So the fight never happened?"

"There was a fight, but that happened a week before."

"So Jude conflated the two nights and remembers Kennedy tearing up the mountain, upset after a fight, but the truth is you don't really know why he was up on the mountain that night."

"We've never known. Merrilee, just what are you driving at?"

"I don't quite know yet, but Jude's been asking that very question and I think he might be looking to Osmena for the answer."

Merrilee rode back to Main Street and was about to turn right toward her house, when she saw Calvin cross the trestle and disappear around the corner up Old Route 9. He'd turned around and disappeared down the railroad tracks after he passed Ms. LaFrance's house. While Merrilee was at the door, she'd lost sight of him. She didn't want to lose him again. She followed him at a distance and dialed Sandra. "Change of plans. Forget Ms. LaFrance. I'm following Calvin up OR 9. Back me up."

Sergeant Roderick woke up with a start at 7 p.m. For a moment he was disoriented by the station, as if he'd expected to wake up in his sitting room chair, then he remembered why he was in there. He'd missed Calvin's passing by half an hour. It was too late. The muscle relaxer he'd taken for his back had made him doze. He knew he was going to need it for his hike in the mountains. Calvin said it was a long haul, so he'd been prepared. He was at the desk going over his plan and the last time he'd looked at the clock it was 6:15. He remembered starting to feel really relaxed and mellow.

Ever since the explosion Roderick had been impatient with the local talk about the VLF and skeptical of their apocalyptic warning: *The End has Come.* But the events of the last few weeks had changed his mind. Somebody else was in control of things, and they were not playing around. That greedy old witch on the mountain had nothing to do with Vermont's new found parity, and he was certain she wasn't one bit pleased about it. His own finances, he had to admit, were a bit better than they'd been before, but who the hell did these Commies think they were, breaking every law of commerce, upending the whole economy, and taking and giving without anyone's blessed consent? They'd never get away with it on his watch, even if he had to ally himself with that wicked old thief herself.

If Osmena were desperate enough, she might be willing to cooperate. Maybe a drive up the mountain would serve as well as a hike in the woods after all.

The lights in the corridor were dimmed to a faint bluish glow that seeped into the dark of Jude's cell. He was alone and everything was silent. Every now and then he heard very distant echoes of closing doors. He had no idea what time it was, and how long they meant to keep him here. Aster and Jet would start to worry soon, but they would never guess where he was, unless...

Merrilee knew he'd been talking to Osmena, and he was sure she'd guessed there was more to the story than he was telling. He could tell by her questions and the way she'd looked at him. He could only hope. There was nothing else he could do.

Jude rolled over on his side in the bed and felt something hard against his thigh. He lowered his feet over the edge of the bed and sat up. He reached into his pocket and found the vial. He'd only taken half because he'd been afraid of what it might do to him. Now, at least he had a secret weapon, something that would give him a burst of super strength. But when should he take it? He went over to the bars. They were solid. He doubted even Osmena's formula could give him enough strength to bend steel, but would he have the strength to lift the grate up enough for him to squeeze under it? It was a risk. If it didn't work he would have wasted his secret advantage, but unless he could get out he'd have no opportunity to use it. The alternative was to sit idly by, while Zephyr went out on her murderous errand and catamounts surrounded Gemini Farm. He shuddered in remembrance of the hellish scream of cats echoing in the darkness down the corridor when Calvin had come for them.

Something else troubled Jude. Osmena had said their lives could be so different. What would it be like for once to be favored? What was really going to happen when the VLF took over? Who was to say Zephyr wouldn't be a hero for helping to take them down? But was she really a volunteer, or had she been forced to take part? Then there was Osmena. Despite everything he'd heard and witnessed, there was a part of him that admired her.

She talked to him like an adult. He had to admit, he liked her and felt like he mattered when he was with her. Her wit, what she knew, the world she inhabited—it was all so rich and mysterious. The way she spoke and dressed. To look at her you'd think she was weak and old, but she was very wise and powerful. If he did get out, he wasn't sure what he would do. If there was no way to keep her from getting the skull back and taking the water she was after, what good would it do to oppose her once she held all the cards? It would be easier to decide, if he knew what and who to believe. Then he'd be free to act, make a decision instead of just going along with the winner.

Merrilee felt she'd been following Calvin in the woods for at least an hour. She could barely keep up with him and she was nearly sapped by the humid heat, but the sudden cool of the mountain gorge refreshed her. She lost sight of Calvin while ascending the trail above the falls, then caught his movement up ahead again and stayed on the trail. She even ran to see if she could gain on him. Then the trail got steep and she had to stop. Had he left the trail? She stopped and listened, strained above the pounding of her heart in her ears for a rustle. She scanned the forest to her left and then her right. In that moment, Calvin's tattooed back, flashed brown and disappeared into the green. She couldn't go on much longer. Even if she turned around now she'd never make it back the way she came before dark. She thought she could find her way back on the trail that went to Route 17, but she'd come all this way and couldn't turn back. She tugged and ripped off a piece of her cotton shirt sleeve and tied it to a branch beside the path. As she took her first steps off the path into the forest, she knew this wasn't taking her any closer to Jude and had a feeling it was probably a big mistake.

"Then I'm going up to Searle's," Jet said. "That girl's got a good head on her shoulders. If she thinks it's got something to do with Miss Searle, then I wouldn't doubt it."

Jet got onto the Mowercar and started the engine.

"Aren't you taking the truck?" Aster said.

"It's too hard to find by the road. I'll just get lost. Now that I have this old girl, I can take Nesbitt 3249 out to Landreaux's logging road. It goes right up onto her land not a hundred yards from her front gates. Besides, you might need the truck."

"Just be careful Jet, please." Aster leaned over and kissed him.

Jet squeezed the throttle, turned on the headlamp and rolled down the drive. He waved to Aster, turned left onto OR 9 and started up the mountain.

⌘ ⌘ ⌘

M ERRILEE WISHED SHE could get closer to hear what Dentremont was saying. She recognized the wild mane of blond hair from the newspaper photo, and he was addressing a group of men mostly, several women too, in a woodland clearing. She had stumbled onto a meeting of the VLF. She didn't know how long they'd been there, but by the deepening shadows in the forest behind her, she didn't think they'd be meeting too much longer. The light in the clearing was better and she could make out Chet Atwood, standing to Dentremont's right. She didn't recognize anybody else. Most of the people had their backs to her anyway.

Calvin was nowhere to be found. Merrilee lost him for good once she'd left the trail, but soon after she'd heard voices. When she came upon the clearing, she knew why he had come here.

A man with dark hair and a beard spread his arms. The men around him stepped away from him until he stood alone. Luc Dentremont pulled out a pistol aimed it right at the man's chest from no more than five feet away. Gasps and fearful murmurs stirred the gathering. Merrilee covered her mouth to keep from giving herself away. Luc fired once. The dark-haired man remained on his feet unflinching. A cry of wonderment replaced the fear. The man lifted his shirt to show he was unharmed. Where the bullet went, nobody knew.

"Oh my God," Merrilee whispered, and, as if those words had been a signal, she was grabbed from behind. A hand covered her mouth, and a powerful forearm was thrust under her neck. She couldn't breathe. Then she felt lightheaded and the forest faded from green to black, as if somebody had the night on a dimmer.

In the clearing, the commotion stirred the gathering to action. Everything broke up at once and in seconds the VLF gathering vanished from the clearing down a trail. The sound of ATV engines starting in unison filled the dusk with their disquieting roar.

The other three members of GEIST glimpsed Merrilee just in time to see her grabbed from behind and carried away by two men—one wearing a mask. They'd found her abandoned bike at the head of a trail and had followed it. Then they'd seen a piece of her shirt tied to a bush, like a marker, and had gone into the forest there.

Cate and Sandra both covered Alison's mouth in reflex to keep her from screaming. They heard a commotion up ahead in some kind of clearing and then they heard the sound of engines, loud at first and then fading away.

"Why did you do that?" Alison said. "At least if we got caught they'd have taken us all and we'd know where they were taking her."

"But who would know where we were?" said Sandra.

"We've got to get back and tell the police that Merrilee's been abducted."

"There's a path out to Route 17," said Cate. "We should get cell reception there, but we'd better hurry, it's getting dark."

The girls turned and found themselves face to face with Zephyr LaFrance.

"Ms. LaFrance, thank God you're here. Merrilee's been abducted. You have to help us find her."

⌘ ⌘ ⌘

MORE TEENAGE GIRLS to contend with. What next, a Girl Scout troop? "One of us should go back and tell the police," said Alison.

That was the last thing Zephyr wanted. She looked around. Well, it was better if she kept the girls with her for now. Once she got them a little further into the woods it would be easy enough to lose them. They'd spend the rest of the night lost and wandering, none the worse for wear and her work would be long finished.

"It's okay girls. You stay with me; I know these woods backwards and forwards. It's the VLF who has her and I know where they are, but you'll have to move fast, because we haven't got much time, and it's going to be dark soon. Okay?"

The girls nodded agreement.

"Ready then? We haven't got a minute to waste."

PART III

25.

The Liberation Front

A BUMP IN THE road rocked Merrilee's head and she awakened. She lay still with her eyes closed. The smell of musty rope, metal and canvas was strong. She opened her eyes and tried to move. Her feet and hands were bound and the tight sensation across her mouth was tape. She was in a pickup bed with a truck cap. The silhouette of two heads bobbed with the bumps against the blue glow of the dash. The sliding window into the cab was open about in inch, and it must have been loose because the panel was vibrating and opening wider as they bumped along.

The men up front were talking and not aware she could hear them.

"What do you suppose the girl was doing there?"

"Followed somebody. Probably that Calvin."

"How did he ever find the clearing?"

"He doesn't know about tonight, so what does it matter? Luc knows about the girl. We agreed to take her to the bunker. So when Luc goes there to explain why she was taken, we'll take him and EG hostage as well."

"What about Atwood, Sokol and Landreaux?"

"Jake said them too. Even if they managed to free themselves they'll never break out of the bunker. Then we'll move on Osmena and Greenway. By the end of the night they'll be history."

⌘   ⌘   ⌘

O NE OF THE cats leapt up, paws on the parlor window, and screamed like a hellion. Everybody jumped back.

"I think we'd better get upstairs," said Raeanne.

Nobody argued. They just turned and went up, glancing back at the menace just outside their windows.

For a while, the Meades' had watched in amazement as the cats patrolled their farmer's porch like posted guards. They could not help but watch, for nobody had seen catamounts in Vermont since before the middle of the last century. Now, it seemed they might actually break through the old single panes of the farmhouse windows. Wild cats wouldn't act like this. They would never be out prowling with people around in the daylight. These cats were used to people.

David and Oscar moved a tall dresser to block the top of the stairs. They'd removed all but the top drawer and loaded it with anything heavy that would fit, so if the cats broke a window and came up after them, the dresser would tip back on them when they tried to clamber over it. The twins were with Oscar in his room. David and Raeanne were in Willa's room with her.

"Doesn't your buddy, Calvin, have a catamount tattooed on his back," said Oscar.

"Yeah, what about it?" Jesse said.

"Did you ever wonder why?" Junie asked.

Jesse didn't answer, but the moment the cats appeared in the yard, it occurred to him it had something to do with Calvin. He had a feeling, one he couldn't explain, as the first cat crept up behind his father, that this had somehow been inevitable. How could it even be true?

"It's just a coincidence."

"Could be," Oscar said. "But it isn't every day you see somebody with ink like that; and then they start hanging around and all of a sudden there are catamounts stalking us."

"It's not like they're wild cats. They had to come from somewhere," Junie said.

"Do we even know who Calvin is? He doesn't go to school here. Who are his people? Have you met them?"

A loud scratching from the porch roof made them look out the window. Oscar went over to look. "No way."

Junie and Jesse popped up and stood beside him. The catamounts, one on either end of the porch, had shimmied up the poles and climbed onto the porch roof. Willa's scream sounded from the room next door.

By the time the boys got out to the hall, David, Raeanne and Willa were there too.

"We'll be safe in the attic."

"But there's no light up there."

"I'll be right back." David headed down to the kitchen.

"Get a jug of water too," Raeanne called after him.

⌘ ⌘ ⌘

T HE ATTIC WAS hot and close. There was a small window on each end of the house, but even with both of them open there was barely any air. They sat near the window and took sips of water from the jug when they got thirsty. It was nearly dark out and the lantern made it feel like they were camping, but they all looked like scared campers who've just heard something wild in the night.

"Do you hear something?" Oscar said.

"Yeah."

Jesse got up and made his way across the attic, under the peak, the only place you could stand up straight and where there was a path so you didn't bump into chairs and boxes, or the brick column of the chimney on your way.

"Turn the lantern off for a minute," Jesse said.

The light went out and the attic went dark. Truck taillights moved away on the road toward their wood lot.

"What is it?" his father said.

"A truck."

"What kind of truck?"

"I can't tell, but it's pretty big and it's going toward the wood lot," Jesse said, with a sinking feeling in his stomach.

"The wood lot?" David said.

"Hey, you and Calvin were in there last week," said Junie.

"And?"

"You sure he didn't find some buried treasure out there while you guys were dowsing?"

"Junie, let up on your brother."

"Come one, Mom," Junie said. "We're being held hostage in our house by catamounts that supposedly don't exist, and now there's a truck on our property doing god knows what, while we're stuck in here. And whose fault is it?"

Raeanne turned the light back on. She looked at David.

"Did anybody bring the cell phone up with them?"

Raeanne shook her head. The boys shrugged.

"I guess we're stuck up here until morning. Well, we can keep an eye on that truck, at least. I've got that Greenway feeling in my bones."

"Ms. LaFrance, wait up," Alison called out again, but it seemed there was no slowing her down. Darkness had fallen and it grew harder to keep from tripping and falling, let alone pick out the trail and keep up with Ms. LaFrance. Cate and Sandra were getting ahead of her as well in their attempt to stay with Ms. LaFrance.

"You guys, I can't keep up."

Cate yelled to Ms. LaFrance. "Just stop for a minute, please, we're losing Alison."

Cate didn't know if Ms. LaFrance had heard or bothered to stop (she couldn't even make her out among the shadows), but she was so angry she wanted to run up from behind and tackle her to make her stop. Cate was about to let out a string of curses, when she practically bumped into Zephyr on the path.

"Now I told you girls, we'd have to move if you wanted to find your friend."

Sandra caught up, and finally Alison. A cool breeze came rushing through the trees like a new presence in the forest. The night air had been changing, but only now, at a moment's pause in their frantic pace, did they sense it. Then the stifling humidity washed over them again. The sky began to glow with the light of the rising moon.

"I tripped and hurt my ankle," Alison said.

"Well, it looks like this is where you all get off the train."

"You're just going to leave us here?" Cate said.

The girls could make out Zephyr's face, but it was too dark to read her expression. She stepped out of a shadow, reached to her side and raised a pistol.

"Do I have to repeat myself?" Zephyr said, pointing the gun at them.

The girls screamed and scattered from the path.

Zephyr fired once into the air and screams rang out from farther away and from different directions this time. Another breezed rushed in and drowned them out. Zephyr replaced the pistol and took off at a miler's brisk pace, as if all she were trying to do was run her own mountain marathon in the dark.

Jude waited until he thought it must be nearly dark before he took the rest of Osmena's formula. If he were going to escape it would have to be under the cover of darkness. Right now he had no idea if it would really give him enough strength to budge that gate of iron. So he waited as long as he could to test its potency, despite his impatience to escape. Every minute was making him crazier. He started pacing around his cell like a lunatic, muttering.

Sit down. Don't waste the juice in your cell like some hamster on a wheel.

Jude returned to the bed, but he felt unable to lie down. He just wanted to get home so Jet and Aster wouldn't worry. He didn't know what he was going to do about Osmena, or the machine, or even what he could do about Zephyr. Even if he were free, he had no way of knowing where she was or how to find her, let alone how to stop her from assassinating her brother.

There was something strangely unreal about an anonymous underground group. When Jude thought of them he couldn't imagine faces exactly. Vermont Liberation Front? He imagined revolutionaries in military fatigues with sweat rags and Che Guevara hats, toting automatic rifles and ammunition rounds in sashes across their chests. It was stupid, he knew. If they were Vermonters they were dressed in Carhartts or denim, maybe hunter's camouflage, and John Deere caps. He'd know exactly how they'd sound too, not with the Latin accents of the movies that made you think the idea of revolution itself was foreign, but blunt Vermont accents, with the T's rounded off, faint remnants of long dead French trappers he'd learned about in American History. And maybe that last trace of a thing that becomes something else, what was now called a Vermont accent, had kept something revolutionary and stubborn in it all along.

There was one face Jude knew, that of Luc Dentremont. Aster had kept a picture of him in her closet. She had known him once. Yet, it might never come to light and there was no proof Luc Dentremont was behind this. If Osmena succeeded, maybe everything associated with the VLF, their sudden presence in their lives, tangible in their bank accounts and the new mood of the people, would just disappear and fade away as if it never existed. Would Zephyr feel like a hero when the brother she'd thought she'd lost ended up dead at her hand?

It had to be an hour now. Jude went over to the cell bars and took hold of a horizontal section and pulled up with all his might like an Olympic weightlifter. Nothing. The bars wouldn't budge. Jude lay down on his back and gripped the bars behind his head and tried to shoulder press them this time. If only he could fit his head through the space in the bars he could push up from his chest instead of from behind his head, but his head was too large. It was no use.

26.

The Best Laid Plans

"**N**OBODY IS GOING to hurt you," Luc Dentremont said.

Merrilee pretended to come around under the bright lights of the underground room. She'd had to concentrate on relaxing so she'd feel like dead weight when they picked her up, but she'd managed to peek for a split second when a hatch in the earth opened and she was taken down below.

It was just Luc Dentremont, she and a young man in a mask, who stood like a watchman by the stairway. Merrilee sat in a large chair, her feet still bound but her mouth was untaped and her hands untied. Luc sat in a chair across from her.

Merrilee blinked and nodded.

"I just want to explain why we've taken you."

"You can't risk being exposed?"

Luc nodded, looked down and the beginnings of an embarrassed smile started. He cleared his throat and his expression became earnest. "Then you know who we are and where you are."

"You're Luc Dentremont. Some people think you're dead. I recognized you from a newspaper photo. So I guess there is a VLF, and we're somewhere in the mountains. Problem is nobody else knows where *I* am. Like my parents."

"I apologize for this truly, but, yes, we aren't in a position yet to come out publically." Up close the wild blond mane was tinged with gray hairs, but his skin was smooth and his eyes a golden brown color. His face was broad and handsome.

"I should say not. Not everything is peaches and cream since you started playing around with all the capital."

"I'm sorry, and you are?"

"Merrilee Rainey. Two r's, one l, two e's."

"Well, pleased to meet you, Merrilee. Luc Dentremont, officially."

"It was your land Osmena stole."

Luc raised an eyebrow at her perspicacity. "How do you know about that?"

"We found out trying to help Ms. LaFrance—"

"Zephyr?"

Merrilee nodded. "She said Osmena stole her father's land. But there wasn't any land owned by LaFrance, but there was by Dentremont."

"The land was in my mother's maiden name—Dentremont. Her family owned it all. I legally changed my name because of my involvement with the VLF, for Zephyr's sake. What's happened to her?"

"She's in deep with Osmena—bad news involving experimentals." Merrilee decided then to trust him and tell him everything. "But, there's no time to explain; your men are going to take you hostage tonight and storm Osmena's compound. I overheard it in the truck on the way here. Any time now."

Luc wore a look of disbelief, the confusion and pain of a knife in the back. Then a look of suspicion crossed his face. "You're sure this is true?"

"I swear it."

"EG, take the skull and go to the cabin."

The young man by the stairway rushed into a small back room.

"The black skull? It's real?"

"Yes. That's what we're protecting, and what's protecting us."

"That's why the man you shot in the clearing wasn't harmed."

EG emerged with something bundled in a small chamois sack.

"Go. Through the tunnel." Luc tossed a ring of keys to EG.

EG opened a padlocked door at the far end of the room and disappeared behind it. Luc went over to the door and snapped the padlock in place again.

"Where does that go?"

"Out to the edge of camp. For quick escapes."

"Shouldn't we—"

"We'll never make it."

"You mean with me?"

"Yes, and I'm not going to leave you alone."

"So the skull is what gave Osmena her power?"

Luc nodded. "Part of it."

The hinges of the bunker hatch squeaked open.

Booted feet sounded and treads creaked under the weight of many men. Chet Atwood and Jasper Landreaux were the first men down. Ivan Sokol was behind them. Their mouths were taped and their hands tied behind their backs.

"What's going on here," said Luc, buying time for EG to get away.

Jake looked at him. "Where's EG?"

"He was tired; I sent him off to get some sleep. What's this is all about?"

Jake nodded at Rene Savage and Gus Penrod. They went into the back room where the skull was kept.

"I'm sorry to have to tell you, Luc." Jake came around close as if to confide in Luc and then raised a pistol and hit him on the back of the head. Luc slumped to the floor. Merrilee screamed.

The door in the back room banged hard against the wall and Gus emerged with an empty metal safe box. "Skull's gone."

"Somebody tipped him off," Jake said.

"You want to bet it was that punk Calvin?"

"He didn't know about it."

"Then who did?"

Jake tossed his head in Merrilee's direction. "Tie her hands up again and tape her mouth so she doesn't make a peep. Tie him up and bind all their feet." He indicated Luc and his men. "And stand a guard over the bunker in case EG comes back."

"We can't just let him get away with the skull," said Gus.

"How will we find him at night? He knows the woods better than most of us. But do you think he actually knows how to use the skull?"

"He knows the invocation."

297

"Does he? By heart? If he forgets a single word, gets the order wrong in any way he may as well be wishing on a star. He has no experience using it. Anyway, he can't reverse our incantation because he doesn't know it; damn near impossible even when you do."

Calvin was breathing hard and drenched in sweat by the time he reached the edge of the encampment, but felt strong and full of vigor. The formula Osmena gave him had worked wonders. Without it, he could never have endured the mountain sprint he'd just run, let alone found the clearing and now the encampment.

Through an arch cut into the dense hemlock canopy, shadows of trees and silhouettes of men in motion leapt in firelight, a carousel of phantoms turning on headlight beams. The echo of masculine commands sounded as blunt and inarticulate as the bark of dogs, and the hum of idling engines rumbled like a bass tremolo through the forest. The air was pungent with diesel and warm pine.

Calvin leaned against a tree and caught his breath. Something big was going down tonight. Could it have had something to do with the girl in the clearing? He had seen her before in the village on her bike, and he had seen her on his way here tonight, for a moment standing outside the door of her house. She had to have followed him. But she couldn't have known anything about him and where he was going.

Something creaked and slammed behind him. Calvin jumped and turned at the sound, expecting to see a VLF jeep on the road. He recognized the mask.

"EG?"

EG jumped and almost dropped what he was carrying. He tucked it under his arm as if to hide it. "Calvin? You're not supposed to be here."

"I think that girl followed me to the clearing; I just wanted to make sure she was alright. What's going on?"

"The men have turned on Luc and are going to storm The Cosmos and take Osmena down. I got away."

The full moon overhead came out from behind a dark cloud. A cool wind whistled through the pines and set off their eerie creaking. Calvin saw the bundle under EG's arm.

"I've got to go, Calvin, and you'd better get out of here before they take you too."

Headlights were coming at them through the hemlock arch.

"The truck is coming out," Jesse said. Junie crowded in at the window to see for himself. Everybody sat forward. The full moon had risen and now the yard and the road to the wood lot were lit with sudden daylight brilliance. You could see everything but the shadowed places and the true color of things. The headlights stuttered, seemed to flash out and dim as the truck undulated on the rutted road and light bounced up and down off the reflective cone behind the head lamps. The effect was like somebody flashing their high beams off and on.

"Can you see what they're carrying?" David said.

"It's like a tanker truck but smaller," Jesse said.

"It's not metal, but plastic," Junie said.

"Then they're hauling water," said David.

"Zenger's old spring?" Raeanne said.

"What about it?"

"Well, the realtor said it was contaminated, so we never even bothered to find it."

"But who would go through all that bother for some old spring water. There's nothing *but* water under ground up here."

The truck passed out of sight around the house, muffling the sound of the engine to a mere vibration. Oscar got up and crossed to the other side to catch a glimpse of it as it pulled away down the drive.

"It's stopped beside another truck."

Junie and Jesse hurried over to get a look. It was a dark pick-up. Under the moonlight you could just about tell it was red. A man wearing a familiar hard hat got out of the passenger side of the tanker truck. He went to the pickup and retrieved a bag from the cab, and then lowered the tailgate. The man turned toward the house, put his fingers to his mouth and whistled. He tossed the contents of the bag into the truck bed. A moment later, the catamounts bounded in and began to devour what the man had left for them. He closed the tailgate, got into the pickup truck and started the engine.

The taillights glowed red. He pulled away, with the tanker following close behind.

"It looked like Greenway," Junie said.

"Maybe we'd better go out to the wood lot to have a look," David said.

⌘　⌘　⌘

ALL WAS DARK in Jude's dungeon cell except the dim blue florescent flutter in the corridor. The faint hum the lights made was the only sound he'd heard in hours. He'd been too sick and nervous to think of food, but he hadn't eaten since the farmer's market that morning and for the first time pangs of hunger started reminding him. Now, he was sorry he'd passed up Osmena's sandwiches.

Jude lay quietly on the bed, listening and doing all he could to conserve his energy. Osmena said exertion triggered the release of the chemical and the more you exerted the more energy it released. It was hard enough to lie still, but hunger was making him more nervous by the minute; so much so, he startled when he heard a noise out in the corridor. He sat up. It wasn't footsteps, but a kind a brief click or scuff. Then, as if appearing without approach, like a ghost, a silhouette passed behind the bars of his cell.

"Who's there? Osmena?"

"Psst." A figure stood at the cell door and motioned.

Jude got up and came forward cautiously.

"It's Stemple. I met you on the lawn when you arrived."

Kept me from escaping was more like it. As if Stemple read Jude's thoughts, he amended his statement. "When you were trying to leave."

Stemple was feeling through a bunch of keys to find the right one and trying the lock each time. Finally, there was a click. He opened the door and led Jude out into the hall.

"This way, Jude. You didn't touch your sandwiches at all, you must be hungry."

"Are you, like, a mind reader or something?"

300

Stemple looked back at Jude, his face blue in the pale light. "Not even Osmena can do that." A moment later he added, "That's about the only thing she can't do."

Jude and Stemple took a different staircase, not the spiral one Osmena brought Jude down. It led up to a tiny servant's kitchen. At the other end, an open arch led into a larger kitchen or pantry. The bread dough and cinnamon smell of a bakery lingered in the air.

The overhead light was off, but a coil shaped bulb burned dimly above a small sink. There was a refrigerator beside the sink and a rectangular café table in the corner up against the opposite wall. Jude took the chair at the end of the table.

"Aren't you going to get in trouble for this?"

"Don't worry, Madam hasn't been too well and retired early, and Mr. Greenway is off on an errand."

Stemple brought out the covered plate of sandwiches Jude hadn't wanted earlier and set it down before him with a glass of milk.

"Thanks." Jude took a sandwich. "Are they brother and sister?"

Stemple nodded. He pulled out the chair to Jude's left and sat down.

"I overheard Calvin calling her Aunty. And I heard about the water."

"Osmena needs it, you see. She's much older than she looks and—"

"That's why they're after the farm? They're my relatives, the Meades, you know."

"I'm afraid I do."

Jude swallowed a bite of sandwich. "Why do you work for her?"

"Why?" Stemple stared at Jude with incredulity, almost amusement. "Do you know where you've been for the past three hours?"

"The Cosmos Correctional Facility?" Jude joked.

"The servant's quarters."

Jude's smile went slack.

"Other than Hilton, the man who grabbed you, I am the only house servant. I lock them in each night when their work for the day is done. In fact, I had just finished my task, before I came to your cell."

"You're like prisoners?"

"That word is never to be uttered on these premises."

"Can't you just escape? I mean there're woods all around."

"It's very hard to do. There are creatures in the woods that will stalk you; and of course, the catamounts, trained to track like bloodhounds, only you can't hear them coming. My brother tried to escape."

"You had a brother here with you?"

"We were born here. Our parent's came with Osmena when she bought this place. That is, they met while in Madam's service."

"What happened to him?"

"My brother? I don't know to this day. I assume he got away because he wasn't captured, but...sometimes I lie awake at night and break out in sweats, gripped with a terror that something terrible happened to him." Stemple looked at Jude. "But what have you done that got you locked up here?"

"I interfered with Madam's plans," Jude mocked Stemple's formality. "I tried to help Ms. LaFrance."

"Ah, poor Ms. LaFrance. And you came of your own accord?"

"Osmena promised to tell me everything about Ms. LaFrance, and to tell me things about the night my brother died."

"You've lost a brother as well. How extraordinary."

"But your brother isn't dead. At least not that you know about."

"It was five years ago in June."

"Freaky. That's when my brother died. The thing is nobody knows why he was driving up on the mountain that night. My parents act like they don't know. Maybe they don't. Maybe I'm paranoid. I mean, I know how you feel at night lying awake, remembering things. Only I keep imagining things were different, or there was some way to stop it."

"Did Madam tell you what you came here to find out?"

"Not yet. She told me about Ms. LaFrance. I have to find a way to stop her."

"It may be too late for that, Jude. But, I think this is a sign. You are the sign. I have to find out what happened to my brother. I will help you escape, if I can come with you."

"On the Byclops? The seat's big enough for two, but it's going to be one heck of a downhill ride in the dark with two of us on there."

The sound of a closing door in a distant room silenced them.

"Mr. Greenway has returned with the water for Madam. Hide under the table. Madam and Mr. Greenway never come in here, and Hilton always takes his night meal in his room. I'll turn out the light. Don't move until I return and say the word 'brother'. They'll be waiting up anxiously tonight for Ms. LaFrance's return with the skull, so we shall have to make our escape as soon as they release me. Hurry, under the table."

⌘ ⌘ ⌘

"MADAM?" STEMPLE KNOCKED on the door of Osmena's bedroom. "Come in Stemple." The bedside lamp was on and Osmena was sitting up in bed when he entered. "Has Zephyr returned?"

"Not yet, Madam. But Mr. Greenway has returned with the water."

Stemple approached her bed with his tray.

"Ah, the water." Osmena grasped the cool glass with her trembling hand. She looked at it for a moment in the lamp light, and then she tilted her head back and drank deeply from the glass. She gasped like someone underwater coming up for air. "My, how fresh and thrilling and cold it is." She drank the rest of the glass.

Stemple set the tray and pitcher on her night table. "There is more, if Madam requires it."

"Yes. Pour me another glass." Osmena handed it back to him and he filled it again. She drank more slowly this time, then set the glass down, half empty, on the tray. "Oh, that does feel better. I feel refreshed, truly. Perhaps not stronger yet, but very soon I'll be right as rain."

The telephone rang and Stemple picked it up before the second ring. "Hello? Yes, Mister Calvin, she's here." He handed the receiver to Osmena.

"Yes, Calvin?"

"Aunty, listen. The VLF is on their way to The Cosmos, with trucks and guns. Dentremont's men have gone against him; I don't know, something happened, but they're coming for you and father."

The smile on Osmena's face froze in a mask of alarm. "Calvin, what are you saying? You're hysterical. Where are you?"

"Route 17. I couldn't get through on the cell. I ran all—"

Calvin was out of breath or the cell service was cutting out. "Calvin?"

"Aunty, get out of there; get in the chopper. I'll be there as soon as I can."

"You should stay where you are, out of danger. And don't you worry about us. I've had some water now and I'm feeling better."

"If something happens though? I'm com—I'll be there as soon—"

"Calvin?"

There was silence on the other end.

"Stemple, get my blue caftan from the closet there and my sturdy shoes. And some of that water to go."

Osmena was out of bed. She picked up the receiver and hit the radio button. "Hilton."

"Yes, Madam."

"The VLF is on their way to take The Cosmos. See that Mr. Greenway knows immediately and follow his instructions. Then take my satchel and go to the vault and take everything in there. All our papers, the maps, everything. We may need to fly out tonight."

"Madam, George is—"

"Mister Greenway can fly us out. See that the chopper is fueled and ready, just in case."

27.

The Assassin's Mark

"I'VE GOT TO stop," Alison said. For a while, she'd been able to keep going and her ankle felt okay, but it was swelling and stiffening up, so that every step caused her foot to throb with pain.

"We are so lost," said Sandra.

"Maybe we should just stay put for the night," Cate said. "Find the trail in the morning."

The girls had tried to backtrack after Zephyr abandoned them, but they must have gotten off on a side trail; for it soon melted into the woods and they were wandering untethered through the mountains in the dark.

"No," Alison said. "I don't want to stay here all night. Just give me a few minutes to rest."

"We should definitely keep going; it's just a matter of time before we hit a road. It's not the Alaskan wilderness."

"Unless we're going in circles," Cate said.

"I don't think we are. It's seems to be less steep here, and we've been heading gradually down."

"Okay, I'm ready." Alison took a step and nearly fell to the ground.

"You aren't ready."

"Wait. We can do this," Cate said. She took off her T-shirt.

"What are you doing?"

"Chill out, I've got a sports bra on."

Cate tore the jersey material down the seam. "Ever been in a three legged race? It's your right ankle, so we just tie your right leg to my left leg at the knee so you can bend it and I'll bear the weight for both of us."

Sandra tied their legs together. "Is that too tight?"

"No, it's okay. It's got to be secure. Let's try it. Just small steps. Swing your left and I'll swing my right together. Then I'll swing my left leg." They stood, each with an arm over the other's shoulder, and stepped forward together with their outer feet, and then Cate brought their tied legs forward. They practiced a few small steps until they got a rhythm.

"Not bad."

It was slow going. Alison and Cate had to stop frequently to keep balanced on the uneven terrain, and to keep Alison's suspended calf from cramping, but they were moving again. The girls came over a small rise and stopped. The ground ahead was flatter and tamer. Through a sparse growth of young trees a purplish glow radiated from a clearing.

"What is that?"

"Some kind of light."

"Out here?"

The periwinkle glow permeated the open growth as they passed through it, slanting in radiant shafts between the trees and rimming their slender silhouettes in its aura. They approached in silence and stopped at the edge of the clearing. It was a mountain meadow covered in bright candelabras of blue Vervain. A million dots of periwinkle light appeared suspended over the tawny grass. They bobbed and swayed under a fresh breeze and all the grass bent forward, releasing the ripe sweetness of the field into the night.

"Look at us," said Alison.

The girls were aglow with the reflected purple light. They started through the meadow and moved amidst the flowers.

"Where are we?" Cate said.

None of the girls dared say what they were thinking. Sandra plucked a stem. "Wow. They even glow after you pick them."

The wood across the meadow was dark and dense, and when the girls reached the other side they paused for a moment, as if they were leaving the safety of enchanted ground.

"Pick some flowers; we can use them like torches to light the way," Sandra said. "The stems are kind of tough; you have to cut through with your thumb nail."

"You pick them for us, we're kind of tied up at the moment," Cate said.

Tulley drove and Roderick gave directions as they wound their way through the mountain roads to The Cosmos.

"I told you that tattooed punk double crossed me. He was supposed to come by the station at six-thirty. No show."

"Yeah, but what's that got to do with Miss Searle? You're after the VLF."

"You know you're right, OB. Thank you for reminding me of that." Roderick reached over and slapped Tulley upside the head.

"Ow. You're welcome, sir. I think."

"Just pay attention to your driving. Here, this left. See, you would have missed it if I hadn't focused you."

"That's what you call it sir? I'm actually a little dizzy now."

"I call it asking for another. Now, don't distract me, OB. The point is, I owe Miss Searle a visit. If I know her, she doesn't like what's going on one bit. Nobody needs her anymore. I'm sure she'd be willing to put an old wrong right if it was to her advantage. If we could help her put things back the way they were."

"Respectfully, sir, I'm not sure I want things to go back to the way they were."

"Oh, you don't?"

"I already paid off an old credit card and if things keep up I'm going to be out of debt for the first time since I finished school."

"They're commies and soon they'll be telling you what to do. You want that, honestly?"

"Right now I'm so hamstrung with debts and bills, and with working two jobs I'm not free to do a darn thing I want to do anyhow. So, yeah, I'll take my chances with the VLF. You can hit me all night 'till I can't see straight, which by the way is assaulting an officer of the law, but that's how I feel about it, sir."

"Well, don't get so high and mighty, Officer Ben. And I am also an officer of the law, acting in that capacity against your insubordination; so, I suggest you shut up and take the next right, before I take you up on your offer. We're almost there."

⌘ ⌘ ⌘

OSMENA STRODE INTO the parlor, her blue caftan billowing behind her as if she'd been propelled through the door by a gust of wind.

Merlin Greenway was waiting there with Stemple and Hilton.

"The helicopter is ready. We should leave while we have the chance," Merlin said.

"Leave?" Osmena protested.

"Yes. As to the servants. What should we do about them?"

"We let them out and arm them to fight. There're more of us than there are of them."

"But, sister, they have the skull."

"Do they? In minutes everything could change. It's too soon to turn and run."

Stemple's ears perked up at the mention of this skull. Could that have been the secret Orest had gotten away with?

"But they'll already have some incantation in place to neutralize our weapons. We'll never stand against them," Merlin said.

"Yes, guns, no doubt, will be useless, but their incantation is bound to miss something. Give them sticks, garden clippers, hedge trimmer, shovels and hammers, weed whackers and chain saws; I don't care. They can hide in the shrubs and attack by surprise. Oh, the skull is very demanding and particular and they will not have found a way to keep us from fighting altogether. Besides, those do-gooders will not be expecting an attack from the servants."

Merlin stood up. "Osmena, please. If they find the place empty and deserted, what can they do? And if Zephyr gets the skull as you say she will, we'll return before they can get comfortable on the furniture."

Osmena put a finger to her lips as if considering, then she shook her head. "No, I'm not giving up this house, or my gardens without a fight. My gardens are the eighth wonder of the world, Merlin. They will trample them without mercy and destroy this house because they hate me. Hilton get the tractor and fill the trailer with every tool you can find that can double as a weapon. Stemple release the servants and line them up on the reception lawn. We're staying and that's final."

Zephyr found the camp deserted and nearly dark. The campfires were dim piles of red embers, diffusing the sharp smell of ash and char into the air. She lifted her head and closed her eyes. There was some presence here yet, but the skull was gone. Something had happened and everything had changed. What she wanted was not here. She turned a slow circle and waited. It had been here, right near where she was standing. She opened her eyes and stepped forward. Yes. She remembered something just then. A room, a place she had been many years ago. The cabin.

Sandra led with her bouquet of candelabra flowers lighting the way. The deep shadows cast by the moonlight would have made the pine forest dark as pitch without them. Yet, they hadn't gone too far before the light of the plucked flowers began to fade.

"If only we could find a trail," said Sandra.

"Just keep heading down."

There was little undergrowth at least. Except for the small bone snap of twigs, the pine needle undergrowth was easy to negotiate and quiet underfoot. The waves of breeze caused little more than whispers in the tree tops. At first, the sound of their own footsteps echoed back between the dark hillsides and they would stop and listen as if they were being followed. They soon got used to this and lost their fear.

"Wait." Sandra bent down to tie her shoe. Three-legged Alison and Cate gratefully rested. That was when they heard a snap that was not of their own making.

"What was that?"

There was another snap, nearer this time. This was followed by a low growl. Sandra held out the dimming glow of the flowers as far as she could.

309

Out of the shadows, a dark creature approached on all fours, its head and cowl low, as if ready to spring.

"Oh, my God, what is that?"

It was dark in color, with brindling on its face and a blunt snout. Its teeth protruded, uneven and densely packed, in a permanent sneer, like a cross between a dog and some gnashing prehistoric beast. Alison screamed when she saw it.

"It's hideous."

"And probably rabid," said Cate.

Sandra stepped forward and thrust the flowers toward it like a torch. The animal flinched for a moment, and then advanced again. The girls stepped back.

Sandra reached down for a stick but it was dead and light as a feather. Beside her the sharp spoke of a dead pine branch poked her in the ribs. She reached out, yanked it from the trunk and swung it at the creature. It snarled louder, but the snarl didn't stop. It was a purr. The purr of a motor.

"Somebody's coming."

"Help! Help us!" The girls called out as the sound grew nearer. Sandra waved the still glowing bouquet of Vervain. Up ahead, advancing from behind the creature, a single headlamp flashed between the branches and grew stronger.

"Help!"

The headlamp swung away as it came upon them.

"Help! Don't go, please!"

The roar of the engine grew fainter for a moment, then burst louder and the headlamp turned again, shining on them and the dreadful creature.

A man got off his machine and started whooping and waving. Caught between them and the light he was just a silhouette of waving arms and stomping feet, glimpsed through a cloud of dust. The creature turned to face him.

"Well, aren't you one ugly beast," the man said.

It growled and woofed like a choking dog. The man growled back. He took a pistol out and shot the ground at its feet. It yelped and choked again and took off like a black blaze into the forest. The man put his gun away.

"You girls alright?"

"I think so," Sandra said, still shaken.

"You look lost."

"We are."

"And injured," said Alison, raising her hand.

"Bad?"

"Just my ankle."

"Sorry, I'm Jet Corgan, I'm looking for my son, Jude."

"You're Jude's father?"

"I'm Sandra. The three legged monster is Cate and Alison."

"Have you seen him?"

"No. Merrilee told us he hadn't come home and we followed her into the woods."

"Because she followed the boy with the tattoo into the woods," added Alison.

"You've lost me, girls."

"And we came upon some gathering up beyond the falls and Merrilee got kidnapped," Cate said.

"Abducted," Alison corrected her.

"Did you see who took her?"

"Two men grabbed her. I think she saw something she wasn't supposed to see."

"Lucky you didn't get taken too. This is no place for you girls. Do you know where you are?"

Alison shook her head, Cate shrugged and Sandra nodded.

"You're on Miss Searle's land. You don't want to be caught trespassing here at night."

"Yeah, what was that thing?"

"Feral dog, I'd guess. Something like it was found dead a few years back in Maine. Weren't like anything I've seen before, but then there've been stories about some strange creatures up here. One of you know how to drive?"

"I do. Been driving a tractor since I was 10," Cate said.

"Then you're gonna pilot this thing. You girls get on in the back."

HARD MAGIC

Sandra untied Cate and Alison's legs. Jet hoisted Alison onto the flat bed facing backwards.

"You'd better sit. Hold onto the rings."

Alison grasped a ring with each hand. Sandra got in behind her and stood facing forward. Cate got into the seat. The Mowercar was still idling.

"It stalled on me halfway here; took me a half-hour to get it going again. I adjusted the RPMs, best I could, but try not to stall it. There's your throttle. Your gears. Don't pull that lever because the mower blade will come down. Your headlight. The pedal stops it. Shift on the fly. Except reverse. Just take this trail right down the way I was going. It takes you to the road outside Osmena's gate, just wait there out of sight for me. You're our ride back. Unless something creepy comes for you; then just hit the road and get out of dodge as fast as you can."

"What are you going to do?"

"Merrilee thinks Jude going missing has to do with Osmena. Something at the market today. I'm going in from here on foot. You girls be careful then."

"Thank you, Mr. Corgan. You saved our lives."

"Well, maybe so."

It was all so strange and beautiful, the way Zephyr remembered, though she hadn't been here in nearly thirty years. Even while running, she could read the land and change direction without pause: a ledge, a dry rill, an old stone wall. She knew where to go. It was like a dream rich with shadow and golden moonlight, the kind where you return to a place you've been so many times before, and though you have no particular memories of those times, all remembrance is contained in that one dream.

Zephyr was amazed she had ever lived without the Assumption Formula. The abilities it granted her; the way she moved and felt. What she knew was what she sensed. The thing that was just and right. Her purpose. She was to get the black skull and kill the man who had taken it from Osmena. Luc Dentremont. As if the two represented a single idea and action. Yet, in this name two realities existed simultaneously. Luc Dentremont was the VLF leader; Luc Dentremont was her brother. As in the working out of a dream, the two could both share and maintain separation in their identity. She could kill one and not kill the other. It was simple. So simple. All were assumed in the assumption. The intoxicating formula.

The moon was so large and brilliant. A radiant medallion. She'd seen it over the last rise, a rocky promontory, without trees to block her view. There also, she'd seen it throw out flames, actual fire, and plummet to the earth like a burning comet. Had she? That was the sign and the way to the cabin. Where the moon had fallen.

The cabin was there when she arrived down the back of that slope, on a nearly level bit of land. A dark block in her vision. The trace of road was there as well. She stepped onto it and the dream deepened. The man. Who was the man holding her hand? And the boy clasping his other hand?

The skull was here. Just out of reach. In that darkened cabin was a frightened man. Luc Dentremont, or Luc Dentremont. The thrill deepened. Just within her reach.

Zephyr approached like a huntress, her pistol drawn, and a flashlight in her other hand ready to blind him. How quietly she walked, not stirring a leaf or breaking a twig, as if she were weightless. She was close enough now to see the door. She must not make a sound until the moment she opened it on him.

Zephyr felt a stone under her foot. The ring of stones around the fire. The campfire. Where the moon had landed. *Stay away from her.* Zephyr stopped. That voice, whose was it? The man in the dream she couldn't see, who was always there. *If I told you her power comes from an old tree, you'd think it was a fairy tale.* Not just the tree. He never knew about the skull!

Zephyr took a step toward the door. The threshold. Old stone. Old skull. *I call it, 'the Will of the World.'* The skull was almost in her hands.

Zephyr threw open the door and turned on her light. She swung the beam around the room. The man was sitting in the corner, clutching an object to his chest. There was something wrong. Was there? The moon had fallen here. The skull was here, but not Luc Dentremont. He wore a mask. The smell of mold and rot was strong. A floorboard caved and she stepped over the rotting wood. Webs as thick as spun silk wrapped the beams, corners and windows in their sheer white fabric.

"Give me the skull."

The man stood up, pressing his back to the corner. "Ms. LaFrance?"

"You don't know me. Give me that skull. You're not him. I don't have to kill you, but I will."

"Ms. LaFrance it's me."

"Wait. You are him, trying to disguise yourself. I know your voice. You can't fool me. And if you think I'm not serious." Zephyr aimed the gun.

The masked man charged her. Zephyr pushed him back into the corner with one hand. His head slammed into the wall and he slid down on the floor, dazed. She stood over him, shining the light down.

"Ms. LaFrance, please."

The man put up his hand, but instead of shielding himself, he removed the black mask and looked at her.

"Oh, my God!" For the first time Zephyr retreated, the pistol still poised to fire. The man in the dream? The boy who held his hand? No. The moon had fallen on his face. *Do you want to stop her?*

"Luc?"

"I'm not Luc."

"But, I know you."

"Yes, you do Ms. LaFrance."

"Do you want to stop her?" Zephyr asked the question, plucked the last words she had heard inside her head. The moon was in the sky again. It hadn't fallen. A wrong assumption. Whose words and meanings was she now?

EG rubbed the back of his head. "That is the plan."

"It is." Zephyr lowered the gun, extended her hand and helped EG to his feet. Her eyes filled up. She pulled him to her breast and held him while they wept in the rotten smelling darkness of the cabin.

28.

The Fall of The Cosmos

FOOTSTEPS SOUNDED THROUGH the big kitchen and entered the servant's nook. Jude held his breath and remained still. The light went on over the sink. "Brother."

"Come out. Something's happened." Stemple pulled out the chair and Jude crawled from his hiding place and got to his feet.

"The VLF is going to storm the compound tonight. Mister Calvin informed Madam."

"That's good right?"

"Maybe. Hurry." Stemple flicked on a light and led the way down the stairs to the servant's quarters. "There was an insurrection in the VLF and its leader was taken hostage. There's no telling what his men have in mind."

"But if Luc Dentremont was taken hostage, that means he's still alive." It gave him hope that Zephyr had not been able to carry out Osmena's plans.

"You're wondering about Ms. LaFrance. Dentremont could still be in danger. Mister Calvin got cut off."

Jude and Stemple reached the corridor where Jude had been held. Stemple flipped on lights as they started down the hall. "Listen Jude. I cannot go with you now." He stopped where the hall turned off to the left. "Madam wants the servants released and armed to fight the VLF."

Jude laughed. "Sorry. I bet you guys are kick-ass ninjas, but do you even have weapons?"

315

"Mr. Greenway is certain the VLF will have protected themselves against firearms at the very least. There's no way of knowing what we'll be able to do. I know. Garden tools aren't exactly one's weapons of choice."

"What's going to happen?"

"I have no idea. Continue down the hall. At the end there is a door. I've unlocked it already. That's the way out. Turn left and head across the gardens; it will take you to the edge of the woods. You don't want to be caught on the open lawn when they get here. Wait for me in the woods with your—"

"Byclops."

"Yes. I'll get there as soon as I can."

"Sergeant Sir, listen, you hear that?"

Roderick sat up in the passenger seat. "Company?"

It was only a rumble at first, but it soon grew into a roar. The vibration shook the dash.

"A lot of company. Feds?"

"The Feds didn't start taking this seriously until the money started changing hands. I suppose Osmena's a person of interest in anything having to do with a lot of money, but I doubt she's even on their radar."

The first truck appeared around the corner stopping short of the gate. Behind the bend, headlights from the other trucks threw fractured bands of light and shadow. Then the gates swung open, and one by one the trucks entered the drive.

"Guests?" Roderick said.

"Let's go in and see."

"Too soon. Let's wait."

"What if they're committing a crime?"

"We can't stop that many men by ourselves. We have all we need to find out what's going on right here."

Roderick switched on the tuner. "All big trucks have radios."

The rumble started first, then the headlights flooded the understory of the locust wood and finally, when they rounded the last bend, the trucks appeared in a line and came up the drive toward The Cosmos. Osmena watched from the balcony of the north carousel. A fresh breeze stirred her blue caftan. She gripped the balustrade and surveyed the gardens below. It appeared that nobody was afoot, but she knew the servants were hidden, lying in wait to strike the VLF as they approached the house.

The trucks split off and circled the perimeter of the estate. Merlin and Hilton were down below arming the alarms. If they got into the house, it wouldn't be long before the police would be on their way. Osmena reached into her caftan for her phone and pressed the number one.

"Yes?"

"They're surrounding us. I've counted ten trucks. How many of them can there be? Surely we outnumber them at least."

"But we don't know what the servants can or will do. We still have a chance to escape if we head to the tunnel now."

"Brother, we will not. They assume because we live outside the law that we aren't protected by it. Tonight the law is on our side."

David Meades shined the flashlight beam into the midst of the Zenger's cellar hole, revealing freshly dug dirt mounds on either side of an old well seal. The smell of broken ferns—a wild and wounded sweetness—and the graveside smell of soil filled the night. The moon was radiant, but wind gusts tossed shadows of the trees darkly over the source.

David, Oscar, and the twins had followed the signs of disturbed vegetation by lantern light and it led them right to the old Zenger spring as they'd suspected.

"It was the water they were after," said Junie.

Oscar set the lantern down beside the well seal. It was not concrete like the new ones, but chiseled stone and very ornately carved : a spreading tree with roots arching like a bridge over a stream. Above the crown of the tree was the name Zenger, and down below the stream there were words curved along the bottom of the circular seal.

David got down on his knees. The lettering appeared to be chipped, but it was dirt caked in the crevices of the letters. He took out his pocket knife and used a tool to clear the dirt out of the letters. *I am the water of life* stood revealed.

"Is this what he's been after all along?" David looked up at his sons. "He went through a lot of trouble to get it. What if he thinks it is just that? The water of life."

"Didn't Mom say it was contaminated?" Jesse said.

"Mom said the realtor said it was contaminated."

"Which may be what the Zengers told the realtor," said Oscar.

"The Zengers were all dead when we bought the property. Well, the local ones. There was a cousin from the Midwest, near Chicago. We met him at the sale. He mentioned some religious mania and rolled his eyes. We never gave it any thought and we never heard anything about the spring. The property was abandoned and deserted for almost twenty years when we moved in. Charbonneau said something about the old man. Of course I thought he was joking. He said, nobody lives that long outside the Bible."

"But Greenway's too smart to fall for some old superstition," said Oscar.

"Unless it isn't superstition," said Junie. He shoved Jesse's shoulder. "I guess Calvin really played you. Some friend."

Jesse shoved him back with both hands. "Shut up. I'm sick of listening to you."

"Sick of the truth."

"The only truth is you're jealous."

"Jealous of your boyfriend?"

"Boys." David was still on his knees about to get up, when Jesse lunged at Junie. Junie lurched backward into David and both lost their balance— David rolling sideways into the mound of dirt, Junie pitching back onto the Zenger's seal. He landed hard with a thud.

"Junie!" David pushed forward and knelt over his son. Junie didn't answer, but lay still with his eyes closed. David laid two fingers on Junie's neck. "We can't move him. Get to the house and call an ambulance."

Oscar ran full speed out of the woods toward the house. Jesse stood frozen as a pillar, pale and open mouthed, gazing at the still, unconscious body of his brother.

⌘ ⌘ ⌘

318

J AKE ALLARD LED his men through the spiral of the gardens, weaving
through the maze of hedges, beds and arbors toward the house. The space
around the hedges was deeply shadowed, while the open clipped bands of
lawn in between were lit by the moon. You couldn't be seen in the shadows,
but you also couldn't see what lay around the next hedge. He held up his
hand to stop the advance of his men. "Fisher Cat, this is Front Man. Any
movement?"

Jake's radio crackled. "This is Fisher Cat, Front Man. Negative."

"Front Man, this is Sugar Man. North side I've seen a light go on in the
house, no movement."

"Roger that. We're forty or fifty yards from the house. Let's go. Approach
and secure the entrances."

Jake broke across the grass, waving his men on. They ducked through
an arch and cut across the open grass. They'd almost reached a back terrace,
when a shout went up, and men popped up from behind a privet hedge bran-
dishing sticks and rakes and shovels.

"Hold up," Jake ordered his men. "Prepare to fire."

The men stood in a line. Some raised handguns, others aimed rifles.

But the people behind the hedge weren't charging them. They were shouting and jumping up and down, raising their tools in the air. They dropped
them, or tossed them aside and scrambled over and around the hedge, some
of them falling and laughing.

Allard said, "Stand down." Osmena had sent out her servants to fight
them, but they had dropped their weapons in an instant. He wondered if
they would have done so without the prompting of an incantation. They were
running everywhere now in the moonlight in their gray institutional uni-
forms doing cartwheels, skipping hand in hand, and ripping plants out of the
flower beds. A woman pantomimed Osmena's outrage on the moonlit lawn.
"Not my Euphorbia mellifera! Oh, there shall be hell to pay for this!" And
then she laughed and ran with a hedge clipper snipping Osmena's favorite
plants. She followed the spiral out, "Not my Cardiocrinum giganteum! I've
waited five years for it to bloom! Five years!"

Allard's radio squawked. He picked it up and listened. "Mountain Fox,
here. What do we do with—"

"Her servants? Let them alone for now, unless they interfere with us. Secure the house. The servants are uniformed. Take anybody else in the house or on the premises into custody without exception. Copy me Fisher Cat and Sugar Man."

"Copy. This is Fisher Cat. We have a man in custody. Caught him approaching the house. He says he's looking for his son."

"This is Sugar Man. We have someone too. Teenage boy trying to leave the premises. Says he's been held against his will."

"Hold him until we can have the place secured. Same with the man."

⌘ ⌘ ⌘

ZEPHYR TOSSED THE stick and heard it land.

"Who's there?" The guard turned and took a step toward the sound. He saw the stick bounce. He went over. Looked up at the canopy. Then bent over to pick up the stick. "Damn twigs are always falling—"

EG grabbed him from behind in a chokehold. In a few seconds the man went limp and slumped to ground. EG rolled him over and shone a light on his face. Dan Boyer. "Sorry, Dan, maybe." He'd have to apologize to the girl, also, for grabbing her back at the clearing.

EG whistled for Zephyr to come out, and together they lifted the hatch. "The hinge is 180," said EG. They laid it on the ground and descended into the bunker.

Jasper, Chet and Ivan were sitting backs against the wall; Luc was lying on his side and Merrilee was in a chair. They were all bound and gagged but their eyes lit up when they saw EG.

Zephyr and EG untied them and removed the tape from their mouths.

"Don't trust her," Merrilee said.

"Zephyr?"

Luc got to his feet and looked at his sister for the first time in more than twenty years. They moved toward each other as if magnetized, the pull starting, edging them closer and then drawing them in irresistibly.

320

"Luc. All this time so close; and you—" Zephyr said to EG, tears coming to her eyes again.

Luc cleared his throat and looked at Merrilee.

"Zephyr's okay, now," EG explained to Merrilee. "She was supposed to get the skull back and kill Luc."

"But?" Merrilee asked.

"But the spell is broken," said Zephyr.

"How did that happen?"

Luc raised his eyebrows at his sister and EG.

EG shrugged. "Case of mistaken identity."

Merrilee stared down over her glasses at the eye holes in the mask. Then she saw the necklace. It must have been tucked under his shirt before, but had slipped outside his shirt neck. The same one that had flashed in the sun and blinded her at Atwood's that day. She knew he was the one she'd come upon and startled. Only now she could see the metal strips up close and see that they were VIN tags. A whole string of keepsakes. A shiver, unlike anything she'd ever felt, ran down her back. She opened her mouth to speak.

Jasper Landreaux said. "I hate to cut the reunion short, but we've got a party to crash."

EG handed Luc the skull. "Yeah, we'd better go."

"Take your hands off of me! This is trespassing! Breaking and entering! Assault! Kidnapping! Armed robbery! At this rate you will never see the outside world again!" Osmena shrieked.

"Just checking to see you weren't tied too tight," said Gus Penrod to his captive. "Unless you want me to make them tighter."

"I set off the silent alarm, you know. It won't be long before the police are here, and then how will you explain your little overthrow to people who live in the real world? This isn't a game of revolution in the woods. You've no right in their eyes to be here."

"Miss Searle. Your alarm isn't going to rouse anybody tonight. We put a lot of thought into our incantation; and that was one of them."

"Where have you taken my brother? I demand to know."

Penrod stopped, opened a cell door with Osmena's keys. "Step in."

"I will not."

Penrod grabbed her arm and pushed her toward the opening. She stumbled in. He closed the door. "We thought it was best to separate you and your brother for tonight."

Penrod took out his radio. "Front Man, this is Mountain Fox. The Empress is in custody."

"Front Man copies. What about Greenway?"

"Ditto. Mountain Fox, out." Penrod started to leave down the hall.

"You're going to leave me here with her?"

Across the hall, Jude Corgan stood at the bars in the cell opposite her.

Jude waved at her. "So glad you could join me," he said.

The squeak and echo of running in the hall made them turn. Penrod looked back. A servant was coming toward them. The man stopped dead at Osmena's cell and stood, mouth ajar, as if he'd seen the glory of God. "How does Madam like the accommodations? Is it time for your tea? Oh dear. Well, past."

"Avery Mason, you are drunk."

"No, Miss Searle, I'm free." Avery leaned and then straightened himself. "And a little drunk."

"If you've gotten into Mr. Greenway's 12 year old scotch he'll be most displeased."

Penrod intervened. "Out of here before you end up in the cell next to her. Go on." The servant turned and ran back down the hall.

"Front Man, this is Mountain Fox, do you read."

"I read you."

"We seem to have lost containment. I thought all the entrances were secured."

Jude remembered the door Stemple had unlocked for him.

"Get out of here while you still can," Stemple told them. There were seven or eight of them in Osmena's apothecary stuffing bottles of her formulas into their pockets.

"Oh, what about the new ones, the batch from the 4th of July."

322

"You're going to end up back in your cells if you don't get out of here. Do you hear me?"

"You're not our boss."

"This stuff is ours by right. We worked all through the night to make it."

"Many nights. What's this? *Assumption Formula.*"

"Don't take that, please," Stemple said. He came around the center table trying to shoo them.

"It must be good if Mr. Stick-in-the-mud doesn't want us to take it. What's this? *Light My Fire.* I'm ready." Clyde, one of the gardeners, unscrewed the cap and chugged the small bottle. "Whooh! That's some hot stuff."

Stemple threw up his hands and left. It was no use. In a strange way it made sense. Their captivity had always been connected to this place and so their first acts of freedom would be in overturning its ownership and rules. Stemple wanted no more of it. It would be too late for him if he didn't leave now. Jude was waiting for him.

"So, tell me what the people think about it?" Luc asked Merrilee. They swayed and bounced in the back of an army truck, seated opposite each other on wooden crates. Luc grabbed the back of his head and winced.

The smell of musty canvas was strong. Through the open back, the forest jostled behind them in a stutter of tree shapes, moonlight and shadows. Merrilee felt like she was heading off on a dangerous campaign.

"Most people are happy as kids at Christmas. The higher ups are about to explode. The government checks have stopped. Hospital billing is a nightmare, and a lot of state workers haven't gotten paid. The investment capital is gone and if it keeps up the state's probably going to plunge into a depression. And the Feds are finally taking you seriously, so you and that skull had better do some fast thinking."

"There's a lot we haven't put into place. It's coming. But, for your information, the capital isn't gone; it's just been distributed more widely and evenly. Workers haven't gotten paid by the state, but they have money in the bank. If a man is dying of thirst, you give him water and then you dig him a well, you don't tell him to lie in the road and wait for the rich man's water truck to go by so he can catch the few drops that trickle into the dust. It's gone too far the other way, and the only reasonable thing is to begin again. Give everybody some chips so they can get back in the game again. If it means the government falls apart, so be it, at least the people will not be without, and as long as they're controlling their own money and have some to control, they're going to be putting it into the economy; and if the economy springs from the ground up it's going to be a real economy. Small scale and organic. Try and let it unfold again and see if we do better this time around."

"Well put. I might even vote for you if you were running for something."

"I'm not running, but I'm elected. And I've got an incantation to recite." Luc removed the skull from its sack, and laid his hands on it.

29.

Ice and Fire

CATE STEERED THE Mowercar through a narrowing in the trail. She ducked the brush, as it gave then snapped back at her, so she didn't catch one in the eye. One branch snapped hard against her wrist. Her exclamation of pain joined Alison's steady aria to bumps and bruises, which modulated up and down with every rut and washboard they encountered.

They rode a long slow curve and then came out to a wide straightaway.

"Shhh." Sandra hushed them.

This was the turn off, and they were not alone. A police cruiser sat in the entrance facing out. Cate braked and threw it in reverse. She backed up just out of sight, killed the lights and shut off the engine. The cruiser was empty as far as they could see.

"It's a Twin Gaps cruiser," whispered Sandra.

"Do you think Jude's father called the police?"

"Maybe. He didn't say so."

"Why else would the police be here?"

⌘ ⌘ ⌘

"WELL, WE MISSED our chance to get inside," Tulley said. They'd picked up the VLF's transmission as they advanced on The Cosmos and

325

had gone to the gate on foot to see if they could get a glimpse of what was going on, but the gate had shut behind the trucks. They headed back to the cruiser.

"We might as well listen in some more. Let them scare the hell out of Osmena first, and then we call in the Feds to take care of this lot of fools."

"Did you hear that?"

"No, I was talking OB. Hear what?"

"An engine or something."

"Probably the VLF trucks."

"No, it was closer."

"Well, do you hear it now?"

"No."

Roderick and Tulley got in the squad car and tuned in the scanner.

"Front Man, this is Mountain Fox. The Empress is in custody."

Roderick slapped his knee and laughed. "That alone was worth the wait."

"Front Man copies. What about Greenway?"

Roderick stopped laughing. "Greenway?"

"Ditto. Mountain Fox, out."

"Greenway and Osmena?" Frederick appeared to be in shock.

"Hey, weren't you taking your marching orders from Greenway? Looks like he had you foo—"

Roderick swung a fist into Tulley's solar plexus.

Tulley lost his breath. His eyes watered and his mouth opened wide, but only a faint airy wheeze leaked out of him. He threw his hands out and gripped the steering wheel, like a drowning man clutching a life ring. His lips moved around silent syllables. Then the wheeze got louder and he began to breathe again.

"What were you saying Officer Ben?"

Tulley blew hard between pursed lips and wiped his eyes. "Pain inflicted in the line of duty is its own reward, Sir?" he managed to squeak out.

"That's the correct answer."

⌘ ⌘ ⌘

M OMENTS AFTER MOUNTAIN Fox had delivered Osmena to her cell, the door from upstairs opened again and more footsteps sounded in the hallway. Two men in fatigue pants and black t-shirts were leading a rather vocal resister down the hall. Jude and Osmena both came to the bars of their cells to see.

"She's got my boy," the man said. The moment sound and sight merged, Jude recognized his father.

"Dad?"

"Jude!"

The men approached the cell. Jet tried to turn, but the men held him fast and kept moving.

"This one gave us a hell of a struggle."

"Jude, are you alright?"

"I'm fine. How did you know I was here?"

"Merrilee figured it out. So here I am."

Jude felt something welling up in his throat, something he hadn't felt in many years. God bless Merrilee for being too smart for her own good, and God bless Jet for coming. Even if he got himself caught, the thing was that he'd come looking.

"Dad—" Jude began, but he couldn't speak.

"That's my son. She put him here. I demand you let us go."

"These men put your son in here; open your eyes, Jet Corgan. Do you think I locked myself up?" Osmena said. "When this is all over we must talk about building my machine."

Jet shouted back, "If anything happens to my son, the only thing I'm going to build for you is a coffin."

Jet and his captors disappeared down the hall.

"Yeah, they put me here after you put me here."

"Nevertheless, true in the strictest sense."

"Yeah, but you never tell the whole truth."

There was yet another commotion coming back up the hall, a metal on metal clatter. Another servant in drab gray streaked past them, running a short metal pipe against the bars. Osmena stepped back as he zithered her cell. In an afterthought, he stopped and returned to address Ms. Searle.

"How is the view of the estate from the basement Madam? Would you like another pillow for your bed? Now don't you worry about a thing, Miss; we're taking good care of your gardens." The servant brandished the pipe like a scythe.

"You scoundrel! Cretin!"

Boots clomped like horse hooves up the hall as a VLF man caught up with the servant, seizing his pole with one hand and grasping the back of his collar with the other. "Come on now; the house is sealed. You come in here again and I'll put you in that cell with her."

The servant looked back, waiting to be marched down the hall, but the man remained in place, holding onto his collar. Osmena stepped forward to see. The man stared straight ahead, his mouth slightly parted around the last word they'd formed, as if frozen. Osmena clapped once and pressed her hands together in a hallelujah, while the servant yanked against the hold, then unbuttoned his shirt and slipped free. The VLF man just stood there holding on to the limp shirt like a human clothes rack.

"Zephyr did it! Clever girl to stop them in their tracks," Osmena proclaimed. She paced back and forth clasping and releasing her hands. She stopped and turned to Jude. "Zephyr has the skull now. How do you like that? And the VLF will soon be history."

"Aunty?" the call echoed down the hall.

"Calvin? I'm over here."

Calvin arrived with his keys, followed by Greenway and Hilton. He let Osmena out and hugged her. "Are you okay?"

"I'm fine, dear boy. Just fine. You see?" Osmena pointed to the VLF guerilla. "The skull is ours again and we shall have it soon. Hilton, drive the water truck and go to Mr. Greenway's and wait for us there. Calvin, you take the cats and do the same. When Zephyr arrives with the skull we will dispose of all these frozen felons once and for all. Then we'll deal with the servants." Osmena turned with a sweep of her blue caftan and led them down the hall.

"What about me?" Jude said. "Are you just going to leave me here?"

Osmena stopped. She turned to face him.

"What about my brother? You promised to tell me."

"So, you really want to know?"

Greenway touched Osmena's arm. "We don't have time for this."

Osmena held up a hand to her brother. "A deal is a deal, I suppose. Very well. I remember your brother, Jude. A beautiful boy really. Not surprising really that Jet Corgan was not his birth father."

Osmena paused to register Jude's shock and disbelief.

"You lie."

"Well, your father is rather plain—attractive in his own way, but, you see, I had a revelation recently. Some clues rolling around in my head tonight: just who your brother reminded me of, only I'd never put one and one together. The truth is that Kennedy was going to meet his birth father that night, but he crashed and died on the way and never got the chance."

"How do you know that? You don't know."

"I have my first hand sources," Osmena said, opening her large eyes wider. "Haven't you figured out what the wrecks were telling you Jude? In all these years?" Osmena turned and walked away.

"What are they saying? Tell me!"

Osmena kept walking. She threw her head back and projected up at the high ceiling. "What you already know, Jude Corgan. Your brother died for nothing. For another dead man."

⌘ ⌘ ⌘

THE RADIOS HAD gone dead for some time. Roderick had a funny squint in his eye and whenever Tulley saw that look he wanted to be out of arms reach.

"What's the matter, Sir?"

"It's been awfully quiet for too long. Something's happened. Drive to the gate."

Tulley pulled out onto the road.

"Park right in front of it."

"You think it's time to call in the Feds, Sir."

"Maybe so, OB. Pull in parallel. Good."

"One thing's for sure. Anybody wants in or out, they gotta go through us."

"Officer Ben, you watch way too much T.V."

The rumbling started again, and a wide headlight glow underlit the canopy an eerie yellow.

"Here we go."

It was a single truck, like the others, only smaller.

"Ready OB?"

"Let's roll."

They got out of the cruiser and stood with their guns drawn. The truck approached and stopped with a squeak of worn down shoes. The driver got out with his hands up. The passenger followed suit.

"Ms. LaFrance?" Tulley lowered his gun.

"Officer Ben," Roderick warned.

"Sir, it's Ms. LaFrance."

"You need to take off that mask," Roderick said to the driver. "And I need to see your license and registration." He unclipped the flashlight from his belt and shined it on the upper windshield. "No inspection sticker either."

"Ben, we think Ms. Searle may be in danger, and maybe others too. If you'll just let us through," Zephyr said.

From behind the squad car, the gate swung open on its iron hinges with a slow even creak. Roderick said, "We know what's going on in there."

"So do we. From the radio. Osmena and Greenway and some others were taken into custody."

"I'm sorry," Tulley apologized. He holstered his gun and went around to the driver side to move the cruiser.

"OB, don't move that car," Roderick ordered him. "Or else."

"But, sir, we can go in now. Sir? Are you okay, Sir?"

Tulley looked over at Zephyr in confusion.

"Don't worry, he's just a bit frozen."

Luc Dentremont appeared with Merrilee Rainey from the back of the truck.

Then three girls emerged from the shadow of the turn off. Two of them arrived arm in arm, legs tied together, like stragglers in a three-legged race.

The girls screamed when they saw Merrilee and the four of them came together in an awkward hopping embrace. They screamed again, in terror, when they saw Zephyr on the other side of the truck. "She's okay now," Merrilee said.

"I'm so sorry about earlier girls, you have no idea. Truly. I was sort of under the influence. Officer Tulley? Would you mind escorting these young ladies home. I think they've had enough adventure for one night."

"But we're supposed to wait for Jude and his father," said Alison.

"They're in there?" said the man with the mask.

"I think so," said Sandra.

"The Mowercar is in the turnoff. Tell him it's there," said Cate.

"Come on girls, pile in."

Tulley helped Alison into the front seat and the rest of the girls got in the back.

"What are you going to do with him?" Zephyr said.

"I know just what to do with him." Tulley went over to the driver's side reached in the window and popped the trunk. "Give me a hand."

EG bent over and grabbed Roderick by the legs and Tulley grabbed him under the arms from behind. Then they hoisted him up, stuffed him into the trunk, long legs and all, and shut him in. Tulley chuckled in his throat, thinking how they'd find Nolan Roderick tomorrow—standing like a catatonic in the island on U Street with a hand up displaying his lost finger, his fly open and a sign taped to his back: I traded my finger for a bigger pistol. And maybe this: Public humiliation in the line of duty is its own reward.

Junie sat up in the hospital bed and took a sip of water through a straw. The back of his head was pounding still, but the drum of pain was duller now. The overhead fluorescent lights in the room hurt his eyes a little and the disinfectant smell of bandages was strong. After the CT scan came back negative for fractures they'd taken him off the backboard and he could move around again. There were no bleeds either, but he did have a concussion and a good sized knot on the back of his head.

Junie had only been unconscious for a few minutes, enough to give them all quite a scare. Everyone had been in to see him except Jesse. Although, he'd been woozy, dazed and not fully aware of everything going on around him for quite a while, so he couldn't be absolutely sure. There were nurses coming and going. The IV line going in his arm. The doctor asking him questions about what he remembered. Now that he felt clearer of mind, he couldn't stop thinking about Jesse, and it was making him more nervous and agitated the longer he lay there. He pushed the call button and a minute later the nurse arrived.

"Everything okay?" the nurse asked.

"Could you ask my brother Jesse to come in?" Junie's mom and Oscar had just gone home to put Willa to bed and keep an eye on things, but he knew his dad and Jesse had stayed behind.

The nurse stuck her head into the waiting room. "Your brother is asking for you," she said.

Jesse had been sitting staring at the TV without seeing or hearing what was happening on the screen. His leg had been jiggling nervously for hours, without his realizing it. Now, everything came to a stop and his stomach seemed to flip with nerves at the summons. He stood up suddenly and felt rather strange, almost mechanical, as if he'd forgotten how to use his legs. The strange out of body feeling stayed with him until he walked through the door and saw the relief on Junie's face.

It wasn't logical, but what Jesse feared most was that his twin brother's face would no longer be just like his own. That what happened between them had somehow changed them both forever. It was why he had put off coming in to see Junie for so long,

"I'm so sorry," the twins spoke at once.

Jesse sat down beside the bed on a rolling stool. "It was my fault."

"I was jealous and I shouldn't have been."

"I feel so stupid about Calvin and the spring."

"Hey, Mom signed his fake petition. So you weren't the only one. It wasn't your fault."

"I never meant—"

"Jess. I know it. You don't have to say it."

"I was so scared that you—"

"Come on. I'm not. It's just a concussion, which means you're going to have to do my chores for a couple of days. I'll milk it for three, if it makes you feel any better."

"Okay." Jesse smiled and gripped his brother's outstretched hand.

When the twins looked at each other, it was like looking in a mirror, but a mirror with a difference. It was a reflection, but a wondrous and spooky kind that didn't always return the same expression, and it was an assurance that as long as they both were in the world together, they would never be alone.

Junie knew it now. He also knew that life would test their bond again and again, but next time he'd be stronger. "Hey, Jess. Don't know what I'd do without you."

Jesse wanted to say what he felt should be true—that Junie should never have to, but all he could say was what he knew and hoped. "Same here."

⌘ ⌘ ⌘

Stemple found the Byclops where Jude had left it, but there was no sign of Jude. He paced and waited several minutes, but Jude should have been here waiting for him. The VLF must have captured him. He would have to go back.

As Stemple stared across the lawn at the moonlit cupolas of the house, a truck roared past him, up the drive toward the house.

"Wait!" Stemple emerged from the wood and ran across the moss, kicking up divots that surely would have drawn Madam's considerable ire. He ran, waved and called after them, but the truck was moving too fast, and in its urgent and voluble rumbling toward the house, neither saw nor heard him.

Zephyr drove the truck with EG and Luc hiding in the cargo. A pair of headlights went on from the parking area just outside the gardens and a vehicle came toward her up the drive. At the first curve it turned almost parallel to her. It was a small tanker. She slowed down and the tanker slowed as they neared each other. They stopped window to window.

Zephyr recognized the driver as the head gardener, Hilton.

"I'm Zephyr LaFrance."

Hilton's eyes lit up.

"I've got the skull and Luc Dentremont is dead."

"Wonderful, Miss Zephyr. Madam will be so very pleased. Drive right in."

"Is everything okay here?"

"Fine, Miss, everything is under control."

Hilton drove on. Zephyr breathed a sigh of relief and continued toward the house.

Calvin tried to take the shortest route back to the trailer where the cats were waiting, but he kept running into frenzied and unpredictable servants. First, he'd startled a couple making out in the grass. They'd looked up at him for a moment, and then went right back at it. Others were armed with garden tools, and made war on Osmena's gardens and hedges. In another lane, Geneva, an assistant to Hilton, ranted and brandished her hedge clippers over the fallen remains of a tall perennial. "Whoever destroyed my Aconitum is going to pay with forty lashes. No, I'll cut off their fingers with these. No, I shall make them eat its poisonous leaves and watch them die!"

"Stop it!" Calvin scolded her. "You're destroying everything."

Geneva dropped the hedge clippers, rushed him, eyes wide with desire, locked her arms around his neck and kissed him on the lips.

Calvin pushed her away. "Geneva, stop it. What's gotten into you?"

Geneva had in her eyes and in her smile the light of a great bursting secret. "Osmena has." Geneva dashed off without her clippers and disappeared into the shadows.

Calvin soon found himself all the way out at the entrance to the gardens, and passed the privet arch in time to see a truck arrive. It had to be Zephyr with the skull. The engine cut and the lights went out. Sure enough, Zephyr LaFrance got down and looked up toward the house. Calvin almost stepped out to greet her, when two men emerged from the back of the truck. It was Luc Dentremont and Ederyck Gannon. Luc held the skull in his hands. Something had gone wrong, and yet such relief washed over Calvin, he wanted to run down the steps to the lot below to greet them. But what if they were coming to harm his father and Osmena?

Calvin hid out of view and punched the number two.

"Calvin?"

"Aunty, something's happened. Zephyr's here, but she's with Luc."

"Impossible. The assumption formula cannot fail."

"It did. Luc's alive and he's got the skull. They're armed and coming in from the visitor's lot. You're going to have to take them by surprise. I'll slow them down, but Aunty, you have to promise me that when you get the skull you won't hurt them."

"I promise."

EG!"

EG turned. Luc and Zephyr stopped. They had reached the stone terrace outside Osmena's parlor. Two VLF guerillas stood frozen in place where they'd been guarding the French doors.

Calvin slowed to a trot as he approached. He was bare-chested as he'd been outside the camp, but not sweating now. Luc nodded. Zephyr waved, remembering him from the police barracks, but she couldn't figure out why he would be here.

"Calvin?"

"You're alright?"

"Yeah, why wouldn't I be?" said EG.

Calvin shrugged. "I got here as soon as I could. When you told me about Allard's plot, I didn't know what else to do. What happened to these guys?"

"It seemed like the best way to put an end to it," Luc said. "They took some people into custody including Osmena and Greenway. We wanted to make sure everybody was safe and, well, get these men out of here with no further damage done. You don't suppose Osmena and Greenway are free? The head gardner seemed to think everything was under control."

Calvin shrugged. "Maybe the gardener didn't know they were in custody. Too bad you didn't freeze the servants. They're tearing up the gardens."

"Oh my. Osmena is not going to be happy about that," Zephyr said.

"We'd better go in and get this done," said Luc. The French doors were curtained and the room behind it was dark. He turned the handle and the doors opened in. Luc and Zephyr went in first, followed by EG and Calvin. They stopped and listened. There were no voices, only the sound of a far-away door closing. They stood uncertainly in the midst of the room. EG sensed something wrong, something about Calvin. If he had just arrived on foot from the camp, why wasn't he sweating, and how had he even found Osmena's place?

The room filled with light, blinding them all for a second. A forearm chokehold took EG and the blunt end of a gun butted his temple. Luc and Zephyr wheeled and drew their guns. Greenway had EG. "Drop them now," he said.

"You can't shoot in two directions," Osmena said from behind them. She held a gun in each hand and she was so close to Luc and Zephyr she could not have missed. "Toss them aside." They obeyed.

Luc hadn't thought to make a protection spell, being concerned with bringing his renegade men to heel, and knowing that Osmena and Greenway were in custody. Yet, somehow they had gotten free. Jake's protection spell would not have extended to him and EG, and most certainly not to Zephyr. He had no choice but to surrender.

"Take the skull," Greenway said, but it was not apparent to whom he was speaking, until Calvin emerged from behind the French doors. He took the chamois sack from Luc's raised hand and gave it to Greenway.

"You pretended all along to be with us," EG said.

Calvin looked at him for a moment, and then lowered his eyes.

"Take them down to the servant's quarters," Osmena said to Greenway.

"I say we just tie them up here. We don't want any mishaps or tricks in transit."

"Very well. But make sure they can't escape. We can't see to them all; let the government deal with them now. It's far too dangerous here and the night too full of surprises for us to remain. It feels like that game, what is it—capture the flag. Well, enough. We leave straightway, Merlin."

⌘ ⌘ ⌘

THE SHIRTLESS SERVANT had just chased Osmena's amorous impostor away with his metal pole, as if claiming the terrace as his own little corner of the estate. The shrubbery was no match for him in a battle of swordsmanship, and the destruction of the gardens seemed to him a bit passé. There were no new challengers to his dominion, and he was soon quite bored. Yet, a tune kept running through his head that spurred him to dance and run. It had words too, but only at the moment he sang them out loud, did he become aware that this music had been the soundtrack of his movements since he'd drunk the formula. He'd been gliding and weaving to it, psychedelically graced by the neo-baroque keyboard passage in his head. Then, he saw the oil torchere at the edge of the terrace. The stand came in two pieces that detached with the push of a button (he'd set them up enough to know). He liberated the top of the torch, took the lighter he'd stolen from a cupboard out of his pants pocket, and set it ablaze. He waved it in the air like a scepter and rushed the patio door. He shattered a pane with the end of the pole and unlocked the door. In he swept, with his blazing scepter, once around a dining table and past the windows, pausing with each cadence of internal music to set a curtain panel on fire. He rushed out into the night and looked back to see the curtains blaze out in sudden conflagration. The flames leapt up, devouring fabric like ravenous, red hot serpents until the entire room was a blazing chandelier.

30.

The Skull and the Mask

J UDE WAS ON the floor of his cell crying, when Stemple appeared at his door the second time. He didn't hear him approach.

"Jude."

"Stemple?"

"Who else? They keep locking you up and I keep freeing you. This time you just have to do better at not getting caught. Good thing there's hardly a soul left to keep the jails full."

Stemple unlocked the cell and held the door open. He stared at the frozen VLF guerilla. "What is happening around here?"

"They had Osmena and Greenway, then the guy just froze, and Calvin came for them."

"They're frozen all over the grounds. That means Miss LaFrance has succeeded. Is that why you were crying?"

Jude nodded, but that was not the only reason. He wiped his eyes. "My father's down here too. He came for me and they captured him, but I don't know where they took him."

"You leave that to me. But this time Jude, don't go through the servant's exit."

"No, I'm staying with you," Jude protested.

"Somebody has set the house on fire, you must leave now." Stemple pointed in the opposite direction. "Follow this until you reach the door at the end of the hall. Go up the stairway to the first landing. There is another door. Go through and follow it. It's a tunnel that will take you out beyond the gardens."

"Where does it go?"

"The helipad clearing."

"What if it's locked?"

"The inside locks with deadbolts only. I assume you can handle those."

"No sweat. I'm juiced up and ready to go."

Stemple eyed him curiously. "Well, don't stand there. Hurry. When you reach the trees, take cover and wait for my return."

Castor and Pollux looked restless in the trailer, despite having eaten only a couple of hours ago. Rigel and Betelgeuse were quiet. Castor let out an ill-tempered snarl at Calvin. He stared back into the dark cage at the restless beast, as if mesmerized by the lashing tail and feral eyes. "I had to. You know I did. And who are you to talk after tonight? All for a big piece of meat. So just quiet down while I drive."

Calvin got into the cab and drove the outer circle of the estate. A glow rose up from the house as if all the lights were suddenly ablaze. Probably the servants at play. He looked again. The light had an unsteady flicker to it. He stopped the truck.

Calvin opened the door, stepped back onto the sill and then stepped up onto the seat. From there he hoisted himself up with his arms to glimpse the house. There were billows of smoke. It was fire. He let himself down and got back in. Calvin stared ahead, while the engine idled and the cats paced. "You can't ask that of me. You can't." He reached for the key and turned off the motor.

The temperature in the parlor had risen. They all felt it, though with their mouths taped they could not have said or speculated about what was happening, but when they smelled smoke they all knew. They could see it in each other's eyes. It was fire and they were trapped.

Luc began to tip his chair. He tried to say, "Get down", through the tape, but it was just a downward modulating moan. Zephyr got it and started to tip side to side. One by one they tipped their chairs and landed with thuds and muffled grunts. If they had any chance it was to get down low out of the smoke.

The whole south wing was engulfed in flames, spreading towards the parlor. Calvin flung open the French doors and smoke billowed out. He hit the floor. It wasn't as bad yet down low. They were all on the floor their eyes shut against the sting of smoke, coughs muffled through tape. They were wiggling futilely on their sides toward the doors. It would take too long to untie the rope. He crawled over to EG and ripped the tape off his mouth. He coughed.

"My blade," EG said.

Calvin found it hooked to EG's belt. He cut the ropes that bound his feet and helped him up. EG ran out bent over, with the chair still lashed to his back. Calvin cut Zephyr's feet and got her up. Last he freed Luc.

Out on the terrace, he cut them free of the chairs. "The whole thing is going up; you'd better get out of here before it's too late."

"But all my men," Luc said.

"Most of them are on the grounds," Calvin said.

"And what about Jude and his father?" Zephyr said.

"Down in the basement. The heat and smoke rises. They might be safe down there."

"Until the burning house collapses on them."

"How do we get down there," EG said.

"You can't go back in."

"Take us," EG said.

Jude ran down the tunnel. The familiar feeling of the formula started again, but the sensation of its power was even purer now with only his legs, and not the intervention of the Byclops, under him. The force was like a drug in itself, daring him to run faster (the tunnel rushing by him in a fantastic blur of blue lights), so fast he almost ran smack into a wall when he reached the end. He stopped himself with his arms and bounced back. It was not a wall but another door. He opened it and followed a winding ramp upward.

He felt cool air on his skin and light streaming around the bend of the narrowing ramp. The feeling of speed was pulsing through him, but he fought it. There were voices chopped and liquefied by an unearthly whooping sound.

The ramp emerged at ground level under the half dome of a shelter. A flood beam shining out above Jude defined the arc of light and shadow. The beam projected light out to a circle of lawn, and two ducking figures—Osmena, her blue caftan billowing wildly, and Greenway—hurried across the grass to a helicopter whooshing noisily on its pad. The sleek Plexiglas nose faced Jude, while the escaping pair had their backs to him.

Osmena and Greenway reached the cabin door. Osmena turned in profile and spoke to Greenway. In her right arm, she cradled something in a sack. Greenway came behind her, took her left hand and placed his other hand on her right hip to assist her into the chopper. She clutched the object tightly under her arm. Was it the skull? It had to be. He couldn't bear the thought of Zephyr turned into Osmena's cold assassin forever. If she kept the skull, she would get to them all eventually, roping them into her schemes at some low or desperate moment.

Jude broke into a run across the grass, pumping his arms and legs harder than he'd ever done in his life. It wasn't far. He'd make it, if only they didn't look now. The blades whooped louder and their wind was furious. Osmena looked down as she stepped up. Greenway watched her. Then he sensed movement, Jude crossing the angle of the flood beam, and he looked up. Jude reached—one long stride, almost a lunge—and ripped the object free from Osmena's grasp, knocking them both off balance with his shoulder.

⌘　⌘　⌘

CALVIN HADN'T SEEN the helicopter ascend. He might have missed it when he went into the parlor, but seeing was believing. Tonight he couldn't take anything for granted. He left Luc and the others at the servant's entrance and headed toward the landing pad.

The flames had risen already to the south cupola. The old dry wood had gone up like tinder and parts of the south wing were already consumed to near transparency, as if the flames themselves were the structure and substance holding up the house.

Greenway was thrown back, but he braced against the chopper and wrapped his arm around Osmena's waist in time to save her fall. He motioned her down and she crouched behind him. He pulled his gun and wheeled, aimed it at Jude's weaving form.

Jude ran faster yet. *He could*—if Greenway faltered—*go*—and was slow—*all*—to find Jude in his sights—*the*—and fire—*way*.

Calvin heard the blades of the chopper as he reached the clearing. He stepped out onto the grass. Something large and fast raced by him into the shadow at the moment he stepped out of it. He did a double take, and then looked over to the helicopter. A shot rang out.

Jude jumped twice (it happened so fast it was hard to say if it was all one moment and one movement), but somebody stepped out of the shadows, almost directly in his path, and then he heard the shot. He was still moving, so Greenway must have missed. He wondered if you actually heard the shot that killed you, or if bullets traveled faster than sound. It didn't matter, because he was running through the trees now with the skull. He waited for another shot, but it never came. Then he heard a faint and distant scream.

Jude stopped. Who or what had stepped in front of him? Stemple or Jet? Coming to meet him? A cold terror rode Jude's back in a shiver.

Jude turned and went back to the edge of the clearing. Loud voices sounded nearer.

"What have you done, Merlin? What have you done?" Osmena and Greenway stood over Calvin, who lay bare-chested and flat out on his back in the moonlit grass.

Merlin Greenway dropped to his knees. "Son, I didn't see you. You were supposed to be taking the cats."

"The house is burning, Dad. I had to make sure you got out. I can't move. Why can't I feel anything?"

"It's in his spine. We can help him, if we get the skull," Osmena said. "Get the skull."

"Am I dying, Aunty? Help me..."

But Osmena and Merlin were helpless. For all they knew, Jude was hundreds of yards away by now— propelled by Osmena's formula—soon to hop on the Byclops and take off down the mountain.

"Jude!" Osmena called. She was crying. "Do you hear me, Jude Corgan? We need your help!"

"Corgan!" Merlin called out. "Please!"

Jude couldn't hear them, but he knew who they were calling and what they wanted. He walked to the edge of the trees. They looked blindly into the shadows for him. He could run away yet and return it to the VLF. Or keep it to himself. Why couldn't it be his? If he gave it back, there would never be another chance. The skull and whatever magic made it so powerful belonged in better hands than Osmena's. Because, if the bullet had dropped him instead of Calvin, would they have used its power to heal him, or would they have let him die? He knew the answer. But, there was Calvin on the grass contemplating death at seventeen. How many times had he imagined scenarios of Kennedy's last minutes, trapped in a burning car, paralyzed and hoping until the very last second that somebody would happen by and drag him from the burning wreck. And then he thought about Calvin up above the falls, laughing and asking for advice about his unfinished tattoo. Somehow, it didn't matter at all what they would have done, because Jude knew what he would do.

Jude stepped from the shadows onto the moonlit grass and held out the skull to them. "Save him. I'd have given up a thousand skulls to save my brother."

Osmena rushed over and took the sack out of his hands. She removed the skull and knelt over Calvin. She closed her eyes, faltering for a moment for words (incantations that once rolled so easily off her tongue) to save her nephew's life. Her hands trembled on the skull. Jude was close enough now to see the dark bullet hole in Calvin's neck. His eyes had closed and his breathing had become shallow.

"Oh, errant bullet in the night; with no intent for one so fair; retract your accidental might; withdraw as if you'd not been there. Young Calvin, say, rest not this night; hard magic, though, you've laid him low; say, stand and live to join the fight; restore the one we love and know."

Calvin remained very still for several minutes. Jude kept waiting for him to come to life, but he'd been so intent on Calvin's face, he didn't notice that the bullet wound had closed. Osmena clasped the skull to her bosom. Greenway took hold of Calvin's hand.

Calvin opened his eyes. They were not weak and fluttery as they'd been before, but wide and clear. He squeezed his father's hand back. Greenway lowered his head.

"Just lie there for a moment," Osmena said. "Your strength will come."

Greenway wiped an arm across his face and stood up. He took Osmena by the arm and raised her up.

It came to Jude, then, that Greenway and Osmena hadn't been thankful like this in all their lives, and still they'd sooner die than thank him.

"Don't mention it," Jude said.

Osmena raised her chin, as if reappraising Jude. She held the skull against her stomach, the way a pregnant woman holds her womb, hands opposed, one over the top, the other underneath, as if it were a part of her.

"What is it, really, the skull? Where does it come from?"

"That is something Luc Dentremont would have done well to ask." Osmena held up a finger, in preparation to recite. Jude had a feeling she knew this one by heart.

"The head of him who took life first; had placed on it a blessed curse; the earth would not yield to his arm; but marked so none could do him harm. He bore a race, a city made; and prospered in his brother's shade. Who finding it is of a mind; so set in stone for all mankind; may turn the curse in latter days; and move the earth in stranger ways. That is all I'll say about it; and this—it is often true that those who prove most worthy of the skull are, alas, unsuited to wield its power."

Greenway extended a hand to Calvin and prepared to raise him to his feet.

"We'll see about that," said a familiar voice.

Two men leapt out of the shadows and grabbed Greenway and Osmena from behind. Calvin fell back onto the grass. Zephyr stepped in and took Greenway's gun. The skull had fallen from Osmena's grasp and rolled in front of Jude's feet. He scooped it up. Zephyr came around, and Jude flipped it to her with the ease of a giant jock in a game of Ultimate Team Handball.

It took Jude a moment to recognize the man who held Greenway as Luc Dentremont. The other man, shorter in stature, wore a mask.

"Then you didn't kill him?"

Zephyr shook her head. "I had a revelation instead."

Overhead a big flaming cinder drifted over the trees and descended on the clearing. The eddy of the helicopters blades stirred the giant ember up again and it flew out and landed on the grass not far from them. The sky behind the line of trees was golden with firelight and a giant black cloud of smoke moved over the moon, dividing the sky between its absolute blackness and luminous midnight blue.

Jude remembered Jet and Stemple as the totality of the fire filled him all with the terror of its possibilities.

Then, from out of the shadows, Jet Corgan appeared, waving one hand in the air. He and Stemple had come around from the other side of the gardens. Jet walked a little stiffly.

Jude ran over and embraced him. "You alright?"

"Yeah. One of them hit me in the knee and it's just stiffening up on me, now."

"We didn't dare go back through the house. You were supposed to stay under cover," Stemple scolded Jude.

Jude shrugged and motioned to the scene behind him. Jet looked puzzled (he didn't have a clue about the skull and Zephyr or anything else), but when he saw Luc Dentremont a look of far away recognition, like the memory of a long ago dream, came over him.

Luc stuck his face right next to Greenway's and said, "I think it's time for you to make your exit. Your ride awaits." He turned Greenway around and pushed him away. The man in the mask turned Osmena around and released her. They walked apace and then turned back.

"Calvin?" Greenway shouted.

Calvin got to his feet, but he didn't follow them. He shook his head.

Greenway shouted something back.

Calvin shook his head, as if he couldn't hear.

"Calvin!" Osmena shouted.

Calvin went over to Osmena. He hugged her and kissed her goodbye.

"Son, you don't know what you're doing."

"I know there are people here who don't even know me, and yet my life means more to them than possessing the power you live for. That's what I know."

"You're making a big mistake. Once you leave, there's no coming back."

Calvin turned, put up his hand in backward salute, and walked away into the shadow of the trees.

Greenway and Osmena stood watching him until he disappeared, then they turned again and boarded the cabin. The helicopter rose straight up into the night. It ascended until it was no longer a helicopter but a couple of pulsing red lights moving through the night sky.

The clearing became very quiet and still in the helicopter's wake. There was a moment when they all stood around saying nothing. Then Luc nodded at the man in the mask.

EG came forward toward Jet and Jude. He looked back at Luc and Zephyr as if uncertain of what to do. "Hey, Judo—Dad, it's me." He took off the mask and dropped it in the grass at his feet.

"Kennedy!"

31.

The End of the Beginning

THERE WAS PURE shock at first—seconds that dragged out like minutes before Jude and Jet could believe their eyes. Then there was joy—hugging and crying and jumping up and down like they were all on springs. What came after that were questions, a flurry of them from Jude and Jet both; and they were angry questions peppered with a lot of curses. Jet was madder than Jude had ever seen him. Jude felt angrier at his brother than he had at Osmena for what she'd done to Zephyr. Still, Jet was so relentless, Jude almost felt sorry for Kennedy. Almost.

"The next time you die and don't tell us you're alive, I'm going to hunt you down and kill you myself. Do you hear me?" At one point, Jet was waving his arms around so much he had to walk way, for fear he might hit Kennedy. And then he cursed himself and punched the air for even feeling like hitting him.

Eventually, things calmed down. Luc had unfrozen his men and they had returned to their trucks and driven back to the forest. Five of his men were unaccounted for and presumed lost in the fire, including Jake Allard. From Luc's expression when he returned, a war between anger and grief was also being waged inside of him that night.

They all sat around on the helipad in a circle, and must have looked like a bunch of weepy New Agers waiting for a space ship to beam them up. They'd built a fire from gathered sticks and red hot embers drifting beyond the

349

gardens and over the trees from the burning house. It was chilly, as the cool front settled over the mountains, and they were much too far from the burning house to feel its heat. Stemple had tried to excuse himself, ever the tactful servant, but they'd all said he should stay since he was as much a part of this now as any of them.

"But I did tell you. I tried to anyway," Kennedy explained. "The wrecks."

"You brought the wrecks?" said Jude.

Kennedy nodded.

"But how?"

"Atwood's salvage. Chet's in the VLF. He helped me with every one. We'd just kill the engine and coast quiet as we could down the last part of the mountain. I'd unhitch it and Chet would roll on by a ways down the road. Then he'd come back and we'd push it into place in neutral. They were bad wrecks, but we made sure they could all roll, and without the engines they were a cinch to push. The only way we could make them that easy to unhitch wasn't really legal."

"Neither is faking your death," Jude said.

"But why?" asked Zephyr. "That's a lot of trouble to go through."

"It wasn't that hard really. A half-day's work every few months or so. It was just nerve-wracking getting them there."

Something about how they pulled it off appealed to Jet, for he started to grin. "I always said, didn't I Jude, that them wrecks were telling us something."

"And what was that?" Jude said.

"God, Judo, I thought for sure you'd get it, the way you are with things like that. I spelled it out for you with the cars. KENNEDY CORGAN LIVES. Minus the E and the S because your friend caught us fixing the Escort. Now, we'll never have to. I thought the Escorts would get you thinking. It was supposed to be a joke."

Jude smiled a little sheepishly. "I never thought of an acrostic."

Kennedy picked up a twig and tossed it over the fire at Jude. "Well, your friend Merrilee did. She told Luc on the way from the compound. It came to her tonight, when she saw these up close around my neck." Kennedy shook the necklace of VIN tags. "You got good taste in friends, Jude, I'll tell you that much. She put herself in harm's way to find you. But, listen, if you'd gotten on the right track with the wrecks, you could've solved it a year ago, soon as you had the L—just like on The Wheel."

"That's four long years of not knowing," Jet said, with a don't-get-me-started tone in his voice. "We could a caught you at it anyhow."

"Mom always said Gabriel's trumpet couldn't wake you out of a sound sleep, and Judo you've got the exact same gene. Anyway, it made me feel close to you."

"But why couldn't you have just come to us and told us you were taking off ?"

"Because I didn't know I was. Listen, none of it, the wrecks included, makes a bit of sense unless you know what happened that night, and none of this ever would have happened if it weren't for A & P class."

"Anatomy and Physiology?" asked Zephyr.

"Yeah. In the spring we were doing blood typing. In class we chewed on rubber bands to make saliva and then spun it in a centrifuge. You test it with drops of antigen to figure out what your blood type is. Mine was AB. If you know your own and one parent's blood type, you can narrow down the other parent's possible blood types. So we were supposed to ask the other parent after we did our type testing and did our figuring."

"I remember that," Jude said. He also remembered what Osmena told him tonight. But was it true?

"Mom said hers was A and you blurted out O positive," Kennedy reminded Jet. "But then mom corrected you and said AB. And we laughed at you for being such a dufus, but you weren't being a dufus were you?"

"No."

"Because you're not his birth father," said Jude.

Kennedy's mouth opened. "You want to ruin my whole story, Judo? God, you're a bigger pain than ever." Then he smiled. "You couldn't figure out the wrecks, but you've got this all worked out?"

"Osmena told me tonight. It's why I came here. She said she knew the truth, but I didn't believe her."

"Well, it's the truth. I didn't have any reason to doubt mom back then. I mean, it's just like something you'd do, dad—forget your blood type. So I didn't think about it for a while."

"By the way, Osmena also said you were dead," said Jude.

"She might have known the whole truth and just didn't want to give you that much satisfaction. But hold on, I'm coming to that," Kennedy said.

That Memorial Day weekend turned out to be a fine one, lots of sunshine and really warm. Aster had the table set and had gone inside to make the burgers. Jude and Kennedy were wiping down the stacking plastic chairs. Under the trailer storage hold, Jet was bumping and banging around looking for the charcoal. He crawled out cursing under his breath.

"Kennedy," Jet whispered to his older son. "There's no charcoal. I looked everywhere. I told your mother we had plenty when she was heading to the store yesterday, but..."

"You were too lazy to check."

"I was sure we had some, but anyway, she'll give me the what for if she finds out. Go in the bedroom and get some cash from my wallet. It's on the night table. Make like you're going to the bathroom and run the water. Something. Then you slip out and go to the store, while she's in there fixing up."

"She's going to hear the engine, and besides I've only got my permit. I'm supposed to be accompanied by an adult."

"Just drive slow and careful—you're a better driver than your mother (don't tell her I said that). Listen, get her some smokes, she's almost out (tell her you noticed). I was under the trailer getting the charcoal, and you just drove off before I could stop you."

"Great. I've got to do your dirty work, and take the bullet too? I'll be grounded."

"Something like that. My hide's already like Swiss cheese."

Kennedy went in past his mother. She stood with a big spoon of mayonnaise poised over the bowl. "Come and taste this. I think it's too dry, but god knows your father doesn't need help clogging his arteries."

"Can't Mom. Gotta pee." Kennedy went down the hall to the bathroom, lifted up the seat and turned the faucet on. Then, he tip-toed out and down a door into their bedroom. At least the wallet was where Jet said it was. He opened it and took out the cash. Aster's footsteps sounded. He looked up and fumbled the wallet, dropped it on the floor. A yellow card fell out. He scooped it up with the wallet, keeping one eye on the door. Some doctor's appointment he'd probably missed from the look of it. No, it was an old blood donor card. It had only one date entered (another of his father's good intentions gone the way of the Incubus). The card was soft and frayed on the edge and it bent when he tried to fit it back into the wallet sleeve. He just flipped it into the cash compartment. That was when the words on the other side of the card caught his eye: Universal donor "O" positive.

Everything seemed to disappear for a moment: the sounds in the kitchen, the birds outside the window, and the footsteps coming up the hallway. Kennedy felt the color drain out of his face and his body felt weak, as though he might fall over at the touch of a finger. He didn't even move when Jude appeared at the bedroom door.

"Dad, says hurry up."

Kennedy just stood there holding the wallet, pale and looking like he was going to be sick.

⌘ ⌘ ⌘

"I DIDN'T KNOW WHAT to do; but I knew things weren't ever going to be the same again. Not after that day," said Kennedy.

"We were going to tell you when you turned eighteen; we never dreamed you'd find out like that. As far as we could tell, only your mother and I knew the truth. There just didn't seem to be much point in telling you about a father who'd been a fugitive for over 16 years and was never coming back. He might have been dead for all we knew. Lots of people thought so."

"And I tried not to think about it, but I couldn't hold it in. I thought for sure you had a reason and were trying to protect me, but I was so angry I was about to burst."

"I remember the fight just before you drove up the mountain," said Jude.

Kennedy shook his head. "That happened a week earlier. You've got the two events mixed up. I didn't know who my birth father was that night. That's what I wanted to know and that's the night I found out."

Luc Dentremont, who'd sat in silence as if lost in distant reverie, came back to the present and rested a hand on Kennedy's shoulder.

"That's why there's a picture of you in mom's closet," Jude said.

"There is?" Jet looked over at Jude.

"She's not into him, don't sweat it. She cut his picture out of Kennedy's obit."

"She did?"

Stemple shifted awkwardly, as if it were the first time he'd ever sat in a lotus position, or on the ground for that matter. A restless mood came over him when Kennedy began his story.

"Osmena said that's why you were heading up the mountain. To meet your birth father," Jude said.

Zephyr gently cleared her throat. "It explains the connection I felt to Kennedy, and I think that also extended to you, Jude. The feeling of being closer to my lost brother. Something in me just responded to that physical similarity. But, Kennedy, I don't understand how you discovered his whereabouts in a week's time. I'd been trying to find him for years."

"Merrilee figured out you were brother and sister, when she found out Luc changed his name. It's kind of cool that we're almost related," Jude said.

Zephyr smiled. "It doesn't matter really, does it? I think we'll always be connected now."

Jude smiled. It felt as though something large and warm were growing in his chest. Then a dark thought crossed over him. "Osmena wanted you to kill your brother? What a witch!"

Zephyr nodded and lowered her eyes.

"Could you stop interrupting?" Kennedy threw another twig at Jude.

Jude made a rather stern and sober face and said in a pompous judicial voice, "I will allow the clarification this time, but in the future, Jude Corgan, keep your superfluous questions to a minimum."

Jet lost it. He snorted through his nose and held his stomach in a sudden fit of laughter. He pointed at Jude and shook his head.

"He can't help himself," Jude explained.

"You wonder why I faked my death?" Kennedy said.

Jet stopped laughing. "Which wasn't a bit funny."

"But, you were saying," Zephyr intervened.

"Well, I'd started working at Atwood's salvage on weekends and sometimes after school, taking apart the wrecks for used parts. You look under the hood or undercarriage of any of those wrecks I left and there's nothing worth keeping or using. So I spent a lot of time up there that week just to get away from home. I asked if I could come up the next day after I found the donor card, even though it was Sunday and they were closed. Chet said sure. He could see right away that something was wrong. He asked me if I wanted to talk. I didn't say anything then.

"I ended up staying the whole day, until Chet finally came out and told to come in and have some supper. That was when I showed him the donor card, told him what I'd discovered, and how I'd confronted my mom and dad the night before. He got real quiet and didn't say a word for a while. But you and mom weren't the only ones who knew. Luc had confided to Chet that he'd gotten Aster pregnant before he fled, and he'd asked Chet to look out for me. So Chet took me out to one of the bays and told me my father was alive and that he knew where he was. I begged and cried and carried on until he agreed to ask Luc to meet me. Chet said he couldn't tell me where my father was, or guarantee a meeting, but he would ask.

"I waited on pins and needles all week, then finally on Friday, Chet said the meeting was on for the following night. He told me to go to the head of the trail of the lookout on the mountain top and walk the trail and wait there.

"It was really late and you were all asleep when I snuck out with the car."

Kennedy's mind had raced as he drove up the steep winding sides of Catamount Gap, and with the urgency of his meeting, the thrill rising inside of him, he'd begun to push the pedal harder and race up the mountain as well. He felt his heart beat in sudden wild bursts; he trembled with nerves and his stomach leapt with surges of adrenalin. Slow down. He breathed and fought to keep himself under control. He'd swiped a beer from the fridge and downed it minutes after leaving home, tossing the can out the window when he finished it, because it was illegal to have open alcohol containers in your car. He'd also slipped some of the Captain into some coke, about half and half, and took it with him in a thermal mug. A buzz had started. He wouldn't have blown a point eight, but he'd had just enough so you could smell the sour of beer and the fruit rot whiff of the Captain on him. Without it, he might have chickened out at the last minute.

About a half mile before the pull-off, the road went into a long winding curve. Leaning hemlocks gave the bend a dangerous closeness, as if he were entering a narrowing chamber in a cave. On the left, a stream ran down a gulley beyond the guardrail, and, on the right, steep mountain rose dark with shadows. The curve broke and the road opened. Something moved in his periphery. It came at him fast, and his reaction was a second slow. Waving arms. A man. It made no sense that the man wouldn't stop, but pitch head-long in front of him, so that he hit broad and square against the car grill in falling. Kennedy swerved to avoid crushing him. The car essed out of control back and forth across the center line before he lost it to an oncoming tree. He braked with all his weight, turned the wheel hard. The nose swung wide, wheels tearing for a hold in the gravel shoulder, and the tail smashed broad into the tree. He sat for a moment dazed. Then he got out and ran toward the man lying in the road.

The headlights of another car spread a dome of pale light over the rise of the mountain top. Instead of driving up, the vehicle veered into the pull-off with the headlights facing Kennedy.

"Help!" Kennedy called out.

A man got out of a jeep and ran over to the two men in the road. Kennedy looked up. It was Luc Dentremont, his birth father. He might have been looking at himself twenty years in the future, only taller and with a wild mane of tawny hair.

"Kennedy?"

"Luc?"

"What happened?"

"He ran down the embankment. He was just waving, and then he didn't stop. He must have tripped. I don't know. Oh, my god."

"So the man you hit is buried in your grave?" Jude said.

Kennedy stared into the fire. It was just red coals with translucent blue flames pulsing around them.

"What made you think you could get away with passing off somebody else's body for yours?" Jet sounded angry again.

"You have to understand," Luc said. "He was sixteen, driving alone with only a permit. He'd been drinking, and had hit and killed a man late at night on a mountain road. It wasn't his fault, but how was it going to look when he shouldn't have been there in the first place? I was a fugitive wanted for setting fire to a federal building. To return and face that meant that both of our lives could be ruined—not to mention the cause I'd been dedicated to for so many years. There wasn't a lot of time to think, and we didn't have many choices. Kennedy could call the police and report the accident and face the consequences. If he called home, you and Aster might have made it there before the police, and it could have been like I'd never been there at all. One of you could have said you were driving. But would you have? We could both flee and go our separate ways, as if neither of us had been there and leave a dead stranger on the roadside."

"But you haven't told us who he was?" said Zephyr.

"We're coming to that," said Kennedy.

Stemple was agitated. "The fire is almost out; I should gather some more sticks. We shouldn't let the fire go out."

"It's okay. Osmena's not going to come out of the bushes; you're officially retired from forced servitude," said Jude.

"But the fire dies, and this story has turned strange. I find it frightening. Choices are a terrible thing; one makes them and then..." Stemple muttered the last part, and nobody heard it.

"Then we noticed Kennedy's car on fire. An idea came to me. The man was about the same height and build as Kennedy, but probably about twice his age at the time. But, if he were to be found burned beyond recognition in Kennedy's car, in Kennedy's clothes, nobody would question his identity. Dental records were the only thing that could prove it wasn't Kennedy, and so we set Dr. Lane's office on fire to destroy them. If all the records were destroyed it would just seem like an unfortunate coincidence. If we broke in and stole only Kennedy's records, the search for a match would have triggered suspicions of foul play."

"So, if you set the fires, then you also gave Dr. Lane all that money," Jude said.

"Technically Chet did that, but it was my money. My father's really," said Luc. "There was an account; he put it in my name when I went into hiding. He knew a day would come when I might need it. I knew before we set the fires, I'd have to restore what I'd destroyed. So I told Kennedy what I was thinking, but I told him it meant he would have to join me underground. It meant he might not see his family for a very long time. It was a huge leap for him. A terrible choice to make under pressure."

Kennedy took over for Luc. "But something happened in those few minutes that I can't explain. I was still angry with you and mom, and I didn't want to go back. I mean, everybody and their secrets; what's wrong with the truth, anyway? Like we can't handle reality. I'm ashamed to say it, but I thought, well how would they feel, then, to have reality turned upside down; like if the non-existent father can suddenly come into being, maybe the living son can suddenly disappear."

"That was downright cruel," said Jet. "What did we ever do that you would just toss us away in a moment?"

"It was cruel. And because I felt cruel, I was also free to leave. At least I can admit it. Do you even have a clue why I'd want to leave? I bet you don't. It wasn't something I came to in a moment. Just look at the way we had to live. The insults every day at school. That was cruel. Being ashamed to stand in front of my house when the bus came by in the morning. That was cruel. Never being able to have friends over. That was cruel. You made us ashamed every day. Yes, Dad, you were cruel, in your own good humored, inept way. And when I found out you weren't my birth father, well, it all made sense, like none of the junk and the waste and the shame had anything to do with me at all. It didn't have to be."

"So you don't want anything to do with us? Is that it?"

"No! You don't know how many times I wanted to come back. Every time we snuck down with a wreck in the night, there was always a moment, just being that close I could almost touch you again, where I'd come alive.

Because a part of me really did die that night, not just to you, but inside of me as well. Maybe I secretly hoped you'd wake up and catch me all along. Who do you think it was you scared into the woods the other night?"

"That was you?" Jude said.

"And it wasn't the first time either. The guilt hit me later, and it's never really left me, knowing how sad I'd made you all. But what I felt that night was more thrilling than anything I'd ever known. Like I had no clue who I was or what I was doing until then. So I said, 'go for it'."

"I broke the man's neck, so it would look like he'd died instantly, or was paralyzed and couldn't escape," Luc said. "Otherwise they might wonder why he didn't crawl out of the burning car. He wasn't trapped."

Zephyr seemed disturbed by the idea of it. "But this man would have dental records too, and family looking for him."

Luc and Kennedy glanced at each other.

Stemple said, "You said, so it would look like he'd died instantly. Did he die instantly?"

Kennedy shook his head. "He was still alive when I got to him."

The man was on his back, lying still in the middle of the road.

"Mister, are you okay? Can you hear me? I'm so sorry. I don't know what happened. You were there and then it was like you were flying. Oh, God. Mister?"

Kennedy put his fingers to the man's neck and felt for a pulse. With his hand trembling and his own blood pounding in his ears, he couldn't be sure what he felt, but he thought he picked up a couple of blips against his fingers.

Kennedy didn't know if he should try to move him; they said you shouldn't in case of spinal injuries, but they were just out there on the dark road like sitting ducks for a passing car.

"Mister, can you hear me?"

The man opened his eyes, a momentary stare that seemed to take in Kennedy's face as if to remember it once and forever, and then a flutter closed them. He opened his mouth to speak. Nothing came out for a moment. He swallowed and said, "Got away from her."

"Away from who? Is there somebody else? Family to call?"

The man's eyes opened through fluttering lids, and his head moved the slightest bit up and down. "Oliver. Stemple. Help." His eyes closed again. He opened them once more, and with great effort, slid his hand over to rest on his pant's pocket. "Osmena. Her power." Then his eyelids closed and rested shut. Kennedy felt his neck again and held his fingers there for a long time. There was no pulse.

Stemple scrambled to his feet and ran off across the grass. He stopped and stood for a moment with his back to them, and then he collapsed to his knees and stared up at the moon. It had risen, crossed above and beyond the path of the black cloud's southward flow.

"Oh, Orest, my Orest! Ohhhhh!" That howl ascended as if across the night to the moon itself, full and glowing with the light of unspoken dreams and promises, so that they all raised their eyes with him then, and saw in the light reflected, and felt in his desolate cry, that cord of memory, loss, and longing that was all of theirs, stretched across a chasm of darkness and irretrievable years. His body shook and he lowered his head and closed his eyes, as if he could not bear even the light of the moon anymore. Calvin was the only one who knew Stemple, but he'd wandered off through the trees with a grief of his own, so Jude got up and comforted his new friend. He knelt behind him and did what he'd wished a thousand times that Jet and Aster would have done for him after Kennedy was gone. He put his arms around Stemple and held him. It felt strange at first, Stemple shaking and Jude's still and stiff, but then it changed, as if Stemple had gradually absorbed the embrace, and Jude's arms had melted into that acceptance. Because the only truly awkward hug was one you didn't mean or feel inside.

Stemple stopped shaking. "Orest would have come for me. I knew he would not have left me alone in that place. In all the world, imagine Jude, his very last thought was for me." He breathed deeper and said, "You'll take me to where he's buried tomorrow?"

"You got it."

"When I told Luc, he'd said Osmena's name and something about getting away, he knew the man probably didn't have any ID or records. I didn't know then that Osmena kept dozens of servants on her estate against their wills."

Now, the group walked the rim of the gardens back to where the truck waited in the visitor's lot, with Luc and Kennedy telling Jude and Jet the rest of the story on the way. Zephyr walked behind with Stemple, who couldn't bear any more of their tale.

Luc said, "But that's what started me thinking about a switch. And, as I suspected, he had no ID. What we did find on him changed everything. In the pants pocket he'd touched before he died. It was such a shock, I could scarcely believe it was real. Without it, I could never have asked Kennedy to do what he did that night, and we wouldn't be here now, because what we found was our eventual return ticket to life. He had in his possession a map that led us to the black skull, and with it, the incantation that allowed us to wield its magic. My father had spoken of the tree as the source of Osmena's power, but nobody knew about a skull, let alone where she kept it."

"But why would she keep it in a tree instead of with her?" Jude asked.

"It was safer there. And more powerful because of the power of the tree," said Kennedy.

Luc added, "We learned the hard way that the tree is protected by a bog that will suck down anything that's sets foot in its treacherous morass. You can only approach from above through the canopy. And anybody who managed to steal the skull without the key to using it, would have nothing more than a lump of fossilized bone. In such an unlikely event, Osmena always had the means to track it down, the way she did with Zephyr tonight. How Orest Stemple ever got a hold of those papers is beyond me, but he did."

Luc held the skull and ran his hand over a mark on its forehead.

"What is that?" Jude asked. It was barely visible in the moonlight, a faint indentation that looked like a jagged sunburst.

"Up until tonight, I wasn't sure."

"Osmena quoted something about it, but I didn't understand it. *The head of him who took life first; had placed on it a blessed curse.* That's all I can remember. What did it mean?"

"I'm certain it's a reference to the mark of Cain. You know who he is and what he did?"

361

"Uh-huh. He killed his brother." A shiver passed down Jude's spine at the dark transformed object in Luc's hand—an ancient skull turned into stone. The first crime and its ancient curse. Tonight, Jude had redeemed the one and reversed the other. "You mean that's his head?"

"Maybe so. What's left of it. Not even knowing that, I wanted to destroy it after those two men died at your cousins' farm. But I was wrong, and I was wrong to take it on myself to decide for all the men who were in this with me. They were wrong for taking matters into their own hands. I'm going back to the compound, and tomorrow we'll talk it all out. That's what we should have done in the first place. It wasn't up to me. Is the mark evil? I don't know, but somebody higher up than me put it there, maybe to show that even something that started as evil can be turned to good. But I know you can't just walk away from power when it comes to you, because it's there, like potential that somebody is going to get behind and use. The only thing you can do is be humble, answer for your actions and hope for the best."

They passed down the steps under the arch of the privet hedge.

"But, what happened with Zephyr? Why didn't she kill you?" Jude asked his brother. "Did the skull save you?"

Kennedy shook his head and shrugged. "I don't know how to use the skull. All I did was take off my mask. And maybe there was another, stronger magic hovering around that old cabin."

Luc and Jet got in the cab and the rest of them piled into the cargo. They passed Calvin, walking alone, at the edge of the locust wood. He'd donned a gray shirt discarded in the grass and they almost mistook him for one of Osmena's servants. Luc stopped the truck.

"Come on Calvin," Zephyr called.

Calvin stared down as he walked, lost in thought.

"Mister Calvin!"

Calvin looked up at the familiar voice of Stemple, quickened his pace and then trotted toward the truck. He planted his hands on the bumper and vaulted into the cargo.

Kennedy reached out, took his hands and helped steady him in the moving truck.

"Thanks," Calvin said. "Do I know you?"

"Kennedy Corgan."

Calvin sat with his hands pressed to the cargo, wearing a look of confusion and shock. He had disappeared before Kennedy had unmasked and told his story. "Weren't you—"

"You knew me as Ederyck Gannon."

"I was going to say dead." Calvin shook his head in disbelief, as at the presence of a ghost, or else he realized how close he'd come to being one himself. "You're not disfigured at all, and I knew that name was phony."

"Yeah. It's just my old name scrambled around."

Calvin introduced himself to them all. Then he said, "Thank you, Jude, for what you did. That was—" Calvin shook his head. He couldn't even put it into words yet.

"You're welcome, I think," Jude deadpanned.

Calvin laughed, like he had that day at the falls. "I guess I've got some making up to do before I'm really welcome."

Behind them, The Cosmos soared, an architecture of fire, like a monument alight. The carousels were traced in flame. A beam caved, then the giant lattice square of a wall swung down like a door, and finally a cupola and its cavalcade of beasts collapsed. The flames flashed higher, and sparks, like salutes at a fireworks display, shot up and drifted down in a scarlet rain.

32.

Grounded

I T WAS ODD after everything, that the Corgan men were all silent on the ride home in the Mowercar. Maybe it was just the time they needed to absorb it all. Maybe it was Kennedy thinking about what he was going to tell Aster. Or maybe being together was enough just then.

But, when the Mowercar pulled into the drive and Aster was already standing on the doorstep with her elbows out and hands on her face, the way she did when she was fretting, it was clear that quiet time was over. Kennedy was still out of sight in the back. Jude said, "Man, you are dead meat." Jet turned his head, "And the worst of it is, you'll live to tell about it. I've been there. But, son, this beats anything I've ever done, or conceived of doing, in the realm of what's inside my poor little head. I'm just preparing you is all. Stay down. We'll go in first."

"Jude?" Aster called.

There was something tremulous and grateful in his mother's voice that Jude had never heard before.

"Mom, I'm okay," Jude said, getting out of the Mowercar and running up the driveway past the truck. It reminded him of his first day of school, how sad and interminable the separation from Aster had felt, and how when he got home, he'd run to the trailer also and wrapped his arms around her waist and hugged her. The lost and lonely feeling had melted instantly away. "Oh, Jude. You're back." Aster embraced him and she began to cry. "I was so worried; I was sick to death with worry. But you're home and you're okay. Thank God you're okay. Why didn't I ever—" Aster started a thought, but finished it by squeezing Jude tighter. There had been the cold and the anger and the terror that filled so much of her. She'd begun to wear them like protection, and barriers worked both ways. It wasn't long before Jude had built his own walls, so there was seldom a moment's peace between them. Yet, all at once, it felt as if the walls of cold and fear had melted away.

Jet hobbled up to the steps and took Aster inside. Jude remained outside. When the door closed behind his parents, he waved for Kennedy to approach the trailer.

Jude listened through the screen door. "Everything's all right, Aster. Better than all right. Look there's somebody who wants to see you. But, just sit down and be calm. Okay?" In his father's voice was the pride of a man who'd gone out to find one missing son and came back with two, the second raised from the dead even. That must have felt pretty darned good, for man who hadn't done a whole lot right in the past five years.

Jude and Jet sat on the step outside the trailer listening to the scene in the kitchen, the reliving of their own emotions. The shriek of joy from Aster was the most thrilling sound their trailer and the doomed, illustrious junk heaps had ever been privileged to hear. Jet sat with his forearms hung over his knees, Jude was leaning forward with his arms across his chest. They just sat together listening and crying quietly. Then there was such shouting the like of which they'd never heard, not even from Aster, and even through closed doors and windows the words pierced them. "How could you do this to us!"

"What you did nearly killed me!" Aster stood trembling, her back to the kitchen sink, eyes wide to bursting, mouth open in anguish. Her voice broke once, then again in brittle sobs. "Days when I could barely get up and dressed. So help me, if it hadn't been for Jude and Jet. So many days I didn't want to go on." She dropped her head and broke down crying.

Kennedy took a step toward her. "I'm so sorry, Mom. I'm so so sorry."

Aster stepped back from him and lifted her head. Her eyes were wild with fury and the closest thing Kennedy had ever seen to loathing in his mother's eyes. "I can never forgive you for what you put me through, and I will never forget it."

Now Kennedy took a step back. He stood blinking back another wave of tears, lips parted in disbelief. "Never, Mom? Not ever?"

Aster's stare of fury and rejection held, flared stronger again, like a fire fanned by wind. Kennedy dropped his head. His shoulders sank, and then rocked up and down in sobs of this new, towering anguish, like those of a golden angel who has been cast out of heaven and told he may never again return. At that moment, when the meaning and full measure of 'never' broke over him, and his anguish found itself in company with hers, Aster relented and rushed to wrap her golden angel in a long-delayed embrace.

"Oh, Kennedy. Not never. Not ever that."

Then there was weeping, both Aster and Kennedy, a most terrible distress of sorrow and regret and tenderness. Jet looked up and squeezed his eyes shut like someone praying hard. The sobbing quieted, and Jet could breathe again. For, he could make out the muffling of a long embrace, like a salve over a stinging wound, and he knew somehow it would be okay.

Finally, there was the familiar cadence of Kennedy's story. He had to tell her the whole thing from start to finish, even though he'd done it once already tonight. That was how stories were. They never really ended, they just found new listeners, and with the listening there was the hope, when the last t was crossed and i dotted, that the teller and the listener would reach an understanding, make some kind of peace about the way it all turned out. So long as Kennedy didn't leave anything important out, he'd be all right.

"Jude, I'm sorry about the way things have been around here," Jet said. "I've been about as useless as all this scrap for a very long time. It's funny, you lose one person in a family and somehow you all get kind of lost too."

"You are absolved my son; say five Hail Mary's, three Our Father's, eight Fluffernutters, and endure unlimited jokes at your expense for all eternity."

Jet smiled, but there was a sad and distant look in his eyes. "I'm not absolved though, really, am I?"

"Shhh!" Jude put his finger to his lips. Kennedy must have finished, because Aster was talking again.

"And I want one, no two, massive dumpsters to haul every last piece of junk off of this property; or get that skull and make it all disappear by magic, I don't care. And another thing—"

But Aster started crying before she could get it out, and it was all an impossible garble to Jet.

"What on earth did your mother just say?"

Jude sighed. Translating Aster when she was in an emotional state wasn't an exact science. You just had to kind of feel your way through it, knowing her, knowing the kinds of things she'd say, whether she was laughing or crying, or throwing a fit.

"Something like: if you were sixteen, you'd be so grounded I'd never let you out of my sight again, for as long as you lived."

Jet thought for a moment and slowly nodded. "Sounds about right."

Close enough.

pg 10 - bottom - "of"
   15 - top - could "n't"
   29 - bottom - "scar(e)s"

Proof

Made in the USA
Charleston, SC
13 November 2012